She was stretched out on his narrow bed, her glorious hair a halo around her face and shoulders. Her smile was a bit shaky, but the hand she held out toward him wasn't.

Neither of them spoke. Maybe that should have worried him, but so far, words had done nothing but hurt the people he cared most about. He'd made Ole cry, he'd made Sadie cry, and he'd come damn near making himself cry, something he hadn't done since he was old enough to walk.

He knelt by the bed to kiss Sadie, wanting desperately to convince her that her decision to share his bed was the right one. At the same time, he had to wonder what she was thinking. Even that little delay had her looking worried, so he immediately brushed his lips across hers. Then he wrapped her in his arms, wishing like hell that he'd never have to let her go.

Come Home
For Christmas

Pat Pritchard

ZEBRA BOOKS
KENSINGTON PUBLISHING CORP.
www.kensingtonbooks.com

ZEBRA BOOKS are published by

Kensington Publishing Corp.
850 Third Avenue
New York, NY 10022

All Kensington titles, imprints, and distributed lines are available at special quantity discounts for bulk purchases for sales promotion, premiums, fund-raising, educational, or institutional use.

Special book excerpts or customized printings can also be created to fit specific needs. For details, write or phone the office of the Kensington Special Sales Manager: Attn. Special Sales Department. Kensington Publishing Corp., 850 Third Avenue, New York, NY, 10022. Phone: 1-800-221-2647.

Zebra and the Z logo Reg. U.S. Pat. & TM Off.

ISBN 0-8217-7792-0

First Printing: October 2005
10 9 8 7 6 5 4 3 2 1

Printed in the United States of America

*This book is dedicated to Faye Rosser—
friend, neighbor, and book lover extraordinaire.
Your friendship means so much to me,
and your unflagging support and interest in my writing is a real gift.
Thank you for always being there.*

Chapter 1

His elusive quarry had finally gone to ground.

Jed Stark smiled with grim satisfaction and swung down out of the saddle. By nightfall, he'd have his prisoner and get to the bottom of this mess. Sliding his rifle out of its scabbard, he took off at a ground-eating lope, ready to have this hunt finally over with. He was damn sick and tired of breathing trail dust and eating cold beans and jerky for three meals a day. Once his prisoner was under lock and key, Jed had dreams of spending a week or more sleeping in a real bed, but only after soaking in a hot bath for hours.

But first, he had a job to finish.

He reached a low ridge and lay down before peering over the top. A smart man learned early not to make an easy target of himself whenever he could help it. Wiggling forward, he ran afoul of a damn sticker bush. Muttering a few heartfelt curses, he backed away and removed the offending nettles from his hand with his teeth, spitting them out in disgust. The little bastard hiding somewhere on the other side of the ridge was going to pay dearly for all of this inconvenience.

Jed hated putting chains on a kid, but the boy's word wasn't worth shit. The first time Jed had cornered him, Hawk had promised to stay put. Then the minute Jed shut his eyes, the boy took off running again. Hell, even the most vigilant of lawmen had to sleep sometime. But it was time to find out once and for all what drove this prisoner to run, especially since Jed knew full well the boy had nowhere to run to.

He studied the view below. Other than a creek winding its way through the tangle of brush that covered most of the valley floor, there wasn't much to distinguish this place from any of a hundred others like it. If Hawk was down there, it would only make sense that he'd be near the water. Jed followed the line of the stream, watching for signs of movement.

Sweat had his back itching, making it hard to remain still, but any movement on his part might reveal his presence to anyone watching from below. His patience was wearing thin, and he could kick himself for leaving his canteen back on the saddle. The sun sparkling off the water didn't help either his parched throat or his mood, another reason he couldn't wait to get his hands on his prisoner.

He settled in to watch. If the boy was down there, Jed would get him. As the minutes ticked by, some of the small creatures that had taken cover at his approach slowly began poking their heads out again. Just down the slope a small ground squirrel darted across the top of a large rock. It stopped, turning its head this way and that, probably looking for lunch.

A sleek shadow, silent and deadly, slid down the

side of the hill. Before Jed could look up, a large hawk swooped down to snatch the small rodent up in its talons. The attack took place some distance away, but Jed clearly heard the shriek of pain as long claws tore into the small animal. The bird's triumphant scream echoed over the hillside. With a few hard beats of its wings, the feathered killer lifted back up into the air with its unlucky prey still struggling weakly to get free.

"Poor bastard."

Jed wasn't sure if he was talking about the squirrel or the kid he was hunting. At least the boy had good reason to know that Jed was on his trail; the poor squirrel had no warning that its life was about to end.

Lying in the dirt wasn't accomplishing anything. Jed pushed up off the ground and started down the rocky slope, his rifle at the ready. He picked his way carefully, the available cover too scant to be of much use. As far as he knew, the boy wasn't armed, but more than one lawman had died by underestimating his foe. At the edge of the small creek, he stopped to listen for any sign that he wasn't alone before risking a quick drink of water. He quickly scooped up several handfuls and then splashed his face and neck before easing back into a stand of willow saplings to resume the hunt.

It was too quiet.

Even the birds had quit making their usual racket. He lingered in the shadows, waiting to see if they would start up again. If not, he'd know that he wasn't alone. His patience was rewarded a few seconds later. The sound of a horse's hoof striking a loose rock came from just upstream. He wished for better cover, but unless the boy happened to be looking in the right direction, Jed stood a good chance of getting a bead on him before he could react.

A heartbeat later, a flicker of movement from across the creek caught his eye as an ugly brute of a horse wandered into sight. Jed liked a good-looking horse as much as the next man, but he admired stamina and speed even more. This horse would never take any prizes for its looks, but everything about it said it could go all day, all night, and still have enough left for a final burst of speed.

He was so taken with the horse, he almost didn't see the boy walking along beside the big bay. It was Hawk. As far as he knew, the kid only had the one name. If he had any family left, they sure hadn't stepped forward to claim him. Jed didn't want to feel sorry for the boy. He did, but it didn't change what he had to do. Knowing he'd have to play this just right, Jed kept his finger on the trigger although he wasn't anxious to resort to gunfire. His own horse was too far away to be of much good if the boy decided to make a run for it again, especially riding that long-legged horse of his.

After the bay drank its fill of cool water, the boy led him back upstream. Jed let them go, following along behind only after he was sure they were still unaware of his presence. He felt like that hawk, soaring in circles high overhead, choosing its moment of attack when its victim was most vulnerable.

It didn't take long to trace their trail back to a small camp set up deep in a stand of trees. The boy had rigged himself a primitive shelter out of branches, and a ring of rocks marked a fire pit although there was no smoke rising from the ashes. Jed waited until both the horse and its owner were settled before stepping into the clearing, his rifle aimed at the dirt near the boy's feet. He wouldn't shoot unless he had to, but the boy didn't need to know that.

"Raise your hands slowly Hawk. In case you've forgotten who I am, my name is Marshal Jed Stark."

The boy froze, his face expressionless as he waited for Jed's next order. As soon as Jed took a step, Hawk made his decision. One second he was standing there, the next he was a blur, running like hell. Jed dropped his rifle on the ground and took off after him, knowing if he didn't catch Hawk before he reached the horse, he'd be condemned to another week of beans while he tracked him down again.

He caught Hawk by the scruff of his collar and tumbled them both to the ground. He probably had a good seventy or eighty pounds on Hawk, but desperation went a long way toward evening out the fight.

"Damn it, boy, quit before one of us gets hurt." Jed managed to pin Hawk down once, only to have the boy twist and throw him off. Finally, Jed mustered a last burst of energy and pulled Hawk back down. This time he sat on his back until he could get the boy's hands tied.

It was embarrassing how much the brief tussle took out of him. He doubled the usual number of knots to make sure Hawk's nimble fingers wouldn't be able to work them loose any time soon. As soon as that was done, he rolled off the boy and jerked him up to his feet.

"You hurt, boy?" He tried to tell himself that he was only asking because an injured prisoner would only slow down their return trip. It sure as hell wasn't because he recognized a lot of himself in the hate-filled expression on Hawk's face. Or that they both had the same pitch-black hair and high cheek-bones.

Hawk spat at Jed's feet. So much for friendly relations. He pushed the boy down on a convenient log.

"I'm going back up over that ridge to collect my horse. You'd better be sitting there when I get back." He picked up his rifle and dusted it off. "It'll go hard on you if I have to run you down again."

He didn't bother to keep looking back over his shoulder. Either the boy would do as he was told or he'd pay for his stupidity. As Jed climbed back up the ridge, he felt every one of the long hours he'd put in since breaking camp before the sun had come up. Glancing at the sky, he decided against trying to make any distance back toward the small town where Hawk was wanted.

Instead, the two of them would stay the night and then head out at first light. With any luck, they'd reach town an hour or two before sunset tomorrow. He couldn't wait to be shed of this mess. A marshal was paid to bring back criminals to stand trial, but it was hard to believe that this boy had done anything that warranted prison, or worse yet, hanging.

Unless he'd stolen that ugly horse. Then there wasn't a court in five hundred miles that would let him off because of his age, especially a mixed-blood like Hawk. The whole affair left a bad taste in Jed's mouth.

His mare had wandered a short distance farther down the far side of the slope. The poor beast was as bone weary as Jed was himself. Well, at least there was good grazing and cool water aplenty for the night. Both of them could use a relaxing evening, even if the mare was the only one likely to get it.

If the boy had moved at all while Jed was gone, it hadn't been far. When Jed rode back into camp, Hawk was still sitting on the log, studiously ignoring Jed's approach. His horse, though, perked up at the approach of Jed's mare; the stallion tasted her scent in the wind and pawed the ground restlessly. She responded with a coy sidestep that almost unseated Jed. Hell, all he needed was for that ugly stallion to take a liking to his mare. Even if he could keep them apart, it could be a constant battle to control the two of them.

Son of a bitch, was nothing ever easy?

He tethered his pinto on the opposite side of the makeshift camp, although he didn't figure it would make for a peaceful night. The boy looked up when his horse snorted and pawed the ground again. It didn't take him long to size up the situation.

"She in season?"

Jed ignored the question. Last thing he wanted was to discuss his mare's mating urges with someone not even old enough to shave. "You got anything to eat around here?"

"Why should I share, lawman?"

He gave the boy credit for sheer gumption. There he sat, all trussed up like a Christmas goose, and still he wasn't cowed. "I only brought enough for myself. If you want to go hungry, that's fine with me."

He made a show of getting out his skillet and starting a fire. Whistling tunelessly, he put some water on to heat for coffee and tried to look as if he were excited about the prospect of another meal of beans and jerky. The smoke drifted right toward the boy, carrying the scent of Jed's dinner with it. There was a slight rustling sound, as if Hawk were shifting his position on the log. Jed wondered whether it was to get a better view of his simple meal or to get away from the fragrant smoke.

"I've got a couple of snares set. I was going to check them when you showed up." The admission was given grudgingly.

"Where?"

The boy didn't try to point with his hands lashed together. "I'll show you."

"Fine. Lead the way." Jed considered untying the boy but rejected the idea. He wasn't likely to take off as long as Jed kept him away from the stallion, but it wasn't worth the risk. He trailed along behind his silent companion, reaching out to steady Hawk when he tripped over a rock and almost went tumbling straight forward onto his face.

As soon as Hawk regained his balance, he jerked away from Jed's supporting hand. Jed took no offense; he didn't much like being touched either. They'd gone about a quarter of a mile when Hawk stopped and nodded toward a cluster of bushes a short distance away from the creek.

"Over there, on the far end of that brush. The second one is about another fifty feet farther down that way near that bunch of big rocks." He must have figured that he'd done his part, because he turned back toward camp.

Jed wasn't about to risk having to chase him down again so soon. "Stay here while I check your snares."

"And if I don't?"

"I'd try to just slow you down a bit," Jed said, patting his revolver with his gun hand. "But, to tell you the truth, when I get this tired, I can't rightly vouch for my accuracy."

Hawk's eyes widened briefly. He actually backed up a step before he could stop himself. "I ain't scared."

Like hell he wasn't, but Jed didn't push it. Sometimes all a man had was his pride. That and an ugly horse were likely all this boy could lay claim to.

"I'll be right back. Let's hope your skill with a snare is better than mine." He walked away without looking back over his shoulder. The boy would stay or run. Either way, Jed would deal with it.

The first snare was empty, although it was torn out of the ground. Either the rabbit had gotten lucky and escaped or another predator had found an easy meal. The second snare was a little harder to find, but his diligence was rewarded with a fat rabbit. Maybe Hawk had been dining regularly on fresh meat, but it would be the first for Jed in far too many days. He quickly dispatched the animal, skinning it out and throwing the entrails out into the rocks where some of the local citizens could fight over them.

When he reached the spot where he'd left Hawk, the boy was nowhere in sight. Jed bit back a curse, sure he was in for another long night. Then he spotted him standing in the shadows a few feet off the game trail they'd been following. There was a brief flare of triumph in the boy's dark eyes, no doubt enjoying his minor victory in their game of chase.

"Do you like your rabbit roasted on a spit or boiled in a stew?" Jed walked past Hawk, letting the boy follow as he would.

"Why do you care?"

"It's your rabbit. Since you're in the mood to share, I figured the least I could do is fix it the way you like it." Besides, the gesture would help keep Hawk off balance. He figured the boy was used to being cuffed around and insulted. Simple courtesy was probably completely foreign to him.

The boy trotted forward a few steps to come abreast of Jed. He muttered, "Roasted" as he passed him by on his way to reclaim his seat on the log.

An hour later, the rabbit was only a fond memory. Jed had waited until the meat was sizzling and crusty before pulling his knife from his boot to cut the ropes off the boy's wrists. Hawk had immediately torn into the plate of food Jed had set on the ground beside him with far more enthusiasm than half a rabbit and a bunch of beans deserved. Evidently Jed wasn't the only one who'd missed a few meals lately.

"You clean up the dishes. I'll water the horses."

"My horse won't let you near him." The claim was made with a great deal of pride. "Last bastard that tried ended up with a broken arm."

The stallion already had its ears flat back as its rear legs sidled toward Jed, preparing to kick. Jed stopped a short distance away and stared right into the horse's eyes. When he spoke, he kept his voice pitched low and soft. "I can see you're a tough customer, big man. But that water looks cool and would taste plenty good right now, wouldn't it?"

The ears flicked forward and back as the horse looked first at its owner and then toward Jed. That was all right. He had the bay's attention now. "I'm not going to try anything stupid like trying to ride you. I just want to let you enjoy some of that cool, cool water." By this point, Jed was almost chanting the words, letting the sound calm the horse's jitters, the way an old friend had taught him when Jed had been just about Hawk's age.

Finally, he slowly reached out to let the horse catch his scent. The bay snorted and backed up half a step. Jed started talking again, keeping his hand thrust forward toward the bay's nose. This time the horse allowed him the privilege of touching his nose before sliding his hand over to pat the animal on the neck. When Jed untied the makeshift rope halter that Hawk had used to tether his horse, the stallion followed him easily down to the water's edge.

While the horse drank its fill, Jed looked back to see how Hawk was handling this obvious betrayal. Once again, Jed felt the surprising urge to explain himself.

"I'm not after your horse, boy. But I need him to trust me since we're going to be traveling together." He gestured toward the mare. "While I stake him out where he can graze, you bring her down to the water. She doesn't much like strangers, either. Be careful and watch out for your fingers. Sometimes she likes a little meat with her dinner." Then he turned his back and let Hawk handle the mare without further comment.

He listened to the murmur of the boy's voice as he coaxed the mare into following him down to the water. It didn't take him long to charm her into doing as he asked. It spoke well of the boy's ability with animals because Jed hadn't been exaggerating. The pinto had been with him for the past three years. In all that time, there'd only been one, maybe two others whom she'd learned to trust.

Once he knew Hawk could handle the mare, Jed walked the stallion a short distance away to tether him for the night. When he returned, he was pleased to see that Hawk had already done the same for the mare and was busy cleaning up the dishes they'd used. Seeing the boy's willingness to help out with chores made Jed hate like hell to have to tie him up again, but he had no choice.

He'd managed to track the boy down once before. That time, Jed had underestimated Hawk's determination to avoid returning to Cutter, the small township where he was wanted by the law. No, he'd tie Hawk's hands even if he'd feel guilty for doing so. The sun had already disappeared behind the low hills to the west, leaving just enough light to see by.

"You ready to turn in for the night?"

"Do I have any choice?" Maybe getting caught again so quickly had taught Hawk something about what it was like to be a prisoner.

"No, you don't." Jed felt the weight of Hawk's gaze as he cut a new length of rope. "Hold out your hands."

Hawk made a motion as if to comply with Jed's orders, but then in the blink of an eye, he was off and running straight for his horse. Jed had been expecting him to make a break for it, so he caught him within only a few steps.

"Let go of me, you son of a bitch!" Hawk twisted and turned, using every bit of his wiry strength to try to break free. "I'm not going back there! Let me go!"

Jed jerked his hand back just in time to keep from getting bitten. "Damn it, Hawk!" He flipped the boy over and jerked his hands up behind his back and quickly tied them together.

His own temper was heating up, so he left Hawk lying in the dirt until he could get it back under control. He grabbed up his saddlebags and stomped down to the creek. The water felt cold now that the heat of the day was gone, but he didn't give a damn. Right now he wanted to wash off some of the dirt crusted on his skin and cool down his anger.

He had a reputation of being ruthless when it came to dragging outlaws back to stand trial and had little sympathy for those who chose to stand on the wrong side of the law. But something about this case stunk to high heaven. He'd never deliberately let a prisoner escape, and he wasn't about to now. That didn't mean he liked treating that boy like an animal.

Looking back, he realized that the sheriff who'd sent Jed after Hawk hadn't provided many details about the crimes the boy had supposedly committed. Once again, Jed felt a surprisingly strong surge of sympathy for Hawk because so much about him reminded Jed of his own miserable childhood.

He scrubbed his skin dry with his dirty shirt before putting on his last clean one. As he did so, he considered his options. The simplest thing to do would be to drop Hawk off in Cutter and not look back. He rejected that idea out of hand. The sheriff might not like it, but Jed would conduct his own investigation into the situation and then decide for himself whether to press charges. Of course, if the locals were all that hot to get their hands on Hawk, he might just lose the boy to a lynch mob before Jed could get at the real truth.

Then there was the little matter of Hawk's obvious mixed heritage. Knowing how strong the prejudice against anyone with Indian blood was, that alone might account for Hawk's real problems with the law. Jed knew he'd never turn the boy over to anyone until he knew more about what had happened. Having made a decision of sorts, he gathered up his gear and returned to camp.

Hawk had managed to push himself back up and was sitting on the log. Jed unrolled his own bedding and sat down on it. "Tell me what happened back in Cutter."

Thanks to the dim glow of the dying fire, Jed could see Hawk's face well enough to see that his request had set off some powerful emotions. He doubted Hawk would trust him enough to tell him everything, but he hoped to at least get some idea of what he was dealing with.

"The sheriff said you're a thief."

The boy's chin came up in denial. "I never took nothing that wasn't mine to begin with."

"That's a pretty strong claim." Jed plucked a piece of grass to chew on. "You telling me you never took food or clothing that belonged to someone else?" He fought back a small grin at the sight of Hawk trying to find a way to avoid admitting as much.

"Well, nothing big. Sometimes I got hungry." His chin came up in stubborn pride.

"Yeah, well, I've been hungry a few times myself." It was no more than the truth. "But stealing a few meals isn't usually enough to land you in jail."

Just that quickly, Hawk shrunk in on himself. "My mother was white. My father wasn't, leastwise not completely."

Once again, Jed found it all too easy to see himself in the hunched shoulders and anger-filled eyes. He didn't bother to ask where Hawk's parents were. They were both dead; he'd bet money on it.

"That's not a crime."

"It is in Cutter."

Jed didn't dispute the truth of that statement. The sheriff hadn't been all that friendly even after he found out that Jed was the marshal he'd sent for. Underneath a thin veneer of upholding the law, the man clearly hated Indians and didn't much care who knew it. Jed's eyes might be silver, but his heritage was written in the harsh planes of his face and in his shoulder-length black hair.

"Even in Cutter, they'd have to have some kind of evidence, even if it's trumped up." He poked at the coals with a stick, sending a shower of sparks up in the air. "What did you do—steal that horse?"

The boy jerked, as if Jed had hit him. "Like hell I did. Me and my father's father raised Wind Son from a colt."

His voice thickened with the sound of grief at the mention of his grandfather. Another blow death had dealt to the boy.

"I'm listening."

"My grandfather had a small ranch outside of town where we raised horses, just the two of us." His eyes stared out through the darkness to where the bay grazed. "We made a little money selling green-broke mustangs to the army, but we knew right off that Wind Son was special. There's no way my grandfather would have sold him to anybody. He was to be the father of our herd."

Jed could believe that. If the stud's strength bred true, a man could get rich from his offspring. If the boy was to be believed, someone had taken a good look at that horse and gotten greedy.

"What happened to your parents and your grandfather?" He hated to ask, knowing the more he learned, the more he was getting tangled up in Hawk's problems.

"My parents died of a fever when I was little." There was only the faintest echo of grief in that statement. "My grandfather was murdered by those bastards back in Cutter." He spat out the words as if he expected Jed to call him a liar or, worse yet, laugh.

"No witnesses?"

"How did you know that?" Hawk's surprise was obvious.

"I've heard this story before. Sometimes it's true, sometimes not."

"They forged my grandfather's signature on a piece of paper that says he sold Wind Son to a neighboring rancher."

"How do you know it was a forgery?" He had to ask even though he already knew the answer.

"He couldn't read or write—not even his name."

"I'll have to take your word on that. Then what happened?"

"Grandfather died on the way back to the ranch." The boy's eyes were dull with remembered pain and grief.

"How did he die?"

"They say he forgot to carry water with him and that the heat killed him because he was an old man. I found him about a mile from our cabin." Grief clouded his voice. "There were bruises all over his face and rope burns on his wrists."

"What did the sheriff say?"

"He said my grandfather got the bruises when he fell on some rocks."

"So you think this rancher beat your grandfather until he signed the paper to sell Wind Son?"

Hawk shook his head. "No, I think he died of a broken heart."

Jed wanted to punch something or, better yet, someone. Unfortunately, the only person within striking distance had been beat up too much already, especially for someone so young.

"Get some sleep, boy. We ride first thing in the morning." He stretched out on his blanket, cradling his head on the hard leather of his saddle. Closing his eyes, he depended on his sense of hearing to know what Hawk was doing. After a minute, maybe two, Hawk stood up awkwardly and slipped inside his makeshift shelter. For the sake of his own sanity, Jed pretended not to hear the snuffling sound of crying. Come morning he'd shoulder the burden of proving Hawk innocent or guilty, but tonight he needed his sleep.

Jed woke up a good five minutes before he could bring himself to open his eyes. It was morning—the warmth of the sun on his skin told him that much. He wasn't alone, or at least he thought he could hear two horses slowly moving around. It took another few seconds for him to pinpoint to Hawk's location. Unless he missed his guess, the boy was talking to one of the horses, mostly likely the stallion.

Damn, he didn't want to start the day off with a chase and no coffee. He pried open one eye and then the other. Not wanting to startle his prisoner into flight, he slowly rolled over on his side and lifted his head. Every bone in his back snapped and creaked, but the noise must not have been as loud as it sounded to him since neither the boy nor his horse even glanced in his direction.

He let out a deep breath. So far, the day was off to a passable start. He rolled up off the ground and stretched his arms over his head. If Hawk had planned to take off on him, he could have done so before Jed woke up. Rather than worry about it, Jed headed off into the bushes for a moment of privacy. Still, he didn't linger. There was no use in letting the boy think he'd gotten lazy.

Hawk was perched back on the log waiting when Jed returned to camp. There were dirt streaks down his face, probably from last night's tears, but Jed wasn't about to mention them. Before breakfast, though, he'd untie Hawk's hands long enough for him to eat and wash up in the creek. Then they'd ride out. There was no question about that, only about which way they'd been heading when they left the valley behind.

He put on the coffee to heat and reached for his skillet.

"That bastard thinks he has me." Hawk sneered at the lawman, but only when he knew he wouldn't be seen. Defiance didn't fit the picture of a broken and scared little boy. And the only way he was going to slip past Stark's defenses was to convince him that Hawk was weak.

He hadn't missed the look on the marshal's face when he saw the tear streaks on Hawk's face. Pity had flashed across his face before he'd quickly erased all evidence of it from his expression. Oh, the tears had been real enough, but they didn't stem from grief, but from rage.

There was no way anyone, not even some marshal with fancy guns and a tarnished badge, was dragging him back to Cutter to stand trial. He'd die first, but not before he turned Wind Son loose to live free. He leaned into the warmth of Wind Son's neck. It would near kill him to give up his one friend, but the horse deserved better than to be given over to a thief.

The horse nudged him with his nose, his way of demanding a good ear scratching. With his hands still bound, he couldn't do a decent job of it, but Wind Son moaned and leaned into him anyway. Hawk felt like smiling for the first time since the hard-eyed marshal had appeared the night before. The feeling didn't last long.

"Breakfast is ready."

"I'm not hungry." It was a lie, but Hawk didn't want to eat another meal with those strange gray eyes staring at him.

"I don't give a damn if you are or not. You'll eat anyway. We have a long ride ahead of us. The last thing I need is for you to starve yourself until you either faint or get sick."

Hawk bit back a mouthful of curses, reminding himself that he stood a better chance of escaping if the man underestimated Hawk's strength and determination. That didn't mean he had to act grateful for a few beans and some jerky.

He walked away from the horse, keeping himself a step or two in front of the lawman. Once they reached the fire, he sat down and waited to see what the man was going to do next. Just as he'd hoped, the marshal pulled out his knife and cut his hands free. Shards of pain shot through his shoulders and arms; he bit his lip to keep from crying out.

"It might not hurt less, but it might stop sooner if you keep moving around."

Although the gruff concern sounded real, Hawk didn't acknowledge it. Instead, he got up and walked around swinging his arms and rolling his shoulders. He couldn't swear that it made much of a difference, but at least it gave him something to do until the pain faded to a manageable level. As soon as he sat down, a plate appeared in front of him.

"Eat up. I don't plan to hang around here all morning." Evidently the lawman had eaten breakfast because he was already packing up his gear.

While Hawk ate, Stark brought his mare down to the creek to drink before saddling her. Not once did he make the mistake of turning his back on Hawk. It didn't matter. He had to blink sometime and when he did, Wind Son and Hawk would be gone.

"You got a saddle for the bay?"

"Yeah."

"Get it." The lawman took Hawk's plate down to the water and scrubbed it with sand before rinsing it clean. Once again, he did everything while keeping a wary eye on Hawk.

Hawk half carried, half dragged the saddle out of his shelter. The lawman picked it up and swung it up over his shoulder in one easy motion. He spread the blanket on Wind Son's broad back and then settled the saddle on top of it, tightening the cinch with one hard yank. It would have taken Hawk two or three tries to get it right.

And the whole time, Wind Son stood rock-still, the same as if it were Hawk or his late grandfather doing the saddling. It hurt to watch.

"Got anything you need to pack up?"

"No." He let a little of his anger show. "Those bastards stole everything we owned that was worth anything."

"Then mount up. The day's a-wasting."

A surge of victory swept over Hawk, making it difficult for him to continue to look properly cowed. One foot in that stirrup and he'd be flying with the wind, leaving the stupid lawman looking like a fool. The fact that the man had already trapped him twice was beside the point. This time Hawk wouldn't stop running until he'd put the entire state of Kansas between them.

That was when he saw the rope and his stomach

and hope went south. So the lawman wasn't the fool Hawk had hoped he was. One end of the rope was tied to a tree, the other around Wind Son's neck. Neither of them was going anywhere fast.

The man wasn't exactly smiling, but something in the set of his jaw looked suspiciously like he'd enjoyed outwitting Hawk. "Hold out your hands."

"I can't ride like this." He tugged at the ropes, knowing Stark hadn't left an inch of give in the knots that held him fast to the saddle.

"It's either like that or across the saddle. Your choice."

Stark walked away to untie the rope from the tree without waiting for an answer. Only a fool would choose to spend hours of misery riding draped across the back of a horse. Until this point, Hawk had considered Stark an inconvenience, but now he hated him almost as much as he did those responsible for his grandfather's death. For the time being, he had no choice but to do as Stark said. He drew comfort from knowing someday he'd be big enough to fight back.

If he lived long enough.

A decision was going to have to be made soon, one Jed didn't relish making. He glanced back over his shoulder toward his prisoner. The boy hadn't uttered a single word since Jed had tied him to the saddle that morning. They were long overdue for a break, but he'd wanted to make up his mind what to do next before stopping.

Hawk clearly didn't like anyone telling him what to do, an attitude Jed understood all too well. No matter what Jed decided to do with him, Hawk wasn't going to like it, not one damn bit. In a way, that attitude only made things simpler for Jed. If he didn't have to worry about pleasing the boy, he might as well make himself happy.

No, happy wasn't the right word, but he had to be able to live with himself. He'd done more than a few things in his life that he wasn't proud of, including a few that kept him awake some nights. He wasn't going to add to the list by turning a kid, even one as surly as Hawk, over to a bigot wearing a badge.

He gave the mare a nudge to pick up the pace. Now that he'd chosen a destination, he wanted to get there as fast as possible before Hawk roused out of his resentment long enough to realize they'd changed directions. Before Jed could convince himself he was making a major mistake. And before he could remember exactly why he'd avoided this particular trail for six long years.

Chapter 2

Sadie stepped out of the barn and pushed her bonnet back off her head to dangle down her back, letting the late summer breeze cool her face. Her back ached, telling her quite clearly that she'd spent too much time shoveling out stalls. There was some satisfaction in knowing the job was done, but it was only one in a long list of things that still needed her attention.

The sun beat down from directly overhead, giving her the excuse she needed to take a break from the endless round of chores. Her father wasn't likely to notice it was time to come in for a meal, so she would just have to take it out to where he was working in the back fields. With luck, she'd be able to convince him to sit in the shade of the trees along the creek for a while. Not long enough to hurt his pride, but long enough to force him to rest a bit. He didn't appreciate her worrying about him so much, but she had good reason even if he didn't see it that way.

She was on her way into the house when he surprised her by walking around the end of the barn, his two dogs running in circles around his feet. She would have enjoyed sitting by the water, but having him come in for dinner would save her time, something she always seemed to be in short supply of lately.

"I'll have food on the table in a few minutes." Her smile felt a bit forced, but it didn't matter. He barely noticed her at all.

She turned back to follow him into the barn. "Is something wrong? Can I help?"

"Sadie, quit fussing like a hen with one chick." He waved her back as he frowned at the scythe in his hand. "This blade is dull. I came back to sharpen it. Nothing I can't handle, if I'm left alone long enough."

His words stung, but she didn't really blame him for being a bit testy. Ever since Doc Hartley's last visit, she could hardly bear to let Pa out of her sight. She knew for a fact that Doc had warned him to take things easier, but Pa was ignoring that bit of advice along with everything else the doctor had tried to tell him.

It wouldn't be so bad if she had been able to hire some decent help, but the last hand she'd brought home had lasted less than two weeks. She was willing to put up with a lot to keep her father from working so hard, but the man had been either drunk or wishing he was and nothing in between. The one before him had been lazy and smelled bad. The list went on and on. However, if her father insisted on putting in such long hours, she'd have to drive into town and try again.

Inside the dim interior of the house the air felt a little cooler. That would change as soon as she added wood to the stove, but she enjoyed it while she could. Reaching for her apron, she tied it on over her work pants. Her late mother would have been scandalized to see Sadie dressed in men's clothing. But if she was going to do men's work, it seemed only practical to dress the part. She couldn't imagine how much harder it would be to take care of the animals and their needs while trying to keep her skirts out of the filth that was a natural occurrence around cattle and horses.

She scrubbed her hands and face clean before setting the table and putting the stew on to reheat. After making coffee, she cut a few slices from a fresh loaf of bread and put them on a plate. She'd fetch the butter from the well on her way out to collect her father from the barn.

It didn't take long for the savory broth of the stew to start bubbling. The steamy scent of coffee hung heavily in the air, making the kitchen almost as hot as it was outside. So much for enjoying a break from the heat. At least she didn't have to do more than warm their meal. Satisfied that everything was under control, she went in search of her father.

Outside, she shaded her eyes with her hand, hoping that she wouldn't see him back out in the field already. Luckily both dogs were stretched out on the porch. Since neither Mooch nor Daisy ever let her father venture far without them, she knew he was still close by. Before she called out his name, though, Mooch lurched to his feet, his hackles rising as he stared down the road. His mate joined him, growling deep in her chest.

Riders were coming. She might not have noticed them at all if not for the early warning from the dogs. Chances were that they were drifters looking for a free meal or maybe a couple of days' worth of work before moving on down the road, but it never hurt to be armed when confronting strangers. The war had left a lot of men restless, most of them decent folks trying to find a new home or some peace of mind. It was the other ones, the kind with polite smiles and cold eyes that had her reaching for her rifle.

The dogs took up a position between her and the slowly approaching strangers. She kept her rifle pointed at the ground but ready for action if the need arose. Neither of the horses looked familiar from what she could see, but riding single file as they were made it difficult to make out much in the way of details.

Although there was something about the front rider that tickled at her mind, reminding her of something . . . no, someone. Then he took off his hat and wiped the sweat off his face with the back of his sleeve. He had black hair, the color of a moonless night. Her heart skipped a beat, sending a shiver of cold up her spine in the noonday heat.

"Pa! Pa! Come out here. Riders coming in." Panic made her voice sound shrill and thin to her ears. Even so, it carried far enough for her father to hear her and come running, his shotgun at the ready.

"What's the matter?" he yelled, as he cleared the barn door.

She pointed down the narrow road that led straight to their house. Her father took several steps in that direction, still cradling his gun. Then he stopped and leaned forward as if those few inches would make all the difference in his ability to see their uninvited guests more clearly. Then he took a slow step in their direction, followed by another and another until he was almost running. The lead rider dismounted and led both horses slowly toward her father.

She trailed along behind, her eyes straining to see what her heart already knew. Then her father confirmed it for all of them as he shouted out the name of someone they hadn't seen for almost six years.

"Jedediah Stark!"

"Ole Johanson!"

Jed dropped the reins and walked right into her father's outstretched arms. The two men met in a flurry of awkward hugs and half-spoken thoughts.

A jumble of anger and relief warred inside her at the sight. Not once in those six years had Jed found the time for a visit. A few letters had straggled in, all addressed to her father, never once to her. In fact, it had been over a year since the last letter—more of a note really—had come, not that she kept track.

She hadn't been the one to worry about Jed. No, that had been her father's job, just as if he needed something else that weighed heavily on his mind. When the letters quit coming, he'd prowled the kitchen late at night, pacing the floor and murmuring Jed's name.

The only reason she'd ever been concerned was the effect that Jed's continued silence had on her father. Ole didn't ask much of the boys who had moved in and out of their home over the years, but he wanted to know that they were all right.

Especially Jed.

But Jed was here now, and she wasn't sure how she felt about that. For her father's sake, she supposed she was happy. For her own sake, well, that was a whole different matter. But until she sorted it all out, she stood back to watch and wait.

There had been a time back when she was poised on that fragile edge of no longer being a little girl, but not quite a woman, when she'd found everything about Jed Stark fascinating. The black silk of his shoulder-length hair contrasted sharply with the pale silver of his eyes. And that straight slash of a mouth that smiled so infrequently, but dazzled those around him when it did.

But then he'd ridden away and not looked back. Not until today. Not until it was too late to heal the wounds his absence had caused. She looked beyond where Jed stood talking quietly to her father to study the second rider. It was obvious even from a distance that he was far younger than Jed, even though there was a strong resemblance between the two. She knew that Jed had no family, so she had to wonder who the boy was.

Jed nodded at something her father said and picked up the reins he'd dropped. The two of them walked slowly toward the house, toward her. Sheer obstinacy had her hanging on to her rifle rather than putting on a more welcoming appearance.

"Sadie, look who has come home!"

She might not appreciate Jed's unexpected arrival, but at least he'd put a spark in her father's eyes that had been missing for far too long.

"Jed." She nodded in his direction.

"Miss Johanson." Jed touched the brim of his hat in salute.

"Sadie, Jed. You always called her Sadie," her father admonished. "She was like a little sister to you."

Neither of them bothered to correct him.

"Sadie, how have you been?"

She wasn't fooled. If he'd really cared, he would have asked long before now. Rather than distress her father, she managed to offer him a civil answer. "As fine as could be expected."

Let him make of that what he would. More to change the subject than because she was really interested in someone who rode with Jed, she turned her attention to the other rider. She walked past Jed with the intention of greeting the youth.

"Hello! I guess we've all forgotten our manners. I'm Sadie Johanson and this is my father, Ole. Would you like . . ." She stopped short when the horse the boy was riding laid back its ears and snorted in warning.

"Get back, Sadie." Strong hands grabbed her shoulders and pulled her stumbling back several steps. "Watch out for that horse."

As if she couldn't recognize an easily spooked animal when she saw one. But why would Jed put a young boy up on a half-wild horse like that one? Then she spotted the ropes that bound the boy to the saddle.

"He's tied up!" She whirled around to face Jed. "What kind of man ties a boy to a horse like that?"

Jed's face was all hard edges. "He's my prisoner."

The boy sneered. "It's the only way the big man could hold on to me. I've been riding like this for the past three days."

The Jed she had known would never have treated someone weaker than he was with such casual cruelty. But after his sudden disappearance from her life, she had to wonder if she'd ever really known him at all. On the other hand, the boy didn't look particularly abused, just uncomfortable. Before she could demand a further explanation, her father took over the discussion.

"What has a boy this young been accused of?" Ole looked at Jed and then at the boy with the same calm expression.

"That's what I plan to find out." Jed ignored her, speaking directly to her father, but making sure the boy heard him clearly at the same time. "I need a place to leave the boy. If that's a problem, we'll ride out."

"All you needed to do was ask, Jed," Ole declared, patting Jed on the shoulder. He began tugging on the knots that held the boy prisoner. "Now let's get this young man inside. I have a feeling you could both use a hot meal and a chance to rest. Tonight after supper will be soon enough to make plans."

He pocketed the short length of rope as soon as it fell free from the boy's hands. The gesture was so like her father, never wasting anything that might be put to another use, even a piece of worn rope. She watched him step back, giving the boy room to dismount, hovering close enough to offer help if it was needed but without crowding him.

"My name is Ole Johanson, boy. What are you called?" He offered his knobby, work-worn hand to Jed's prisoner, just as if he were an honored guest rather than a wanted criminal in the custody of a marshal.

For a moment she thought the boy was going to refuse to answer, but even this angry boy couldn't resist her father's patience. Those he couldn't immediately charm, he wore down with his soft voice and gentle ways.

"My name is Hawk." His smaller hand was swallowed up by her father's, but the gesture from one man to another had him standing straighter.

"Well, Hawk, let's go inside and sit down. My Sadie there, she's one of the best cooks for a hundred miles around."

He led the way into the house with Jed right on their heels. No one seemed overly concerned about what she did, so she hung back content to let the three of them help themselves to the meal she'd thrown together for her father. Her appetite had faded as soon as she realized that Jed Stark had suddenly reappeared in their lives.

She supposed she shouldn't be surprised that he only remembered the way back to the farm because he needed something from her father. She didn't know about her father, but she definitely had mixed feelings about Jed's request. True, they could certainly use some extra hands around the farm, but not this boy with his hard eyes and bitter anger. Perhaps ten to fifteen years ago, when her father was in his prime, it would have been all right. Back then there had been a steady march of orphans through their farm, taken in to help with the work, but also to give those needy children a place to call home until they were ready to move on. Jed had been the last one.

For an only child like her, it was like having an ever-changing group of friends and adopted cousins to play with. She'd learned early on not to get too attached because it hurt so much when they left. But with Jed, she'd let down her guard. Despite the hard life he'd lived prior to arriving on their doorstep, he'd eventually learned to trust her father and mother, giving them both the respect they deserved.

She supposed he'd considered her to be a pesky little sister, tolerating her following him around the farm. But she hadn't looked at him as a brother for long. Even now, her cheeks flushed with embarrassment at the memories. Jed had never said a word, but he must have suspected that she was infatuated with him. But if that was all that it had been, she would have eventually gotten over it. He'd left before she'd had a chance.

Mooch leaned against her leg, holding his head up in an unspoken request for some attention. She obliged him by scratching under his chin. The big hound's eyes drifted closed as he moaned in pleasure. The comfort of the dog's simple love went a long way toward soothing her badly jangled nerves.

Her father appeared in the doorway. "Sadie, it's rude to keep our guests waiting. Quit petting that dog and come eat."

She thought about refusing, having no desire to walk into the kitchen and see Jed sitting at his old place at the table. But her father would either get angry or fret over her unseemly behavior, so she pushed Mooch away and walked toward the door, an obedient daughter as usual.

On the way in, she instinctively patted her hair to make sure it was neat and tidy. She never bothered when it was just her and her father and resented the impulse just because Jed and Hawk were there. At least she didn't feel the need to quickly change into a dress before joining the others. If Jed didn't approve of a woman wearing men's clothing, she really didn't care.

Much.

On her worst day, Sadie was a better cook than Jed had ever been. The simple stew with fresh bread was the best meal he'd had in weeks. He considered telling her, but she didn't seem to be in the mood to listen to anything he had to say.

Already, she'd said at least three times as many words to Hawk than she had to Jed. So far, the friendliest she'd been was when she'd asked him to pass the butter. He couldn't say he was surprised, but he'd harbored some hope that she would be willing to be friends again.

Figuring she wouldn't appreciate being stared at, he did his best to concentrate on the intermittent discussion between Ole and Hawk. The old man hadn't lost his light touch with a skittish youngster. Looking back, Jed figured he'd been far worse off than Hawk at the same age. At least Hawk had his memories of his grandfather and some vague ones of his parents. He might only have one name, but it was one his family had given him.

Jed had no idea of who he was or where he'd come from. The closest he'd come to having a real home was the few years that he'd lived with the Johansons. When he'd tried to think of a safe place for Hawk to stay, this farm was the only one he could think of. Hawk might not appreciate the gesture, but Jed didn't give a damn. If the boy wanted justice for his grandfather, he'd have to do exactly as Jed told him. One wrong move on Hawk's part, and Jed would slap him behind bars in Cutter and consider himself well rid of the whole mess.

But for now, he'd soak up a few memories of good times spent sitting at this same scarred table while Mrs. Johanson sewed and Ole read the newspaper. He looked around the kitchen, wishing that Olga Johanson were still there, her smile bright and welcoming. He knew she'd died a year or so ago, but he'd found out too late to come back for the funeral.

It bothered him to see how frail Ole seemed. Jed had been gone for over six years, but his friend seemed to have aged twenty. In part, he figured it was due to the loss of Ole's beloved wife, but that didn't account for the lines of pain that bracketed his mouth or the bony feel to his shoulders when Jed had hugged him earlier.

He'd ask Sadie about her father if he could get her alone. That might prove difficult judging by the way she was avoiding even the smallest glance in his direction. Leaning back in his chair, he took the opportunity to study her face while she was ignoring him.

The young girl he had known was still there in this woman who had become a stranger to him. The bright blue eyes were the same, as was the yellow gold hair. But the mouth was different—she used to smile easily and often. Now there were faint lines on each side of her mouth, the kind that spoke of hard times.

He turned away before she could catch him studying her. After all, he was there for Hawk's sake, not to renew an old friendship. Yeah, and if he kept saying that maybe he'd believe it. It had taken most of his strength to ride away from the Johanson farm six years before and the rest of it to stay away. And now, he was right back where he'd started. Old hurts and old dreams.

His coffee was cold, but he drank it anyway. Once he was sure Hawk would stay put for a while, he'd be free to ride away again. Maybe the second time would be easier.

"Let's see to that horse of yours, boy." Ole pushed away from the table. "Come introduce me to him." He waited at the door for Hawk to join him.

Hawk immediately jumped to his feet and followed Ole outside, probably surprising himself as much as everyone else. Even though he hadn't been invited along, Jed knew he'd be more welcome in the barn than he was feeling in the kitchen. Perhaps later there would be time for him to make peace with Sadie, but right now she clearly didn't want to talk to him.

He picked up his hat. "Thank you for feeding us."

"You're welcome." Sadie busied herself clearing the table.

Rather than leave it all to her, he stopped to scrape the plates clean and stacked them for her. Just that quickly he felt the years slip away when he and Sadie had done their fair share of cleaning up after a meal. Of course, back then the kitchen had belonged to her mother. If he closed his eyes, he could still see Olga sitting by the fire, rocking and humming as she stitched yet another patch on the knee of his overalls or a button on Ole's shirt. But now the rocker was empty and there was little warmth left for him.

"I was sorry to hear about your mother, Sadie. She was a good woman. I know you and Ole must miss her." He wanted to touch her shoulder in a show of sympathy but doubted the gesture would be appreciated. Shoving his hands in his pockets, he waited a few seconds to see if Sadie would respond. Finally, he headed for the door.

"She loved getting letters from you." Sadie kept her eyes trained on the pot she was scrubbing. "She read them often."

Maybe her comment was meant to make him feel better, but more likely to remind him how rare those letters had been He'd been on the move from the day he'd left, at first looking for a job and then tracking down outlaws as a bounty hunter and then as a U.S. Marshal. It wasn't much of an excuse, but it was the truth. Rather than try to explain himself, he left the house and went in search of Ole and Hawk.

He found them in the barn. It didn't surprise him at all that his old friend had managed to soothe both of the horses as well as Hawk. He'd never been able to put his finger on what it was about Ole that allowed him to get past the mistrust and skittish nature of high-strung animals and frightened boys. He only knew he wished he had the knack himself. It would make his job easier when it came to dealing with the likes of Hawk.

He had no doubt that Ole knew he'd come into the barn, but Hawk had yet to notice. Rather than interrupt the conversation, Jed hung back and listened in. Perhaps the boy would let slip some more details about what had driven him from Cutter on the wrong side of the law.

"My grandfather raised the mother from a filly. Her markings were almost identical to his." He pointed at the stallion's stockings and the crooked streak of white down his nose. "But he got his color from the stallion." For the first time Hawk's face reflected none of his usual anger. His hands were flying as he talked, pointing out the various attributes of his beloved horse.

"His father was a wild one. He was only in our area for a short time, but my grandfather's mare got out of the corral and ran with his herd for a few weeks before we could get her back." He grinned. "Grandfather was sure enough mad about almost losing her. When Wind Son was born, though, he forgave her. He was worth risking everything for."

Then his voice dropped and the grief was showing in the set of his shoulders. "We were looking for the right mare to breed him to, but my grandfather died before we could find her." He eyed Jed's mare. "My grandfather would have liked the looks of the lawman's horse."

"Jed always did have an eye for fine horseflesh. I bet he likes your stallion as much as you like his mare." Ole glanced back over his shoulder and smiled toward Jed. "Am I right about that?"

Hawk was not nearly as welcoming, but Jed ignored him. Instead, he joined Ole locking into the stall where the stallion was busy eating fresh hay and oats.

"He's an ugly beast." Jed ignored Hawk's gasp of outrage. "But if I could design a horse built for a comfortable ride, good speed, and lots of stamina, I don't know that I could do any better than him."

"Maybe your mare . . ." Ole started to say, but Jed was already shaking his head.

"Don't even think that way. I need her in my work." Jed spent more of his time sleeping on the ground than he did under a roof, but he didn't see the need to mention that. Ole had always made his hopes clear that Jed would find a place and settle down for good, preferably within spitting distance of this farm.

"When the horses are through eating, Hawk, you can turn the stallion loose out in the corral for a while." Ole walked across the barn and picked up a scythe that was lying on the floor. "I need to sharpen this and then get to work back along the creek. I could use some help." His look said quite clearly that he wanted Jed to come along.

"I need to keep an eye on him." Jed jerked his head in Hawk's direction. "Last time I turned my back on him without tying him up first, it took me an extra week of hard riding to find him."

"Nonsense. That boy's not going anywhere today. You're smarter than that, aren't you, Hawk?" Ole met Hawk's gaze with calm conviction. "He's tired, and he needs a good night's sleep. But more importantly, he knows his horse is about to throw a shoe. Until I can get the farrier out here to fix it, he can't go far on that stallion without risking him going lame."

Jed hadn't noticed any such thing, but Ole

wouldn't lie to the boy about his horse knowing how important Wind Son was to Hawk. Even if the stallion weren't everything Jed had said and more, the animal was Hawk's last tie to his grandfather. He wouldn't endanger the horse in order to get away from Jed.

"I'll stop in town when I leave and ask the farrier to make a trip out here in the next few days." By then, he hoped that Ole would have worked his usual magic and convinced Hawk to stay put without resorting to ropes or chains to keep him from taking off.

Ole had finished putting a new edge on the scythe. "Well, that grass isn't getting any shorter out there. Let's go, Jed, before Sadie tries to convince me that I shouldn't work so hard."

Maybe she had the right of it, but it was too soon for Jed to risk siding with her against her father. Once he had a chance to talk to Sadie, though, he'd find out more about Ole's health. He hoped his suspicions were wrong, but he was sorely afraid that something was wrong beyond the weight of a few more years.

The thought made him sick. But for now, he would follow his friend out to the field, trusting his prisoner wouldn't bolt while his back was turned.

Hawk watched the two men leave. As soon as their voices faded out of hearing, he joined Wind Son in his stall. Murmuring a lot of calming nonsense, he ran his hand down the stallion's legs, lifting each foot for a thorough examination. He was on the verge of calling the old man a liar, but then he took a second look at Wind Son's right front hoof.

Sure enough, the nails were working loose.

He'd been lucky that the shoe hadn't already caused Wind Son some problems. As long as the horse didn't carry much weight or go any distance, he'd be fine until the farrier came. So until then, Hawk was little better than a prisoner on this farm, even without the cold-eyed lawman watching his every move.

After turning Wind Son loose, he climbed up and sat on the top of the corral fence. The restless stallion made several circuits around the enclosure, getting the feel of the place before dropping to the ground and rolling in the dust. For the first time in days, Hawk felt like laughing. His horse might look like a tough hombre, but at heart he was still a little boy who liked to get dirty.

"He's quite something, isn't he?"

The woman's voice came from his left. She was standing close enough to make conversation easy, but far enough away not to crowd him. He wondered if her chosen position was deliberate and decided that it was. Just like her father, she seemed friendly without being pushy about it.

She turned to look at him then, as if she'd been aware all along that he was staring at her. Either it didn't bother her or else she was willing to let him get to know her on his terms. Somehow, her curiosity didn't bother him. Rather than talk about himself, though, he spoke about Wind Son.

"My grandfather said he was born to run with the wind." Hawk let his gaze stray back to his four-legged friend. "He also said that it was a blessing of the spirits to be allowed to run with him. Rather than seek to break the horse like the white man would do, I should seek to be his companion, not his master."

"He looks like the wind would have a hard time keeping up." Her smile showed more in her eyes than it did in the curve of her lips. "Your grand-father sounds like he was a wise man."

"He was." There was more he could say, but the wounds were still too new to speak of his death so easily.

"I need to be weeding the garden." She stepped back from the fence. "I could use some help." Then she walked away, leaving it up to him whether he would follow or not.

Hawk considered his answer. These people had fed him and his horse. Her father had offered to have Wind Son's foot seen to. Although he fully planned to leave as soon as it was safe to ride his horse long and hard, until then he should earn his keep. After all, his grandfather had taught him to return kindness with kindness.

For now, Wind Son was content to doze in the afternoon sun and didn't need Hawk's company. The yellow-haired woman with the sad eyes did. He climbed down off the fence and went in search of the garden and its crop of weeds.

It wasn't the first time Jed had slept in a barn, and it probably wouldn't be his last. He shifted a bit, trying to find a more comfortable position, although that wasn't what was keeping him awake. Tired as he was, his thoughts were too tied up in knots for him to slide easily into slumber.

For years he'd wondered what it would feel like to come back to the Johanson farm. Out of sheer stubbornness, he refused to think of it as home, although it was as close as he'd ever come to having one. Olga and Ole had opened their house and their hearts to him.

He rolled over on his back and stared up at the

dim outline of the rafters overhead. Well, he'd gotten his answer. Even after all this time, it hurt to see the place, mostly unchanged despite the years he'd lost, and know that he couldn't stay. He planned on hanging around a couple of days to make sure Hawk was settled; at least that was his excuse.

But then he needed to hit the trail and get back to his job. He wasn't sure that his boss would appreciate him spending so much time on this particular case. There were far more deadly criminals to be brought to justice than one half-grown boy with an ugly horse. But sometimes a man had to make decisions that he could live with and not just follow the letter of the law.

If the horse truly belonged to someone else, Jed would see to it that the big stallion was returned to his rightful owner. That didn't mean he was also going to hand Hawk over to the fine upstanding citizens of Cutter. The boy deserved a chance at a real life, with or without Wind Son. It might take some hard work to convince him that his best shot for a decent future was with the Johansons, but Jed could only hope that Ole was up to the job.

Some of the changes Jed saw in his old friend could be put off to the normal wear and tear on a man who worked the soil for a living. Kansas summers were blistering hot and the winters cold enough to freeze a man's bones. But there was something else wrong with Ole, something that had Sadie's blue eyes full of worry. Jed worried about them both, not that there was a damn thing he could do to help them.

Giving up on sleep for the time being, he reached for his shirt and slipped it on without buttoning it. He climbed down the rickety ladder and opened the barn door only wide enough to slide through sideways. The last thing he wanted to do was disturb anyone else.

Outside, he was about to walk down to the creek when a slight movement on the porch caught his attention. He stepped back into the shadows to watch to see if he saw it again. Had he been wrong to think Hawk wouldn't try to escape again until after Ole had the stallion shod? Surely the boy wouldn't risk harming his horse.

His patience was rewarded, although he would have missed the movement this time if he hadn't been watching for it. Someone was definitely on the prowl, but they were headed in the wrong direction if it was Hawk planning on running again.

Jed decided to do a little investigating before he raised the alarm. Keeping to the shadows, he worked his way around to the far side of the house. His quarry was definitely on the move again. Whoever it was knew the terrain, ruling out Hawk. Ole was unlikely to do much wandering at night, and if he did, he would doubtless take a lantern with him.

That left Sadie. Where in the world would she be going this late at night? Could she be meeting someone? The thought that she might have a secret lover made his gut burn. What kind of man would entice an innocent like Sadie into a late-night rendezvous? If the bastard were a real suitor, he'd come around in the daylight, not skulk about in the darkness.

Jed trailed Sadie until he knew where she was going. The creek that cut across the farm widened out into a deep pool about fifty yards down the trail she was following. It was the perfect place for a late-night adventure. The moon overhead would make the deep, still water shine like polished silver. The cluster of willows along the bank would offer sheltered privacy.

Well, not tonight. He had no claim on Sadie other than past friendship, but he owed it to her father to run off any man who would treat her in such a shabby manner. If only he'd thought to bring his gun with him. He'd take great pleasure in peppering the bastard's backside with a load of buckshot.

Sadie had reached the edge of the pool. He hadn't thought there was much left that would shock him, but realizing she was wearing her nightgown had his jaw dropping. What could she be thinking of? He dropped down behind a fallen log and waited to see what happened next.

She reached for the hem of her gown and started to lift it. Surely she wasn't going to . . . but she was. And he felt like a fool. Sadie hadn't hiked down to the pool to meet someone. Instead, she'd planned on taking a bath. And if he didn't say something soon, he was going to see far more of Sadie than either one of them would be comfortable with.

"Uh, Sadie, you might want to stop right there."

Chapter 3

Jed rose up out of the darkness, more shadow than substance. The unexpected sound of his voice sent Sadie staggering back a few steps before she recognized him. She managed not to scream, but just barely. Fighting to catch her breath, she glared at Jed. Then she noticed that he wasn't looking at her face because her gown was still hiked up to her knees. With a sigh of disgust, she dropped the soft fabric, letting it swirl back down to the ground.

Embarrassment made her lash out in anger. "What are you doing out here in the middle of the night?"

His teeth flashed whitely in the darkness. "I thought my prisoner was escaping."

"To do what? Take a bath?" She picked up the bar of soap and towel that she'd dropped on the ground. "That boy you dragged in is sound asleep, just like you should be. Go on back to the barn."

"You shouldn't be out here alone," he told her, stepping clear of the log he'd been hiding behind. "It's not safe."

As if she hadn't been making the same trip out to the pool since she was a child. "I'm fine by my-self. Now leave so I can finish what I came out here to do."

She halfway expected Jed to refuse to go, but finally he walked away. She waited until he blended back into the darkness, the sound of his footsteps fading away. After giving him plenty of time to make it back to the house, she eased into the silver coolness of the water. For the first time all day, she tried to relax, hoping the soothing slide of water over her skin would wash away the day's frustrations.

As if anything was going to take away the ache that started somewhere in her head and settled suspiciously close to her heart. She closed her eyes, but even that didn't help. Not when Jed insisted on reappearing in her life with no warning. But in truth, she probably wouldn't have handled it any better if she had known he was coming.

She drew some comfort from knowing that he wouldn't stay. If he hadn't found a good enough reason six years ago to make the farm his permanent home, what was there to offer him now? She had too much pride to hope that he'd finally look at her with the same longing in those hard eyes and see a woman worth loving.

He hadn't asked about her father yet, but he would. Her one fear was that once he knew that Ole was dying he'd feel obligated to stick around. She needed help around the farm, but she didn't need his. Not now. Not ever

She reached for the cake of soap she'd brought with her. She lathered her hair twice, finally rinsing it clean. Some of the day's heat carried over to the night air, but the water took on a delicious chill. The cool water felt like heaven, going a long way toward improving her mood. She lingered, dreading the walk back the house, back to the never-ending worry. As long as she could float in the cool and quiet world of midnight, she could pretend that none of her problems existed.

But she could only stay so long. Morning came early no matter what time she got to bed. And with two more mouths to feed, there was just that much more for her to do.

A slight twinge of guilt had her up and wading back to shore. Yes, she would have to crack a few more eggs and make a bigger pot of coffee, but Jed was no stranger to hard work. Even as a boy, he'd done more than his fair share of the chores. And his prisoner, Hawk, had pitched right in to help her weed the garden. If they eased her father's workload, even if for only a few days, she would be grateful.

She kept to the deepest shadows near the water until she'd dried off and slipped her gown back on. The thin cloth clung to her damp skin, but the warm night air would make fast work of drying everything out quickly. Wary of snakes, she slipped her feet back into her boots before starting back to the house.

A shadow detached itself from the trees ahead. This time, Jed's sudden appearance didn't startle her. She trusted him not to have peeked as she bathed, but she should have expected him to stay around to escort her back to the house.

"You didn't need to wait." She walked right by him, not caring if he followed her or hid out in the woods all night.

He fell into step beside her without saying a word. His silence was as irritating as a constant stream of chatter would have been, but she wasn't going to be the one to strike up a conversation. The time for talking between them had ended six years ago. Back then, she would have listened to his reasons for leaving. It would have hurt her, but she would have listened.

But now, after all this time, she simply didn't care. Much. At all, if she were smart.

"Do you always race back from the river?"

She hadn't realized that she'd been all but running. Rather than answer, she slowed to a more reasonable pace, not that she wanted to spend an extra second in Jed's company. But the path ahead was rocky with roots jutting out at just the right height to send an unwary person tumbling headlong into a tree trunk. It was bad enough that she was outside in a damp nightgown and her father's old boots without embarrassing herself even further.

Despite her resolve to ignore her companion, she couldn't. He made her skin ache with unfamiliar awareness. Well, not unfamiliar, but almost forgotten. It had been six long years since she'd felt this way. She knew the preacher's sermons were full of reasons why she shouldn't hate someone, but at that moment, she didn't care. She had no other name for the powerful emotion that sat on her chest like an anvil, making it hard to simply breathe when Jed stood near her. And she had good reasons for feeling the way she did.

When Jed left all those years ago, he'd taken her heart with him, and with it, most of her joy in living. Without it, she'd grow bitter and cold. The farm and hard work provided all the things her body needed to keep on living, but she no longer dreamed of a bright future. Tomorrow and maybe the day after was as far forward as she ever bothered to look. When each day was the same as the one before and the one to come, why bother dreaming?

The shadows faded into the clearing that surrounded the house and barn. She made an abrupt turn for the porch, hoping Jed would return to the hayloft and his bed without speaking. His fingers closed like a vise around her arm, once again thwarting her plans. She glared down at his hand, not so patiently waiting for him to let go.

He did so, but only reluctantly. Even then, he stood within inches of her. "Can we talk for a minute?"

"We have nothing to talk about." He was no longer a part of her life, his choice originally, not hers. Now she wanted to keep it that way. She made herself meet his gaze and waited to see what he had to say.

Damn, she was stubborn. And angry. That temper of hers made him want to do a hell of a lot more than stand out in the yard and argue. He bet she would show a man the same fiery temperament in bed. That is, if he could get past all those prickly thorns to kiss her without her drawing blood. If she even suspected how much he wanted to get his hands on her, she'd come after him with her pa's shotgun.

It was time to get to the point. "What's wrong with Ole?"

"Do you care?" Her chin came up, demanding an answer to her question before she'd answer his.

He jerked his hat off his head in frustration and crumpled the brim in his hands. "I care, Sadie. I've always cared."

"You have a funny way of showing it. Staying away for six years and then coming back just so you can dump that boy off on us." She started for the porch again.

Jed stepped in front of her. "Would you rather that I had taken Hawk back to Cutter where they'd just as soon hang him?"

That stopped her. Her eyes were wide with shock. "Hang him? He's just a child."

"That's what happens to horse thieves." He kept his voice dispassionate. "Sheriff there says the boy's grandfather sold Wind Son to a local rancher. Of course, the old man died before he could tell Hawk about it. From what Hawk says, his grandfather had been beaten. The boy stole the horse and took off. That's when they sent for me."

"And as a marshal, your job is to hunt down children?"

She made it sound as if he made a habit of it. "No, my job is to bring criminals in for trial." He glanced past her toward the house. "When I find out the truth of what really happened, I'll be back for Hawk."

"Even if they'll hang him?" She threw her towel down and balled her hands up in fists.

He didn't want to talk about it anymore. Turning the conversation back to the original topic, he asked, "What's wrong with your father?"

All of the starch went out of her. She slumped back against the porch railing. "If you must know, he's dying."

The words cut through him like a knife even though he'd been expecting something of the sort. It was just that Ole had always seemed bigger than life, a permanent part of the land that he loved. Logic should have warned Jed that the man who was the closest thing to a father he'd ever known would age and eventually die. But not yet, not by a long shot. There were too many boys out there that needed him.

He made himself ask, "How soon?"

Sadie shrugged. "I asked Doc the same thing. He said he wasn't God, so it wasn't up to him to know such things. He ordered Pa to slow down and not work so hard unless he was in a hurry to die." She gestured out toward the pasture. "You saw him out there today. Did that look like slowing down to you?"

Before he could answer, she was gone. The door closed behind her with a quiet click, as if she'd taken great care not to disturb those sleeping within. He bent down to pick up the soap and towel she'd dropped. Sleep was out of the question, at least until he managed work off some of the pain Sadie's answer had caused.

She wouldn't appreciate him using either her soap or her towel, but that was too damn bad. He needed to cool off more than he cared about making her happy. He followed the trail back down to the river where she'd bathed. There, he stripped off and threw his clothes over a bush to keep bugs and other unwelcome company from crawling into them. After setting his boots on a handy boulder, he waded into the river up to his waist and let the cool water work its magic.

He listened to his daughter's footsteps overhead as she paced back and forth in her room. If she knew he could hear so much, she would stop. But he allowed her the sense of privacy that she needed, especially now. He loved her as much as any man loved his daughter, but he wished she didn't take everything so hard.

She would hate knowing that he'd overheard

every word she and Jed had exchanged outside the house. He honestly didn't know which upset her more—Jed's unexpected return or her admitting that her pa was dying. At this point, she probably didn't know herself. Maybe she had a right to be angry with Jed, but she was just as angry with God, and that wasn't right.

A man was born, a man lived, and a man died. It was the way of all things, and part of the good Lord's plan. To rail against it was pointless, although he sure enough understood how she felt. Olga's death still hurt so badly sometimes that he felt as if he would die from the pain. Doc's dire prediction that Ole wouldn't live to see next spring didn't frighten him as much as it should have, not with Olga already there and waiting for him.

If only Sadie would find someone to love her, he would meet his maker with a cheerful heart. If she couldn't find a man, maybe she could make a family with that boy sleeping in the small room off the kitchen.

Except for Hawk's dark eyes, it was like looking back over the years and seeing Jed's face for the first time. Never before had Ole seen such desperate anger in one so young. He knew pride was a vice in God's eyes, but Ole took some pride in taming that one. It had taken months to coax that first heart-stopping smile from Jed, but the wait had been worth it. Jed had never learned to smile easily; trust was even a harder lesson.

But he'd grown up to be a man who knew right from wrong, which was why Hawk was here instead of jail. And if Jed could clear the boy's name, maybe Hawk would be willing to make the farm his home, a place to breed strong horses out of that stallion he loved so much. He hoped so because Sadie would need someone to fuss over when Ole was gone. It would be better if that someone would share her bed and give her babies, but he would be satisfied with the boy.

The clock in the hall chimed the time, reminding him that the hours were slipping through his fingers. He hated to waste them sleeping, but his worn-out body had its own opinions on the subject. Rolling over to face the open window, he pulled the covers up over his chest and listened for Jed to return from the river.

When he heard the barn door shut, he let himself sleep.

"Boy, I want to talk to you." Ole leaned on the pitchfork and waited for Hawk to look up. "I'd like to make you an offer."

They'd been feeding the stock and shoveling out the stalls for the past two hours. Despite his young age, Hawk had worked hard without complaining. Someone had done a fine job of teaching the boy how to pull his own weight.

Hawk stepped out of Wind Son's stall. His dark eyes narrowed with suspicion and distrust. "My horse isn't for sale."

"I'm not talking about your stallion. I'm talking about you." He moved to sit down on an old bench, putting himself more on the boy's level. "A smart boy like you has probably already noticed that there's a lot more work around here than I can get done by myself." He leaned back against the wall, glad of the chance to take a break.

Hawk nodded. "That's not got anything to do with me. I've got my own plans."

"I'm sure you do, but it's hard to accomplish much without money in your pocket." Ole took off his hat and ran his fingers through his thinning hair. "I thought you might be interested in a job."

That caught the boy's interest. "You'd pay me? Real money?"

Ole could almost see the big plans forming in Hawk's mind. It wouldn't do to smile. "Part of your pay will be money, but part will be a stall for your stallion, a bed for you, and home cooking. How does that sound to you?"

Hawk straightened his shoulders and stood taller. "I think that sounds fine, sir. But what about that marshal? He plans on hauling me back to Cutter."

"Only if I find out you stole that horse."

Hawk jumped back about three feet and stumbled over a bucket. He came up spitting mad. "I did not steal Wind Son. I get tired of telling you that."

Jed held up his hands in mock surrender. "Then you don't have to worry about me dragging you back to Cutter, do you?" Jed held out his hand for the pitchfork Ole had been using. "I told you I'd do the heavy work."

Ole ignored him. "So, boy, I don't want to hire a man I can't depend on to stay. Do I have your word that you'll stay through spring planting?" If he had him that long, chances were that he'd have him for a lot longer than that. He'd settle for help with the fall harvest, but it would be nice to have someone to do the planting for Sadie. Ole couldn't count on being around that long.

"I'll stay until the crops are in. After that, we'll talk." Hawk stuck out his hand to seal the agreement.

Ole stood up and took the boy's young hand in his gnarled one. "We need to let Sadie know that we've hired us a hand. I'm sure she'll be pleased."

He took a chance and put his hand on Hawk's shoulder. The boy flinched but stood his ground. "Why don't you go tell her what we've agreed to and bring back a pitcher of cool water for us to drink and maybe a handful of those cookies Sadie baked this morning?"

"Yes, sir." Hawk made sure to avoid stepping too close to Jed, but then he took off at a run.

Jed waited until he was sure that Hawk was out of hearing. "You haven't lost your touch, Ole. I thought you might have to hog-tie him at night to keep him from running off."

It felt damn strange to be jealous of an orphan finding a place to live. But then, he had firsthand experience in how good it felt to have Ole Johanson invite you to live in his home, to share his food, and to sleep safe at night. He genuinely hoped it worked out for Hawk. At least he was too young to be tempted by Ole's daughter.

"And how about you, Jed? Are you going to stay on to help with the harvest and the planting? Hawk will be a big help for Sadie and me, but he shouldn't have to do it all alone." Ole waited in that quiet way of his for Jed to answer.

"I can't." He had a job to do. He had to find out the truth about Hawk. He had to keep his distance from Sadie.

"You mean you won't, Jed. You didn't lie to me as a boy. Don't start as a man."

Ole picked up his pitchfork and went back to work, leaving Jed staring at his back and wishing he could deny the truth of what Ole said. Not for the first time he cursed the bad luck of getting saddled with Hawk and his problems. Until he'd looked into his dark eyes and seen himself, he'd been able to do his job without thinking about all he'd lost when he'd left the Johanson farm behind.

He wished he had the guts to yank that pitchfork out of his friend's hands and take over shoveling shit out of the stalls. It would certainly suit his rotten mood, but Ole would take it wrong. He'd think Jed thought he could no longer do the job. True as that was, he didn't dispute the man's right to work as long as he was physically able. If Ole gave up trying and sat down in Olga's rocker, he'd shrivel up and die that much sooner.

"I'm going to do a little target practice." It would solve nothing, but a lawman lived longer if he kept his skills sharp. "Send the boy if you need me." Then he dug a box of ammunition out of his saddlebags and headed down to the river. Maybe he'd even get lucky and bring back some fresh meat for the dinner table.

The air felt cooler by the river. He leaned his rifle against a stump and pulled out his revolver. Some men prided themselves on their fast draw, but experience had taught him that a careful aim went a lot further toward keeping him alive. He aimed at a knot in a sapling across the river and pulled the trigger six times, one right after the other. After reloading, he went for speed while trying not to sacrifice accuracy.

When he'd run out of extra bullets for his revolver, he slipped it back in its holster and picked up his rifle. With as much noise as he'd been making, it was unlikely that there was any game left in the area. But if he went some distance, he might find a couple of rabbits or even a turkey. No one would miss him if he stayed gone for hours.

Or even forever.

She jerked the curtain closed and glared at her hand as if it belonged to someone else. It was the third time in the last hour that she'd caught it pulling back the kitchen curtain so she could see if Jed had returned. It wasn't her business what he was doing. After all, she'd gone six years without knowing where he was. Just because he'd chosen to come back didn't mean she had to start caring again.

Maybe her father knew where Jed had gone, but he hadn't seen fit to tell her. And she wasn't going to ask. It couldn't have been far because she could see that pretty pinto mare of his dozing in the shady side of the corral. Well, fine. It didn't matter one whit to her if she was supposed to set a plate at the table for him or not. In fact, it would mean fewer dishes for her to wash.

Not that she had quite decided on what to fix for their evening meal. Earlier, she'd picked a bunch of greens and a few ripe tomatoes. If it were just her, that would be enough. As hot as it was, she was in no hurry to stoke up the stove to cook something. However, her father needed more substantial food to keep up his strength, and Hawk was a growing boy. She smiled. For a skinny kid, he sure ate a lot.

There should be enough of the ham left for another meal, especially if Jed didn't come back. Again.

She was reaching for her favorite cast-iron skillet when the door swung open. Without even looking, she knew Jed had returned. Telling herself that it wasn't relief she was feeling, she slammed the skillet down on the stove with a little more force than was necessary. Why didn't he walk on past her to the parlor where Ole sat reading his Bible? Or back out to the barn where he slept?

Finally, she gave up and made herself turn around to face him. "Did you want something?"

"I thought we might have squirrel for dinner." He'd already skinned and gutted four of them. "I can cook them, if you'd rather."

"Do you still burn everything?" When he'd lived with them, her mother had done her best to teach him enough to get by. It had taken days to get the burned smell out of the house. The shared memory made her want to smile, but Jed had either forgotten the incident or how to smile. Or, more likely, both.

He tossed the meat down in the sink. "Where do you keep the flour?"

Fine. Let him act as though he'd never set foot in this kitchen. The flour was in the same place where it had always been. Just like her. Well, she didn't need him getting in her way.

"I'll cook them. Go wash up." She began cutting up the squirrels, getting them ready to fry as Jed stood by and watched. After doing her best to ignore him, she finally asked, "Was there something you needed?"

"No."

"Well, thank you for doing this. It's been a long time since I've had squirrel." That much was true. Pa didn't often have the time or energy to go hunting anymore, and squirrel was one of her favorite dinners. Had Jed remembered that much about her? "It will be a nice change from chicken and ham."

She couldn't read the expression that crossed his face and then was gone as quickly as it had appeared. Abruptly, he left without a word, maybe because there was nothing to be said. And despite her best efforts, she wished there had been.

Hawk scratched that spot right behind Wind Son's ears that always made the big horse groan in pleasure. When anyone else came near the stallion, he always acted like a big tough hombre, kicking and trying to bite. But with Hawk, he was as gentle as a lamb. A hungry lamb. Hawk shoved the horse back.

"You've already had your treat. Quit trying to talk me out of another carrot." He kept his voice low, not wanting Sadie Johanson to find out that he'd raided her garden. "The other one is for your lady friend outside."

"She'll like that."

Damn! Hawk stepped back, careful not to get caught between the railing and Wind Son. The horse wouldn't deliberately hurt Hawk, but accidents could happen. If the lawman startled the horse into sidestepping, the big bay could easily break Hawk's arm or ribs. Hawk glared at his captor, tired of feeling like a mouse with one big cat playing with him.

And how did he move so silently? That wasn't the first time he'd managed to get within spitting distance without Hawk hearing him. His grandfather had known just about everything there was to know about tracking and hunting, and not even he could move with such silence.

Stark came over to the stall and put his boot up on the lowest rail and leaned on the top. "Sadie know you've been raiding her garden?"

No use in lying. "No. Figured she wouldn't miss a few carrots." He hoped not. She'd been nice to him; he should have known better than to steal from her.

"Her ma caught me doing the same thing." His silver eyes focused on something only he could see. "She told me that if I wanted to waste good food spoiling my horse, the least I could do was plant my own carrots."

"I'll talk to Sadie about it at dinner tonight."

Standing there with the lawman made Hawk nervous. He picked up a currycomb and started working on Wind Son's already gleaming coat. The familiar routine was soothing to them both.

After a bit, the lawman stirred. "My mare needs some exercise. If Ole doesn't have chores for you after dinner, do you want to run her for me?"

The offer shocked Hawk into almost dropping the comb. Was the lawman trying to tempt him into escaping? He felt more like a mouse than ever. "Why?"

Stark shrugged. "I've noticed the way you've been watching her, wondering if she's as good as she looks. I figure you can take my word on it or you can find out for yourself. Your choice."

Then he walked away, leaving Hawk staring after him. No matter what the man was up to, he wasn't going to miss his chance to ride that pinto. Until the farrier came out to fix Wind Son's shoe, he didn't want to ride him. This would be his first chance to learn more about where this farm was. With luck, it wouldn't be too far from the nearest town. Once he got the lay of the land, he'd be better prepared to make a run for it if that should become necessary.

He wished he hadn't been so quick to give his word to Ole that he'd stick around until at least the harvest was done. Not that he minded helping the old man out. But if Marshal Stark were to come riding back, ready to haul Hawk back to Cutter, he wanted to know which direction offered him the best chance of freedom.

Free to go where? The thought of that cold-eyed lawman dogging his footsteps filled him with a sense of dread. He still hadn't figured out why Stark had changed his mind about taking him back to Cutter. Instead, he'd brought him to these people, another puzzle in itself. It was obvious that the old man was glad to see Stark again.

But his daughter, now, that was another matter. She'd been real nice to Hawk, but she clearly wasn't happy about Jed hanging around. That brought a smile to Hawk's lips. He'd make a point of showing that lawman which one of them belonged there on the farm. After all, he had a nice bed in the house while Stark was sleeping in the barn with the horses and the milk cow.

Feeling better about everything, he patted Wind Son's neck. "I'm going to give your lady her carrot. I'll make sure to tell her that it's from you." Visions of handsome colts and fillies, some with the mare's coloring, some with Wind Son's, filled his head. A man could get rich with such fine horses to sell.

If he didn't get hanged for stealing a horse that was his. His eyes burned, but he wouldn't cry. If he hadn't let the tears fall when he found his grandfather's beaten and broken body, then he wasn't going to fall apart now. But it wasn't easy. He scrubbed at his eyes with the back of his hand to make sure that none of his sorrow had leaked out where Sadie or her father would see it. Or worse yet, those sharp eyes of that damn lawman.

Chapter 4

Dinner was a quiet affair. Jed ate enough to fill his stomach, but he hadn't tasted a thing. He wasn't sure how long he could continue to sit across the table from Sadie without doing something rash. He had no business wanting to brush that loose tendril of hair back behind her ear or trying to capture one of her bright smiles for himself.

She was wasting them all on his prisoner. Hawk had suddenly decided to turn into a chatterbox. Jed wouldn't think much about it, except twice he'd caught the boy giving him a look that made him clench his teeth. Somehow the kid had figured out that it would bother him to see Sadie smiling and even laughing with Hawk when she wouldn't even talk to Jed.

The kid was smarter than Jed had given him credit for. Well, he had better things to do than provide entertainment for a half-grown thief. Rather than watch any longer, he pushed his plate away and stood up.

Ole protested. "Sit, Jed. There's more to eat."

"I'm not hungry." At least for food, but that wasn't

something he was going to confess to his old friend. "I need to saddle up the pinto."

"You're leaving?"

It was Sadie who asked. She looked as surprised by that fact as he was. Maybe she was starting to get over some of her anger. He didn't know if that was a good thing or not.

"No. I promised Hawk here that he could take her out for a run. She's been cooped up too long." So had he, but he'd be moving on soon enough. Right now, he'd settle for getting Hawk away from Sadie for a while.

"Now that's a good idea." Ole nodded in approval. "A young boy should have a chance for fun."

Hawk carried his plate to the sink. "I'll be back to help with the chores."

He beat Jed to the door, heading for the corral at a dead run. Ole didn't move nearly as fast, but he wasn't going to be left behind. Jed hated leaving Sadie alone to clean up after the three of them, but he doubted she would appreciate his help. He asked anyway.

"The boy can saddle the mare. Do you want me to help with the dishes?" He wasn't sure whether he wanted her to accept his offer or not.

"No, I can handle it. Go help my father or he'll try to do everything by himself." She was already busy scraping the plates clean.

"Dinner was good. Thank you."

She glanced at how much he'd left on his plate, giving the lie to his compliment. As she scraped it into the slops for the hogs, he wished he'd just followed the others out the door.

"I'd better go make sure that the mare doesn't try something stupid. She doesn't much care for strangers."

Sadie laughed. "Tell me, have you ever seen a skittish animal that my father couldn't handle?"

"No. I should have said that I want to make sure that Hawk doesn't try to take off with my mare permanently." He watched Ole and the boy from the door. "I've already hunted him down twice. I don't want to do that again."

Sadie sidled closer, just like one of those skittish animals she mentioned before. If he made the wrong move, she'd put more than the table between them. He stood still, waiting to see what she wanted.

"Do you like what you do? I mean, hunting men like animals? You wear that gun like it's part of you." There was a note in her voice, suggesting she wasn't asking out of idle curiosity.

"I don't know that *like* is the right word, exactly." He struggled to find the right words to make her understand what drove him to wear a badge. "Most of the men I hunt down are little better than animals. Murderers, thieves, and worse. The only way we can stop them is being faster and smarter than they are." And meaner and colder, but he wasn't going to say that.

"Pa always thought you'd make a good farmer."

He would have laughed if that hadn't been a secret dream of his. He had few close friends outside of the Johansons, but none of them would ever have considered the possibility of him hanging up his guns any time soon. Not when he spent his free time, rare as it was, playing poker and hanging around in saloons.

Him, a farmer? No, not because he would hate the endless days of work that it took to keep food on the table. His problem was that he couldn't imagine working any farm but this one. With this woman.

"I'd better get out there."

This time she let him go without asking any more questions he didn't have answers for.

He had to leave tomorrow, the day after at the latest. For one thing, he needed to send a wire to his boss to let him know where he was and that he'd have to go back to Cutter. One way or another, he was going to make sure that no one else came after Hawk. If the boy was right about someone killing the old man to steal the horse, then Jed had a real crime to investigate. With or without the local sheriff's help.

Jed might not be Hawk's favorite person, but he was all that stood between the boy and jail. He'd wait until Hawk disappeared around the bend in the road before telling Ole his plans.

"When are you leaving?"

It shouldn't have surprised him that Ole guessed his intentions without him having to say a word. The man always had been uncanny that way. Jed couldn't count the number of times that Ole had managed to figure out what was bothering Jed, half the time before he'd figured it out for himself.

"Tomorrow, the next day at the latest." He didn't bother trying to sound sorry. As much as he would like to stick around to do what he could to make things easier for Ole—and Sadie—he had a job to do. At least that was the excuse he gave himself.

"Sadie won't be pleased."

Ole's bright blue eyes dared him to deny the truth of that statement, but Jed wasn't going to argue. She wouldn't be pleased; more likely, she'd be ecstatic to see him ride out, especially if he promised not to return. She'd made it all too clear that he wasn't welcome. He turned away, partly to watch for Hawk's return, but also to keep Ole from seeing too much.

"I'll come back when I can. Soon." He wondered if that little promise surprised Ole as much as it did him. He'd been known to lie when the occasion called for it, but never to this man.

Ole put his hand on Jed's shoulder, one of the few people whose touch he could tolerate. "Was it so hard coming back?"

The hard part was leaving in the first place, but he wasn't going to say that. He'd had no choice but to go, but his soul bled each step he'd taken down the road he'd gone. The wound had never completely healed, but he'd learned to ignore the occasional flare-up of the pain. Ole waited patiently for an answer when Jed had none for him.

"Send for me if Hawk proves to be a problem for you."

"He gave his word to stay through the harvest. You heard him." Ole left the corral, leaving Jed to tag along behind him like he'd done as a boy. "He'll be fine until then."

Jed wished he had Ole's confidence in Hawk's word. But short of tying him to the saddle again, he didn't have much choice but to ride out and pray the boy would stay put. He'd be a fool to walk away. Hawk was insolent and angry; he wasn't stupid. He would have offered to help pay for Hawk's keep, but he knew Ole would refuse.

"I have to check on a few things before I get back to Cutter. As soon as I know more about what happened, I'll let you know."

The two of them went into the barn. Jed did a quick sidestep to pick up the pitchfork before Ole could get to it. Ignoring the older man's frown, he began tossing hay into each stall. He wouldn't always be around to do the heavy work, but for tonight he could. It wasn't much, but it would have to be enough.

The two of them worked through the chores, falling back into habits that hadn't been part of Jed's life for a long time. The familiar routine felt good but bothered him for that very reason. It would be so easy to . . . What? Turn his back on his job? Forget the reasons he'd left in the first place?

"I know Wind Son is a big horse, but even he would have trouble eating that much hay."

Ole stood nearby, grinning from ear to ear. He was right. Jed had almost buried the big horse with hay. Son of a bitch, now all he needed was for Hawk or Sadie to see what he'd done for his evening to be complete.

"Maybe I think the haystack would look better over here." He started shoveling the excess back to where it came from. At least, he could count on Ole keeping the little joke to himself. He understood Jed's need to not look foolish in the boy's eyes. And Sadie already thought badly enough of him.

Ole carried in one last bucket of water. "Hawk is coming."

A little of the tension in Jed's gut eased. He'd been almost certain that Hawk would come back, that his love for Wind Son and the promise he'd made Ole would make sure of that. But there'd been that small piece of doubt that had kept him on edge. He leaned the pitchfork against the wall and stepped outside the barn.

It was hard to decide who was having the best time, Hawk or the mare. The mare was prancing, ready for another run. And right up until Hawk spotted Jed waiting for him, he had a big, wide grin spread across his face. He looked younger, allowing Jed a glimpse of how the boy would have looked all the time if life had been a bit kinder.

Hawk tried to guide the mare closer to Ole, but she'd have none of it. As soon as she caught Jed's scent, she fought against the reins to stop near him. He reached out and grabbed her bridle to calm her down. Hawk finally admitted defeat and dismounted.

"What did you think?" Jed led her back toward the corral. He'd already shared her more than he liked to. He'd take care of cooling her down and grooming her.

"I've ridden better." Hawk stood nearby, his hands shoved into the front pockets of his overalls. He managed to keep a straight face for a few seconds before the excitement bubbled up again. "But only Wind Son! She can almost fly."

Jed carried her saddle into the barn and slung it over a rack. "I like her speed, but I like her smooth gait even more. When a man spends most of his life on the move, that's as important as endurance or how fast a horse can run."

He rubbed her down with a burlap bag and then started working her over with a currycomb. Gradually, she settled down, accepting that her fun was over for the day. Jed nodded toward the barn. "You promised Ole you would help with the chores."

"Goldarn it! I forgot!"

Hawk took off at a run. Jed allowed himself a small smile. He knew from personal experience that the boy would have to learn to watch his cursing around both of the Johansons. A few more slips like that around Sadie, and she'd be after him with a bar of soap. In his own case, it had been her mother, Olga, who'd taught him to choose his words carefully, at least within her hearing. To this day, whenever he cut loose with a string of cusswords, he swore it left a taste of her homemade lye soap in his mouth.

He checked the mare's feet before turning her loose in the corral. He'd already filled the trough with fresh water and the feed box with oats and fresh hay. She was used to living outdoors and would be fine in the corral.

The sun was finally disappearing over the horizon, easing some of the heat that made the air feel heavy. He wiped the sweat off his face with a bandanna and stuffed it into his back pocket. Another bath in the pool upstream sounded like a good idea. He'd wait until Ole and Hawk turned in for the night before going. Maybe he'd even take along some of his clothes and wash them, too. They'd dry quick enough spread out over bushes. It would be nice to have his shirts clean again before riding out.

With that in mind, he headed into the barn to collect his saddlebags. He'd have to stop in town to buy supplies on his way back to Cutter. And as long as he kept his mind on the details, he would have to think about how much he didn't want to be the one riding out.

She stopped to listen. Just as she feared, someone was in the pool up ahead, and she knew exactly who it was. She'd had to boss Hawk into washing up back at the house, and her father only made an occasional trip upstream, preferring to bathe with a bucket of cold spring water from the pump.

That left Jed. How like him to invade not only her home but also the one spot she'd claimed as her own. She tried to draw some comfort from knowing that his intrusions would last only until he rode out again. She gave him one, maybe two days before they all watched him disappear over the horizon.

An unexpected sound caught her attention. She angled her head, listening to see if she heard it again. Her wait was short. She recognized what it was the second time, but it definitely came as a surprise. Unless she was sorely mistaken, Jed was washing his clothes in the river, scrubbing them with soap and then pounding them on the rocks before rinsing them out.

Did he think she wouldn't have done it for him? A couple of extra shirts and a pair of pants wouldn't have made that much more work for her. Of course, she hadn't told him that. Shame made her shrink back into the shadows. He'd been nothing but polite since his arrival. She'd been the one who snapped and snarled whenever he got near.

He deserved better from her. Even if his presence on the farm left her feeling out of sorts, her father was thrilled that Jed had come back home. She couldn't remember the last time Pa acted so energetic and cheerful. Maybe it was because he had another lost boy who needed him, but more likely it was because of Jed.

Bracing herself, she eased forward, still not sure what she was going to say or do.

Jed saved her the trouble. "I wondered how long you were going to hide."

"I wasn't hiding."

She was lying, and they both knew it. Jed didn't bother to contradict her; instead, he gave her one of those looks that made it clear that he expected better of her. She knelt down beside him and reached for one of his shirts and dunked it in the river.

"You don't have to do that." He picked up a bar of soap and began rubbing it on the knees of the pants he was washing.

"I know that." She held out her hand for the soap. "I figured the sooner you got done with your wash, the sooner I can take my bath."

"I was going to take one as soon as I get these washed." He kept his eyes on what he was doing, as if washing a pair of wet, soapy pants needed his complete attention. "You're welcome to stay."

All her good intentions disappeared. Even if he was teasing, the last thing she wanted was to think about him swimming in the river, naked in the moonlight. The surge of anger had her back on her feet and walking away, after slamming his wet shirt back down in the water where it could float away for all she cared. She didn't bother to hurry, though. Jed would follow after her, and even if she ran, he'd catch up with her within a few steps.

He moved to stand in front of her. That didn't mean that she had to look up at him. The nice thing about being a bit on the short side, everyone else was taller. If she looked straight ahead, she'd get a close-up view of the middle button on Jed's shirt, nothing more.

"Look, I'm tired. I'm going back to the house." She was proud of how calm she sounded.

He ran his fingers through his dark hair in frustration. "Sadie, give me a minute or two to finish up, and I'll get out of your way." He stood there, solid as an oak. It wasn't exactly an apology, but she knew it was as good as she'd get from him.

Her anger drained away. "Let's not argue about it. You got here first. Finish your laundry and take a swim. I'll be fine."

"Then I'll walk you back to the house." He stepped aside to let her pass.

"Don't be silly, Jed. I'm perfectly capable of getting there on my own. This is where I live, remember?" She made the mistake of looking up, his light eyes capturing her gaze and holding it prisoner. There was anger and something else that made her skin feel hot and shivery at the same time.

"Believe me, Sadie, I've never forgotten that, not for one damn minute." He reached out as if to touch her face, but then dropped his hand back down to his side, before stalking off, leaving her to stare after him.

When the sun came up, he was gone.

He urged his horse back into a canter, knowing they couldn't keep up this pace for long. But he needed to put as much distance between him and the Johanson farm as he could. He kept telling himself that if he went far enough, fast enough, he'd outrun the pain of leaving. Again.

Lies were lies, no matter how much he wanted to believe them. But that didn't matter. If he hadn't left when he did, it would have only gotten harder and harder to saddle up the pinto and ride away. At least there was a town a few hours' distance away, one that boasted of a saloon with cheap whiskey and pretty women to serve it. It wouldn't be the first time that he took solace in hard liquor and a whore's arms. He always woke up the next day sick to his stomach and sick at heart, but right now he didn't give a damn. Tomorrow would take care of itself.

A flash of silver off to his left caught his attention. Even if he didn't need to stop, the mare could use a break from the grueling pace he'd set since before sunrise. A cool drink of water and a few minutes of rest wouldn't hurt either one of them.

Once they reached the side of the creek, he dismounted and loosened the cinch to let the mare breathe a bit easier. He led her down to the water and let her drink a little. Once she was cooled down completely, he'd let her have more. For now, he turned her loose to graze for a spell, knowing she wouldn't stray far. Since they were stopping, he took his saddlebags and dumped his wet clothes out on the ground. The night had been warm enough for them to dry most of the way, but they'd been still damp when he packed them up. It was as good a time as any to let them finish drying.

He figured he would take an hour, maybe two at the most, before he would pack up again. Time for a cold drink and a short nap. He knelt by the creek and drank deeply. The water tasted good, washing away the dust in his throat. After splashing a few handfuls on his face and the back of his neck, he looked around for a comfortable place to sleep. On the far side of the water, a handful of willow saplings cast a small patch of shade on the ground. He hopped from rock to rock to the other side to find the least rocky spot and stretched out. Concentrating on the soothing sound of the shallow stream slipping past, he forced himself to relax.

It didn't work.

His mind kept circling around and around, always coming back to Sadie. He'd tried telling himself that he'd gone to the river last night because he really did need to wash his clothes, that he needed them clean before he could ride out. But he'd had all damn day to do his wash; instead, he'd chosen the one time he knew that Sadie was almost certain to find him. Instead of getting mad, she'd knelt down and tried to help him.

Hell, he didn't want her doing his laundry for him, touching his shirts and pants, leaving her scent on them where he'd be tormented by it, even if it was all in his imagination. Instead, he'd been deliberately rude, lashing out to drive her away like some half-crazed wounded animal would do.

He gave up on sleep and sat up. Guessing by the sun's position, he figured it was near noon or just after. If he were back at the farm, it would be time to eat. Unfortunately, in his haste to leave, he had yet to get any supplies. His stomach rumbled, reminding him how long it had been since he'd raided Sadie's kitchen for a couple of slices of bread and a piece of ham. He'd done without coffee, settling for filling his canteen with water from the well.

All the more reason to move on to the next town and the one after that. He'd stop for a night, gather up the necessary provisions, and ride on until he reached Cutter. Once there, he'd find out who was lying and who was telling the truth. If those bastards had banded together to rob the boy and his grandfather, there would be hell to pay.

After that, he'd wire headquarters to get a new assignment. Something, anything to keep him from returning to the Johanson farm. He'd promised Ole he'd be back, sooner than the six years it had taken him last time. His old friend didn't have six more years to wait for Jed to get up the gumption to come back again. So he'd come and he'd go until Ole was gone.

"Son of a bitch."

He had to be moving, moving on. After whistling for his mare, he gathered up his clothes and stuffed them back into his saddlebags. Stopping only to tighten the cinch, he swung up in the saddle and urged the mare into a fast trot.

And didn't look back. Not once.

* * *

As towns went, Cutter was a damn poor example: hardly more than a handful of buildings clustered around a wide patch of dust. What passed for a street was deeply scored with wagon wheel ruts and littered with piles of horse droppings. The town saloon was the first building he came to; Jed didn't bother to look any farther. It was also the only two-story structure in town, although it looked as if a good stiff breeze would blow the damn place down. The roof sagged tiredly, and the hot summer sun had bleached the last bit of life out of the wood.

It fit his mood perfectly.

He figured on getting a stiff shot of whiskey under his belt, find a hot meal and a place to sleep. Tomorrow would be soon enough to go looking for the sheriff. But luck wasn't with him. As he stepped up on the porch, the man in question shoved his way through the batwing doors. Jed ducked his head, hoping the man wouldn't recognize him in the fading evening light.

Unfortunately, the sheriff had a good eye for horseflesh. He recognized the pinto. "So, Marshal, you finally made it back." He looked up and down the street. "I don't see your prisoner. Did that big, tough boy prove to be too much for you?" His laugh was nasty.

"I have him." He slung his saddlebags over his shoulder, careful to keep his gun hand free.

"So where is the little breed? I've got a cell all ready for him." The man reeked of whiskey, which explained his careless words. He'd have to be blind not to notice that Jed's own heritage was the same as the boy's.

Jed ignored the man's questions and his bigotry. Some things never changed. If he lost his temper every time someone made a similar comment within his hearing, he'd be fighting all the time. "Is there a hotel in town?"

"No." The sheriff spat a stream of tobacco juice on the ground. "The saloon rents out a couple of rooms upstairs, with or without a roommate, although that costs more."

A feminine laugh rang out from above their heads, sounding a bit drunk and forced. Whoever she was, he doubted if he'd be interested in having her share his room or his bed for the night. He had some pride.

"I'll be by to talk to you in the morning." He hoped that would be enough of a dismissal to keep the sheriff from following him back into the saloon. It didn't work. Jed ignored him as much as he could.

Just his luck. The sheriff decided to play host. "Hey, Paddy. The marshal here is looking for a room."

The bartender looked up from the glass he was polishing with a rag only slightly cleaner than the bottom of Jed's boots. "Got one left. Upstairs, second door on the right."

Jed wondered if the sheriff would try following him up to his room. He hoped not. "I'd like some whiskey and something to eat. Any suggestions?"

Paddy pulled a half-empty bottle out from behind the bar and set it down beside the glass he'd been polishing. "My wife will bring you a hot meal, as long as you pay up front."

Jed hoped the man's wife kept her kitchen cleaner than her husband did the saloon, but he wasn't in a position to be picky. "See if she'll deliver breakfast, too. Let me know when that runs out." After tossing a gold piece down on the bar, he picked up the bottle. "I'll be upstairs."

The sheriff grabbed Jed's arm. "You going to tell me about the boy? I need to let the judge and the witnesses know when he'll be here to stand trial."

Jed stared down at the hand and then slowly looked up at the sheriff's face. If the bastard hadn't been half drunk, he would have known better than to do something so stupid in the first place. It wasn't worth killing the man over, but the thought was tempting.

Something in Jed's expression must have made an impression. The sheriff jerked his hand away and backed up several steps. The brief taste of fear made him angry. "Listen, I asked a simple question. When are you bringing that brat back to stand trial?"

Rather than answer him, Jed tossed the whiskey bottle back to the bartender. The unexpected move had Paddy juggling to keep the bottle from smashing on the bar. Meanwhile, Jed drew his gun at the same time he grabbed the sheriff by the front of his shirt and slammed him up against the bar.

"First, you don't ask the questions. I do. Second, keep your hands to yourself or I'll be forced to teach you some manners." He jammed the barrel of his pistol against the sheriff's fat neck. "Now, I'm willing to forget all this happened if you walk back out that door without saying another word. What do you say?"

There was a healthy amount of fear in the man's eyes as he nodded. But there was enough anger mixed in with it to warn Jed that he'd just made an enemy. Too damn bad. He'd dealt with enough men like the sheriff in his life. He'd have to watch his back as long as he was in town, but that was nothing new.

He stepped away from the flustered lawman. "I will see you in the morning."

The sheriff shot him another nasty look before stumbling toward the door. No one in the room said a word as Jed held his hand out to retrieve his bottle from the bartender's shaking hands. He tucked it into his saddlebags. "You said the second room on the right, didn't you?"

"Y-yes, sir. Upstairs. Second on the right." Paddy immediately busied himself at the far end of the bar.

"I need to see to my horse."

Paddy was only too willing to be helpful. "There's a corral just past the last building on the far end of town. The owner will see to it that your horse gets water and hay." He cleared his throat. "For a price, that is."

No surprise there. Everything had its price. "Thanks. I'll be back in a few minutes."

He stepped out onto the porch and took a careful look around. Chances were that the sheriff was already safely behind closed doors, but there was no use in being careless. His mare shook her head and snorted. He wasn't the only one well overdue for a good meal and a night's sleep. They'd both been pushing hard for the past three days.

He patted her nose. "Come on, Lady. Let's get you settled in." She followed along behind him, her head hanging down in weariness. He knew just how she felt. Luckily the stable owner lived next to the corral and came out as soon as he heard Jed swing the gate open.

"Who is out there?"

"I'm Marshal Stark. I need to stable my mare."

"Turn her loose in there for the night. I should have a stall for her tomorrow." He stepped closer to the fence. "I can store your saddle in my tack room, if you'd like."

"Thanks. How much do I owe you?"

"Not a thing, Marshal. The town will take care of the charges." He closed the gate after Jed and led him around to the tack room.

On his way back to the saloon, Jed wondered if the townspeople would be so eager to pay to stable his horse once they realized that his intention was to clear Hawk's name. Probably not, but that was too damn bad. They'd be lucky if a couple of their leading citizens didn't end up dangling at the end of a rope by the time he finished with them.

Because if Hawk was innocent, someone else was guilty of both murder and horse theft. Tomorrow morning, he'd start to work. Not just for Hawk, but for Ole and Sadie as well.

Jed arrived at the jailhouse just after sunrise. He figured on catching the sheriff early enough that he wouldn't be completely awake. Lack of sleep and the effects of last night's whiskey might make the man careless. He was right.

While he helped himself to some coffee, he kept his voice friendly as he asked his first question. "Which judge is coming?"

Sheriff Nolan stretched his arms overhead and yawned. "What judge? We're not expecting..." He snapped his mouth shut when he realized what he'd let slip. "I mean, we're not expecting him for another week or so. Judge Hartley normally covers this area. He should be along presently."

So, contrary to what the sheriff had said the night before, they hadn't contacted the judge at all. Interesting.

"I'd like to talk to the rancher who claims he bought Hawk's horse from his grandfather." The coffee was mud thick and tasted like tar. He poured himself another cup.

"I'll take you out there later this morning."

"No need. Just give me directions. I don't want to take you away from your regular duties." He took a long drink of coffee, ignoring the taste, and set the cup back on the woodstove.

"But—" He was waking up enough to bluster.

"Don't worry about it, Sheriff. I'm sure the man at the stable can give me directions."

Then he walked out, hoping the man wouldn't follow. Nolan wasn't dressed, which would give Jed a little extra time. If he hurried, he could be gone before Nolan had a chance to catch up with him. Putting two fingers in his mouth, he gave a shrill whistle that brought the pinto running. He got her saddled and ready to ride before the stable owner came outside. Still no sign of the sheriff.

"Morning, Marshal. You're out early. Pleasure or business?"

"Business. Sheriff Nolan asked for help on a case he was investigating. Thought I'd start talking to some of the people involved." It wasn't actually a lie. Nolan had asked for help dragging Hawk and his horse back to Cutter There had been no mention of an investigation of any kind. The sheriff hadn't wanted a lawman; he'd wanted a bounty hunter.

"I've forgotten the rancher's name who made the complaint against the boy." He glanced back toward the jail. "I didn't want to disturb the sheriff."

"Well, you'd be wanting to talk to Mitch Grant. He's the one who claims to have bought that boy's stud." He pointed to the east. "Ride that way for about three miles until you hit a good-sized creek.

Follow it upstream and you'll run right into his place."

Interesting way that he'd phrased it, saying Grant only claimed to have bought the stud. Might be not everyone in Cutter believed Grant's story even if the sheriff seemed to.

"Did you know the boy or his grandfather?"

"They didn't come to town much." His eyes shifted down the street behind Jed. Maybe toward the jail, but it was hard to tell. "Some folks make it tough on Indians and such. They always paid their bills on time and did a damn fine job breaking horses. I bought a few from them myself."

"Did you get a bill of sale from them?"

"Hell no. We did business with a handshake. The old man had no use for paperwork of any kind. Never had any trouble because of it."

Now wasn't the time to press the man too much. The longer Jed stayed in town, the better the chance Nolan would catch up with him. Unless the sheriff had sent word to Grant last night, the rancher wouldn't be expecting Jed to show up on his doorstep. Considering no one seemed to be expecting him to do an actual investigation, maybe the rancher wouldn't have hidden his trail very well.

For Hawk's sake, Jed hoped so.

Chapter 5

Two hours later he had his answers including the forged bill of sale supposedly signed by Hawk's grandfather. As soon as he saw the neat signature, he'd commented how nice the handwriting was, considering he had a reliable witness that the man could neither read nor write.

Just like most bullies, Grant was a coward at heart. Jed had pushed him hard enough to trigger the man's considerable temper. After accusing Jed of siding with Hawk because of their shared heritage, he took a wild swing at him. It didn't take much effort for Jed to have him flat on the ground with his hands tied behind his back. Grant would have a few bruises that were absolutely necessary, but they gave Jed some satisfaction.

Several of Grant's men came running, but at the sight of Jed standing over their boss with gun in hand, they slowed down. He'd been in this same position more times than he could count. So far, he'd survived.

"Stay back and he won't get hurt."

One of them was stupid enough to make a play

for his gun. Jed made sure it would be a good long while before he'd have full use of his wrist again.

"Maybe I should have said, stay back and no one will get hurt. Now, we can do this one of two ways. One of you can go saddle a horse for your boss and lead it out here or I can drag his worthless hide all the way back to Cutter. It makes no difference to me."

He was pleased to see that they were taking him more seriously. Two of them tore off toward the barn. In record time, they returned leading a good-looking sorrel. Jed stepped away from his prisoner and mounted up, careful to keep his gun aimed right at Grant, who was struggling to stand up. Jed tossed a rope to the ground, while keeping one end in his rein hand.

"Loop that around his horse's neck and then toss Grant up in the saddle."

Grant tried to jerk free from his men's attempt to help him. "Listen here, you half-breed bastard, Sheriff Nolan will see you hanged for this!"

If he was hoping Jed would get careless because of a few insults, he was mistaken. As far as Jed knew, he *was* a half-breed bastard. The truth didn't make him a fool.

"You've got thirty seconds to get up on that horse before I start shooting."

"You won't live long enough to take down all of us," Grant snarled. Brave words coming from an unarmed man whose men were staying a healthy distance away from him.

"Your men are smart enough to realize that I won't be aiming at them, Grant. You'll be the first one dead and they know it. Do you pay them well enough to risk their lives?" He grinned, showing lots of teeth. "I doubt it. Men who try to steal horses from little boys aren't known for being particularly generous."

From the look on their faces, this was news to the men. Jed pressed his advantage, shaky as it was. "I take it that it was Sheriff Nolan who helped you with that little deal. Indians might not be treated the same as white people around here, but most folks draw the line at stealing horses. After all, it's a hanging offense."

Two of the men held their hands up to show they weren't going for their guns. Between the two of them, they wrestled their employer up onto the horse. One of the others slipped the rope around the sorrel's neck so Jed could lead him back to town.

"Anyone stupid enough to try to rescue Grant, keep in mind he'll be the first one shot. A dead boss can't reward such loyalty." Jed spurred his mare forward, breaking into a run. His prisoner wobbled in the saddle, damn near falling off before he managed to catch his balance. If there was time, Jed would stop a safe distance from the ranch and tie him to the saddle, much as he'd done for Hawk. But maybe not. The bastard deserved little in the way of fair treatment.

When they finally slowed to a safe pace, Grant cursed Jed and his traitorous men with equal fervor. There wasn't anything he was saying that Jed hadn't heard before. That didn't mean he liked it, but he'd long ago outgrown the need to use his fists because of words. The man would pay dearly enough for his crimes. Jed would be satisfied with that.

Of course, he still had to get his prisoner safely tucked into the local jail, along with his good friend, Sheriff Nolan. Seemed fitting that they share the same cell until the judge passed sentence on them. Then they'd either spend a long time looking out of prison bars or they'd dance at the end of a rope.

Either way, justice would be done. And that was enough for Jed.

Sadie stood on the porch and watched her father and Hawk working on some harness. Pa was probably explaining to the boy how important it was to make sure that everything was in good condition before time to start harvesting the wheat they'd planted. Although Hawk was still quiet and reserved, if not a bit surly at times, he seemed to hang on to every word her father said. Maybe Ole reminded him of his grandfather. The boy hadn't been living with them more than a couple of weeks, but already it seemed as if he'd been with them forever. And despite her earlier misgivings, she was grateful for his continued presence. There was considerably more life in her father's footsteps these days.

Of course, Pa was convinced that Hawk would stay on indefinitely and that Jed would be back any day. After all, he'd promised as much, but that was before he left without saying good-bye to any of them. She knew her father believed in Jed's good intentions. For his sake, she hoped Jed had been telling the truth. But for her own sake, the thought of seeing Jed return made her pulse race and her stomach churn.

She'd replayed the last night of his stay over and over in her head, wondering what she'd done—if anything—that had resulted in his abrupt departure. She'd refused his invitation to swim in the river with him, but that was hardly an excuse for such behavior. Her father was willing to forgive Jed most anything, but leaving without even a word had hurt his feelings. When he did return, she planned on giving him an earful about his lack of common courtesy.

It was time to start the evening meal. She planned to put some soup on to simmer before going back outside to weed and water her vegetable garden. For the next hour, the nearby trees shaded most of it, making it marginally cooler than it would be later in the sun. She was turning to go inside when something caught her eye.

Blinking her eyes several times did nothing to change what she saw. Rather than watch Jed's slow approach, she took the coward's way out and pretended she hadn't seen him Inside, she added another couple of potatoes to the pot, along with extra carrots. That was as much of a welcome as he was going to get from her.

But despite her resolve, she stepped back out on the porch. It was too hot to be inside, was the excuse she gave herself, but that was a lie. Rather than standing on the porch, however, she forced herself to start weeding the garden just as she'd intended.

A shadow fell over her as she started to set her bucket down to fill it for the second time. The pump handle clanked loudly as cool water started gushing out. It was too much to hope that Hawk had decided to help without being asked. The shadow was too long and the boots she could see out of the corner of her eye were too big.

"You're back."

She picked up the bucket and walked away. She half expected him to try to carry the water for her, but he didn't. Instead, she heard the pump handle working again. She risked a quick peek back over her shoulder and almost dropped the bucket on her foot. As it was, she lost almost half the water, most of it spilling down her skirt.

Lord of mercy, Jed had stripped off his shirt and was holding his head under the running water while Hawk pumped the handle for him. When he straightened up, he shook his head, sending a shower of water flying from his shoulder-length black hair. She could only be grateful he was facing away from her; otherwise, he would have caught her staring at his smoothly muscled back with her mouth hanging open like a fish.

The effect on her came as a surprise. After all, he'd lived with them long enough for her to have seen him without a shirt before. But that was before he'd come into his full growth and she hadn't been looking at him with a woman's eyes and a woman's thoughts. Then she noticed the ugly scar high on his shoulder that made her wince—she hadn't seen many bullet wounds in her life, but she recognized the scar for what it was.

She closed her eyes and fought down the nausea that threatened to embarrass her. How close had he come to dying without them even knowing it? Would they ever have found out? It hurt to think he could have gone to his grave without her there to mourn him.

And that scar wasn't the only evidence of the violent life he'd been living since he'd left their farm behind. A crooked slash cut across his ribs to disappear around toward the front of his chest. Who had come after Jed with a knife in his hand and murder in his eye? She didn't really want to know. The good Lord said to love her fellow man, but she couldn't quite bring herself to feel that way about someone who had tried to kill Jed.

She must have made some little noise or else

Hawk had said something, because Jed stopped using his shirt as a towel and looked back over his shoulder. His eyes flicked down at her wet skirt from where she'd spilled her water.

"Do you need me to get out of your way?" He stepped away from the pump.

She nodded, glad for the excuse he'd offered her. "Yes, I'd appreciate it." She quickly set her bucket back under the pump, hoping that neither Hawk nor Jed noticed how unsteady her hands were. Hawk gave the handle a couple of quick pumps, topping off the bucket for her.

This time, she picked it up and walked straight toward the safety of her garden on the far side of the house. She kept her eyes firmly on her destination, walking slowly and steadily and without spilling a drop. There she finished weeding before picking a few ripe tomatoes and a handful of carrots. Now that the mare was back, Hawk would need twice as many to slip to the horses when he thought she wasn't looking.

Finally, she poured the water, stretching it as far as she could. She wasn't sure she could face another humiliating trip back to the pump, especially if Jed was still there. When she'd stretched her time in the garden to its limit, she picked up the bucket and her hoe. Rather than put them back inside the barn, she left them on the front porch.

Inside the kitchen, she felt more in control of herself, finding the common routine of setting the table and serving up the simple soup soothing for her overwrought nerves. Now that Jed was back, she needed every minute of peace and quiet that she could find.

* * *

The cold-eyed lawman was back. If he had news about Hawk's fate, he hadn't shared it yet. No, he was too busy pretending not to watch Sadie when his eyes secretly followed every move she made. Why didn't Ole notice the ugly hunger in Stark's gaze? If Sadie were Hawk's sister, he would come after the man with a gun for daring to be so bold.

For a marshal, he didn't seem to have his mind on his work. Was he here to arrest Hawk? Or to try to take Wind Son away? He'd hoped to have some warning before Stark returned, ready to decide Hawk's fate once and for all. The cocky bastard didn't seem at all worried about Hawk making a run for it, especially since the farrier had replaced Wind Son's loose shoe. Ever since the day his horse had been declared sound to ride again, Hawk had taken the stallion out for a daily run. He'd learned a great deal about the surrounding area and had an escape route all picked out, not that it would do him a bit of good.

He kicked a rock, sending it flying across the corral. If only he hadn't made the promise to stay through harvest with Ole and his daughter. His grandfather's spirit would not rest easily if Hawk were to break his word so easily. So, here he sat, caught in the trap of his own promise and the lawman's threatening presence.

"We need to talk."

Hawk wanted to ignore Jed, but he knew the man would have his say one way or another. "So talk."

"I went back to Cutter." The tall lawman stepped closer to Hawk. Once again he put his boot up on the low rail and rested his arms on the top one, obviously a position he found comfortable.

It made Hawk feel crowded. If the man wanted

him to ask him to continue with his story, he'd have a long wait.

"I saw the bill of sale that Grant swore your grandfather signed. Seems the only witness to the sale was Sheriff Nolan." He had a piece of grass in his mouth. "For a man who could neither read nor write, your grandfather had a fair hand."

"That paper is a lie! Those bastards tried to steal my horse and murdered my grandfather!" Tears stung Hawk's eyes. He swiped at them, hoping the marshal didn't notice. "And if you don't believe me, you're as much of a bastard as they are."

He clenched his fists, wishing he was big enough to punish Stark for believing the wrong people.

"I can't really say I'm a bastard for certain, but I've always figured I was. However, I didn't say I believed either of them. In fact, that's what took me so long to come back. It took over a week for the judge to come to Cutter to hear the evidence against both Grant and Nolan. A couple of the townspeople testified that your grandfather had always done business with a handshake because he couldn't read."

"What did the judge say?" Did he dare hope that a white judge would take Hawk's side?

"The judge sent both of them to prison for forging the bill of sale." Jed looked down at Hawk. "Without witnesses to the actual murder of your grandfather, the judge wouldn't sentence them to hang." There was real regret in the lawman's voice, but he looked away again. "I'm sorry about that. I tried."

"Was it because my grandfather is . . . was an Indian that he couldn't get a white man's justice?"

"I could say no, but I would be lying. Or at least,

I can't swear that it wasn't why. This judge is normally a fair man, so it is hard to tell." He shrugged.

"And Wind Son?" Hawk's voice came out as a squeaky whisper. "Is he mine?"

"Yes. As you are your grandfather's only kin, the horse is yours." Jed pulled a piece of paper out of his pocket and held it out. "I had the judge put that in writing so there's no doubt. You can read it for yourself."

Hawk took the paper, but didn't look at it. His grandfather wasn't the only one who couldn't read. If the lawman suspected that was the case, he didn't say so directly, but his next words strongly hinted that he did.

"You might have Ole read over that with you later, boy. In case there are words you don't understand."

Then Jed walked away, leaving Hawk alone, his head full of questions he had no answers to. He had no desire to return to Cutter, not by himself. At least he had a home for another few weeks here with the Johansons. That would give him some time to make plans now that he had a future to look forward to.

There was only one thing that stuck in his craw. He didn't want to feel grateful to Stark. He knew full well that one reason that Ole and his daughter had accepted Hawk into their home so easily was that he reminded them of Jed Stark. He didn't want to be a substitute for anyone, especially the lawman.

Hawk could only be grateful that some of the townspeople had spoken up for his grandfather, and therefore Hawk. Otherwise, he had no doubt that Stark would have dragged him back to stand trial without a second's hesitation. The Johansons might have been sorry to see him go, but they wouldn't have stopped their good friend.

No, he didn't owe the marshal a damn thing. He stuffed the judge's letter in his back pocket. It might prove helpful sometime, but he only had the marshal's word about what it said. Maybe he would have Ole read it over for him, to make sure that it wasn't something else entirely.

"Supper is ready!" Sadie's voice rang out over the yard, calling them all in to eat.

Hawk patted Wind Son on the nose, promising to come back later. Maybe they'd even go for a long run before it got too dark. He needed to get away for a while. He liked and respected Ole Johanson, and his daughter had been nothing but kind to him, even if she did nag him into bathing far too often. But he was used to spending a great deal of time outside and alone. Now that the marshal was back, he felt caged in even if the lawman said that Hawk was no longer wanted by the law.

He stopped at the pump to wash his hands and face, another concession to Sadie's cleanliness requirements. Ole was there ahead of him, talking to Jed about something. Evidently, they both knew they wouldn't be welcome at Sadie's table with dirty hands and sweat-stained faces, as if that made the food taste any better.

He considered skipping the routine to see if she would even notice with Jed at the table. But no, she was standing on the porch to make sure that no one tried to slip past her guard.

"Here, boy, I will pump for you and then you will pump for me." Ole reached for the handle, but Jed stepped in front of him.

"I'll do it. You two go ahead."

Ole frowned, clearly not happy to have his plan

overridden. "I can pump water, Jed Stark. Don't think I can't."

"But this time you don't have to. I need to earn my keep somehow." With a couple of quick movements, he had the water flowing. "Hurry before the food gets cold and Sadie blames it on me."

Ole's appetite was not what it used to be, but he made himself eat enough to keep Sadie from fussing at him. She seemed to be convinced that if she fed him enough she could heal what ailed him. He couldn't tell her that no amount of soup, however delicious, would ease the bone-deep weariness that followed him around like a black storm cloud.

Some days were better than others. Today was one of the good ones, with the sun to warm his old bones and the people in this world whom he cared about the most all safely at home. While he toyed with his food, he studied each of the others sitting around the table in turn.

Hawk, the newest member of Ole's extended family. The boy had suffered some heartbreaking losses in his short life, and it showed in his dark eyes and the somber set to his mouth. Given time, though, his rare smiles would come more often. Rebuilding his trust in other people would be trickier, but it could be done if they were careful.

Now that Jed had cleared the boy's name, Hawk was free to do as he pleased. But whether he knew it or not, Ole intended to hold him to his promise to stay through harvest time. By then, they would have either won his heart or sent him off with their best wishes.

Ole noticed that Sadie had stopped eating to stare at him. Dutifully, he picked up his spoon and took another bite of food. He wished she wouldn't worry so, but the time would come soon enough that he wouldn't be there for her to fuss over. If eating more than he wanted made her happy, it was little enough to ask.

His Sadie was a strong woman, just as his beloved Olga had been. A man could do far worse than to wed a woman who would stand shoulder to shoulder with him against all that life could bring—good times and bad. He studied her face from across the table.

Her eyes were the deep blue of the cool early morning sky, but they could darken to the edgy color of a spring storm. And her smile brightened the darkest days and eased the heaviest heart. It was no wonder that a man full of shadows and black memories like Jed would be drawn to her. Ole smiled. Of all the men he'd ever met, Jed Stark was the hardest one to read.

He and Olga had done their best to soften his rough edges and to ease the anger that had been burned deep into Jed's soul. But despite their best efforts, he'd hung on to that hard shell that kept most people from seeing past it to the good man underneath. But Ole knew. And if Sadie would let go of the hurt that Jed's leaving six years before had caused her, she would know it, too. Then, maybe with the fading time that Ole had left, the two of them could convince Jed to see it for himself.

Well, he'd been lost in his own thoughts for too long. Four people sitting around the same table and breaking bread together should not be so silent. If none of the others would speak first, then he would.

"Hawk, Jed has told me about the judge's decision. I know that it won't bring back your grandfather, but you are now free of the burden of worry."

He smiled at the boy first to show that he was indeed pleased for him. Then he gave Hawk a stern look. "I am sure that you remembered to thank Marshal Stark for risking his life in order to save yours."

Jed's hand froze halfway to his mouth, his eyes narrowing in disapproval. Ole didn't care. Hawk needed to learn manners. And whether he knew it or not, Jed needed to hear that at least someone appreciated the extra effort he'd taken to clear the boy's name. Ole didn't know any other U.S. Marshals, but he suspected at least some of them would have dragged the boy and his horse back to Cutter and considered the job well done.

After giving him a puzzled look, Sadie turned her attention to Hawk. She gave him an encouraging smile. Hawk kept his eyes on her even as he spoke. Jed, on the other hand, shot a dark look in Ole's directions, telling him without words that he neither wanted nor deserved Hawk's gratitude.

Hawk managed to mumble, "Thanks, lawman." He immediately took an enormous bite of bread to keep from having to say anything else.

Ole shot Jed a look, arching an eyebrow to remind Jed of his manners, too.

"You're welcome." He went for more soup rather than the bread, but his motivation was the same. As long as his mouth was full, he didn't have to engage in any more dinner conversation.

"Jed, you will stay a few days." Ole made sure it sounded like a statement of fact rather than a question. He didn't miss the quick look Jed gave Sadie before answering.

"I will try." He pushed his plate away and stood up. "If you'll excuse me." He didn't wait for an answer before he disappeared out the door without looking back.

Hawk mimicked his action except that he went into his room and closed the door, leaving Ole alone with Sadie. He considered making a quick retreat himself because he recognized the look on his daughter's face. Unless he missed his guess, he was in for a scolding.

"Pa, I know you mean well, but you can't force those two to like each other." She began clearing the table. "No matter how much you want them to."

"I never said they had to like each other, but I do expect them to watch their manners." He leaned back in his chair and waited for her to have her say.

"Jed doesn't want to be here. You shouldn't shame him into staying." She took his plate. "He left for his own reasons six years ago, strong enough reasons that kept him gone all that time."

The sadness in her lovely eyes hurt his heart. Jed had never said in so many words why he had felt it necessary that he leave, but Ole had his suspicions. He hadn't missed the way his too young daughter had taken to following Jed around the farm, her heart's desire there in her big eyes for anyone to see. Perhaps he and Olga should have stepped in and tried to warn her off, but it simply never occurred to them to try. The only one who objected to Sadie's interest in Jed was Jed himself. Noble fool that he was, Jed probably thought he wasn't good enough for Sadie, partly because she was so young, but mainly because of Jed's own background.

It was nonsense then and it was nonsense now. Ole wasn't about to let another six years go by without trying to bring Jed home to stay. He didn't have six months, much less six years, left to waste. He'd given Jed the freedom to leave once, hoping he would realize that his heart and home were here on the farm.

"Maybe Jed doesn't know what's good for him." Ole knew his daughter would rise to that bait quickly enough.

She glared at him from across the room, hands on hips and a spark of fire in her eyes. "And who says you know any better? You won't listen to Doc about what you can and can't do. You won't listen to me, either. And that somehow makes you an expert on what's good for that boy in there? Or for Jed?"

She threw her towel down on the table and stomped up the stairs to her room. Well, he'd managed to stir up a hornets' nest, that's for certain. Maybe if none of them were talking to him, they'd talk to each other. He didn't want to sit by himself in the kitchen. After considering his options, he decided that Jed deserved his company. Pleased with his evening's work so far, he finished clearing the table before heading out to the barn.

Jed eyed his saddle and considered whether or not he should take the coward's way out of the mess he was in. He'd done what his conscience dictated and cleared Hawk's name. Despite what Ole thought, gratitude wasn't necessary for doing the job he was paid to do. Hell, as long as he walked away from a hunt without bleeding, that was all the thanks he wanted or needed.

He looked around the barn, needing something to keep his hands busy, his mind occupied. Finally, he decided that whether or not he decided to leave, his mare needed a good brushing. Maybe she'd prove to be better company than his own dark thoughts were. He led her from her stall and reached for the hoof pick. Before he had one foot done, the door of the barn slid open.

Damn it! The last thing he wanted right now was company. Without looking up, he ran his hand down the mare's right foreleg and lifted her hoof. She stirred restlessly, warning him that someone else was getting too close. Jed looked up long enough to see that it was Ole and not Hawk or Sadie invading his territory. He supposed that was good news.

He moved on to the back legs, hoping that his old friend would take the hint and leave just as quietly as he'd come in.

"There you go, girl." He gave the mare a good ear scratching before picking up the brush. The repetitive long strokes along her neck and chest soothed him as much as they did her. For the first time all evening he felt like smiling when her skin twitched as he hit a ticklish spot, causing her to snort loudly near his ear.

"She's as touchy as you are." Ole sat down on the bench behind Jed. "I can see why the two of you are so fond of each other." Never one to sit idle, he'd brought along his scythe and a sharpening stone. Jed watched the elder man run a fingertip along the edge of the blade. "Wish I knew why this thing won't hold an edge."

"Maybe it's too old to work anymore." As soon as he said the words, Jed wished he could take them back. Even though he'd been talking about the tool, it sounded as if he'd been referring to Ole himself.

"Old doesn't mean can't, Jed Stark. Sometimes it just means that the job takes a little longer." His words were calmly said, but there was a spark of anger in Ole's faded blue eyes. "But we weren't talking about this tool, or me, for that matter. We were talking about you and that horse."

"No, *we* weren't. You were." Jed pulled out his pocketknife and cut a couple of burrs out of the mare's tail.

Ole used the stone to point across the barn to where Jed's saddle sat next to the door. "So, tell me this, Jed. Were you going to say good-bye this time or ride away without a word like a coward?"

That did it. Jed would never raise a hand to Ole, but that didn't mean he could always keep his temper under control. The curry brush slammed against the far wall while he fought the urge to kick something.

"If I was going to leave, I would be gone by now." He didn't admit to how close he'd come.

"But you sure enough thought about it." Ole looked toward the saddle again. "Seeing your gear sitting by the door makes me think you came pretty close."

Ole always did see more than Jed wanted him to. He turned the mare loose in her stall and gave her an extra scoop of oats. "I'm still here, aren't I?"

"So you are." Ole checked the edge on the blade again. Still not satisfied, he gave it a couple more strokes before setting it aside. "You didn't like Hawk thanking you for clearing his name."

"No, I didn't, not that I believe for a minute that he meant it. You shouldn't force the boy to say things he doesn't really feel." He retrieved his saddle from where he'd left it and slung it back over the rack where he normally stored it. Then he picked up the brush he'd thrown and put it away, not that he was sorry for his little show of temper. But if he hadn't picked it up, Ole would have, silently making Jed feel ashamed. Once it was safely back up on the shelf, Jed shoved his hands in his back pockets to resist throwing it again.

Ole leaned back against the wall and chuckled. "So now you're an expert on how young boys think and act?"

"Hell no, I'm not. But I do know forcing him to do stuff he doesn't want to do is not the way to keep him here." He looked around for something else to do. He wondered if he'd be in Sadie's way if he went up to the river for a quick swim.

"I'm not treating Hawk any differently than I treated you at the same age."

"But you're forgetting, Ole. I didn't stay."

No longer able to stand to be closed in by four walls and his friend's eyes, he walked out of the barn without looking back. Outside, the gathering darkness fit his mood better than the warm glow of the lantern in the barn or the lamp in Sadie's kitchen. Or upstairs in her bedroom. He shut that thought down, not letting it get too far into his imagination.

He watched for several seconds to see if he could see her moving around in the house. Someone walked between the lamp on the kitchen table and the window, but he was too far away to see for certain if the shadowing figure belonged to Sadie or to Hawk. Hoping it was Sadie, he walked around the porch and followed the narrow trail up to the river.

Even if he didn't go for a swim, he could sit on the bank upriver a ways and listen to the quiet sounds of the woods. He kept going past the pool in case Sadie came out until he found a secluded spot. He dropped down onto the ground and leaned back against the trunk of a willow tree and let the silent darkness settle down around him. The thoughts he'd been ignoring filled his mind, making him wish he'd thrown that brush a few more times.

Did Ole really think he was a coward for not wanting to stay? No matter how Ole felt about Jed's visit, it was pretty damn clear that Sadie wasn't particularly happy to have him there. He closed his eyes and let his head drop forward. This small farm was the one place in the world he wanted to be and the last place he could let himself stay.

On nights like this, old memories stirred around in his head. Even with his eyes closed and the drone of crickets and cicadas filling his ears, he couldn't shut out whispers from his past. They grew louder and louder until they screamed with remembered pain and humiliation. No amount of time passing or hours spent soaking in hot baths or the gentle touches of Ole and Olga could erase the ugliness he'd endured as a child before coming to this farm.

He'd never told Ole how bad it had been for him. Ole had never asked, not in so many words, but he must have had his suspicions. Both Ole and Olga had been careful in the way they approached Jed, never reaching out to touch him too quickly or from behind. He still didn't know why they hadn't sent him packing the first time he'd lashed out at them, more like a wild animal than a civilized human being.

Maybe their patience alone would have won him over in the end, but it was Sadie with her huge blue eyes and bright smile who had somehow slipped through the barrier of his pain to win his trust. Why her parents ever let a rough character like him within a hundred miles of her, he'd never know. But from the first, she'd followed him around, getting in his way, getting into his heart.

She was still there, although he'd fight to his last breath to deny it. He'd had his fair share of women interested in him, mostly for the wrong reasons. Some liked lawmen. Others wanted to see if his Indian blood made him a savage in bed. Still others were drawn to the edgy feel of danger that clung to men who made their living with their guns, no matter which side of the law they were on.

Only Sadie had looked at him, really looked at him, and seen something worth caring about. Even when she was still a little girl all legs and big eyes, he felt like a king when she smiled up at him. He loved being a hero in her eyes, even if all he'd done was coax her favorite kitten down from a tree.

But then slowly the look in her eyes had changed. He didn't remember when he'd first noticed the difference, but suddenly her following him around bothered him. He'd never been comfortable with people touching him, but Sadie had always been the exception. Hell, maybe it hadn't been her at all, but him, who had sensed a change in their relationship.

As much as he'd tried, the changes in her body became too obvious for him to ignore. She was growing up, turning into a beautiful young lady. It was one thing for her to worship him as a friend or even like an older brother; it was quite another for her feelings to turn into something more. Especially when he knew his own feelings for her teetered on the same sharp edge of emotion.

He'd tried to discourage her from spending so much time in his company, hoping that Olga or Ole would step in and fix the problem before it got out of hand. All he'd accomplished was hurting Sadie's feelings and forcing her to become more sly in finding ways to spend time in his company. He'd always wondered if her parents had even noticed. And if so, would they have cared if their only daughter had chosen him to marry?

They should have. Hell, he wanted better for her than that, even if they didn't.

And when he couldn't find the words to ask Ole for help in keeping Sadie at arm's length, he'd fumbled along trying to find a way to protect her from him and from herself. When that didn't work, he gathered up what strength he could and rode away. It had taken six years for him to find an excuse he could live with to come back, hoping to find Sadie married with a passel of kids at her feet.

But no, that wasn't what he found. Instead, she'd grown into a lovely woman, but with dark shadows in her eyes. Life had been hard for her, losing her mother and now her father was fading away. Why hadn't she found someone to marry? He hated that small part of him that rejoiced that she had never looked at another man the way she used to look at him.

Of course, she didn't look at him that way anymore either. Not that he deserved it. He used his gun skills on the side of the law, but he'd killed more than his fair share of men. Whether they deserved killing or not, he had too much blood on his hands to touch a woman like Sadie.

A snapped twig broke the quiet behind him. He managed not to draw his gun, but only just. Even as his hand reached for it, his mind recognized the sound of Sadie's step. He closed his eyes and listened, hoping she wasn't looking for him. As usual, his luck was all bad.

Chapter 6

"Jed?"

Her voice carried on the night air to send a shiver of awareness along his skin. Sitting in the darkest shadows along the river as he was, she wouldn't find him unless he wanted her to. Half an hour before, he would likely have stayed still and all but invisible. But he'd always had a hard time denying her anything within reason.

"Jed?" This time her voice was louder, with a touch of exasperation in it, making him grin. His Sadie had grown up with a bit of a bite in her personality.

"I'm here." He didn't stand up, but he did wave his hand to attract her attention. "Look a little more to your left."

As soon as she spotted him she walked straight for him, waiting until she was within only a few steps to speak. "I thought you might be taking a swim."

He wasn't above doing a little teasing. "Hoping for a little peek?"

"No!" She sounded as if she might be blushing.

Maybe he hadn't been too far off the mark. "I wanted to talk to you while my father wasn't around to listen."

Jed tried not to be disappointed that she hadn't sought him out for herself. He moved over to make room for her, making sure that she could sit down without touching him. He knew he shouldn't touch her, but that didn't mean that he didn't want to. "Is something wrong?"

"Nothing new, but I have a few things you need to hear." She turned to face the river, telling him without words that whatever she had to say wasn't going to make him happy.

"Go on, Sadie. Just say it and get it over with." He picked up a handful of pebbles and tossed them into the water. The noise they made wasn't half as satisfying as the one the brush had made back in the barn. Maybe he needed bigger rocks.

"I want to thank you for bringing Hawk to us." She echoed his action, throwing rocks into the water. "He has given my father new purpose, something to think about other than his illness. I even heard him whistling a song this morning."

Although they sat shrouded in darkness, the moon was clearing the tops of the trees along the river, giving just enough light for him to see her face. Her mouth was curved up in a half smile. Bearing the burden of her father's illness had been hard on her if Ole's off-key whistling make her smile.

"Are you sure it wasn't a pair of the barn cats fighting? Ole's whistling never sounded much like a song to me." He allowed himself a small grin to let her know he was teasing.

Her smile widened. "Yes, well, it did sound pretty bad, but at least he was whistling."

"I'm glad for you, Sadie." He let the silence simmer between them again, aware of the way she chewed at her lower lip and stared out at the water rushing past them. She had something else on her mind, something he wasn't going to like. He was in no hurry to find out what it was.

A sharp intake of breath warned him that she'd gathered up her courage to speak again. "Pa thinks you're finally going to come home, Jed." She looked up at the moon rising over the river. "You know, to stay."

She held up her hand to keep him from interrupting her with the denial she knew was coming. "I know your life is out there." She waved her hand toward the west. "But he's never given up hope that you'd finally settle here"

"But you and I both know that's not going to happen." He didn't offer reasons, just the bald truth.

She drew a shuddering breath before looking at him again. "I figured it out when you stayed gone for so long. There's something out there that you need and can't get here." One single tear trickled down her cheek.

Actually, it was the other way around, but he wasn't going to tell her that. He reached out to catch the tear before it disappeared. If it helped her to accept his desertion to think he left for selfish reasons, he wasn't going to tell her different.

"If it were up to me, Jed, I would tell you to go and never feel like you had to come back." Her hand flew to her mouth in shock. "I didn't mean that the way it sounded. I just meant . . ."

He allowed himself to touch her other hand— just once—to reassure her. "I know what you meant, Sadie."

She looked down at his hand covering her much smaller one. "I need you to come back . . . at

least when you can . . . for my father's sake, you
understand, until he . . ." Her voice trailed off as
the tears came in earnest this time.

His arms were around her, drawing her close for
comfort, although he wasn't sure if it was for her
sake or his. She buried her face against his chest
and let the tears come. And it wasn't pretty. Her
sobs came in huge hiccuping gulps, as if a dam
had broken and the floods were set loose upon the
land.

Her grief was his grief. Her pain, his as well. Ole
had been the cornerstone of Jed's life and even
more so for Sadie. Facing a future without him in
their world made him feel as if he were a child instead of a grown man. He let her cry out her pain,
patting her awkwardly on the back. One of the
drawbacks of not liking to be touched was that he
didn't know how to offer someone comfort.

Could he do what she was asking? Come and go
for a few months? He'd have to be a selfish bastard
to say no, not if it kept Ole happy and, by default,
Sadie. He waited until the tears slowed and her
sobs quieted before speaking. He tipped her face
up from his chest with the crook of his finger.

"I'm still a U.S. Marshal with a job I need to do.
I can't stay for long at a time, Sadie, but I'll come
when I can." He might as well go for broke. "I'll
write more often."

At first he thought she was crying again when
she buried her face against his chest again, but
then she looked up again, revealing the real truth.
She was laughing. He honestly didn't know what
he'd said that she'd find funny, but it didn't matter. Anything was better than her heartbreaking
pain.

"All right, share the joke."

"I shouldn't laugh, but your promise to write

more often struck me as funny. Does that mean you're going to write more than once a year, if that? How will you ever bear up under the extra work?" She giggled again, but then the tears were back.

He pulled her onto his lap this time and wrapped his arms around her. She had every right to doubt his good intentions, but he didn't have to like it. Once again, he waited for her to regain control.

When she did, she pushed away, putting a small bit of distance between them. "I'm sorry. I shouldn't have said that." She accepted the bandanna he offered her and wiped her face. "Sometimes I don't know what's the matter with me. I normally don't cry at all, much less like a water pump."

"I suspect you've been holding all this in, trying to hide it from your father." He didn't phrase it as a question. He knew her too well to think otherwise. "Have you talked to anybody about what's been going on with him?"

She shook her head. "Pa doesn't want folks to know. He made Doc promise not to tell anyone in town. Didn't want everyone treating him differently."

Jed understood Ole's thinking, but it was shortsighted. Obviously Ole didn't want their sympathy or even their help, and maybe it was his right to make that decision. But had he thought through the effect it would have on Sadie? She had no one to talk to and no shoulder to lean on when everything ganged up on her. Except his, and he wasn't there enough to be of much help.

"I'll talk to Ole. Maybe he'd let you talk to the pastor."

"No, don't. I'll be fine. Pastor Ludwig is a good man, but he would feel obligated to do more than just listen." She eased back off Jed's lap, drawing the darkness and pride around her as she stood up. "I'd better be getting back."

Jed let her step away, reaching for another handful of pebbles to keep from reaching for her. "I'll stay another two days and then I have to go." The small rocks plopped into the water, disturbing the ripples for a few seconds before sinking out of sight. He wished he could do the same thing.

"But you'll be back?" Her hand rested on his shoulder.

He closed his eyes and enjoyed the warmth of her touch. "I'll be back as often as I can."

"It would mean a lot if you'd tell Pa that you'll be here for Thanksgiving and Christmas at least. He does better when he knows he has something to look forward to."

His heart hurt. "And you, Sadie? Would that give you something to look forward to if I come . . ." He caught himself just in time. He didn't want to think of the farm as home. "If I come here for the holidays?"

"This year, what I want doesn't matter." Her hand was gone from his shoulder, giving him his answer. "It's enough that it will make my father happy."

Then she walked away, making Jed wish like hell he hadn't promised to stay for two more days. The peaceful murmuring of the river grated on his senses. He waited long enough to make sure that Sadie had had time to reach the house before following the path back to the barn and his makeshift bed.

Sadie watched from her window until she saw Jed cross the yard and disappear inside the barn.

She kept vigil until she was sure that he wasn't going to saddle up and ride out again. Not that there was anything she could do to stop him if he was determined to leave.

But he'd given his word to stay two more days this trip and to return as often as he could, right up through Christmas. She counted off the weeks and days that she would still have Jed Stark in her life and wished that it didn't matter so much. She'd learned to live without him once; she wasn't sure she could again.

Her eyes felt gritty and burned with the sting of tears that hadn't quite stopped flowing. She glanced down at the bandanna clutched in her hand, feeling like a schoolgirl with her first crush. But then, maybe that description wasn't so far off the mark. What would Jed think if he were to find out that she had a small box tucked away in her dresser with all the little mementos he'd given her over the years that he'd lived with them? A bird feather, dried flowers, a ribbon, and now a bandanna would join them once she laundered it.

Only the late hour and her utter weariness kept her from dragging the box out of its hiding place to touch each item in turn. How many times had she done just that, as if holding on to them were the same as holding on to Jed himself?

Too many times to remember; far too many times considering the pain it still caused her.

She forced herself to lie down in bed rather than to stare out into the darkness, trying to see through the walls of the barn to where Jed slept in the hay. Or maybe their little encounter along the river had left him restless and unable to sleep as well. It would only be fair that she not be the only one whose blood still tingled with the memory of being held in Jed's arms.

There was such gentle strength in the man, although she suspected he would be the first one to deny it. Nothing had really changed after her bout of crying against his chest, but deep down inside, she felt better. Lighter, as if some of the burden she'd been carrying alone was now no longer only hers to bear. Perhaps it was an illusion, but it had felt so good to have the rest of the world held at bay for the few minutes he'd surrounded her with his warmth.

How long would he have continued to sit there holding her if she had not made the first move to leave? She gave up trying to keep her eyes closed and stared up at the ceiling. The truth was that she'd been afraid to stay wrapped in his arms for too long, afraid to know how wonderful it felt.

She rolled over on her side, away from the window. Maybe if she concentrated on what she did have instead of what she didn't. Pa was feeling better, even if only for a little while. Hawk was settling in. He hadn't mentioned riding off for several days, at least in front of her. Despite his reluctance to thank Jed, the boy had to be feeling better knowing that no one was on his trail, set on dragging him back to that town.

And finally, she had Jed's word that he would return off and on for the next three and a half months. For the first time in ages, she had something to look forward to. If Hawk stayed on past the harvest, they'd have a real Thanksgiving dinner with all the trimmings. In past years, it had been too much of an effort to make for just Pa and her. And then there would be Christmas, with gifts to make and pies to bake, and best of all, Jed sitting at the table right where he belonged.

Pastor Ludwig, with his big booming voice and

cheerful grin, always claimed that Christmas was the season of miracles, when the most amazing things happened. She knew no amount of praying would cure what was wrong with her father, but it wasn't too much to ask that he be well enough still to celebrate the holiday one last time. Fancy phrases and flowery words weren't her style, but she didn't think the good Lord required that his people be poets when they needed his help.

She clenched Jed's bandanna in her hand and whispered in her mind, *Please, God. Let us celebrate this one last time as a family, with all of us here under one roof. Amen.*

She listened in the quiet of her room, hoping for some small sign that her prayer had been heard, that her request would be considered. She settled for the comfort in knowing that she also had things to be grateful for. She had her father still, snoring loudly enough to rattle the windows in his room below. For now, she had Hawk, the younger brother she'd always wished for. And as her breathing slowed and slumber gradually claimed her, she smiled because she still had a little piece of Jed in her hand.

Jed wished like hell that they would have let him just ride away without all three of them gathering on the porch to wave good-bye. He could have avoided the whole situation if he'd gotten under way earlier. The sun had only been the faintest of promises in the east when he'd pulled on his boots, ready to face the day.

There was a hotel that served decent food within an hour's ride, so he hadn't needed to wait for Sadie to cook breakfast for him. But he'd hung around, starting the morning chores for Ole. Hell, he'd even watered Sadie's garden for her without being asked. So, he laid the blame for his late start squarely at his own feet.

The first two times he'd ridden away from the Johanson farm had been under the cover of darkness. The pain of separation had almost killed him, especially six years ago. He kept telling himself that it would go easier on all of them if he left with their blessing, knowing he was welcome to come back.

He fought the urge to kick his mare into a gallop, to get the leaving over with. A few minutes one way or the other wouldn't make much difference for him to get back on the job. But as long as Sadie was watching, he didn't want her to think he couldn't wait to get away from her.

When he reached the last bend in the road before the farmhouse and those who lived in it disappeared for good, he reined the mare in long enough to stop and wave one last time. At least two of them were still on the porch watching. He would have felt damn foolish to wave at no one other than the few chickens pecking in the front yard.

He wasn't going all that far before stopping for the night, just as far as the nearest town to the west. The day before yesterday he'd driven Ole into town to get supplies. After dropping him at the mercantile, Jed had made a quick trip down to the telegraph office to send a short message back to his boss to let him know where he was and that he was available for an assignment.

He was hoping to have a response waiting for him when he reached town. Once he knew where he was going and whom he was after, he'd know better what supplies he would need before hitting the trail. If there was no answer yet, he'd get a room at the hotel and wait rather than ride back to the farm for another night. Sooner or later the marshal would send Jed out on another search. One cheery good-bye had been hard enough to face.

Hawk threaded the reins through his fingers and waited for Ole to give him the signal. His stomach felt as if it were filled with a bunch of hungry grasshoppers, keeping his breakfast from settling completely. He moved to the center of the seat on the wagon, trying to look more at ease than he really felt. This would be his first time driving a team of draft horses all by himself. He and his grandfather had maintained a small garden much like the one Sadie had out behind the house, but they had raised horses, not crops.

But Ole had a field of wheat that needed harvesting and hay to be brought in for winter feed. Then there was the feed corn waiting its turn. No wonder the old man had asked Hawk to stay on through the harvest. A few neighbors were supposed to stop by to join in; in return, Ole and Hawk would be expected to help at several of the surrounding farms.

Hawk's job would be to drive the wagon slowly through the fields, stopping to let the workers load it up. Then he was to bring it back to the barn where another crew would empty it back out. Sadie had told him several times how important his job was, keeping the crews busy on both ends of his route. She'd been up since before dawn cooking the huge amount of food necessary to feed everyone who was coming. But she'd taken the time to pack up a few cookies and a jar of spring water for him to carry in the wagon.

He wasn't sure that growing boys really did need to eat more than other folks, but Sadie sure enough seemed to think so. She was always hunting him down to slip him a few cookies or an apple to eat.

"All right, boy. Do just like I told you. Release the brake and then give old Bill and Buck a sharp slap on the back with the reins and keep them walking steady." Ole backed away from the wagon to give Hawk plenty of room. "They're the best team in these parts, so you'll do just fine."

"Giddyup, Bill! Move out, Buck!" Hawk tried his best to sound like the boss, but he wasn't sure how successful he'd been. The two huge geldings held their ground for a few seconds, worrying him that they'd recognized his inexperience and wouldn't take orders from him.

But then Buck stepped out, with Bill following a heartbeat later. The traces pulled tight and the wagon moved forward with a lurch, almost knocking Hawk off his seat. He managed to brace his feet against the front of the wagon to hold his position. But then the two horses fell into step together and the ride smoothed out. Just as Ole had told him, he guided the horses down the road to the last bend before gradually turning back toward the barn.

He already knew to pull back on the reins a bit to keep the horses moving at the same slow pace. They wouldn't have been the first horses to catch sight of the barn and decide to make the return trip in half the time.

When they neared the house, Sadie came out on the porch. Her smile made him sit up straighter, trying to look as if this weren't the big deal it really was. Then he gave up trying and grinned back at her.

"You look like you belong up there, Hawk." She stepped down off the porch, wiping her hands on a towel. "Are you sure you've never driven a team of draft horses before?" She gave him a mock suspicious look before laughing again.

He guided the wagon back to where Ole stood waiting. The old man had the same smile as his daughter. "I need to check on a few things in the barn, boy. You drive up and down a few more times until either you or the horses get tired."

"Yes, sir."

Hawk watched Ole walk away, not sure how he felt about the man's unspoken trust that Hawk would be careful with Buck and Bill. He was no stranger to hard work and liked working with animals, especially horses. But the longer Hawk hung around the Johanson farm, the more comfortable it felt. He'd already lost one home; he didn't want to go through the pain of losing another one.

With the harvest almost upon them, his time here was running out. He wanted to ride away feeling that he was leaving behind a job and friends, not a home and family. Deciding that it might already be too late for that, he snapped the reins and went back to work.

Jed shoved his prisoner through the cell door and slammed it shut behind him. Billy Joe Thatcher managed to catch himself before he fell. Barely. He spouted a mouthful of obscenities as he whirled around to charge the door. It rattled a bit, but that was all, giving testimony to the strength of its construction.

"You son of a bitch, I'm going to kill you for this!" His words might have carried more weight if he looked old enough to shave.

This time Billy Joe kicked the door. Jed ignored the insult as well as the threat, just as he had for the past three days while he dragged the pitiful excuse for a man back to stand trial. Oh, he believed Billy Joe meant every word of it, but unless the judge was feeling generous, it would be several years down the road before Billy Joe would walk free of a jail cell. If he was still mad at Jed when they turned him loose, Jed would worry about it then. Hell, if he lost sleep nights over who might be carrying a grudge against him, he'd never get any rest.

The front door of the jailhouse swung open. Jed reached for his gun more out of habit than any real sense of danger. As soon as he recognized who was walking in, he snatched his hand back from his gun, but not before his boss saw him. Nothing much ever flustered Marshal Bart Perry, certainly not seeing one of his own men being cautious.

"I see you caught up with him." Bart accepted the cup of coffee that Jed was holding out to him. "That didn't take long."

Jed shrugged. "He wasn't hard to find. You'd think that if he was smart enough to rob a stage, he'd be smart enough to wait until he was a safe distance away before stopping to spend the money."

Bart sat down at his desk and shoved a chair toward Jed with his boot. "And I bet he just had to do some bragging."

"You guessed it." Damn, he was tired. "He was busy gambling and trying to impress some of the working girls at one of the saloons in Abilene. I caught him with his chips down."

The marshal laughed, just as Jed had expected him to. "I don't suppose you managed to recover any of the money."

Jed pointed toward a sack lying next to his saddlebags sitting by the stove. "Not all of it, but enough to make the stage folks happy."

"Nice work, Jed. I can always count on you to get the job done." He leaned back in his chair and propped his feet up on his desk. "You want to leave right away or take a couple of days off?"

"I hate to ask it, but I need to take more than a couple of days. I've got some family business to take care of." He held his breath and waited for the questions to come because Bart didn't much like surprises, especially coming from a man who had been working for him as long as Jed had.

Bart's eyes narrowed as he opened a drawer. He pulled out a couple of cigars and tossed one to Jed before lighting his. After several deep puffs, he said, "I don't rightly recall you ever mentioning any family before. In fact, I distinctly remember you saying you were an orphan."

"They're not really my family, but I lived with a farmer and his wife and daughter for a few years when I was a kid." He tucked the cigar in his shirt pocket for later. "They own a farm about three days' ride from here."

No one ever said the marshal was slow. "That's where you took that boy Hawk, isn't it?"

"Yeah. I need to check to see how he's doing or if he's still there. If he's already lit out on that stud horse of his, Ole will need my help bringing in the crops." He'd been staring at the wall behind the desk, hoping to avoid answering all of the questions that Bart had to be wanting to ask.

"Take as long as you need, Jed. You've got time

coming." Bart blew a smoke ring. "Just in case, though, leave me the family's name. I promise not to bother you unless absolutely necessary."

"Ole Johanson." Jed wasn't used to sharing his problems, but Bart was one of the few men Jed called friend. "The local doctor says Ole doesn't have long to live. There's just him, his daughter, and Hawk. That is, if he's still there."

"I'm sorry to hear that, Jed." This time it was a bottle of whiskey and two glasses that Bart pulled out of the desk. He poured each of them a stiff shot. "How old is the daughter?"

Jed stared into his glass, wishing he hadn't started this whole line of conversation. "Sadie is about twenty."

"Not married?"

"No."

"Interested in her yourself?"

"Hell no!" Jed could have bitten his tongue. That little flare of temper probably convinced Bart that Jed was lying. Of course he was, but that was no one's damn business, not even a friend's.

"When do you want to leave?" Bart allowed himself another half shot of whiskey and then held the bottle up to see if Jed wanted more.

"No, thanks." Jed set his empty glass back down on the desk. "I should be able to finish up here tomorrow morning. Unless you need me for something, I thought I'd ride out after lunch."

"Shouldn't be a problem." He looked back toward the cells. "We won't need you to testify at Billy Joe's trial. Hell, short of a signed confession, there's not much else he could have done to make sure we knew who robbed the stage."

"Don't have to be smart to be a crook, I guess."

"Not unless you want to be a successful crook.

Billy Joe wouldn't know much about that." Bart finished the last of his whiskey and put the bottle and glasses back in the drawer. "So this Sadie, is she pretty?"

The sudden change in topics surprised Jed into answering more truthfully than he would have if he'd had time to think. "Yes, she is. Blond hair, blue eyes."

"And you're definitely not interested?" A small smile played around the corners of Bart's mouth.

"Why the hell do you care?" Jed was tired enough to not have a good handle on his temper.

"Their farm isn't all that far of a ride. Thought maybe I'd keep you company and see her for myself. Winter's coming, and it gets damn old living by myself."

Now what should he say to that? There was no way in hell he wanted his handsome boss anywhere near Sadie. Bart was a good man, one whom Jed would trust with his life. But not with his woman. Not that Sadie was his, he reminded himself, but damned if he was going to let Bart get mixed up in her life.

"She's not the kind of a woman that a man trifles with."

Rather than being insulted, Bart laughed and dropped his feet to the floor. "You've sure got it bad, Jed. Go on and get out of here. I'll stay until Clark shows up for the night."

Jed wanted to protest his innocence, but that would only serve to convince Bart even more that Jed felt more for Sadie than he was willing to admit, even to himself. Especially to himself. He picked up his saddlebags.

Bart followed him to the door and locked it behind him. "I'll have your pay ready for you if you want to stop by in the morning." He clapped Jed on the shoulder. "I know it's not due for another week, but you might as well get it early."

"Thanks." The cash would come in handy, but he wondered if Bart thought that maybe he might not be coming back. He thought about turning down the offer, just to make his intentions clear to both of them, but Bart had already closed the door. Somehow, he didn't have the energy to argue the point anymore.

Jed stepped out onto the sidewalk and stopped, keeping his back to the wall. Habit had him looking up and down the street with a lawman's eyes, watching for the first hint of danger. Nothing caught his attention. He turned right and headed toward the boardinghouse where he stayed when he was in town. The rooms were small, but clean; the food plentiful and cheap.

As he walked along, he made a list of what he needed to do before leaving for the farm. He would settle his bills, pick up his laundry, and then stop in at the barbershop for the works—a haircut, a shave, and a hot bath. It was nice to have a plan. Maybe it would keep him so busy he wouldn't have time to think about spending time at the farm and how much harder it was for him to leave each time he made himself go.

Damn Bart, anyway, for making him admit that Sadie mattered to him, but then maybe the only person he'd been fooling all these years was himself. Rather than think about it anymore, he went back to making his list.

Pick up supplies. Eat dinner. Sleep. Eat breakfast. Hell, then there were the things he needed to pack up. If he tried real hard, he could keep himself entertained right up until he turned in for the night with all the things he could think of to do before saddling up and riding out.

That didn't change a thing. No matter how much he didn't want to think about Sadie, he'd made a promise to her, one he'd keep at the cost of his own soul if that's what it took. If it helped Ole to have him come home, then he'd be there.

Chapter 7

The neighboring men had started arriving just after sunrise, some of them having left home well before dawn. Sadie's back ached, and her arms were numb, but the food was ready. Looking around the kitchen, she took some measure of satisfaction in knowing that she was ready to feed everyone who showed up to help.

Wiping her hands on her apron, she decided that everything was under control enough that she could take a short break. A breath of fresh air and a cold drink of water would help restore her lagging energy. She might even sit a spell out on the porch until it was time to start carrying food out to the table her father and Hawk had made out of lumber and sawhorses. Two good friends had promised to come along behind their husbands to help.

She sat down on a bench and leaned back against the house, letting her eyes drift shut. There was enough of a breeze to make the day pleasant, making it easier on everyone. Several minutes passed while she hovered on the near side of sleep, leaving her mind free to wander.

To think about Jed Stark and where he might be and what he might be doing. Whatever it was, she hoped he was safe. She used to not worry so much about how dangerous his job was, but now she seemed unable to forget it for more than a few hours at a time. At least, he d promised to return when he could, and she knew he'd meant it. They had even received letters from him, at least one a week. Did he have any idea how much those pieces of paper meant to her father? Or to her?

They knew from his last letter that he'd been sent out to bring back yet another criminal. She had to wonder what drove him to hunt down so many bad men. Surely there was another way for him to make a living that wouldn't entail guns and killing. Like farming, for example. Had he hated life here on the farm so much? Up until he left without any warning, she had thought he was happy working alongside her father.

And even though she'd been wondering about those same questions for the past six years, she was no closer to answering them. Well, she had more important things to be doing than lazing on the front porch and worrying about things that she couldn't change.

When she opened her eyes, she almost jumped out of her skin. Jed was walking toward the house, his pinto trailing along behind him. She considering rubbing her eyes, sure that she was still dreaming. But if she had been, she wouldn't have put those weary lines around Jed's eyes or those sweat stains on his shirt. Even so, he looked so very good to her.

She wasn't sure he'd seen her yet, sitting as she

was off to the side on the shady side of the porch. Just in case, she stood up, ready to greet him. Not for the first time, she wished she could run to him and throw her arms around his neck as she had when she was a little girl.

Now she would have to settle for a tentative smile. "Welcome back."

He stopped short of the porch. "Where is your father?"

She did her best to ignore the jab of hurt when he didn't return her greeting. "He's out in the back pasture. The neighbors are here to help him bring in the hay. I'm expecting two friends to be along any minute to help feed everyone. You might remember Meg and her mother, Alice."

Jed nodded as he took his hat off, wiping his forehead with the sleeve of his shirt. "I'll put the pinto up and head out to help them."

His face was gray with exhaustion, making her wonder how much help he'd actually be. On the other hand, she knew her father would be pleased to see him, no matter what he could or couldn't do to help.

"If you wait a few minutes, you can probably get a ride out to the field. Hawk should be along with the first load any minute."

That perked Jed right up. "So the boy stayed." He nodded, as if that pleased him.

"He's still not committing past the harvest, but Pa has hopes." The jingle of a harness caught her attention. "In fact, there he is now. Why don't you turn your mare loose in the corral? Maybe you can help unload the wagon before going out to catch up with the others."

"I might just do that."

She would have watched him unsaddle the pinto, but a motion down the road caught her attention. The women she was expecting had just come into sight.

"When you get out to the field, tell Pa that we'll be ready to eat soon."

Jed checked his watch. "All right."

She allowed herself the excuse that she was waiting for the women to come the rest of the way to watch Jed for a few minutes longer. If he was aware of her gaze, he gave no sign of it. By the time Hawk drove the wagon into the barnyard, Jed was outside waiting for him.

It wasn't hard to see that the boy wasn't particularly happy to see Jed. There was a tension in his bearing that hadn't been there before. She wondered why that was. It wasn't as if Jed was there as a lawman. Any interest he might have in Hawk had nothing to do with his job, not anymore. Well, that was for the two of them to deal with. She had her own problems with Jed's return without having to take on Hawk's resentment, too.

Rather than dwell on it, she walked out to greet the two women who were just pulling up in front of the house. Mother and daughter, they were much alike in both build and personality. Alice had been her mother's closest friend, so Sadie and Meg had grown up together. Although the farm claimed most of Sadie's time, she and Meg still enjoyed getting together whenever they could. Of course, now that Meg was married, those occasions were rarer.

"Sadie! Good morning!" Alice climbed down out of the buggy first. She enveloped Sadie in a lavender-scented hug. "It has been entirely too long since we've seen you, young lady. You and that father of yours need to come to dinner once the harvesting is done."

"I would like that," Sadie told her truthfully.

The few times she got away from the farm to spend time with her friends were the only relief she had from worrying about her father's health.

Meg was in the process of lifting a pair of heavy baskets out of the backseat of the buggy when Jed walked up to the buggy.

"I'll take those for you, ma'am."

His sudden appearance surprised Meg into losing her balance. She plopped back down on the seat, looking a bit stunned.

Jed reached out to steady her. "Sorry, I didn't mean to startle you, Miss Meg."

"Uh, that's all right, Mr. Stark. No harm done." She looked past him at Sadie, all sorts of questions in her eyes.

It was time to take control of the situation. "Jed, just set those baskets on the porch. We'll take them from there."

"Yes, ma'am. I'll see to their horse, too, if that's all right, Miss Sadie."

At least Alice managed to summon up a smile for him. "That would be right neighborly of you, Mr. Stark."

He touched the brim of his hat in salute to the two visitors and picked up both baskets. As he walked away, he shot Sadie a knowing look, telling her without words that he knew she was rushing him away from her friends.

Had she hurt his feelings? Surely not. But even so, she'd handled that badly. She certainly hadn't meant to treat him like she would a hired hand instead of a member of her family. But that was part of the problem with Jed. She'd never been sure exactly where he fit into her world.

Her friends followed her inside the house. Once Jed was safely out of hearing, they rounded on her as she'd known they would.

"So, missy, when were you going to tell us that Jed Stark came back?" Alice was busy unpacking her basket, but that didn't keep her from demanding answers.

"He only arrived a few minutes before you did. We weren't exactly expecting him." That much was true. Sort of. True enough, anyway.

"How long is he going to stay this time?" This time it was Meg asking.

They both knew about Jed bringing Hawk to stay with them. After all, they had to explain the boy's sudden appearance in their lives. For Hawk's sake, though, they'd kept the details of the situation private. Even though Hawk had been proven innocent of all charges, there were some folks who would always think the worst. Meg and Alice weren't among them, but she'd promised Ole that she wouldn't tell even them.

Meg had moved to the window. She was watching Jed and Hawk as they unloaded the hay from the wagon. Sadie knew that because she'd been looking in that direction herself.

"It's been years since I've laid eyes on Jed Stark, but I'd forgotten how striking he was, what with those light-colored eyes combined with that pitch-black hair." She looked over to where Sadie was slicing bread. "He was a good-looking boy, even if he never smiled at all. He always looked so fierce. Still does, I have to say."

He had smiled back then, just not around many people other than her parents and her. Sadie almost said so, but managed to keep the words to herself. She didn't particularly like this unexpected need to defend him, but also she knew her friends would read more into her comment than she wanted them to.

No one knew how devastated she'd been when

he'd left six years before. Meg might have had her suspicions, but other than a few subtle hints to that effect, she'd never pressed Sadie for details. The last thing she wanted was to stir up any of those old memories.

"Do you think I've cut enough bread for everybody?" There wasn't much hope that her attempt to change subjects would work, but she had to try.

Meg answered for her mother, who was still staring out of the window. "Looks like plenty to me."

"You know, that boy looks enough like Mr. Stark to be his brother . . ." Her voice trailed off. "You know, if I didn't know better, I'd almost think he could be Mr. Stark's son." She suddenly found it absolutely necessary to rearrange the stacks of dishes needed outside on the table. There were twin spots of blush staining her cheeks.

There was no way Sadie wanted that rumor to get started. "I know there's a strong resemblance, mostly because of their coloring, but Hawk is twelve years old, and Jed was still living with us back then."

Alice looked relieved. "Oh, that's right. What was I thinking?"

Sadie chose not to answer that particular question. "Did I mention that Jed is a U.S. Marshal? He brought Hawk here after Hawk's grandfather died." She picked up the sheets she intended to use on the table and headed for the door. "For Hawk's sake, we don't discuss the details of his life. It's still a very painful memory for him. You understand."

Alice's face softened as she looked outside again, this time in Hawk's direction. "That poor boy. Well, your Mr. Stark did the right thing by bringing him here."

"He's not my Mr. Stark." The words slipped out, sounding defensive and a bit too insistent, before she could stop them. "I mean, Jed was just one of the orphans my father and mother took in. It's only logical that he'd think of us when he found a boy in such need."

Once again, Meg came to her rescue. "I don't know about you, Mother, but I'm getting hungry. I imagine the men are more than ready to take a break from all their hard work."

"Jed and Hawk will take the wagon back out to pick up the men after they empty the hay."

Sadie stepped out onto the porch and was relieved to see the wagon already a fair distance on its way out to where the men were working. They should have just about the right amount of time to get the table set and bring out the food before they returned.

Meg helped her spread the sheets over the tables. They anchored them down with a couple of rocks at each corner until they could bring out the dishes. Alice brought them out and began arranging them to her liking. It was times like these that Sadie missed her mother the most. Days spent like this one, working shoulder to shoulder with her mother and the other women, were some of her most cherished memories. She'd learned so much listening to them chat about husbands and children and living in general.

The scent of roses from the garden drifted past on the small breeze, another reminder of her mother. Those few bushes held the place of honor at the end of the porch. They commanded a fair amount of Sadie's time in making sure they were well tended, because to lose one of them would be like losing her mother all over again.

Alice slipped her hand around Sadie's shoulders and gave her a soft squeeze. "I miss her, too, Sadie girl. Her dying left a mighty big hole in all our lives." Then she smiled. "You know Olga gave me cuttings from those very same bushes. I cherish them most of all my flowers because when they bloom, I know we still have a little bit of her here with us. I've already started some cuttings for Meg to plant at her place."

Sadie had to blink several times, fighting off the tears that always threatened when she thought too hard about her mother. It had been hard to learn to live without her; it was doubly hard now with her father's illness. How could she face being completely alone?

"Oops! The men are coming in and here we stand dawdling. We'd better get the rest of that food on the table."

It took several more trips to get everything laid out and ready. As soon as the wagon pulled up by the barn, the men all piled out and headed for the pump to wash up a bit. Without realizing what she was doing, she stopped pouring cups of cool water to set at each place to look for Jed. She didn't see him at first but then spotted him leading Buck and Bill away from the wagon. He probably figured they needed a breather, too.

Or he wasn't feeling comfortable with the other men.

She didn't hear her father walk up beside her. "You've done a good job setting a bountiful table for all of us, daughter. I know I'm hungry." He pulled out the closest chair and sat down. The fact that he didn't wait for the others told her a lot about how he was feeling.

It never did any good to tell him that he was working too hard. The last time she tried, he'd snapped at her that he was going to have eternity to rest all he wanted. For now, he was going to work as long and as hard as he could. His words broke her heart.

The others drifted toward the table as they finished washing their hands. When they were all gathered close together, Ole led them in a prayer. They all echoed his "Amen" before filling their plates and then looking around for a place to sit. She didn't have nearly enough chairs to go around, but these men were used to finding a spot of shade or a comfortable rock to sit on. Once they were settled, she made the rounds pouring more water or offering seconds.

For a while, it took all her attention to see that everybody got their fair share of the food. After setting the last platter on the table, she was about to fill her own plate when she realized that Jed had yet to eat. She finally spotted him over by the corral.

Why was he avoiding the others? Had someone said something to offend him? Her first instinct was to fill a plate and take it to him. If he was going to spend the afternoon laboring under a hot sun, he needed to eat. But she changed her mind. Part of the reason people had always been a bit uneasy around Jed was his fault. If he'd relax and let them get to know him, they'd accept him easily enough. Most of these men respected hard work over anything else. An extra pair of hands was always welcome.

Instead of taking him food, she went to fetch him back to the table whether he wanted to come or not. She would have sent Hawk, but he probably would have refused to speak to Jed. All her father would have to do was ask, and Jed would have come running. Now that her father was sitting down and resting, she wasn't going to disturb him. That left her.

After setting down the two plates she'd picked up, she wiped her hands on her apron and braced herself to approach him. She made sure to walk slowly, stopping to speak to folks as she made her way to the barn, figuring she'd draw less interest that way. Once she'd passed the last of the men, she headed straight for Jed.

"Aren't you going to eat something? I went to an awful lot of trouble for nothing if you don't."

Jed dropped the piece of grass he'd been chewing on. "If you cooked all that for me, you outdid yourself." He should have known that Sadie wouldn't let him get by without nagging at him.

"Come on back and sit down, Jed." She joined him at the railing. "You know Pa won't eat right if you don't."

Since he could clearly see her father already at the table and eating, Jed thought about calling her on the small lie. If she wanted to hide her own concern behind her father's, he wasn't going to point it out.

"I won't believe you if you claim you aren't hungry. I grew up with you, remember? My mother used to claim that there wasn't enough food in the entire county to keep you filled up."

She looked so cute, glaring up at him that way. He couldn't deny the truth of her claim, though. Olga had always made sure there was something left for him to eat whenever the urge hit, night or day. Maybe it came from all the times in his life when he'd gone hungry. Early on, just knowing that plate of cookies or gingerbread or beans was waiting for him had kept him from running away from this place as he had from so many others.

"How about you? You haven't eaten yet." He took his hat off and wiped his brow. "Judging by the way that table is loaded down, you must have started cooking yesterday."

Sadie rolled her shoulders as if to relieve tired muscles. "Actually, the day before, if you must know. Now, come and eat. I don't much appreciate men who don't do justice to my cooking."

Most of the time she didn't much appreciate him at all, but he didn't say so. Instead, he let her think she'd convinced him although he'd been about to head that way on his own. The other men had been working for hours longer than he had. He'd offered to see to the horses so they could get started. But it felt good to have Sadie fussing over him, even over something as little as fried chicken.

Back at the table, she hovered nearby until she made sure that he was capable of filling a plate on his own. She handed him a cup of water to wash the food down before picking up her own plate. It was too much to hope that she'd sit near him. Maybe that was for the best because what he was hungry for had nothing to do with her excellent fried chicken and everything to do with the woman herself.

He found an empty spot in the shade and sat down. No one was doing much talking right now. These farmers had hours of hard work ahead of them and knew enough to rest when they could. To a man, they'd nodded and waved when he'd shown up out in the field with Hawk. It was hard to remember that he'd once been accepted as one of them, mainly because of Ole's efforts to civilize him.

But he'd never let himself get used to belonging to the group. He'd lived in other towns, ones where he'd been hated and despised because of the color of his hair and his skin. A dog didn't

have to get kicked more than a time or two before
it learned to keep a healthy distance between it
and anyone wearing boots. As a kid, he had felt the
same way. If you didn't let people get close, they
couldn't hurt you.

If he didn't get attached to a place, he wouldn't
miss it when he had to move on. And as much as
he loved this farm, it wasn't his home. Not anymore. He knew Ole didn't understand his reasons,
but then he wasn't all that clear on them himself.
His friend was wise in a lot of ways, but Ole had no
real experience with all the ugliness in the world.
Jed, on the other hand, knew it too damn well.

If it weren't for Ole and Olga, he knew full well
he wouldn't have joined up with the U.S. Marshals.
Hell, the way he'd been headed when they took
him in, it would only have been a matter of time
before his name was on the list of cutthroats and
killers the marshals brought to justice. So if he
couldn't stay on the farm, then he would stand
guard outside.

He shook his head. Here he was, a mixed-breed
bastard, setting himself like some kind of hero.
That was a laugh. There wasn't much difference
between him and the killers he dragged back to
stand trial and hang. He wore a star on his chest
and had the law to back him up, but he made his
living with his guns just the same.

Being around all these decent people made him
uncomfortable because they were so damn clean,
even when their clothes were stained with sweat
from an honest day's work. They set down roots
and lived their lives raising crops and kids.

His only skills were a fast gun, the ability to kill,
and the willingness to do so when the need arose.

Damn, he wished he'd never agreed to come
back. Him showing up and pretending to be a

farmer again wouldn't keep Ole from dying. And being around Sadie hurt like walking on shards of glass. He looked around the yard, not letting his eyes rest on any one person very long. Except for two people, no one was paying him the least bit of attention. Hawk glared at him and moved a few inches closer to Ole. Jed smiled just enough to aggravate the boy a bit, knowing he had no use for Jed. He supposed Hawk was jealous because Jed had known Ole first, but he was no threat to the boy's position here on the farm. If he could get near Hawk long enough to talk to him, he'd tell him so.

It was the other pair of eyes watching him that Jed didn't know what to do about. If Sadie wasn't careful, there'd be talk. Meg and her mother were good friends, but even they had to wonder why Sadie had never found a man to marry. If they got it in their heads that he had anything to do with that, he wasn't sure what they'd do. Yet another reason he shouldn't be here.

Despite Sadie's excellent cooking, he wasn't hungry, at least for food. He took his plate back to the table and set it down near Ole. "I'll get the team hitched up again."

Ole's faded eyes never missed a thing. "You didn't eat much."

"I wasn't hungry." He made sure to look the man straight in the eye when he lied. It didn't work. Like always, Ole saw more than you wanted him to.

He nodded in the direction where his daughter sat with her friends. "I saw you two talking. Did she say something to upset you?"

"Not at all. She was worried that I wasn't eating."

Ole stared up at him and then patted him on

the arm. "Go on and see to the horses. I'll make sure that she saves you some pie."

Jed walked away and didn't look back.

The last man—Martin Finney—rode out of sight. Like the others, he'd promised to come back at first light to finish with the hay. The day after, they would all move on to his farm. Long about tomorrow night Ole figured on having a fight with his daughter about whether or not he should go. What kind of excuse could he offer for not showing up after the man spent two whole days helping him? Short of telling his friends about his health problems, there was no way he could avoid helping each and every one of them bring in the crops. Helping friends when they needed it was what a man did. And he sure as hell had raised his daughter to know that.

She didn't understand that he was building up memories for when he was too sick to work the farm. He couldn't tell her that it was his way of saying good-bye to everything—the farm, the animals, old friends, and her. But she wasn't ready to hear that any more than he was ready to tell her. So he'd fight against her need to coddle him as long as he had the strength to do so.

"I'll get a meal on the table. You three go wash up." Sadie disappeared into the house. The door closed with a tad more force than was necessary.

"What's got her all riled up?" Hawk was sitting on the porch step whittling. As far as Ole could tell, the boy was carving a pile of wood shavings, but it kept him busy. Hawk twisted around to look up at Ole, clearly expecting a reasonable answer to his question.

Before Ole could answer him, Jed spoke up. "I

suspect she wants Ole here to sit and rest for a day or two." Jed was leaning against the railing. "Hawk, if you ever figure out which one of them is the most stubborn, I'd appreciate you letting me know. I've never been able to make up my mind on the subject."

Hawk started to laugh but quit when he remembered who was doing the teasing. He turned back to his whittling without a word. Ole shook his head. He wished the boy would get over his resentment of Jed. He'd tried talking to him, but none of it sank in. Jed had one thing right—Sadie had gotten her short temper and hard head from him. But the two on the porch with him had their own fair dose of both.

He let the quiet settle around them. Jed never had been one for talking much, and Hawk had his own long silences, too. That didn't matter. The important thing was having Jed back where he belonged, even though he was already looking down the road and wondering how soon he could ride away and not look back.

Ole made a habit of not asking Hawk how long he planned on living under his roof. If he pushed too hard, Hawk and Wind Son would be gone for good. If Ole didn't manage to pull off a miracle between now and, well, the then he never wanted to think too much about, Jed would leave, Hawk would leave, and his poor Sadie would be alone on this big farm.

He'd thought about selling the place now while he had the chance. Sadie would have enough to live on for a good long time until she figured out what she wanted to do with her life. Maybe with him out from under foot, she might find a decent, hardworking man to settle down with. He'd always wanted to dangle a few grandchildren on his knee, but that wasn't going to happen now. But this wasn't about what he needed any longer. He needed to provide for Sadie, come what may.

He'd been sitting too long. The longer he sat, the harder it would be for him to get his stiff old bones moving again. "I'm going to check on the horses. Tell Sadie I'll be back in a few minutes."

Hawk stuck his knife in the step and started after Ole. Jed reached out and stopped him by grabbing him by the shoulder.

Hawk froze and then jerked free of Jed's hand. "Keep your hands to yourself, lawman." He made sure that he was beyond grabbing range. "I've already seen to the horses. There's no need for him to go check on my work."

Had he ever been that angry and always ready to assume the worst of people? Hell, he'd been so much worse.

"Ole isn't checking on your work. He just needed to get away by himself for a few minutes." Jed resumed his position on the railing, saying without words that Hawk could do what he wanted. "Besides, has he ever once made you feel like he didn't trust you to do a job once he knew you were capable?"

Hawk cocked his head to one side and gave the matter some thought. "No, he hasn't." He sank back down on the steps and tugged his knife free of the step. After a few seconds, he was back to making sawdust.

Jed wished he had something to keep his hands busy. When he was on the trail, he did some target shooting to keep his skills up. He usually had a book or two tucked away in his saddlebags, but he'd already finished the one he brought with him. For the next week or so, he'd be busy enough helping with the harvest in the daytime. It was the long hours of the evening and night that made him restless.

The river was calling him, but he'd have to wait until after dinner to go upstream. He thought about asking Sadie if she wanted to go, too, but he didn't want to crowd her. He could always watch from the barn until he either saw her leave the house or knew for certain that she'd turned in for the night.

She looked every bit as tired as her pa did. After all, she'd been cooking for three days solid and still had another day to go before she was done. Of course, knowing her, she'd already volunteered to help out at some of the farms over the next week. Olga had always done that, and Sadie would likely feel obligated to do the same.

He didn't know how he felt about that. Since he'd be working right alongside Ole and the others, it meant that he'd see more of Sadie than he would if she were to stay home. One part of him, the selfish part, wanted to spend every minute he could around her, knowing the time was coming when he'd ride away and not look back.

If he were the man he wished he was, he'd stay as far away from her as he could. After all, he was here for Ole's sake, not Sadie's. Or at least that's what he kept telling himself, wasn't it? Sadie chose that moment to open the door, saving him from having to answer his own question.

"Where's my father?"

Hawk jumped to his feet. "He went to the barn. You want me to fetch him for you?"

"That would be nice, Hawk. Thank you. Tell him supper is on the table." As the boy scampered away, she called after him, "Make sure you both wash up!"

Hawk shot her a disgusted look, probably because he didn't like being reminded.

"I swear that boy avoids soap and water more than anybody I know." Her smile was short-lived. "I'm afraid Pa is overdoing it. What do you think?"

"I saw to it that he took a few breaks this afternoon." Short ones and not as many as he would have liked, but at least he could offer her that little bit of comfort.

Jed hated the worried look that never seemed to leave her eyes. It made him want to find some way to take her away from all of this. He bet she'd never been farther than the next town or maybe the one after that. Would she like to see what life was like beyond the narrow confines of this farm? She used to have dreams, ones that she shared with him when she was a scrawny little girl. He seemed to remember wishes for beautiful dresses, fancy horses, and a big house somewhere. Although his experience was pretty limited, he suspected that she wanted the same things that most girls did.

At the time, he couldn't imagine wanting to leave this small farm. He knew the world outside it was a violent, ugly place at times. She was much better off right where she was, but he had no idea if she knew that.

"He's glad you came back again." She stood close enough that he could smell the lavender she used to scent her clothing.

"I know." Honesty made him add, "But I can't stay for long. Just until the majority of the harvest is done."

"Is it that hard for you to be here?" The words were hardly more than a whisper, as if she hadn't really meant to say them aloud at all.

Before he could decide whether or not to answer, she spun away from him and disappeared back into the kitchen. Rather than follow her inside, he headed for the water pump. He'd already washed up once, but another splash of cool water gave him a good reason to stay out of the kitchen for the moment.

He waited at the pump for Ole and Hawk so he could follow them into the house. Ole smiled his thanks for the rush of clean, cool water. Hawk took it as his due, but at least he stayed long enough to return the favor for Jed. From the way Ole and Hawk were moving, he had to think they were every bit as tired as he was. Maybe he wouldn't need that trip upstream in order to get to sleep. Part of the problem was that in the course of his job he spent most nights sleeping outdoors. Even the loft in the barn seemed to close in on him, especially with the new crop of hay crowding him even more.

In contrast to outside, the interior of the kitchen seemed dim and shadowy. He had to blink several times for his eyes to adjust. Luckily, he knew the room so well that he found his way to his seat at the table without tripping over anything. Weariness hung on his bones like a well-worn shirt.

Sadie offered them all a small smile. "I hope you all liked what you ate at noon, because we're having more of the same."

Hawk reached for the platter of chicken. "Anything is all right with me as long as it's filling."

Jed fought the urge to laugh. As compliments went, it wasn't much, but at least it was honest. He glanced at Sadie to judge her reaction. Although she wasn't smiling, there was good humor in the lines around her eyes and the set of her mouth.

She glanced in his direction and winked when she saw he was looking at her. "Then I'm sure you'll love this meal, Hawk. There's plenty to go around."

"Whose turn is it to say grace?" Ole asked.

Hawk's hand froze, his fork halfway to his mouth. Jed had just picked up a bowl of potatoes. He kept it hovering in the air for fear that any noise he made would draw unwanted attention from Ole.

"You said grace earlier, Pa, and I said it at breakfast this morning." Sadie sat back in her chair, looking rather smug. "Shall we pick by age or size?"

Jed set the bowl down, figuring he was the loser either way. Hawk sank down low in his chair, his eyes firmly on the plate in front of him.

"All right, I'll do it this time," Jed conceded, looking straight at Hawk. "But that means your turn is coming."

The relief on Hawk's face was short-lived. He sat up taller and folded his hands, waiting for Jed to get started.

Meanwhile, Jed struggled to remember at least something close to the prayers he used to hear sitting around this same table.

"Dear Lord . . ." He paused, figuring he was off to a good start. "Thank you for this food to nourish our bodies and give us strength. Thank you for good neighbors who ease our burdens."

He opened one eye to peek in Ole's direction. His friend had been watching for Jed to do exactly that. He gave Jed an encouraging nod before bowing his head again. Evidently there was something more he thought Jed should be saying.

Finally, he just blurted out, "Thank you for Ole, Sadie, and Hawk. Amen!"

Jed looked up in time to catch Hawk rolling his

eyes, but Ole gave him a big smile. Sadie, on the other hand, looked more surprised than pleased.

At least no one laughed. Considering he hadn't had to perform that little chore since he'd left six years ago, Jed figured they were lucky he even knew how to begin and end the prayer.

For the most part, the rest of the meal was eaten in silence. Hawk was the first to excuse himself, saying he wanted to check on Wind Son before turning in for the night.

"He seems to be doing all right here." Jed pushed his chair back from the table to give himself more room to stretch out his legs. "Has he given you any problems to speak of?"

Ole shook his head. "He gets a little moody now and then, but that's to be expected. His whole life has been turned upside down in a pretty short time. But he does his chores and doesn't complain about it."

"That's more than you could have said about me at that age." Looking back, he figured he must have caused Ole more than a few of the gray hairs on his head.

"You always did think you were worse than you really were." Sadie started gathering up the dishes. "Pa, I'd suggest you head off to bed, but you'd only accuse me of nagging."

"See the sneaky way she still has her say?" Ole gave his daughter a dirty look. "But in this case, she's right. I'll see you both in the morning."

Jed considered making his escape, too, but old habits die hard. He'd always helped with the dishes, partly because the kitchen was his favorite room in the house and partly to spend more time with Olga and now Sadie. At least she didn't object to his help.

He dried the dishes as she washed them. "Are you going to try to keep Ole home from helping the others?"

"Wouldn't do me any good to even try. He's already promised the others he'd be there." She rubbed her eyes with the back of her hand.

Damn, was she crying? Just in case, he offered her what comfort he could. "I don't know if this helps or not, but Alice's husband made sure that Ole had the lightest workload. He never asked me outright about your pa's health, but he said a couple of things that made me think he suspects something is wrong."

"That's good." Sadie sniffed a couple of times. "I know Pa has his pride, but he can't do everything, not like he used to."

Jed wanted to ask what she was going to do when Ole couldn't work anymore or, worse yet, when Ole was gone. He sensed she wouldn't react well to his questions, especially considering he wasn't going to stick around to help her himself. His life was out on the trail, doing his best to keep the world safer for people like Ole and Sadie. He knew some lawmen married and even had children, but that was no life for a woman. Not when there was a better than fair chance every time her man walked out the door, he wouldn't come walking back in.

He tossed the towel down by the sink. "I'd like to take a bath in the river, but if you want to go first, I'll wait here."

Sadie stacked the last of the plates on the shelf. "I'd appreciate that. Let me put these few dishes away and then I'll gather up what I need." She took off her apron and hung it on a peg by the stove. "In fact, why don't you walk up with me and sit up where we were the other night until I'm finished? It always seems so much cooler by the water."

He wanted to refuse, but then she stopped him cold.

"I'd appreciate the company." She busied her hands straightening an already tidy shelf.

Hell, how was he supposed to keep his distance if she wouldn't let him? Given time, he could probably have come up with an excuse not to go, but she was waiting for an answer now. "I'll meet you out by the porch, say in about five minutes."

"That'll be fine." She hurried toward the stairs, as if anxious to be off on their stroll through the woods together.

What was he thinking?

Admittedly, he was a little surprised and more pleased than he liked to be that she seemed more eager than usual to spend time in his company. But then he was the only one other than her father and the doctor who knew what she was going through. Maybe her reason was nothing more complicated than that with him she didn't have to be so careful about what she said or did.

And once again, against his better judgment, he'd accepted another excuse to spend more time in her company. Damn, it was too late to change his mind, not without lengthy and awkward explanations.

What would she do if she found out how much he wanted to wipe away her tears and hold her in his arms? Or that he dreamed of joining her in that cool river water, naked and needy? Maybe if he told her, she'd finally tell him to saddle up and ride as far and as fast as his horse could carry him.

He considered doing just that. But then, what if she said yes? That thought scared him clean through and through. He would walk with her because he had promised to, but after that he would make more of an effort to keep his distance. Because if he didn't stay the hell away from her, he didn't know how he was ever going to leave.

Chapter 8

She shouldn't have asked him, but she didn't regret it, at least not much. But ever since that first night when he'd tracked her to the river, she'd spent a fair amount of time remembering how his voice sounded in the shadows. He was a dangerous man, she knew. The danger was there in the way his gun fit against his hip, well worn and ready to use. The hard edge in his eyes had been honed to a new sharpness by the years. A man would be wise not to cross him.

But a woman, especially her, would be even more of a fool to mess with Jed. He wasn't a forever kind of man, not in the way her father had been for her mother. Jed would lay down his life for her without a second's hesitation, and she knew that kind of loyal courage was rare in this world. But he wouldn't spend his life with her, and that bit of knowledge hurt her something fierce.

And as sure as the sun would be up in the morning, he was working himself up to leave again. A few more days at best, and she'd be looking at the back of him riding away. Each time her heart ached to see him go, even if she understood that it wasn't in him to stay.

She didn't want to be alone for the rest of her life, she surely didn't, but she'd never met another man who made her feel the way Jed did. Not that he'd ever done so much as kiss her, not in the way a man kissed a woman. Even though more than a few men had partnered her at the dance every harvest time, none of them had come calling more than once or twice. Pa always thought it was her fault for not making them feel more welcome.

Maybe she should have picked the best of the lot and married him. But it hardly seemed fair to take a vow to love and honor a man when she knew it would be a lie from the start. From watching Meg and her husband, she had seen firsthand how a woman in love with the man she married acted. No one she'd ever met made her feel that way.

Except Jed.

Maybe if he'd stuck around six years ago she would have gotten over him, but he hadn't. Or maybe her girlish mind had built the memory of him into something no real man could possibly compare to. If that were true, though, his recent return should have served up a healthy serving of disillusionment.

That hadn't happened.

So she'd made a decision and then a plan, ones that she wasn't sure she'd be able to follow through on, but she was going to try. Every year, when the majority of the harvesting was done, everyone gathered together and celebrated with a potluck dinner and a dance. This year it was being held at Meg's place, partly because it was more or less in the middle of everyone's farms and partly so she and her husband could show off their new barn.

It was likely that Jed had forgotten about the annual event, but she was going to remind him on their way up to the river. She'd work it into their conversation and casually mention how excited her father was about taking Hawk to his first dance and that Jed would be there for the first time in years. Jed might be able to refuse her invitation, but not her father's.

Her conscience tweaked her a bit for twisting the truth, but she honestly couldn't figure out another way to make sure that he'd stick around long enough to come. One dance was all she wanted, and then she'd get on with her life. Somehow.

Did Jed even know how to dance? And who would have taught him? Had there been a special woman in his life out there beyond the horizon who had kept him from coming home sooner? Some questions were better left unasked and unanswered, she decided. After picking up the small basket with her soap and towel in it, she looked out of her bedroom window to see if Jed was waiting for her. She spotted him just leaving the barn.

She hurried down the steps to the kitchen. Jed wasn't known for his patience, and there was no sense in putting him in a bad mood before she asked a favor of him. A big favor. One he was likely to refuse no matter what kind of mood he was in. But just in case, she was ready and waiting when he reached the porch.

"That didn't take long." She sounded breathless and knew it.

"You didn't have to run. I would have waited for you."

It was nerves and not hurrying that had her needing to catch her breath, but he didn't have to know that. Not at all.

"I know, but it's already getting late, and tomorrow will be another long day for all of us."

When he reached for her basket, she let him take it. For a second, she was afraid he'd also offer her his arm and was relieved when he didn't, knowing his touch would make her too jittery to think straight. Keeping her eyes on the narrow path ahead, she considered how best to break the news about the dance to him. Knowing the trail widened out into a small clearing about fifty feet farther along, she tried hard to come up with the right words to use in a hurry.

In the end, she simply blurted it out. "There's a dance at Meg's farm on Saturday. I'd like you to come."

She'd counted on using the darkness as a shield to hide behind so that Jed couldn't see her disappointment if—or more likely when—he turned her down. Her face felt hot from embarrassment mixed with fear, afraid he wouldn't come and fearing that he might. But as they reached the small clearing, the moonlight seemed to intensify, bathing them both in stark relief.

Jed's steps stuttered and then stopped. "A dance? Why?"

Her stomach sank. She had expected a simple answer, either a yes or more likely a no. Instead, he'd turned the tables on her, demanding in that quiet voice of his an explanation.

"We're all going." She shuffled her feet before forcing herself to meet his gaze. "Pa and Hawk and me. It will be Hawk's first time going." And, as far as she could remember, Jed's, too.

"Hawk won't care if I'm there. Your father will spend the evening in a corner with his friends." He stared down at her, his light-colored eyes holding hers prisoners. "So why do I need to be there?"

"I want to dance." There, she'd said it.

"So dance. You don't need me for that. I can't

believe that there aren't some single men around here who wouldn't line up to dance with you." He started to walk again, leaving her no choice but to follow him.

He wasn't wrong. The men all seemed to know which women came alone or needed dance partners. No woman was left out if she wanted to dance. But that wasn't the same as dancing with that one special man, even if it was only for one dance on one night of her life.

She finally hurried her steps enough to reach out and grab his arm. "Jed, stop for a minute."

He stopped midstep and waited, unmoving and rigid. The silence around him was blacker than the night. He'd already given his answer. It was up to her to speak her piece.

"All right. The truth is, Hawk won't care if you're there. He may even be happier if you aren't. My father will be pleased if you come, but he'll understand if you stay home." She made herself add, "Or if you've already left again."

For a second, he wavered as if he were going to abandon her to the woods and the river, but then he was still again. He didn't want to listen to her, she realized, but he would if she insisted.

"I'm the one who wants you there. Just this once. Just one dance." She expected him to walk away again, but he didn't.

He shocked them both by reaching out to gently cup the side of her face. The warmth of his touch made her want to whimper with the sweetness of it. When his hand dropped away, she leaned closer to him in protest.

"I don't think that's a good idea, Sadie." His voice was soft and gentle and filled with regret and good-bye.

Now, when she so wanted to see his face to see

better what he was thinking, they were standing in the darkest shadows of the woods. She turned the tables on him. "Why, Jed? Why shouldn't I ask for one dance from you?"

He looked skyward, as if seeking wisdom from the stars or else some way to escape this painful conversation. "Because I'm not the sort of man a girl like you should be dancing with."

She took refuge in temper. Hands on her hips, she glared up at him. "First of all, I'm not a girl but a woman full grown, Jed Stark, which you'd know if you stuck around here long enough to take a good look at me. And out of curiosity, just what kind of man should I dance with?" She suspected that he knew as well as she did that neither of them was really talking about dancing, which made the conversation hurt her heart even more.

"A man who makes his living with his hands instead of a gun."

"I don't care about that. You are a deputy U.S. Marshal, Jed. You should be proud of what you do. I know I am. We all are."

"You think I should be proud of hunting down a child like Hawk? Holding him at gunpoint and tying him to his saddle? Remember how you looked at me when I brought him here trussed up that way?"

And it had hurt him, she realized with surprise, although there hadn't been any indication of it at the time. "Well, I was wrong to act the way I did. I'd like to think it was only because of the shock of having you come back."

"I should have stayed gone."

"No, you should have come back sooner. We needed you here. *I* needed you here." She closed the distance between them and put her arms around his waist. At first it was like hugging an oak tree, but slowly he responded until his long arms crushed her against his chest

For the longest time, they stood together, drawing what comfort they could from the simple embrace. But as the fireflies danced around them and the crickets sang, the nature of the hug changed. She became aware of the soft feel of his shirt against her face. Each breath she took teased her senses with the scent that her mind remembered as belonging to Jed, his strength and surprising gentleness that he'd always reserved for her.

Although she liked being held against his shoulder, it wasn't nearly enough. She lacked the boldness and experience to ask for more, but she tipped her face up toward his, hoping he would know what to do next. Once again, his strong fingers cupped her face, tilting it to just the right angle as he dipped his head down to settle his lips on hers.

If she could choose a single moment of her life as the most perfect, the one she would relive over and over again, this first real kiss from Jed Stark won hands down.

The woods around them and the river that murmured and babbled over the rocks disappeared from her world, narrowing it down to the warm circle of Jed's arms. She needed nothing else. If there was a desperation to his kiss, she ignored it. For the first time, and perhaps the only time, in her life she felt desired by this one man. She knew full well that there was nothing easy about Jed; he was too intense and often too angry for that.

Not that she feared him. From the moment he came into her life she'd known despite his anger and bitterness that she had nothing to fear from him. She'd waited years for this very moment, when she could show him what he meant to her.

He teased at the corners of her mouth, daring her to offer him entry. As their tongues touched and mingled, he tasted raw and powerful. A small part of her wanted to protest that it was too much, too fast, but she refused to listen. She'd waited years without hope, without dreams, wanting to get over this man. She had known the pain of living without him, and she would know it again, probably all too soon. For now, she would take this moment and make as much of it as she could.

She savored the touch of his hands skimming down her back, tracing the curve of her waist, as if he were trying to commit her to memory. He left streaks of heat everywhere he touched, slowly overwhelming her with sensations new and wondrous and strange.

Heat pooled in her breasts before seeping lower to settle between her legs. There wasn't room for a breath of air between them, but still it was too much. She raised herself up on her toes to loosen the narrow strip of leather that held Jed's hair back from his face.

The black silk slid down over her fingers, smooth and soft, the sensation making her smile. "I've wanted to do that for so long."

Jed kissed his way down the line of her jaw and then lifted her high in his arms to nuzzle his way down her throat to her breasts. His breath left a damp trail in its path. Anchoring her to his body with an iron-hard arm under her bottom, he used his other hand to gently squeeze one of her breasts. He suckled the other through the thin cotton of her dress and chemise, stoking the fire that burned deep inside her.

Everything was spinning out of control, leaving her completely at his mercy. Although she trusted him not to hurt her, she felt as if she were about to explode into a million pieces.

"Jed, please!" His name was a moan and a prayer.

He froze, still and quiet and distant, despite the way he held her cradled in his arms. Slowly, so slowly that she thought time had stopped, he lowered her to the ground. Then he took a step back and then another. She started forward, but he held up a hand as if he were fending off an attack.

"Jed?" His silence hurt her. When he spoke, it hurt even more.

"Stand back, Sadie. Don't touch me."

His voice was unnaturally calm, as if they were discussing the weather or some other inconsequential topic. But anger was there between them, as real as the drone of the cicadas in the trees around them.

"Go back to the house. Now."

He might not remember, but she could meet him temper for temper. And maybe the night's shadows gave her courage. "I don't take orders from you. Not anymore." She took a small step in his direction and took perverse pleasure in seeing him back up again.

"Damn it, Sadie, don't do this!"

"Don't what, Jed? Make you admit that you're not immune to me? That I'm not the only one who feels this?" She waved her hand between them even though she wasn't sure how much he could even see.

"Shut up, Sadie. Don't talk that way!" He wasn't so calm now.

"I might have started this when I hugged you,

Jed Stark. But I wasn't kissing myself and it sure wasn't my hand squeezing my . . ."

Just that quickly, he was gone. She sank to her knees in the dirt, tears burning down her cheeks. The hem of her skirt served as a handkerchief to scrub away the evidence of her pain and to muffle her cries. It was foolish to hope that Jed would come to his senses and return, but still she waited far longer than she should have in hopes that he would.

Finally, alone and lost, she pushed herself back up to her feet and tried to decide which way to go. If her father or Hawk happened to see her in this condition, they would demand answers to questions she didn't want to hear. So that left the river. After fumbling a bit, she managed to find her basket where Jed had let it fall while they were . . . She shut that thought down. As wonderful as it had started out, the aftermath had left her raw and bleeding.

She headed toward her spot by the river. The moon was high overhead, giving her enough light to see her way. The beauty of the night was all but lost on her as she stripped down and waded into the water. On this night, she didn't take the time to let the water wash away the day's cares because it wouldn't have worked, not this time. She scrubbed at her skin, taking no pleasure in the process. But no amount of soap and cool river water was going to erase the memory or ease the pain. She settled for washing her hair and rinsing it clean.

Then she tugged her dress back over her head, not bothering with her chemise because she would go straight to bed as soon as she reached her room. All around her the normal voices of the night seemed muted. Did the crickets and cicadas and whippoorwills somehow sense her mood? Or maybe they were singing their hearts out and she couldn't hear it because hers was broken.

It didn't matter. Tomorrow would come whether she wanted it to or not. At the break of day, she would be in the kitchen cooking for the crowd of men and women who were coming to help again. She didn't have a prayer of getting enough sleep to cover up the ravages of her sorrow. Her father would likely be too busy to notice, but she couldn't hide from the sharp eyes of Meg and Alice. What could she tell them?

It was too late, and she was too tired to worry about it for now. She stepped up on the porch, avoiding the loose board that squeaked. Inside, she walked through the darkness with the ease of familiarity. She'd lived every one of her days in that house and knew each inch of it. Once in her room, she stripped off her dress and dropped it in a damp heap, wishing she could burn it or at least throw it in the ragbag. She knew every time she wore it that she would remember the sweetness of Jed's kiss and the agony of his rejection.

She started to turn down her covers, but something drew her to the window. She thought about ignoring the urge to look toward the barn, as if she could see Jed and draw some comfort from knowing he was as miserable as she was. But he wasn't in the barn. He was standing beside his horse, tightening the cinch on his saddle. He froze, as if he could feel the weight of her gaze. He turned slowly to stare up at her window. Maybe he waved, but she wasn't sure. Her vision blurred from the tears welling up in her eyes. She tried to wave back, but he'd already turned his back to mount up. She halfway expected him to tear off down the road in his haste to leave her behind.

But he didn't. Maybe he was afraid the sound

would wake her father, or maybe he was afraid of injuring his horse out of carelessness. But what she wanted to believe—needed to believe—was that he was finding it damn hard to leave her behind.

Chapter 9

He rode as far as the edge of the next town and turned back, cursing himself for a fool each step of the way. Right now the last place he wanted to be was back at the farm and the temptation of Sadie Johanson. As Lady plodded along in the dark, Jed tried to come to terms with what had almost happened between them. If he were a cad, he would point all the blame at Sadie. After all, she was the one who had thrown her arms around him. But as much as he wished he'd been the one wronged, that would be a lie. Granted she had put her arms around him, but she'd been seeking comfort, not a surge of lust from him.

He closed his eyes, trying to forget the sweet taste of her mouth or the way her breast fit his hand so perfectly. How had he let things get so far? She deserved so much better than to have his filthy hands on her.

And had he apologized? No, he'd turned tail and run. He'd been many things in his life, but he'd never thought of himself as a coward. More times than he could count he'd faced down hardened criminals and known killers. Hell, he'd personally brought down one of the most vicious gangs of rustlers in the Indian Territory. And that with a festering bullet hole in his shoulder.

But one blue-eyed girl could bring him to his knees with something as simple as a kiss. He wished like hell that he had someone he could talk to about it. He'd never been able to talk to Ole about Sadie. The man was her father, but he was less protective of her than Jed was. If he'd done his job right as her father, Ole should have banished Jed from the farm from the first day. Instead, he'd allowed his only daughter with those huge innocent eyes to tag along behind Jed without hesitation.

Even as a boy, Jed had seen and done things that Ole would be shocked and disgusted by. And now, even though he wore a badge, his job involved a lot of ugliness and guilt. There was blood on his hands and death on his soul. But those few minutes in Sadie's arms, when he let himself forget who and what he was, he had caught a glimpse of what life could have been like if things had been different.

If he had been different. Such thinking was getting him nowhere.

He looked around to get his bearings and realized he was almost back to the farm. Lady raised her weary head and sniffed the wind. She stepped out at a faster walk, a clear sign that she was more than ready to see the inside of her stall. Since they were both living in the barn these days, he left it up to her to get them there safely. He was so damned tired, the kind of tired that no amount of sleep would help.

And unless he was seeing things, the sky had a definite pink cast to it in the east. He was going to be one sorry-looking son of a bitch when Ole and the others got ready to head out to the fields. There was no way he could sleep in without raising eyebrows. Ole might not ask questions directly, but they'd be there in his eyes.

Jed vowed to make it through the day because he had to; both his pride and his conscience demanded it. Hell, it was no different than tracking a killer for thirty-six hours straight. If he could still draw his pistol fast enough to get the drop on a fugitive with no sleep, he could harvest hay alongside Ole and his neighbors.

At last the barn loomed up out of the night. He dismounted as close to the door as he could get, not sure how long his legs would support him. After dragging the saddle off his mare's back, he turned her into a stall, promising to be up at first light to feed and water her.

Then he climbed the ladder to the loft, took off his gun belt and boots, and collapsed. He was asleep almost before his head hit the hay.

It felt as if the sun overhead had singled him out for special torment. He scrubbed at the sweat streaming down his forehead with his sleeve, but it didn't help. Dust from the hay combined with the salty sweat to make his skin itch something fierce. At least the misery it caused kept him awake, a miracle in itself. He made his way back to the wagon where Hawk was doling out drinks of water from a bucket of fresh water he'd brought from the house. Jed's hand was shaking so badly that most of the water sloshed out of the ladle and onto the ground.

Hawk sneered. "What's the matter, lawman? Mowing hay too hard for you?'

Jed bit back the obscenity that was his first response. Instead, he scooped up another ladle of water and drank deeply, holding it steady out of sheer cussedness.

"I can work you into the ground, boy." Even if it killed him. Considering the condition he was in, it just might. With grim determination, he went back to work. It was a poor day, indeed, when he couldn't keep up with an old man and a young boy.

A short time later the clang of a bell rang out over the field, coming from the direction of the house. It was Sadie and the other women calling the men in to eat. He almost fell to his knees in relief. It might take more energy than he could muster to eat, but he didn't care. As long as he could quit swinging that damn scythe for an hour or so, he'd be grateful.

Jed broke into a shuffling run to catch up with the wagon. Hawk had already gathered up the others, but Jed knew it was too much to expect that the boy would wait for him. Ole and one of the others held out their hands to pull him up beside them. He slumped back against the sweet-smelling hay and took a deep breath. If he didn't watch it, he'd be snoring before they reached the house. Hawk would never let him live it down.

"What's the matter with you, Jed?" Ole kept his voice down, probably not wanting Martin and the others to hear.

"Just a little more tired than usual." Jed kept the brim of his hat pulled low enough that Ole couldn't get a clear look at his face.

His friend looked disgusted. "Sadie looked almost as bad this morning. You young people think you don't need sleep. Well, you'll learn differently."

Jed forced himself to stay relaxed, afraid that if he didn't Ole would realize that there was a connection between how tired both he and Sadie looked. He'd hoped that she had been able to get some rest after he'd ridden out last night.

But, a small voice reminded him, Sadie had watched him leave. Just before he'd mounted up, he'd risked a look at her bedroom window. She'd been little more than a vague outline from where he'd stood, but he'd seen her all the same. He'd made her cry in the woods, but he suspected he'd hurt her even more by riding out. Did she know he had come back? He hadn't been brave enough to ask. Hell, as far as he knew, neither Hawk nor Ole was aware that he'd spent most of the night out riding. Sadie was the only one who knew, just as she was the one who would be most hurt by seeing him leave.

He sat up and straightened his hat, trying to look as if he had enough life left in him to make it through the rest of the day. Besides, he wanted to see the look on Sadie's face when she saw him riding in with the others. Considering everything, he'd be damn lucky if she didn't come after him with one of her sharper knives. The thought made him want to smile, but he didn't. Ole would want to know what he found funny and he had no intention of telling him.

Hawk had a good hand with the horses, making a smooth turn to deposit his passengers right by the water pump. Jed decided to let someone else see to the horses this time. He had enough to do just getting himself through the meal and facing Sadie.

She spotted him almost as soon as he jumped down off the wagon. He tried to guess what she was thinking, but it was as if her face had frozen.

She looked straight at him and then deliberately looked away as if it didn't matter to her one way or the other that he was there.

He should have been relieved, but he wasn't. He was mad; in fact, he was furious. Here he was, all but exhausted because he'd lost an entire night's sleep because of her and her feminine wiles. And there she stood, looking for all the world as if she didn't have a care in the world.

He knew he should walk away rather than confront her. Hell, maybe he should have kept going instead of turning back. But he figured the least she could do was acknowledge his presence, giving him credit for staying on to honor his promise to her father.

"Is that plate for me?" He stood less than an arm's length from her. "I'm really hungry for some reason."

She ignored him, handing the heavily laden plate off to someone else. Fine, he'd try again.

"Can you fix me a plate like that? I'm hungry."

Sadie turned away. "We all are. What makes you so special?"

"Sadie!" Her friend Meg was wide-eyed with shock. Neither of them had realized how close by she was.

Rather than have to explain anything to her friend, Sadie picked up a plate and began heaping food on it, far more than Jed could eat. He accepted it without comment other than a mumbled "thank you." Then he stalked away, knowing both women watched him leave and not giving a damn.

"What was that about, Sadie?" Meg set down a bowl of hard-boiled eggs. "What did he do to upset you?"

Leave it to her friend to assume that it was Jed's fault that Sadie was snarling at him. Sadie appreciated her friend's loyalty, but she felt a little guilty for not setting her straight. Jed wouldn't care what Meg thought about him, and she was just too tired for long explanations.

"Don't let him bother you, Meg. Sometimes he growls when he doesn't really mean to." She managed to drag up a smile meant to reassure Meg that everything was fine. She wasn't very successful, judging from the look her friend gave her. Rather than face any more questions, she grabbed up an empty bowl and started back toward the house. "I'd better get more corn bread."

Meg made a move to follow her, but then Meg's husband called out to her. Sadie took advantage of the distraction to make good her escape. Inside the kitchen and blessedly alone for the moment, she set the bowl down, all thoughts of refilling it with corn bread forgotten for the moment.

When had Jed come back? And why? Even now her stomach ached with grief from watching him leave during the night. There had been something so horribly final about the way he'd looked up at her window before turning his back and riding off into the darkness.

All morning, she had been avoiding her father, not wanting to explain that it was again her fault that Jed had gone this time. And part of her wished that he had stayed gone. Each time Jed left, it hurt worse, perhaps because she suspected that each time was easier for him. And once her father was gone, there would be no reason for Jed to return.

Except that last night, it hadn't been her father out in the woods with Jed. She shivered in the heat of the day, remembering how it felt for those few glorious minutes in Jed's arms, with his hands on her body, his taste on her tongue. The soft curves of her body had felt cherished cradled against the hard planes of his. She might be an innocent in many ways, but she'd been raised on a farm. She'd recognized the meaning of that hard ridge of flesh hidden behind the buttons of Jed's pants. He'd wanted her as much as she'd wanted him.

The realization pooled inside her, liquid and hot. She wasn't given to using curse words; her mother had taught her better than that. But damn him, anyway, she couldn't go on this way, hungering for a man who had no intentions of being part of her life other than as a memory.

But her father certainly enjoyed Jed's company. In fact, when Jed was around, Ole seemed more like his old self, more energetic and cheery. For his sake, surely she could endure Jed's visits without complaint. After all, she had no doubt that once her father was gone from her life, Jed would be as well. At that moment, she wasn't sure which idea hurt more.

She'd always thought that she was lacking something that other women had. The men she had met were always respectful to her. A few had even showed some interest in courting her, but none of them had ever made her feel the way Jed did in the woods last night. If her mother were alive, Sadie would have been able to talk to her about it because she knew Jed as well as she did Sadie. Out of friendship, Alice had offered herself as a substitute once Olga was gone, but Sadie wasn't sure the other woman would understand the jumble of emotions Sadie was feeling.

Between her father's illness and Jed's reluctant presence, she felt as if everything in her life was out of control. And the worst part was, she wanted to drag Jed right back into the woods to see if last night had been a fluke or if they could rekindle the blaze of passion they'd shared so briefly. If Jed was the only man who could make her feel like a woman, did she want to let him ride away without experiencing that passion to the fullest?

A scary question, one she didn't have an answer for. Rather than continue to chase such thoughts in circles, she turned her attention back to feeding the crowd outside. At least slicing corn bread was something she knew how to handle.

Dinner was a quiet affair. The men had worked extra late to finish bringing in the hay. Tomorrow, they would all move on to the next place to do more of the same. Right now, no one around the table had the energy to do more than lift a fork.

Sadie was grateful for the quiet, even if it felt a bit strained whenever she happened to meet Jed's gaze across the table. Finally, she excused herself and stepped out on the porch. The air was hot and sticky, but she preferred it to the company in the kitchen. The peace didn't last long. She knew without looking that it wasn't her father or Hawk who'd joined her.

She was tired beyond reason. But until she got a few things straight with Jed, she wouldn't sleep. "Let's take a walk."

At least he followed after her without arguing. Rather than risk the temptation of the woods, she walked along the narrow road that wound its way away from the farm. Jed fell into step beside her, maintaining a careful distance between them.

"I saw you leave last night. You came back." It wasn't as much a question as an accusation.

Jed kept his eyes on the distant horizon where the sun was preparing to disappear. "Seemed like I should."

"Which one? Leave or come back?"

He didn't give her an answer, maybe because he didn't have one.

They walked on in silence until they were well past a deep bend in the road and out of sight of the house. They were far enough from the house now that they could talk without risk of either her father or Hawk overhearing them.

She took a seat on a fallen log and patted the space beside her. "There are things we need to talk about."

Ignoring the invitation, he chose instead to lean against a nearby tree after plucking a piece of grass to chew on. She wondered how many times she had seen him do exactly that over the years.

He stared off into the distance, seeing things she could only imagine. With obvious reluctance, he turned to face her, his silver eyes tarnished and tired. "I can't imagine what we'd have to talk about."

She tasted her temper rising. As tired as they both were, it probably wasn't the smartest time to try to hash things out between them. But now that they were here, she was going to try.

"You almost left because of what happened last night in the woods."

He dragged his attention from the horizon back to her. The gray in his eyes darkened. "What happened last night shouldn't have. At all. Ever."

She knew things had gotten out of control, but surely he'd savored the sweetness of their first kiss as much as she had.

"I know I don't have much experience in such things—"

"Honey, you have no experience in such things."

That did it. "Jed Stark, you've got no call to insult me. I may not have dallied with many men in my life, but you certainly weren't complaining last night."

She startled a laugh out of him, the first real one she'd heard from him in far too long. He didn't bother to hide his smile. "Dallied? Is that what we were doing? Hell, I thought we were about to strip down naked and—"

She jumped to her feet and shoved him. "Stop it right now, Jed. I won't have you making me feel cheap." She drew a ragged breath. "This was a mistake. I'm sorry." With luck, she'd have enough control left to reach her room before she broke down completely.

Jed knew he should let her go. He'd manage to insult her and likely made her cry. If his goal was to make sure she avoided him for the rest of his stay, he'd probably succeeded. It should have pleased him. Instead, he hated himself for daring to treat her that way.

Before he even knew he'd made the decision to follow after her, he was already reaching out to catch her arm.

"Look, Sadie, I'm sorry." If she had any idea how rarely he felt the need to apologize, she'd be impressed. But she didn't know, and she wasn't.

She glared at his hand on her arm as if it might carry some kind of horrible disease. "Let go of me. Now."

He weighed his options. If he tried to hold on to her long enough to make her listen, she would likely only get madder. If he let go, she'd walk away. He settled for standing in front of her, blocking her path back to the house.

"Speak your piece." He folded his arms over his chest, his feet planted wide. "I'm ready to listen."

Sadie's eyes narrowed; her sweet mouth was set

in a stubborn line. "I have nothing left to say to you."

For such a little thing, she sure had a temper. It was cute, although he knew better than to say so.

"I never thought you were a coward, Sadie. You're itching to tear a strip off my hide. Here's your chance." He would wait all night if that's what it took.

She held her ground for a time; then her shoulders slumped in defeat. He hated the sorrow that washed over her face and hated knowing that he was partly responsible for her feeling that way.

He tried again. "Tell me what you want to say. I promise to listen." Moving slowly, he reached out to take her hand and led her back to the log. This time he sat next to her, hoping to offer what comfort his presence might give her. She sat quietly, staring at nothing in particular, her hands clasped in her lap in a vain attempt to hide the trembling.

"Sadie, just speak your mind. Hell, scream at me if it will help." He knew he shouldn't, but he put his arm around her shoulders and pulled her closer. He wasn't sure which of them it was supposed to help.

"It hurts so much." She burrowed in against his chest. "Pa's dying, Jed, and we just keep pretending that everything is just fine. Hawk has been a big help, but he's already lost one family. What's it going to do to him to lose another?"

Her tears burned liked acid straight through his shirt and into his heart. His gut churned with regrets. She hadn't mentioned his role in her misery, but he'd definitely added to her already considerable burden.

He made himself ask, "Would it better if I left and didn't come back?"

She raised her tear-streaked face and shook her head. "No, Pa feels better when you're here."

"Damn it, Sadie, that's not what I meant. I wasn't asking about what your father needs or Hawk needs. I'm asking if *you* want me here."

The sniffling stopped, and the silence felt like a summer storm waiting to break. He knew her answer was going to cost him, maybe more than he had left to give.

"I've always wanted you here, Jed. Even when I hated you for leaving."

Life had taught him that words could be twisted and turned to mean anything until it was impossible to tell the truth from the lies. But Sadie's bald statement rang with an honesty that cut right through him.

His first impulse was to apologize, but he wasn't sure what he'd be apologizing for. He'd left for her sake, not his, and he still thought he'd done the right thing. Even so, he hadn't realized that by trying to protect her, he'd managed to hurt her anyway. Enough so that she still hurt after six long years.

So did he, but he wasn't about to admit to that. "I'm sorry, Sadie."

She shook her head. "At least be honest with me, Jed. You're not sorry you left. You're sorry you came back." She made a move to stand up, but he tugged her back down beside him.

"If I am, it's only because my being here has caused you more problems." Not to mention a few for himself. Sadie had plagued more than a few of his nights over the years when he dreamed of holding her in his arms. How much worse was it going to be now that he knew the sweet taste of her kisses?

And how could he make it all up to her, knowing that he was still going to ride away one day and never return? He did the only thing he could.

"I'll come to the dance."

He didn't wait to see her reaction. Whether or not she was happy, he wasn't. Without looking back, he walked away, wishing like hell he was anywhere other than where he was.

The music was loud and boisterous. Jed braced himself and slipped around to the back door of the barn. Most folks entered through the front, but he wasn't most people. Meg and her husband had arranged a row of lanterns to light the way for their friends and neighbors. The warm glow of the lights was intended to make everyone feel welcome.

Jed had been invited, but he wasn't sure he was welcome. He'd thought to slip in unnoticed, but he'd walked right into a knot of men, all of them young, passing a bottle around. He didn't recognize any of them, but that didn't mean anything. During the time he'd lived with the Johansons, he hadn't done much socializing.

Olga had tried her best to entice him to various outings, but he'd avoided most of them. Although the Johansons might have seen past his black hair and dark coloring, other folks hadn't always been quite so accepting. Very few of them had come right out and said anything, but it was there in the way they looked at him and then made sure their daughters were kept a safe distance away.

But these men, most of them barely old enough to shave, stood their ground and blocked the door. Damn, there wasn't anything he hated more than dealing with a bunch of idiots depending on alcohol for their courage.

"We don't want your kind here."

He wasn't sure which one of them had spoken, but it didn't matter. If one of them felt that way, the rest of them would feel obligated to back his play. He forced himself to stay calm, not wanting to provoke a fight with a show of temper.

"I was invited."

"Like hell you were!"

The voice came from the back of the small crowd. The others parted, as the speaker pushed his way through. Jed eyed his challenger, judging him to be about his own height, but the farmer outweighed him by thirty or forty pounds. Just big enough and dumb enough to think size made the difference in a fight. It did, but a cool head and solid experience in fighting dirty went a lot further in determining which man ended up bleeding in the dirt. It would be no contest; the drunken fool just didn't know it yet.

Jed widened his stance and waited. If there was going to be trouble, he wasn't going to be the one who took the first swing.

"Who would invite a half-breed to a dance with decent folks?" The man swayed forward.

"As a matter of fact he was invited by me, Carter." Another voice entered the conversation. Meg's husband, Martin, walked out of the barn. "Marshal Stark, I'm glad you could make it." He held out his hand as another show of support.

Jed gladly shook his hand. The last thing he wanted to do was spoil everyone's evening by getting into a fight, even if he wouldn't have been the one to start it. "I guess I came in the wrong door, Martin."

"I'm glad you came, no matter which way you came in. It's always an honor to have a U.S. Marshal join us." Martin gave the others a narrow-eyed look. "I'm sure all of you have something better to do than drink that poison. Too much of it will make you act like fools." He grabbed the bottle away from the closest man.

Several of the men slunk away into the shadows, either out of embarrassment or because Martin had snatched their bottle and they were off to look for more. Either way, the moment was past. Once Jed and Martin were safely inside, he thanked his companion.

"Thanks for helping me out. I probably could have handled the whole bunch of them, but it definitely would have gotten the evening off to a shaky start." He took off his hat for a minute and looked around the barn. "You've got a really nice place here."

"We like it." Meg had joined her husband. "Ole was looking for you, Marshal. He was wondering where you'd gone." She pointed off to his left. "He's waiting for you over there."

"Thank you, ma'am. I'll go find him." And hopefully find a quiet corner to hide in, at least until he knew if anyone else in the barn took exception to his presence.

"Jed, there you are!" Ole was sitting down with Hawk by his side. "We're sitting here enjoying the music." He scooted over, making room for Jed on the bench. "Sadie wasn't sure you were going to make it, but I told her you'd stick by your promise."

A promise he'd come damn close to breaking. All the way there, he'd tried to come up with an excuse that Sadie would both believe and forgive. But there weren't any runaway wagons he had to run down, nor was there a convenient fire that required his immediate attention. So here he was, feeling out of place and wishing he dared bolt back out into the safety of the night.

The musicians moved smoothly from one song right into the next. One of the local farmers called the dance, doing his best to keep all the dancers moving in and out, laughing when they got it wrong. Jed vaguely remembered the farmer and thought he lived a fair piece out on the other side of town. Martin and his wife should be pleased with the large turnout.

He'd yet to see Sadie, though. Trying not to be obvious about it, he tried to pick her out of the crowd. She'd left for the dance earlier than he and her father had in order to help Meg with the last-minute preparations. He didn't even know what color dress she was wearing.

Ole must have noticed him looking around, because he elbowed Jed in the side and pointed toward the group dancing at the far end of the barn. "She's dancing with Meg's cousin David, there at the back."

Sure enough, Sadie and her partner were just turning a corner. She was flushed from the exertion, but the big smile on her face looked genuine. He knew he was being purely contrary, but even if he didn't want to dance, he didn't want her to have a good time without him.

When the music wound down, he was on his feet heading straight for her. Luckily for him, her partner saw Jed coming and had the good sense to make himself scarce. Jed didn't know what excuse David offered her, but it must not have made much sense because Sadie stood staring at his retreating back with a confused look on her face.

"Did he desert you?"

Sadie tipped her head to one side to consider

her answer. "I suspect you had something to do with that."

Jed protested his innocence. "I never said a word to him."

Sadie gave a very unladylike snort. "As if that made any difference. You probably gave him that narrow-eyed look you like to use when you're trying to intimidate someone."

That didn't seem to upset her though. To his surprise, she looped her arm through his. "I'm thirsty. Let's get something to drink, before I drag you out on the dance floor."

He let her lead him through the crowd to the makeshift table in the corner. She poured each of them a cup of punch. He didn't really want it, but it gave him something to do besides stare at Sadie. Had he ever seen her all dressed up? He couldn't remember, but he suspected the image would have been burned into his memory forever, considering how good she looked. The dress she'd chosen to wear was the exact shade of blue that brought out the color of her eyes. And somehow, she'd managed to banish the shadows that had been haunting her lately. When she smiled up at him, she looked as fresh and beautiful as a field of spring wildflowers.

The urge to kiss her right then and there was a powerful one. He kept his hands wrapped firmly around his punch cup to prevent that from happening.

"What's wrong, Jed? You look like you've just swallowed a toad." Sadie grinned up at him. "I made that punch myself. I know it's not that bad."

"The punch is fine, Sadie." He tried to focus on a spot on the wall behind her, hoping she wouldn't notice that he wasn't looking directly at her.

She glanced over her shoulder to see who or what held his interest. When she didn't see anything, her smile faded away. "You really don't want to be here, do you?" She meant with her, even though she didn't say so, but he heard it anyway.

He owed it to her to do better. "I've never spent much time at affairs like this. I'm not sure how to act." That much was true. But even more important, he didn't know how to act around her.

Sadie looked shocked. "They don't have dances wherever it is you spend all your time?"

"I'm a U.S. Marshal, Sadie. I spend all my time hunting down criminals. They rarely want to dance with me." Sometimes they ended up dancing at the end of a rope, but this wasn't the time or place to be thinking about that. His small joke, though, had brought back Sadie's smile.

"So are you really going to dance with me tonight?"

"And how about me?" Meg strolled up to them, her arm linked through her husband's. "Martin hates dancing, and it's all I can do to drag him out on the floor for one or two songs all evening."

Martin staggered back a step, his free hand over his heart. "You wound me, my dear. I'm only trying to protect your delicate feet from being stepped on unmercifully."

His wife rolled her eyes. "I've never complained, have I? You just use that as an excuse to get out of doing your duty."

"Meg, now you know I've never once complained about doing my husbandly duty." He stopped abruptly when his wife cleared her throat loudly and nudged him with his elbow. A dull flush crept up his neck as he struggled to finish his sentence. "I mean, I don't mind a dance. Or two."

Jed bit back the urge to laugh. He never objected to a little earthy humor, but he suspected that Meg was trying to protect Sadie, an unmarried woman and therefore an innocent.

"I'd be honored if both of you lovely ladies would save a dance for me." He didn't know who was more surprised by his offer—him or Sadie. But he was here for her. One night of his life, he could dance as long as no one objected.

The band was gathering again at the far end of the barn. There was no reason to delay the inevitable. "Shall we?" He offered his arm to Sadie.

She rewarded him with a smile that warmed him all the way down to his boots. He felt it necessary to remind her, "I'm not sure I can follow all the steps."

"I won't complain." Then she giggled and added, "Much, anyway."

The band struck up a waltz. The steps would be simpler, but it meant holding Sadie in his arms. He hoped she wouldn't mind his sweaty palms as he took her hand. After a false start or two, they finally got the rhythm of the music and joined the other couples swirling slowly around the dance floor.

He held her close, telling himself that it was because the place was so crowded, but that was just an excuse. He liked the way the scent of lavender and lilac teased his nose, making him want to bury his face in her hair. The simple touch of her hand in his made him ache to crush her against his chest and kiss her again. That wasn't going to happen because he wouldn't let it. The risk was too great for both of them. If he was going to be able to ride away again when the time came, he had to content himself with the unexpected pleasure of dancing. Each dip and sway, even the texture of the material in her dress, was stored away in his mind, creating memories to feed his dreams on all the lonely nights to come. He hoped it would be enough.

Chapter 10

Sadie closed her eyes and let the music fill her mind. Contrary to Jed's claims, he was a wonderful dancer, at least in her eyes. Other women looked on in envy, although he seemed to be unaware of the attention the two of them were drawing. Even Meg, who was so obviously in love with her husband, Martin, had demanded not just one, but two dances with Jed.

He had been good-natured about the entire evening, more relaxed, in fact, than she could ever remember seeing him. When she and Meg had taken a break from the dancing to replenish the food at the table, Jed had joined Martin and her father talking with a large group of men. If anyone had acted less than welcoming, she hadn't seen any evidence of it.

Maybe her parents hadn't done Jed any favors by letting him stay home from such gatherings when he'd come to live with them. Maybe if he'd been made to feel welcome back then, he wouldn't have left.

But then again, maybe he would have. She quickly shoved that thought away. Tonight was for laughter and fun. There would be plenty of time later to think about all the things in the world that hurt.

"What's wrong?" Jed's voice was a rough whisper near her ear. "Did I manage to stomp on your foot again?"

She forced a smile on her face before looking up into his face. "Nothing's wrong, Jed. I was just dreading the moment when the music stops."

His expression softened. "I have to admit that despite a rough start, this evening has turned out to be better than I expected it to."

She frowned. "Rough start? What happened?"

Jed kept his eyes focused just above her head. "It was nothing."

Temper made her steps falter, almost tripping them both. Jed's quick reflexes saved them from a nasty fall. She wasn't at all satisfied with his curt answer. "If it was nothing, you wouldn't have mentioned it in the first place. Now tell me what happened."

"You never give up, do you?" He waited until they turned the corner at the end of the floor and started back in the other direction. "A few of the young bucks were sharing some whiskey out back when I came in. They questioned who invited me. Martin straightened them out."

"Why would they do that? I'd bet there's not a single person here who knows everyone's name." She knew him well enough to know he wasn't lying to her, but maybe he wasn't telling her the whole truth either. Should she try to pry it out of him and risk making him mad? Normally, she didn't fear his temper, but they'd been having such a lovely time, she didn't want to risk spoiling it.

But if someone had hurt him, she wasn't going to stand for it, either. "What did they say?"

When he didn't immediately answer her, she all but dragged him to the side of the dance floor. "That tough lawman look doesn't work on me, Jed. Now answer my question."

"Let's take a walk." He stopped dancing altogether and led her toward the front door of the barn. Once they were outside, he let go of her arm to put more distance between them.

She let him set the pace as they walked in silence until they were some distance from the others who had stepped outside the barn for a breath of fresh air. Did Jed realize that most of those who had left the bright lights of the barn were couples? She supposed that shouldn't surprise her, considering how few opportunities young people had to spend time together away from the prying eyes of their parents.

What did bother her was that this was the first time she'd gone for a stroll with a handsome man. That seemed a bit sad to her. And wondering if there was a girl somewhere who had slipped off from prying eyes with Jed didn't bear thinking about. Not that she was fooling herself that Jed wanted time alone with her to do a bit of spooning. He was looking for privacy to talk, as if they couldn't talk at home any time they wanted to.

He was frowning again. A woman's laugh rang out through the darkness, coming from over behind several of the wagons. "We should go back."

Sadie was in no hurry to get back to the noise and the overheated barn. "I thought you were going to tell me what happened earlier."

"I was and I will. But I didn't think about how this would look if the two of us were seen walking out here." He moved to stand a little farther away from her.

"What difference does it make what people

think? Are you actually worried that people will think we're more than just friends?" She came to a complete halt. "Unless, of course, you're ashamed to be seen with me."

He didn't like that comment one bit. "Don't be ridiculous, but you know as well as I do that some people might take it wrong for you to keep company with a man like me."

What was he talking about? Then it hit her. Someone had taken exception to his Indian blood. She wished she'd been there because they would have gotten a piece of her mind. But then, he wouldn't have wanted her to leap to his defense. He had a prickly pride that she didn't want to offend.

"I'm sorry, Jed. I didn't think." She hated knowing someone had attacked him with such hurtful words and small minds. "We can go back in, if you'd like. Pa may be getting tired and need to go home." Which would give Jed a legitimate excuse to leave, too, if that's what he wanted.

But to her surprise, he shook his head. "Hawk can drive your father home if he wants to leave. I'm willing to do a little more dancing, if you're of a mind to."

"That sounds wonderful to me." The thought of spending more time in Jed's arms had her skin tingling. She rested her hand on Jed's arm as they reentered the barn.

"Your pa is still over in the corner. Why don't I go check on him while you pour us each another cup of punch? If he's ready to go, we'll make sure he and Hawk get started toward home." He started to walk away, but then abruptly turned back. "Wait a minute. Don't you need to ride home in the wagon with them?"

"I don't have to, if I want to stay longer. I rode over on my mare. I was planning on tying her reins to the back of the wagon because Pa didn't want me coming home by myself late at night. But I can ride with you, if that's all right."

For a second or two, she thought he was going to refuse, probably out of some misguided need to protect her reputation. It made her mad enough to want to scream at all the narrow-minded people in the world and then at Jed for listening to them. Didn't they know that a person's character was far more important than hair color or who your parents were?

He took his work as a lawman seriously, risking his life to make things safer for others. That should count for something. But again, he shouldn't have to wear a badge to be treated with common courtesy.

"If you're sure, I'll go tell your father."

"I'm sure. I'll be waiting over by the table with your punch. Hurry, though. I don't want to miss the next waltz." She gave him a bright smile, not caring one whit what anyone might think.

"I'll be back."

Then he disappeared into the crowd. She waited and watched until he reached the other side of the barn before hurrying over to the table to get their drinks. Meg was there checking on the refreshments.

"Do you need any help?" Sadie asked as she reached for the ladle in the punch bowl.

"No, I've already set out the last of the baked goods. Martin went to fetch one more tray of cookies. When the food supply gets low, I figure more people will start heading home. Several of the families who live the farthest away have already gone."

She leaned back against the wall and sighed. "I don't know which part of me is the most tired, but I think it must be my feet." Meg gave Sadie a conspiratorial grin. "I've been on them all day getting ready, and having Martin step on them half a dozen times on the dance floor didn't help. Not that I'm complaining, mind you. At least he was willing to dance this time without me having to beg."

"I thought he was kidding about how bad he was." Sadie knew she shouldn't be laughing at poor Martin, but it was funny. "He only trod on my toes once."

"Your Mr. Stark was a better dance partner than he let on." Meg fanned herself with her hand. "He's handsome, too, but don't tell Martin I said that. He might not mind Jed being a better dancer or better looking, but not both."

"I keep telling you, Meg, that Jed isn't mine. Leastwise, not the way you mean. We've been friends, but that's all." As much as she would have liked things to be different.

"I've seen how he looks at you, Sadie. He feels far more than just friendship for you."

"You're wrong about that." She glanced back toward the corner where Jed stood talking to her father. "He thinks of me more like a kid sister."

Meg crossed her arms over her chest and raised one eyebrow. "I don't like to argue with you, Sadie, but look around this place. How many men over the age of ten do you see wasting their entire evening dancing with their sisters? Not a one that I can see."

"He's going to leave again, Meg." She tried to hide the pain that idea caused her but failed miserably. "He has a job to go back to."

Her friend looked disgusted. "A job is mighty cold comfort, if you ask me. Besides, Martin said he thought Jed was a born farmer. Coming from him, that's high praise, indeed."

Sadie had always thought Jed was happy on the

farm, but if that was the case, why did he stay away so long? It was a question she had no answer to. But rather than let the whole mess spoil what was left of the evening, she mustered up another smile.

"That was nice of Martin to say. I know Jed likes him, too. Maybe we can get together again some evening before it's time for Jed to leave again."

"That sounds fine with me. Why don't the two of you come to Sunday dinner next week?"

"I'll ask him and let you know."

"If not, Thanksgiving is only a few weeks away. Martin and I were going to invite you and your father and that boy Hawk over for the day. If Jed is around, bring him, too."

Planning for the future, even only a few weeks at a time, was a tricky proposition considering her father's health and Jed's unpredictable presence. "That's very kind of you, Meg. I'll discuss it with Pa, but he may want to eat at home. Can I let you know what our plans are later?"

"That will be fine. Just know that you would be welcome." Her smile brightened. "Here comes your friend, Sadie. I'd claim another dance with him, but I'd better rest my feet in case Martin decides to take me galloping around the dance floor again."

Sadie giggled at the image that made. "I think you're too hard on poor Martin, but I'm just as glad you feel that way. I don't want to waste a single chance to dance with Jed." It had taken too many years to get him to this one. She might be old and gray before she got another opportunity.

"Ladies," Jed murmured as he touched the brim of his hat in salute to the two of them. "If you'll give me a minute to drink this," he said, holding up the cup of punch Sadie had held out to him, "we'll see what the band has up its sleeve to play next."

Sadie hoped they would play all waltzes, just so she could feel Jed's arms around her. Then, after the music ended, she'd have the long ride home with Jed to look forward to. A special night, indeed.

Sadie waited until everyone else had left before changing back into the pants she'd worn when she'd come early to help. Her good dress was rolled up and tied to the back of the saddle. She ached with the kind of tired that went all the way through to her bones. Fortunately, they didn't have all that far to go to get home and with the moon lighting their way, it should be a pleasant ride. Meg and Martin stood on their front porch and waited as Jed brought his mare up beside hers.

Meg stepped forward. "Thanks for coming, Mr. Stark. I hope you enjoyed yourself."

Jed touched the brim of his hat in salute. "That I did, ma'am." He nodded in Martin's direction. "Send word if you need any more help bringing in your crops."

"I might just do that. I can always use an extra pair of hands."

"Well, good night. Sadie and I had better get on our way, or Ole will start fretting."

"Good night, Meg. I'll see you at church." She accepted Jed's boost up into the saddle. "By the way, it's my turn to bring refreshments."

Martin lit up. "Are you bringing some of that gingerbread I like so much?"

"I'll bring it specially for you in return for dancing with me tonight."

"Maybe I'll have to dance more often if that's what it gets me."

Meg shook her head. "I wish I'd known that baking was all I needed to do to get you to dance without complaining."

"You didn't ask. You'd be surprised what I'm willing to do for some of your pie."

Meg rolled her eyes and then giggled. "I'd better get to bed before he tries to chain me to the stove. You two take care."

Sadie waved good-bye again, wondering if Meg was going to be spending a lot more time in her kitchen. She doubted her friend would mind all that much. It was hard not to be a little bit jealous of their obvious happiness. She wheeled her mare away from the porch and started down the road toward home.

Jed came up beside her. "You have nice friends."

"Martin told Meg that he thought highly of you." She didn't bother to point out that her friends would be his as well if he'd stick around long enough to get to know them better.

"He's a good man."

He nudged his horse to move a little in front of hers. Sadie took it as a signal that he didn't find the topic of conversation to be a comfortable one. She was too tired to want to provoke an argument, so she accepted his unspoken request. The night settled around them. It was peaceful, but hardly quiet. A few tree frogs were singing their hearts out down by the river, backed by the drone of cicadas. A few lightning bugs flickered in and around the trees.

"Damn!" Jed swung down out of the saddle and lifted his pinto's front hoof.

"What's wrong?"

"She's developed a limp. She might have picked up a stone, but it could be something else."

Sadie dismounted. "How bad is it?"

"I can't tell in this light." He ran his hand down the mare's leg. "There's no swelling, but I don't want to risk making it worse. I guess I'll be walking home."

Normally, she wouldn't mind a leisurely walk with Jed, but he had to be every bit as tired as she was. "Why don't we ride double? My mare can carry that much weight if we go slowly." She held her breath, waiting for Jed to answer. Wrapped in darkness, riding double would seem intimate, no matter which way they rode—either her behind him with her arms around his waist or riding across the saddle in front of him.

Jed looked around them, as if searching for any other possible solution to the problem. "Are you sure?"

She wouldn't have offered if she wasn't willing to ride with him. What was he thinking? No doubt he was worried about her reputation again. If that were the case, she thought disgustedly, she should let him walk home. "No one will know, if that's what you're worried about."

"I'm not worried about us." He looped his rope around his mare's neck and then tied the other end to the saddle on Sadie's horse. "Do you want front or back?"

"Whichever you think will be easier on the horse."

Jed swung up into the saddle with a grace she had always envied. She wasn't a bad rider herself, but he'd always seemed to move as if he were part of the horse. Once he was settled, he held out his hand to lift her up on the saddle in front of him.

"Comfortable?" He was so close she could feel the warmth of his breath against her skin.

"I'm fine." More than fine. Once again she found herself surrounded by his warmth, reminding her of the way it had felt to waltz with his gentle strength guiding them both around the dance floor. She leaned against his chest, letting the steady beat of his heart lull her back into a better mood.

"Your mare has good gaits. How long have you had her?"

"Pa bought her for me about two years ago. She's a real sweetheart." Would Jed notice if she traced the muscles in his chest with her fingertips? Probably. Too bad.

At first he ignored her, but then he caught her wandering hand in one of his. That was fine. Holding hands with him was nice, too. But he held on to her hand only long enough to guide it back down to her lap before letting go. Next she shifted enough so that she could put one arm around his neck, which had the effect of tugging his face down closer to hers.

Should she kiss him? It sounded like a good idea to her. She teased her way across his cheek to the corner of his mouth. When he turned toward her, no doubt to tell her to behave, she captured his face with her free hand and settled her lips directly on his.

Perhaps it was the cocoon of darkness that separated them from the rest of the world that made her feel so daring, or maybe it was the silver glow of the moon overhead affecting her. Either way, it didn't matter. Nothing had ever felt so right to her than being in Jed's arms and kissing his stern mouth.

At least he wasn't trying to fight her off, exactly. He pulled back to look down at her. "You're playing with fire, Sadie. All my good intentions will go to hell if you keep that up."

She supposed she shouldn't take such pleasure in knowing that she had the power to weaken Jed's iron control, but she did. What woman wouldn't be flattered to have the attention of such a handsome man?

"Kiss me, Jed. Please."

He scowled and then planted a quick kiss on her forehead. That was not nearly good enough. "Not like I'm some child being put to bed."

"When I think about you and bed, Sadie, I'm not picturing you as a child."

She didn't know which one of them he shocked more with his confession, but she wanted to hear more about it. "What do you think of when you think about bed and me?"

At Jed's signal, her horse came to an abrupt stop. If Sadie hadn't been holding on to Jed, she might have fallen to the ground. Before she could shift a bit to feel more secure, Jed lifted her high in his arms and turned her to face him, her legs draped over his. She should have been shocked by the unfamiliar feel of her legs rubbing against the rough cloth of his trousers.

He held her there with one strong arm while he used the fingers of his other hand to force her gaze up to meet his. Even in the dim light of the moon, there was no mistaking the strong emotions glittering in the silver depths of his eyes, but she wasn't sure if it was desire or anger she saw there.

"Sadie, I've tried every way I know to prevent this from happening, but I can't be strong for both of us."

Her heart hurt. She didn't mean to cause either of them such pain. She reached up to touch his face but jerked it back when he flinched. Enough was enough. "Set me down, Jed. I'll walk."

He did as she asked, his powerful hands lifting

her as if she weighed nothing. But as soon as her feet touched ground, he was standing right there beside her.

"I said that I'd walk. There's no use in both of us getting sore feet."

"We're not going anywhere yet." He stood in front of her, as immovable as an oak tree.

A shiver of not quite fear slithered down her spine. She'd started this, but it appeared Jed was determined to finish it. Despite the warmth of the night, something cold roiled deep inside her, making her long for the comfort of Jed's embrace. He stood only a step or two away, but it felt as if he were on the other side of the world from her.

"We can't stand here staring at each other all night long, Jed. What do you want from me?"

Several answers flashed through his mind, several of which might just finally scare Sadie enough to run as far and fast as she could. He settled for part of the truth and another warning. He took a long step toward her, deliberately crowding her a bit more than she liked.

"I want to strip you down where you stand and taste your mouth and your skin, for starters. Then we'll see where that takes us next." His body's response to that idea was immediate and almost painful in its intensity.

"You mean you want to be my lover." Sadie's voice cracked a bit on that last word, but she stood her ground. "Why?"

Hell, leave it to her to ask a question he had no intentions of answering, at least not the way she wanted him to. "Does it matter?"

She actually gave it some thought before answering. "No, I don't think it does." This time she was the one to move closer to lay her head against his chest and slip her arms around his waist.

It was like seeing the gates to heaven open, but knowing if he took one step toward them, he'd been on the slippery road to hell. Did she not understand that a few hours of sweaty sex was all he had to offer her? Somehow he would find the strength to offer her one more chance to escape. But first he would kiss her. He deserved that much.

He wrapped her in his arms and kissed her forehead again, this time gently as a prelude to more. When she looked up to complain again, he captured her lips with his. She deserved a gentle touch, to be coaxed along the path to passion, but that wasn't going to happen. He tasted her sweet lips with the tip of his tongue and then pushed past to claim her mouth for his own

He was probably shocking her with the strength of his demands, but she made no effort to escape. Instead, she tangled her fingers in his hair and moaned deep in her throat, a primitive sound, as if she were staking her claim on him as well. The last threads of control were slipping through his fingers.

"Sadie, we've got to stop." He felt as if he'd been running for hours, with his heart pounding and his legs feeling weak with the need to lay this woman down where she stood.

"No, not this time, Jed. Don't start pushing me away."

He could feel the sweet crush of her breasts against his chest; his greedy hands slid down the curve of her back to cup her bottom. Had he ever held a woman dressed in work pants? He couldn't remember. It should have felt strange; instead, it was unbelievably erotic. When he lifted her, she wrapped her legs around his waist, further fanning the flames of fire between them.

"Jed, please!" she moaned and leaned back, offering up the graceful arch of her neck to him.

He ran his tongue along the edge of her jaw and down to the sweet pulse at the base of her throat. One of them whimpered; he was afraid it had been him. He managed to carry her to the side of the road to press her against the rough trunk of a tree. He guided her legs down to ride lower on his body, pressing the center of her need against the hard ridge of his. As he rubbed against her, new sensations rocked through them both.

It was too much, and yet again it would never be enough to satisfy.

Calling himself a fool and a hundred other names, he fought to catch his breath and his control over this driving need. He'd wanted this woman for far too long to take her like an animal in the woods, no matter how badly he wanted to. She deserved better, even if he didn't.

"Sadie, I'm going to set you down." He did his best to do what he'd promised, but she wouldn't let him.

"Jed, if you're doing this out of some misguided sense of honor . . ." she protested. "This can't be wrong. It can't be."

His laugh was ragged. "Honey, if it felt any more right, we'd set everything we touched on fire. But this isn't the best time or the place. If we stay gone much longer, your pa will come looking for us or else send Hawk."

That got through to her. She loosened her legs and slid down to stand on her own two feet. Even so, she leaned against him, as if she were unsure if her knees would hold. He let her take her time, running his hand up and down her back with long strokes, trying to find the courage to speak his piece.

"Sadie, you know I won't be staying here. I can't. This place isn't for the likes of me." He felt her flinch as his words hit her. He hated hurting her; hell, he hated himself for doing so.

She kept her face buried against his chest, muffling her words. "You're not telling me anything new, Jed. I don't understand why you can't stay, but I believe you when you say it. That doesn't change the fact that you're the only man who has ever made me feel this way. Even if it's wrong, I want this between us."

So did he, but at least he knew what the risks were. She probably had some romantic idea of what it would be like if they carried this to its logical conclusion. No matter what she said, Sadie really wanted poetry and flowers and to make love. All he could offer were his rough ways and sex, plain and simple. They would couple in the woods like the rest of God's creatures, and then he would move on.

"If you still want this, meet me at the river tomorrow night after your father and Hawk are asleep." He held her out at arm's length. "Think long and hard, Sadie, because there is no going back. If someday you do marry, what will you tell your husband if he asks if you've ever been with another man?"

He didn't even want to think about the other possible outcome—a child born of their reckless passion. The very idea should have him running away as fast as he could go. Instead, the image of Sadie round with his child made him want to hold her close and smile.

Damn, he must be more tired than he thought.

Her eyes looked solemn and too big in her pretty face. "We'd better get moving, Jed. I'd hate Pa to be out riding this time of night."

He mounted up first and then pulled her up to sit behind him. It still made him painfully aware of her pressed along the length of his back, her arms wrapped around him tightly. But at least this way, he might manage to keep his hands to himself. They plodded along in silence for a while before she spoke.

"Thank you for coming tonight, Jed. I know you didn't want to, but it meant a lot to me."

"I had a better time than I expected to."

She giggled. "Considering you probably thought it would be as much fun as having a tooth pulled, that's not saying much."

"I can honestly say that it was way better than that." He suspected every time he heard a waltz, he'd be remembering the scent of Sadie's hair and the sweet feel of her in his arms.

"Meg asked me to invite you to Thanksgiving dinner at her place." She didn't even pause, probably aware that he didn't know how to answer that. "I told her that I didn't know where you'd be for certain, but also that my father may want to eat at home."

"Your father should let you tell at least Meg and her mother that he's ailing. Eventually, they're going to find out anyway." He figured he didn't need to be more specific than that.

Sadie sighed and laid her head against his back. "I feel like I'm lying to them all the time, but Pa doesn't want anyone feeling sorry for him. And I think that carrying on like nothing is wrong is what keeps him going from day to day."

He couldn't think of anything to say to that. Ole was a good man, but he had a stubborn streak running wide and deep through the heart of him. That wasn't necessarily a bad thing. Without it, he would never have managed to break through the shell of anger and mistrust that Jed had built around himself. Whenever he looked back, he figured Ole and his wife had saved his life.

"I'll stay as long as I can, Sadie." Just not forever. He closed his eyes against the pain that truth caused him. After a bit, he drew what comfort he could from laying his hand over hers where they rested against his chest. They rode in silence the last half mile or so to the barn. As they dismounted, Hawk came stalking out of the barn.

"Where have you two been? Your father has been pacing the floor for the past hour or more." Wind Son poked his nose out of the barn door, all saddled up and ready to ride while Hawk went on complaining. "I was already asleep when Ole poked his nose in my room and asked if I'd go looking for you."

Jed didn't like explaining himself at the best of times. He wasn't about to justify the delay to this bad-tempered kid. His plan was to ignore Hawk, but Sadie took matters into her own hands.

"We're sorry you lost sleep over us, Hawk. But Jed's mare developed a limp, so we had to ride double. We didn't want to risk hurting either one of the horses by going too fast."

Hawk might not have much use for Jed, but Lady was a different matter. "Bring her into the barn and I'll light a lantern. I hope it's nothing serious." He shot Jed a look that said very clearly whom he would hold responsible if the mare's injury was anything to worry about.

Sadie slid down off the back of the saddle and held up her hand to take the rope from Jed's hand. Their fingers touched briefly, sending another jolt of awareness through him. Damn, he had it bad.

He dismounted and followed Sadie into the

barn, leading her horse behind him. Hawk was already lifting Lady's foreleg.

"No swelling." He set her hoof back down as carefully as if he'd been handling fine china. "No stone either." Hawk looked at Sadie and then back at Jed, his dark eyes narrowing in suspicion. "I didn't notice any limp, either."

"Well, she was sure limping when we left Meg's place. We both saw it." Sadie was busy unsaddling her own mare. "Or at least Jed said he did."

If Hawk had thought Jed was up to something before, now he was convinced of it. Not that Jed gave a damn what Hawk was thinking, but he didn't want the boy to go telling Ole stories.

"Sadie, you'd better go let your father know everything is all right. I'll take care of the horses. We don't want to worry him any more than we already have."

"If you're sure." She turned her bright smile on Hawk. "Thank you for being willing to come check on us for my father. I would have hated to have him out riding this late at night."

The lantern cast a small circle of light and a mess of shadows around the barn, making it hard to read the expression on Hawk's face. Finally, he nodded toward Sadie. "It's all right. But you'd better go talk to him."

Something in his voice must have caught her attention, because she gave Jed a worried look on her way out the door. There wasn't much he could do to change things. The mare had been limping. If Hawk didn't believe him, too bad. But if Sadie started having doubts, he wasn't sure what he could or even should do about it. Maybe it would even make her stay clear of the river tomorrow night.

He wished he could feel glad about that, but he didn't. The truth was, he wanted their one shot at a night of passion every bit as much as she did. Maybe even more. And the last thing he needed right now was one angry boy giving him dirty looks.

"I'll finish the horses. Go to bed."

"Go to hell, lawman." Hawk stalked out of the barn, slamming the door shut behind him.

Jed waited until he was out of hearing to answer him. "I've already been there, boy." And he'd be there again once he rode away from this place for the last time.

Chapter 11

"Hawk, sit down. I want to talk to you, but you're wearing my neck out watching you pace."

Ole examined the piece of harness he was working on. He'd already replaced the stitches that had come undone, but he could see a few more weak spots along the length of the strap. He picked up his needle and went back to work. Either Hawk would sit down and listen or he wouldn't. Sometimes you had to let the young make their own decisions.

Like his daughter, for instance. It would have been better for everyone all around if she'd set her sights on an easier man than Jed Stark. But from the time she first laid eyes on him, no other man stood a chance with her. That was all right with Ole. Jed was a good man, one who could be trusted with the care of his only daughter.

If only Jed would trust himself.

But right now, Jed wasn't the problem. Hawk was. The boy was gradually working his way around to sitting down. Any sudden moves on Ole's part or if he tried to rush him, Hawk would be off and running again.

"What do you want to talk about?" Hawk dropped down to sit cross-legged on the floor at Ole's feet. "I did all my chores."

The note of defensiveness brought a small smile to Ole's face. "That you have, Hawk. I swear, I don't know how we kept up with everything before you came here." He meant it, too.

"Your grandfather would be proud of you, Hawk. From what you've told me about him, he was a man who valued an honest day's work."

There was still grief in Hawk's expression at the mention of his grandfather, but it wasn't as immediate as it used to be. The boy still missed his closest relative, but maybe the pain wasn't quite as sharp as it had been for him. That would be a good thing for Hawk. Once he came to terms with his loss, he'd be better able to move on with his life and find his place in this world.

Which brought Ole back to the matter at hand.

"The harvest is in. You've kept your word to me." Ole kept his needle working in and out, aware that Hawk's eyes were following every move he made. "So, now it is time to decide what you want to do next."

"Next?" Hawk echoed the word as if he didn't understand what it meant.

Ole held the strap up closer to his face, wishing his eyes weren't failing him along with everything else. A few more stitches and he'd be done. "The next step in your life, Hawk. If you were given free choice about where you'd like to go or what you'd like to do, what would it be?"

Hawk immediately looked down at the dirt floor. He used a piece of straw to draw patterns in the dust. He wasn't ignoring Ole, but giving serious thought to the question.

"I want to raise horses like my grandfather." He looked over his shoulder to where Wind Son stood dozing in his stall. "I already have a good stud to start a herd with. A mare, too, if that lawman would let me breed her." He stabbed the straw into the ground. "He doesn't take good care of her."

Ole had a great deal of patience with angry boys and angry men. That didn't mean he would let Hawk attack Jed for no reason other than jealousy. "Hawk! That is not true." He pointed a knobby finger at his young charge. "I have known Jed Stark for a long time. I grant you that he is not an easy man to be around sometimes, but I have never known him to hurt an animal. He did not mistreat that mare." He bit through the thread and set the repaired strap aside.

Hawk's chin came up. "He said she was limping the other night. She seemed fine when they got home."

No doubt Hawk was more upset about Jed riding double with Sadie than any perceived neglect of the pinto. "You know if she picked up a stone and then it fell out on its own, she might have limped only for a short time. I hardly see how that shows he doesn't take care of her," Ole said.

Rather than let that particular discussion continue, Ole guided them back to the original topic. "So you would breed horses. Where would you want to do this?"

Hawk's head came up, and he took a long look around the barn. "As long as there is pasture and a sturdy barn, I guess I could breed horses anywhere."

Ah yes, so he was thinking about staying on. "I built this barn to last a good long time."

"I can see that. And the stalls are roomy and

solid. Wind Son seems happy in his." No longer able to sit still, Hawk stood up and went to pet his friend.

"And you, Hawk? Are you happy here?" Ole smiled. "I know your room isn't much bigger than that stall, but it's warm and dry."

"My room is fine. And Sadie is a great cook, much better than my grandfather was." Hawk looked a bit guilty about that little admission. "But he was good with horses."

"God gave us all different talents, Hawk. My Sadie is a good cook and keeps a nice home for us. She's also a fair hand with horses, but she wouldn't ever claim to be an expert with them." Ole pushed himself up off the bench, his old bones not happy about staying in one spot too long. It was time to quit dancing around the issue at hand.

"I won't ask you to answer me right now, Hawk, because I want you to give this some serious thought. Would you like to make your home here with Sadie?" He paused. "I know that you didn't come to live with us by your own choice. But it is your choice whether or not you want to stay." He approached the boy with some caution, not wanting to crowd him into a rash decision either way.

He patted Hawk on the shoulder on his way past. "Don't lose track of time. Sadie said supper would be ready soon."

Ole wasn't quite to the door when Hawk spoke up. "How about the lawman? Will he be living here?"

"That is for him to decide, Hawk. It was his home at one time. It might be again someday. But you have to make your decision based on what's best for you."

"Why is he here so much?"

Because Hawk sounded more curious than resentful, Ole decided to answer him truthfully. "I think he's here because he suspects I am dying. He is here for Sadie's sake as much as mine."

Hawk looked stricken. "You are dying?"

He hadn't wanted to have this come up so soon, but then maybe it was fairer to Hawk to let him know the truth. "I'm an old man, Hawk. The doctor in town thinks there is something wrong in here." He patted his chest. "Maybe it's my heart, maybe something else. But Doc, he doesn't know everything. Only God does. So until he calls me home, I plan to go on living. That's as much as any man can do."

He looked back toward the boy. "Personally, I prefer to look forward to things, not worry about stuff I have no control over. For example, Thanksgiving is only a few weeks away. There's nothing I like better than a day set aside to be grateful for everything the good Lord has given us. After that, it's only a few short weeks until Christmas. I have so many good memories of the way Olga always celebrated the birth of our Lord with such joy." He smiled at Hawk. "A man can never have too many good memories. I hope to build a whole new bunch this year—with Sadie, you, and Jed."

He'd said enough to give Hawk a lot to think about. "Like I said, get washed up soon." Before he'd gone two steps, he heard Hawk say something, so he stopped to listen.

"So if this doctor fella is right, though, Sadie is really going to need my help." Hawk had turned back to his horse, and that's who he was talking to. "We want to stay where we're needed, don't we, Wind Son?"

Ole slipped out of the barn, his heart, failing or not, feeling lighter than it had in a long time. Hawk had a good head on his shoulders. He was right about one thing—a man should stay where he was needed. Maybe it was time to have another talk with Jed.

Ole looked at his daughter and wanted to shake his head. He wasn't one to complain about the food set before him. However, the mashed potatoes were lumpy, and those lumps were hard and undercooked. The biscuits were almost black on the bottom. He wanted to put it off to her being out so late the night before, but she acted jumpy and nervous, not tired.

"Do you want another biscuit, Pa?"

She passed the still-full basket with a puzzled look. Normally her menfolk fought to beat each other out to get the last light and fluffy biscuit. Hawk quickly handed off the basket to Jed. He took one, but made no effort to taste it. Ole accepted one, figuring he owed it to his daughter for all the good meals she'd cooked in the past.

What was on her mind? He took another bite of the potatoes. Whatever it was, it wasn't her cooking.

Jed, at least, seemed to have a good appetite. He'd already cleaned his plate, including the extra biscuit he'd taken. But his thoughts were also a long way from where they sat around the table. Lord knows Jed wasn't a talkative sort to begin with, but he'd been unusually quiet all day, even for him. Had something happened last night at the dance? Or perhaps on their way home together?

Ole didn't know what to think, but he also wasn't about to pry into their business. They were both adults and entitled to their privacy. That didn't keep an old man from being curious. Judging from

Hawk's expression, Ole wasn't the only one to think something strange was going on. And as usual, he assumed that Jed was the cause.

Maybe he was right this time.

After all, Jed and Sadie had spent most of last evening together and then there'd been that long, slow ride home. Each of them had danced with others, but only a few dances. Most of the time—and all of the waltzes—they were together out there on the dance floor. He wasn't so old that he didn't remember what it had felt like to hold his best girl in his arms as the music surrounded them.

"Hawk, we'd better go finish the chores. I don't know about the rest of you, but I plan to turn in early tonight." He waited at the door until the boy set down his fork and stood up.

"May I be excused?"

When Sadie didn't respond, Jed did. "Sure thing, Hawk. Go ahead with Ole."

As usual, Hawk did not appreciate Jed's interference. "I wasn't asking you," he snapped. "I asked her."

Sadie had been so lost in thought that she missed the entire exchange. All three males in the room stared at her until at last she looked up from her plate.

"What? Did I miss something?"

Her totally bewildered look had Hawk shaking his head. "I asked if I could be excused."

"Oh, I guess I didn't hear you. Sure, go on. I can handle the cleanup in here." She immediately started to stand up, but then looked around as if not sure what she should do next.

Jed asked the question that all of them wanted answered. "Sadie, are you all right?"

Hawk had been about to walk out the door before Ole, but he turned back to hear her answer.

Sadie, on the other hand, seemed to be surprised by the question. "I'm fine, but why are you asking?"

Ole didn't want to be in the line of fire if Jed was foolish enough to point out the burned biscuits or the lumpy potatoes. Far better, he decided, for all of them if he and Hawk were well away from the kitchen right now. At least they had the excuse of having chores that needed their attention.

Maybe later he could ask Jed about what she'd said. But then, he suspected that Sadie's odd mood probably had something to do with Jed himself. As her father, he might worry, but she was an adult, as was Jed. It was up to them to work out the problem, whatever it might be.

He could only hope that neither of them got hurt in the process, but the future was in God's hands, not his. Even so, perhaps it wouldn't hurt to pray for a Christmas miracle or two.

"Sadie, sit down."

She did as he said, still looking distracted and a bit confused. Jed began clearing the table while she tore one of her inedible biscuits into crumbs. Every so often she would briefly look in his direction before sliding her eyes away.

"Something on your mind that you want to talk about?" He took the rest of the biscuit from her hand and then moved her plate out of reach. Of course, he figured he knew what direction her thoughts had taken.

Tonight, the river, him.

She deserved to make her own decision with no pressure from him, but he was mighty curious how the argument she was having with herself was going. If she had a lick of sense, she'd stay home.

He hoped she was feeling reckless and not in the least bit sensible. And just that quickly, his body's opinion on the subject was making itself known. He turned to face the sink to hide the evidence.

He began scraping the dishes. Sadie made no effort to help, but he didn't care, because he was grateful for something to keep his hands occupied. He wished like hell that washing dishes required his complete attention, anything to keep him from thinking about what might happen later. Even as his hands slid over the dishes in the hot soapy water, he wondered what it would be like to touch Sadie's smooth skin from head to toe—and everywhere in between.

Damn, he had to quit thinking that way. He was by no means certain that she would show up, and even if she did, he wanted to teach her the steps in this whole new dance with care. It wouldn't do to lose control because he'd been letting his imagination run wild.

After he'd washed the last dish, he reached for a towel to dry them. When he started setting the clean plates back on the table, Sadie seemed to finally come alive. She stared at the dishes with a puzzled look on her face for several seconds and then looked around the room.

"How long have I been sitting here while you cleaned up?" She began putting the dishes away while she waited for his answer.

"Not all that long." He used his fingernail to scrape off a stubborn spot on a fork. "Maybe ten minutes or so. Your father took Hawk out to finish the evening chores."

"I'm sorry. I don't usually neglect my duties."

He shook his head and smiled. "It won't kill me to wash a few dishes, Sadie. Your mother made sure I knew how, if you'll recall. She thought a man needed to be able to look after himself, if needs be." Meaning if he had no woman to take care of him.

"I still miss her."

"Me too."

Sadie shoved the last few dishes onto the shelves. "I'm going to take a walk outside." She walked out without looking back.

He was tempted to follow after her but decided that she likely needed some space. Their talk last night had left both of them feeling out of sorts with each other. The whole incident had changed their relationship completely, and neither one of them was comfortable with their new roles.

His one big fear was that if she decided not to follow him to the river, she'd no longer feel at ease with just being his friend. Of course, he also worried about the same thing should she decide to take him for a lover.

He should be shot for even thinking such a thing, but he knew he wouldn't have the strength to turn her away again. He'd wanted her for too long. He was feeling as edgy as Sadie was, but he'd had years more practice of hiding his thoughts from others. If he starting pacing outside, Ole and Hawk would wonder what had both him and Sadie upset. That was a question he wasn't about to answer. So rather than risk it, he walked out to the barn, forcing himself to take his time. But each step of the way, he prayed the remaining time before sunset would pass quickly.

The crickets were chirping, the cicadas were droning, and Sadie's hands were shaking. She sat on her bed, dragging a brush through her hair and wishing she were somewhere else. Anywhere else.

But she wasn't, and the time had come to make her decision.

In the next five minutes, she needed to either blow out her lamp and crawl into her big, lonely bed or else walk upstream to where Jed waited for her. She stood up and then just as quickly sat down again, determined to make her final choice. Again. For the hundredth time in the past hour. She'd never thought of herself as indecisive, but this time she sure enough was.

Giving herself to a man for the first time was something that could never be undone. And Jed, determined to be honest at all costs, had told her to think about that. He'd made it most clear that while he was willing to be her first lover, he wouldn't be her last. He would leave because he had to. She would stay and try to build a life without him.

It was time to go, before he gave up on her and came back. How could she face him if she turned coward and hid up here in her room? He'd understand and forgive her, but she wouldn't. Yes, it was time to go.

This time she made it all the way to her door and to the staircase. At least she'd remembered to carry her basket with her. Chances were her father was sound asleep by now, but in case he wasn't, she wanted everything to look as normal as possible.

The stairs seemed to stretch out forever in front of her as she walked down them, holding on to the railing. The wood had been worn smooth from years of use, and she drew comfort from the familiar feel slipping past her fingertips. The kitchen was blessedly dark. Even if her father were to come in, he wouldn't be able to see her face. He knew her so well, she was convinced that he would have been able to read her intentions written across her forehead.

The night air felt heavy, but perhaps that was just the weight of her conscience on her shoulders. She straightened up to her full height, determined not to let anything slow her down now that she was on her way. Tomorrow would be soon enough to worry about regrets. Right now her man was waiting for her.

Jed might never settle in one spot, but she knew in her woman's heart that he belonged to her in ways he'd never belong to anyone else. For tonight, and as many nights as he could give her, they would belong to each other. Her steps quickened, as did her pulse.

She'd gone only a short distance up the path when Jed stepped out of the shadows.

"I wasn't sure you'd come."

"I wasn't sure I would, either." She smiled and held out her hand, needing his touch.

He wrapped his long fingers around hers, but made no move to close the remaining distance between them. Rather than wait for him to make up his mind, she made the first move, tugging him farther along the path toward the river.

"Come on, Jed. We don't have all night."

He let himself be led. "You deserve a man who can give you all night, every night."

"We've had this conversation before, Jed. You can't stay. I know that as well as you do. I'm just asking you for tonight."

They'd reached the safety of the thicket of trees along the river. When she set her basket down, Jed surprised her by pulling her into his embrace, his arms clamping around her like a vise as his mouth plundered hers. She reveled in the sudden rush of heat that simmered deep inside her.

All indecision was burned out of her in just that single kiss.

His hands—his wicked, wicked hands—moved over her, learning her touch and molding her body to fit against his. He reached down to lift her leg to wrap around his, pressing the center of his body more firmly against hers. How had she lived this long without ever knowing such waves of pleasure?

It felt as if he was staking a claim on her very soul.

"Do you want to swim first?" he murmured as he nibbled his way up the curve of her jaw. The tip of his tongue tickled as he blew gently in her ear. She needed more, so much more.

She managed to nod, all ability to string together words in a sentence gone by now. He stepped back and began stripping off his clothes. Although she knew soon she would do far more than look at his naked body, she wasn't quite ready for that. She turned her back, ignoring his throaty chuckle as she did so. When she heard the splash of water, she gathered up her courage and reached for the hem of her gown.

"Look the other way." She knew that she would join him in the river even if he ignored her request.

"I am."

Trusting his word, she drew her gown over her head and laid it aside. Then, as she had on so many other nights, she waded into the river. But for the first time, she walked straight into her lover's arms. The feel of his wet, slick skin sliding over hers sent chills straight through her. The heat of his kiss contrasted almost painfully with the cool water that surrounded them.

"Sadie, I've thought so long about this." Jed brushed her hair back from her face. "If I'm dreaming, I hope I never wake up."

His words shredded the last of her nerves, giving her the courage to do some touching of her own. She slid her fingers over his shoulders and down his sides and then up the solid strength of his back. He let her take her time getting used to the unfamiliar touches and textures of a man's body. After a bit, he turned her around and pulled her back against his chest.

He cupped her breasts, kneading them gently at first and then with more urgency. Her small moans of pleasure pleased him, knowing she was learning to trust that he wouldn't hurt her or rush her.

It was her decision to face him, wrapping her legs around his waist. He lifted her high enough to bring her breasts to his mouth. Sugar had nothing on the sweet taste of her nipple on his tongue. Suckling one and then the other, he slowly drove both of them to the brink. Then he slid a hand down the valley between her breasts, down across her stomach, and down to the warm heat that was waiting for his touch.

He tested her readiness with one finger, a soft caress that startled her at first, but then she moved against his hand, asking for more. It was time to move to the blanket he'd spread out for them on a pile of boughs he'd cut earlier. It wasn't the same as a real bed, but they'd be surrounded by the fresh fragrance of pine as they made love.

Sadie loved the power of Jed's arms as he lifted her up out of the water and carried her back to the shore. He slowly lowered her to the ground onto a blanket she hadn't noticed earlier. That he had taken the time to prepare a place for the two of them pleased her greatly.

And when he lay down beside her, with one long leg nestled between hers, she gave herself up to the wonder of his loving. She tugged him closer for a long kiss, one that mimicked the act that was to follow. His tongue glided in and out of her mouth, each stroke rekindling the heat that they'd shared in the river. Feeling a bit bold, she reached for his hand and moved it down her body, asking him to pet her again because she ached for his touch on her—and in her.

His fingers worked their wicked magic. The sensations were new to her, threatening to overwhelm her. She bucked against his hand, pleading without words for him to ease the empty hunger throbbing deep inside her. She hovered at the edge of need, needing this man—her man—to complete his possession of her body.

He withdrew his touch, using his hand and knee to spread her legs apart. Before she could protest, he moved up and over her to settle in the cradle of her body. He guided his erection to the core at the apex of her legs, poised to break through that last barrier to complete their joining.

She tried to pull him closer, hating even the smallest of distances between them. "Jed, don't stop, not now."

"I don't want to hurt you, honey, but I will." The regret in his voice warned her he was talking about far more than the pain that came when a woman was bedded for the first time.

She stared up at Jed, wishing the moonlight were brighter so she could better gauge his meaning. "That doesn't matter." Maybe later it would, but not yet. "I want you. Now."

He kissed her deeply, once again using his tongue to show her what he would do next with another part of his body. As all the sensations she felt centered low in her body, Jed pushed himself up, angling his body more directly against her. Then with one powerful thrust, he joined their two bodies as one. He trembled with the stress of holding still long enough for her to accommodate the piercing possession.

It felt as if her body was being stretched beyond endurance, a burning akin to pain. Then Jed moved, slowly withdrawing and then just as slowly back again, each time with a little more power, each time a little more speed. He slid his hand down her left leg, lifting it high around his waist. He did the same with her right. The new angle allowed him to seek greater depth with his quickening thrusts. His hand grabbed her bottom, holding her still for his onslaught.

The pain was by now only a dim memory as he kissed her again, stopping occasionally to suckle her breasts. She wished she knew what to do next, but all she could do was dig her fingers into the shifting muscles of Jed's back and hold on.

Then he eased his hand between them, petting her again as he had done before. The sweet touch, combined with the tug and pull of his body inside hers, had her whole body shuddering and then exploding in wave after wave of glorious heat. Before the flow of contractions began to ebb, Jed thrust hard again, once, twice, three times before he went rigid in her arms as he spilled his passion deep within her.

For what seemed like an eternity, she was oblivious of everything but the slick sweat of Jed's skin, the pounding of her heart, and a musky scent that mixed with the smell of pine boughs. Jed had yet to move or speak or even look at her. She wasn't sure she wanted him to, not until she managed to regain some control over her emotions.

Then he shifted to the side, withdrawing from her body, but keeping her tucked in close to his chest.

"Are you all right?" He pressed a kiss against her forehead and then her mouth.

She wasn't completely sure. Her body felt different, but not bad exactly. If she thought too hard about her wanton behavior as Jed had taught her the meaning of passion, she wanted to bury her face in her hands. Certainly she was grateful for the darkness surrounding them, especially since they had yet to retrieve their clothing from where they'd dropped it by the river. It would take time to sort out how she felt, but Jed needed her reassurance now.

"Sadie?"

She could feel new tension in his body. "I'm fine." She lifted her head off his shoulder long enough to plant a quick kiss on his cheek.

"Are you sure?"

When his fingers trailed down her cheek in a gentle caress, she nuzzled the palm of his hand. "I'm sure."

"I'm glad." He shifted a bit, turning on his side to face her. "I want you to know I could lie here all night with you, but I'm afraid we probably should be heading back soon."

"I know. I'd hate it if Pa got worried or Hawk got curious about what was taking me so long." She closed her eyes and listened to the steady beat of Jed's heart. If this were to be her only night in his arms, at least she would have only good memories to take with her. Maybe they could create a few more before time ran out on them.

"Kiss me."

"Yes, ma'am. That would be my greatest pleasure." Jed rose up over her again. The night had grown too dark for her to see many details, but she knew he was smiling. She could hear it in his voice.

When his mouth settled over hers, she wrapped her arms around his neck and held on. Now that she knew more about how he liked to be kissed, she immediately invited him to deepen the kiss. Once again, the woods and the night receded, leaving her alone with her lover.

He was going to hell for this, but at the moment he was in heaven. His Sadie was a quick learner, her kisses enough to drive him right to the edge again. When he lifted her high against his chest, she tangled her legs with his. Then she lifted herself up, offering up her sweet breasts to his mouth for attention.

How was he supposed to get her safely back to her room before anyone got suspicious? As he swirled his tongue around the peak of one breast, he couldn't resist testing the heat between her legs. She was ready for him again, which his body sure as hell thought was a great idea. Maybe a few minutes longer wouldn't matter one way or another.

"Sadie, we either need to stop now, or we . . . I won't be able to." He didn't know if he was being noble or a total fool.

"I don't want to stop." She punctuated each word with a kiss. Temptress that she was, she let her hand trace a direct path down his chest, down his stomach, straight to the part of him that most needed her touch.

If she wanted to be adventurous, he wasn't about to stop her. In a quick move he lifted her above him so that she straddled his body. The immediate contact between her damp heat and his shaft was almost his undoing.

"Lift up a bit." His words sounded as if he'd been running a long distance. Maybe he had. He helped her take him deep inside her body again. She seemed unsure what to do next, so he took her hips in his hands and showed her.

"Jed!" His name sounded like a prayer coming from her lips.

As she rocked faster and faster, he kneaded her breasts with his hands. Sadie responded by arching her head back, pressing herself more firmly into his hands. It was too dark for him to see her clearly, but it didn't matter. Touch alone was enough for this night.

The first tremors of her climax sent him flying right along with her. Then she collapsed on top of him, warm and loving in his arms.

As he'd already told himself, he was going to hell for this. But for the second time, Sadie had taken him all the way to heaven.

Morning came too damn early. The sun was barely over the horizon when the sound of a horse being ridden hard and fast woke him out of a sound sleep. Since it was damned unlikely that anyone was looking for anyone but him with such urgency, Jed pulled on his pants and grabbed his shirt and boots before climbing down the ladder.

Just as he stepped out of the barn, the rider was dismounting.

"You're out early this morning." He leaned against the barn wall to pull on his boots.

Evidently, he wasn't the only one who'd heard the stranger's approach. Ole charged out of the house, his shotgun in hand. Hawk was right behind him. "What's going on out here?"

"I'm looking for Marshal Stark. Is that you?" The man nodded in Jed's direction.

"Depends on why you're asking." Although the

man would have to be blind to think a marshal would be as old as Ole or as young as Hawk.

"I've got a telegram for you. The instructions said to deliver it to you first thing." He held out a folded piece of paper at arm's length, as if leery of getting too close.

Jed wanted to curse, but he didn't. The man was only doing his job. Besides, Bart wouldn't send for him unless it was important.

"I'm Stark." He held out his hand for the telegram, knowing he was going to be sorry he did.

Chapter 12

The first time he read through the words they didn't make sense. The second time, only slightly more so. By the third time he reached the end, his blood ran cold and his temper ran hot. He was only marginally aware that the messenger was still standing there.

"What do you want?" He didn't mean to growl, but his control was shaky at best.

The man backed up a step. "I'm sorry, Marshal, but they said I was supposed to take back an answer."

"Tell them I'm coming." Then he walked away, leaving everyone staring at his back.

She wanted to throw up or scream or break down and cry. He was leaving with no warning and no promises. She made a few of her own, such as not expecting any more from Jed than one night in his arms. She'd lied, not just to Jed, but to herself. She wasn't sure which was worse.

She crammed a few more things into a sack and

carried it out onto the porch. If she'd had even a few hours' warning, she could have put together something better than a few basic supplies. Maybe some fresh bread or even some cookies. Instead, she was sending the man she loved off to face armed killers with two-day-old bread and some beans.

She carried her meager offerings out onto the porch. If only there was a way that she could have a few minutes alone with Jed before he left, but that wasn't possible. Not with her father and Hawk hovering outside the barn, waiting for Jed to finish saddling up.

He hadn't yet told them what the telegram had said, but it was bad news. Maybe very bad news. She'd never seen Jed look so grim, so hard, so cold. If she didn't know him so well, she might even have found him to be a little frightening. Instead, she sensed he was in the throes of some pretty strong emotions. Most people got louder when they were upset, but Jed had always closed in on himself.

Maybe a more experienced woman would know how to offer him some kind of comfort, but all she knew how to do was stuff food in a sack. It was a pathetic effort at best, but he probably wouldn't accept more from her anyway. So she'd smile and wave and tell him to hurry back, even though that wasn't enough.

He led the mare out of the barn. Her father patted the horse on the neck, and then in a surprise move, he managed to catch Jed unaware with a hug. Jed didn't exactly return the gesture, but at least he didn't immediately step away. Her father wouldn't ask for more.

Hawk hung back, watching Jed with his usual barely concealed hostility. Sadie would have thought that he would be happy to see Jed leave, but he actually seemed madder that usual. Maybe later she'd talk to him about it, but right now her attention needed to be focused only on Jed.

And when he would return. She wouldn't let herself think about the fact that he might not return, not out of choice but because of the danger inherent in his job. For a man who professed to not care about anyone, he spent his life upholding the law and protecting innocent people. She was so proud of the job he did even as she hated it for taking him away from the farm and from her.

Would he stop by the house to talk to her or ride away without looking back? She couldn't bear the thought of that happening, so she stepped off the porch, glad for the excuse the bag of supplies gave her for approaching him. Before she reached him, he went back into the barn. Her father stopped her before she could follow him.

"His friend, the marshal, was shot two days ago. They don't know if he'll live."

The sick feeling in her stomach worsened. She set the bag down by the horse.

"Go say your good-byes, daughter, but don't make leaving any harder on Jed than it already is. He has enough trouble right now." Then he walked away, motioning for Hawk to follow him out to the pasture where Wind Son was pacing along the fence. She even smiled a little when her father stopped to pull a few carrots on the way.

A noise from inside the barn was enough to get her moving again. She stepped through the doors, blinking to adjust her eyes to the dim light inside. Jed was just climbing down the ladder from the loft with his saddlebags thrown over his shoulder. She waited near the bottom, wishing for the right words to send him on his way with her blessings when what she really wanted to do was beg him to stay. He'd already been hurt enough in his life.

But then, if those words would work, he wouldn't be the man he was.

He seemed surprised to find her standing there. They wasted another handful of seconds staring at their feet trying to get past last night to the moment at hand.

"I brought you some supplies. It's not much, but it will hold you a day or two." She realized she'd left the sack sitting outside in the dirt. "I set it down by your mare."

"Thanks." He lifted his saddlebags off his shoulder. "I need to get to Rosser in a hurry. Not having to stop for supplies will make it easier."

"I'm glad to be of help." Lord, this was even harder than she expected. Despite last night, she had hoped they'd still be friends. Instead, the tension between them was painful.

He dropped the saddlebags onto the floor with a muttered curse. "Look, Sadie, about last night . . . about us . . ."

There was no "us" to discuss; they had both agreed to that. This was the talk she didn't want to have, especially now with him riding into danger. Even without knowing the details about what had happened, she knew that much.

"Jed, now isn't the time to talk about last night. I have no regrets, and I don't want you to either. It was special. Leave it at that."

She took a half step forward, hoping he would do the same. He held his ground, but then something in his gray eyes softened, giving them back some of the warmth that had been there the night before.

"I have to leave. Now."

"I know. Pa told me what happened."

She started to reach out with a hand to comfort him but let it drop back to her side. He might have accepted a quick hug from her father, but not her. Not now. Not after last night. Still, he made no effort to walk away, his face grim, his eyes staring down at her. Was he even seeing her at all? There were lines bracketing his mouth that hadn't been there the night before, the clearest sign of the pain he was in.

"Have you known this marshal fellow long?"

"Long enough." He blinked twice, as if finally remembering she was standing there.

"What's his name?" Maybe if she kept him talking, it would help him somehow or at least delay the moment when he rode away.

"Bart. Marshal Bart Perry. He deserved better than to be shot from the back." The telegram says he might lose his leg. Jed shuffled his feet a bit. "Look, I need to leave. Your father seems to be holding his own for now, but send word if he . . . well, you know. I'll come if I can."

Once again his job won out. He'd missed her mother's funeral. If he missed her father's, she wasn't sure she'd be able to forgive him. But there was no use in getting mad beforehand. Just as Jed had said, her father seemed to be doing better. For now.

"Will you be back for Thanksgiving? Just so I can let Pa know?" And so she'd know how many marks to make on the wall in her room as she checked off the days until his return.

"You already know that I can't promise. All I can say is that I'll try."

When he started to reach for his saddlebags, there was so much she wanted to tell him, but she choked back the words. He had enough to worry about right now without her falling apart. Instead, she took a chance and took those last two steps and wrapped her arms around his waist. Slowly, so slowly his arms enfolded her. They stood in silence, letting touch say what words couldn't.

She would have stayed there, just as they were, for as long as he would let her. But she knew time was passing, each minute stolen from the time he needed to reach his friend's side. It was time to hurry Jed on his way. Despite her reluctance, she was proud of the fact that she was the one to ease back, signaling her willingness to let go. It almost killed her.

Jed yanked her right back against his chest, his arms feeling like bands of steel wrapped around her. She looked up in confusion with the sudden shift in his mood. Then his mouth crushed down on hers and all her questions were answered.

He should let her go. Hell, he should have been gone half an hour ago. He'd meant to be. But he wasn't finding it as easy to ride away from the farm this time, even with Bart hurt and maybe dying. Yesterday, he could have mounted up, waved goodbye, and headed down the road with few regrets.

But last night had changed everything. He couldn't bring himself to regret bedding Sadie, but nothing was the same now. If only he had the words to tell her, but he didn't. Keeping his emotions and thoughts to himself was a habit far too ingrained in his soul for him to change now.

Her sweet embrace had been meant to comfort, but his body wasn't taking it that way. All it took was the briefest of touches and he wanted to drag her back out to the river and pick up where they'd left off last night. One minute they were holding on to each other in the quiet of the barn; the next they were kissing with enough heat to burn the place down.

What the hell was he doing? Ole was pretty tolerant of Jed's actions, but even he would draw the line at letting his only daughter take a vagrant lawman for a lover. It took every bit of willpower Jed could muster to yank himself free. He held Sadie at arm's length, but it was nowhere near far enough to remove the temptation of kissing her again.

"I've got to leave." His words came out in ragged breaths. "Now."

Her lips looked bruised and swollen. He cursed himself for not being more gentle. He brushed her mouth with his thumb. "Did I hurt you?"

She was sweet enough to shake her head when he knew better. "I'm needed. It's up to me to find the . . ." He fumbled for a word that wouldn't offend her. He tried again. "I need to find the ones responsible."

"Be careful, Jed." A single tear trickled down her cheek. "I'll be praying for your safety."

He'd given up on the whole idea of God watching over him years ago, trusting to his own skill with a gun instead. But maybe Sadie had more influence than he did. Either way, if she took some comfort in doing so, it was fine with him.

"Thanks."

He picked up his saddlebags, really leaving this time. Sadie stayed rooted to the same spot as he turned his back on her and walked away. He almost made it to the door without looking back. But before stepping out into the bright sunshine, he stopped and turned around.

"Thank you for last night, Sadie."

She nodded and bravely tried to smile.

Then he walked out, leaving her looking awfully damn alone. Outside, he picked up the sack she'd left for him and hung it on his saddle. Mounting up almost took more energy than he could muster. His mare sidled away from him, clearly not liking him just standing there. Maybe she felt the urgency he should be feeling.

Damn, he didn't want to leave and knew he couldn't stay. He put his foot in the stirrup and swung up into the saddle. That was all the signal the mare needed. She hit full stride before they reached the end of the corral, tearing him away from the one place he most wanted to be.

And despite the bright sunshine, the day held no warmth for him.

Every bone in his body ached and he hadn't slept more than a few hours in almost three days. Chances were he wouldn't do much better in the foreseeable future. The only good thing was that he could see the outskirts of Rosser in the distance. A hot meal and an even hotter bath would help some.

Finding out if his boss and friend was still alive would help more. He slowed the mare with a tug on the reins. Suddenly, he wasn't in such a hurry to reach town. If the news was bad, he was already too late to do his friend any good. His killer's trail was already cold; a few more minutes wouldn't matter much one way or the other.

If the news was good, maybe he'd stay long enough to get a good night's sleep before hitting the trail again. The idea brought a grim smile to his face. It didn't matter who had the pulled the trigger or why. The man would be brought to justice one way or another. Either he would surrender to stand trial or he'd die wherever Jed found him. Jed didn't care which because it was just a matter of time before the cowardly bastard paid for pulling that trigger.

Jed's hand slid down to his holster, as if he were making a solemn promise to avenge his friend by swearing on his gun. His skill with the six-shooter had earned him a certain reputation, one that he took some pride in. He wondered what Sadie would say if she realized his best skill was killing. He might do so in the name of the law, but that didn't lessen the blood on his hands or the chill that surrounded his heart.

Only losing himself in Sadie's sweet arms had made him feel warm and wanted. And if her God was listening, maybe he'd let Jed find a way to find his way back to the farm for Thanksgiving, if only to make her happy.

He dismounted at the first sign of civilization to lead Lady the rest of the way into town. It felt good to stretch his legs, and the horse deserved a break from carrying him. She'd put in a couple of long, hard days in a row to get him that far. As they got closer to town, he noted several new houses under construction, a sign that Rosser continued to grow. He paused outside the first saloon in town. A couple of shots of cheap whiskey sounded right good about then, but he continued on.

If Bart was well enough to receive visitors, he deserved better than having Jed show up drunk. As tired as he was, one drink would probably have him staggering down the street. He veered off the main street and headed for the stable, figuring at least Lady could get a good meal and some rest. His own day would likely drag on for several hours yet.

Inside the stable, he yelled for the owner. "Lucas, where are you?"

The heavyset blacksmith came lumbering out of his shop in the back. "Jed! Sure glad to see you back." He took charge of the mare's reins and led her toward her favorite stall. "It's a damn shame about Bart, that's for certain. We all are depending on you to catch the man who shot him. I hope the bastard ends his worthless life dangling at the end of a rope."

Cold chills of dread settled in Jed's stomach. Had he arrived too late? He followed the smith into the stall, his fists clenched in fear. "I haven't heard any news in three days. Is he dead then?"

Lucas was already dragging the saddle off the horse. He stopped midmotion to look at Jed. "Aw, damn it, Jed, I wasn't thinking. I sure didn't mean to scare you like that. Doc says Bart has a fighting chance since he's made it this long. His leg is bad, though. Real bad. He's up at Miss White's boardinghouse down the street."

Relief left him feeling a bit shaky. "Thanks, Lucas. I'll head over to check on Bart and talk to Doc myself. I appreciate you seeing to my horse." He picked up his saddlebags and all but ran the three blocks to the town's only boardinghouse. He kept a small room there himself, so he knew it was clean and the food good. If anyone could nurse Bart back to health it would be Miss White. She often took in patients for the doctor when the need arose.

He clomped up the three steps to her door and barged in. Normally, Miss White expected her gentlemen boarders to come and go quietly. He figured she'd understand his rush this time. Inside, he bypassed the stairs that led to his room on the third floor, heading instead for a room off the parlor that she reserved for the patients that Doc sent her.

The door was closed. He set his saddlebags down on the floor and listened for several seconds. There was more than one person talking, but the voices were muted, leaving it impossible for him to tell who was there. If it was the doctor, he didn't want to interrupt anything. Indecision warred with his need to know how his friend was doing.

Finally, he knocked softly and waited. The door swung open almost immediately to reveal both Miss White and Doc Davidson. From where Jed was standing, he couldn't see his friend's face, just the outline of his legs under the blankets. Jed drew some comfort from seeing that he still had both of them.

Miss White looked pleased to see him. "Marshal Stark! We're so glad you're back." She shot a frowning look back toward her patient. "Marshal Perry has been fretting some over your being gone. Come on in."

She stood back, making room for Jed to ease past her into the small room. Even though he was relieved to know his friend was able to have guests, he was worried about how badly hurt he was.

Doc was busy packing a few things back in the black bag he always carried on his rounds. He met Jed's gaze and nodded. Jed wasn't sure what he was trying to tell him. That it was all right to come in? That Bart was doing as well as could be expected? Jed would find out soon enough when he tracked Doc down after he had a chance to clean up and get a meal under his belt. The doctor was known to be a bit surly most of the time, but he knew his business and took good care of his patients.

Jed braced himself for the worst as he prepared to greet his friend. Years of practice made it possible for him to school his expression not to show the shock of seeing the grim change in Bart since he'd last seen him only a short time ago. The marshal's color was sallow, and his eyes were sunken in with dark circles under them. Still, at least he was breathing. Some of the load of guilt that Jed hadn't been there to protect his friend's back eased.

No one who knew Jed ever expected him to be lighthearted, but he did his best to smile. "Well, partner, I see you finally figured out how to loaf all day and have a pretty woman wait on you."

Miss White, a handsome woman in her thirties, rolled her eyes at Jed's comment. "I'd far prefer to have the marshal sitting at my table than lying in this bed, Marshal Stark. However, I will say he's been an easier patient to take care of than you were."

She softened her criticism with a quick smile. "Doc was on his way out when you knocked. If you'll sit with the marshal for a bit, I'll go fix both of you a tray. His appetite hasn't been all that good, but now that you're back maybe you can encourage him to eat more. And judging by the condition of your clothes, you haven't taken the time to eat or sleep for the last few days."

"You're not wrong. I'll be glad to sit down for a while."

Doc walked around the end of the bed. "Don't wear him out talking, Jed. Stop by the saloon later, and I'll buy you that drink I owe you."

He didn't owe Jed any such thing, so evidently he wanted to talk to him, too, but he didn't want Bart to know. "I'll be looking forward to it, Doc."

Once Doc and Miss White left the room, Jed closed the door and sank down on the chair sitting near the head of the bed. Bart slowly turned his head in Jed's direction and gave him a wan smile. His voice was a harsh whisper, but still there was some strength in it. "Sorry to cause everyone so much trouble."

"You always were trouble," Jed told him with no real rancor. "Personally, I think you did this just to get me back here because you missed me."

"How is your friend doing?" Leave it to Bart to worry more about a total stranger than he did himself.

"Ole seems to be doing better. I think Hawk being there has given him something to think about other than himself." He frowned down at his hands. "Although, damn it, you'd think his daughter would be enough reason for him to hang on. Sadie deserves that much from him."

"Still think she's pretty?" Bart managed to put a world of meaning in that one word. He didn't care what she looked like; he'd picked up on the tension in Jed's voice. Hell, he should have kept Sadie's name out of the conversation. But Jed answered the question because it gave Bart something to think about besides the pain.

"Yeah, she is. All that blond hair and the brightest blue eyes I've ever seen. I've known her since she was a little girl." The memory of that little girl trailing after him all day long was etched in his soul.

"Not a little girl anymore." Bart's wheezy laugh started him coughing.

Jed lifted Bart's head and held a glass of water to his lips, trying to help him. After a bit, he settled back on the pillow.

"I'm in a hell of a mess here, Jed. You'll have to take over for a while." His breathing gradually eased up. "Now tell me about Sadie and you."

Jed wished he could tell Bart everything, but maybe now wasn't the time. "I forgot how much I liked working on the farm. I helped a bunch of the neighbors bring in Ole's crops and then helped them with theirs."

"Always knew you were a sodbuster at heart. Now tell me about Sadie." Apparently no matter how bad Bart felt, he was still relentless in the pursuit of the facts. "Does she like you?"

"How is that any of your business?" Jed shook his head and smiled. "We went to a dance, if you can believe that. I thought I'd feel out of place, but she wanted me there. She always did have a way of wheedling me into doing something foolish. Some of the neighbors weren't too pleased when they got a good look at me, but Sadie's friends told them to back off. After that, everything went all right."

"You went dancing?" His astonished disbelief was clearly expressed with the arch of an eyebrow. "Wish I'd seen that."

Bart had every right to think that was odd. In all the time they'd known each other, Jed had never done anything so out of character. Hell, he never even danced with the girls who worked in the saloon down the street, not even when he was planning on spending some time upstairs where they did a hell of a lot more than dance if a man had enough money.

"We danced." He looked up at the ceiling, wishing he had the words—or the guts—to admit how much those dances had meant to him. Luckily for him, Miss White was back with the promised tray.

She had a bowl of broth for Bart, and some great-smelling stew for him.

"I'll feed some of this to the marshal so you can eat yours while it's hot. Then maybe you can spell me. In a few minutes, I really need to get supper on for the other boarders."

The three of them sat in companionable silence while Jed filled some of the empty space inside him with fresh bread and the stew. But there were other holes, most notably near his heart that needed more than Miss White's good cooking for him to feel satisfied.

Damn, he missed Sadie. He'd hoped that putting some miles between them, he'd be able to lessen her hold on him. So far, his plan wasn't working worth a damn. The memory of the time they'd shared on a bed of pine boughs by the river was still too vivid. It only made him ache for more.

He sopped up the last of the stew with bread and then set his bowl aside. "No one makes stew as good as yours, Miss White. I appreciate you fixing it for me."

"You're welcome, Marshal. Now, if your friend here would eat like you just did, he'd be back to his old self a lot sooner." She thrust the rest of the broth into Jed's hand. "I'll let you feed him now. I'm sure you can handle his cantankerous behavior just fine." With her back to Bart, she allowed Jed to see how worried she really was. "He'll fall asleep after he's eaten. I'll have water heating for you if you want to clean up."

"I'd appreciate that."

"Behave yourself, Marshal Perry." She gave her patient a bright smile and a pat on the arm before leaving the room.

Jed scooted his chair a little closer. "Open wide,

COME HOME FOR CHRISTMAS 241

Bart. I'm not about to take this bowl back to the kitchen unless it's empty. It doesn't pay to make the cook feel as if her efforts aren't appreciated."

"Too tired."

"No excuses. Like she said, you need to build up your strength." He held the first spoonful to Bart's lips.

"Nag," Bart muttered before accepting the broth.

"I don't know if you're talking about me or Miss White, but too bad. Eat and we won't have to nag." He fell into a rhythm of spooning up the broth as fast as Bart could take it in without choking or dribbling on the quilt.

Neither man said much. Bart was too weak, and Jed was never one for idle conversation. Finally, though, the spoon was scraping the bottom of the bowl. He set it aside and then did his awkward best to help his friend get comfortable. By the time he had the blankets pulled back up across Bart's chest, he was asleep.

Jed stood by the bed, staring down at his friend. Damn, he hated seeing Bart brought down this low. His leg must be truly bad to weaken him like this. It only strengthened Jed's resolve to get revenge, no matter what the cost. For now, though, he'd get cleaned up. Later, after supper, he'd meet up with Doc to see what he wanted.

Then it would be back here to the boardinghouse for a good night's sleep. Come morning, he'd be in better shape to start his investigation. If Bart continued to improve, he'd hit the trail in pursuit of the fool who'd dared to ambush a U.S Marshal.

He slipped out of the room quietly, closing the door behind him. It was time to fetch the hot water Miss White had promised him. He rarely ventured into the kitchen, knowing his landlady considered it her personal domain. She'd never said so in so many words, but it was easy to tell that she preferred to have one room that gave her a respite from her all male boarders.

He hesitated in the doorway until she noticed him. "Don't be shy, Marshal. Come on in."

That was when he noticed that she'd dragged out a large tub into the middle of the floor. He gave her a questioning look.

"I thought you might appreciate a bath, or as much of one as a man your size can take in that tub. I've set out a towel and soap for you. Get some clean clothes while I pour in the rest of the hot water. I need to pick up a few things at the store, so you should have plenty of privacy while I'm gone."

Her thoughtful gesture shocked him. She'd always been polite, but not overly friendly. He could understand her attitude, what with her being a single woman with men living under her roof.

"I really appreciate this."

"Well, this whole thing with Marshal Perry has made folks more aware of the risks you gentlemen take to keep all of us safer. It won't hurt us to show our appreciation a little more often. Besides, some soap and hot water isn't much to offer you."

Maybe not, but it sure enough sounded good to him. The last bath he'd taken had been in the cool water of the river. With Sadie. Damn, he didn't need to be dwelling on that memory again.

"I'll get my things."

"Before you go, how did you do feeding your friend?" The worry was back in her voice.

"He finished the broth and then fell asleep." He braced himself to ask a hard question. "How bad is his leg?"

She hesitated before answering, perhaps judging whether to sugarcoat her response.

"Tell me the truth of it. How bad?"

"Doc can tell you better, but I know he's still worried about the marshal. On the other hand, he's survived this long. With as much blood as he lost, we were afraid he wouldn't make it through that first night. Each day gives us more hope."

She untied her apron, but didn't hang it up right away. From the way she was gripping it until her knuckles showed white, her next words weren't going to be good news. "His leg, though, is badly infected. He lay in the dirt for a good hour or more before someone happened to find him. Doc stops by at least three times a day to change the dressing and check for . . . well, to check on it."

Jed's blood ran cold at the thought of Bart losing his leg. He'd seen gangrene before and never wanted to again. "Is there anything I can do to help?"

She gave him a smile as she finally hung her apron on a peg. "Just your being here will help. You know the marshal. He's been fretting over things not getting done. He can relax and concentrate on getting better now."

"I can't stay in town for long. Someone has to go after whoever did this. Every day that I wait, he gets that much farther away." He considered his options. "I can wire for more help."

"I think the mayor already has. We're going to need someone to take over for the marshal for a while. Our sheriff does his best, but he's not very experienced. Dealing with petty theft and a few drunks who get rowdy isn't the same as tracking a hardened killer." She gathered up her things. "Now, I'd better be going. No use in letting all the hot water get cold."

Jed followed her to the parlor to collect his saddlebags. "Thank you again for everything." He glanced toward Bart's room. "Especially for everything you've done for him."

"He's a good man, Marshal Stark." She adjusted her hat. "For that matter, so are you."

Before he could respond to that surprising statement, she was out the door and on her way.

Jed patrolled the streets, mostly because he was restless. He knew full well that the town sheriff, although young, was more than capable of handling any problems that arose within the city limits. But Doc's comments on Bart's injuries had left Jed feeling unsettled.

He planned to talk to Bart in the morning about what had happened. Doc warned him that Bart's memories of the night he was shot were pretty vague, but anything he could remember would help with Jed's investigation. He'd already talked to the sheriff to see what he'd been able to discover.

It wasn't much. Bart had been riding back from a neighboring town where he'd taken a prisoner to stand trial. A stagecoach driver had run across Bart's horse standing in the trail and had stopped to investigate. If he hadn't, Jed had no doubt that his friend would have bled to death all alone.

The thought sent a chill up his back. If he didn't need to wake up with a clear head, he would have been tempted to head back to the saloon for some more of that good whiskey he'd had earlier with the doctor. He'd come damn close to losing one of the very few men he called friend.

The realization that he himself might very well end his days dying alone with a coward's bullet in him didn't help. If that were to happen, how long would Sadie keep waiting before she realized that he was never coming back again? Months? Years? The rest of her life? That was a hell of a thought.

He took an abrupt turn back toward the saloon at the edge of town. Maybe a shot or two of that whiskey wasn't such a bad idea after all.

Chapter 13

There was a definite nip in the air, making Sadie shiver as she went out to collect eggs. Judging from the way all the hens sat huddled with their feathers fluffed out, she wasn't the only one noticing a hint of winter in the air. All around, the fall colors were rapidly fading away, leaving only the pines still giving the woods any real color.

She hadn't been up to the river in weeks. The excuse she gave herself was that the drop in temperature made bathing in the chilly river water unappealing. But even if the weather had remained warm enough, her longtime hideaway was no longer hers alone, not since she and Jed had created their private little spot with the sky for a roof and pine boughs for a bed. And without him, she simply didn't want to be there.

It seemed that she was always staring out at the horizon, hoping to catch the first glimpse of Jed coming home. She'd tried not to look, telling herself he'd be there when he got there. If he got there. He wasn't going to suddenly appear just because she wanted him to. The joy they'd shared, or at least she thought they had, had faded into a heavy feeling sitting on her heart.

Thanksgiving was only three days away. Pa had refused to consider Meg's invitation to join them for dinner, claiming that it was important for him to spend the time at home. More and more, Sadie saw him staring off toward the small hilltop where her mother was buried. Sometimes, he'd abandon whatever he was working on and disappear. She knew without looking that he was having another long talk with her mother.

It would have bothered her, but he always seemed to be happier, more content when he returned to the house.

A movement off near the barn caught her eye. Hawk and his horse were coming out the barn, obviously going for a ride. The stallion needed the exercise and Hawk needed the time out running his horse across the fields, his hair blowing in the wind, a big smile on his face. Most of the time, he was too solemn. It was only with his four-footed friend that he seemed happy.

She waved and smiled at him, grateful for all the help he gave her father and her. Did he miss spending time with children his own age? He never complained, but she thought he spent too much time alone or with grown-ups. His long dark hair had her thoughts turning back to Jed. When he was Hawk's age, he'd been more like a wild animal raised in captivity, one who was all too likely to bite if provoked.

She made one more quick trip through the hen-house to make sure that she hadn't missed any eggs. She'd need all she could find to make a proper Thanksgiving feast. For her father's sake, she'd go through all the motions, making a meal to remember.

Her eyes sought out the horizon again. As much as she wanted to curse Jed's name, she couldn't bring herself to do so. It was hardly his fault that his job kept him away from the farm. He had taken the time to send them a short note to say that his friend—Bart, she thought he'd said his name was—had been badly injured. Until he was strong enough to resume his duties, Jed was having to fill in. So far, he'd been unable to track down the man who'd shot the marshal, but he would. Although she'd been relieved to hear from him, there'd been a decidedly grim tone to the letter.

More and more, she realized it took a certain kind of man to stand up for the law, making a target of himself every time he rode out. She respected Jed's decision to be one of those rare men. But she feared for his life, especially now. Before he'd come back to the farm, she'd known what he was doing, but it hadn't seemed real. Now, with his friend so gravely injured, she worried all the time, especially at night when she lay alone in her bed.

Back in the kitchen, she set the egg basket down on the table and hung her coat back up on the hook. She was mixing a batch of biscuits when the door slammed open, startling her into spilling the milk. Her father stepped over the threshold, his face red from the wind.

"I didn't mean to scare you, Sadie. The wind caught the door just as I opened it." His coat joined hers on the wall. "If I didn't know better, I think it felt like snow out there. I know that it's too early in the season for it, but I think I'll bring in another load of wood before supper."

"Good idea, Pa." She cleaned up the mess and started over on the biscuits. "I hope Hawk doesn't stay gone too long. I know it's early for winter to set in, but that wind is awfully cold today." She shivered just thinking about it. "We may need to buy him a warmer coat. The way he's growing, he'll be out of that one before Christmas."

Ole nodded. "Maybe that would make him a good present. Next time we go into town for supplies, we should see what the store has or if we need to order one for him."

She liked hearing her father making plans for the future, even if it was only a few weeks at a time. "When I get these biscuits ready for the oven, I think I'll make myself some tea. Would you like a cup?" She patted the dough out into a flat circle and reached for her biscuit cutter, making quick work of cutting them out.

"Tea sounds good." Her father took a seat at the table. His faded blue eyes twinkled a bit. "Add a little extra sugar to mine. I've got a hankering for something sweet."

She laughed. When it came to sweets, her father was worse than Jed and Hawk combined. He was always snooping around her kitchen, looking for any cookies that she might have hidden from him. Over the years, it had become almost a game between them. If it were up to him, she'd spend all her free time, what little she had, baking for him.

Considering everything, a few extra cookies now and then weren't much for him to ask for. She noticed his shirt was fitting him more loosely, an indication that he'd lost more weight. He seemed to tire a little more easily, but on the whole he was still able to keep up with the never-ending round of chores it took to keep the farm going.

She set the pan of biscuits aside and put the kettle on to boil. As she moved about the kitchen, she could feel her father's eyes on her. She turned to look at him over her shoulder "Is there something you want to talk about?"

His eyes slid to the side, unwilling to meet her gaze. "We got another letter from Jed today. Doc brought the mail with him when he stopped by."

That brought her up short. "When was Doc here? And why? Did you send for him?"

Her father held up his hand to count off the answers to her questions. "He was here while you were in the house this morning." He pointed to the next finger. "He had business in this area and thought he'd do us a favor and bring the mail." And finally, he ticked off the third. "I did not send for him, for the good reason that I feel fine, so don't go jumping to conclusions. Doc has been a friend of the family for a long time, so sometimes he comes just to be neighborly."

"I'm sorry, Pa. I know I tend to fuss and worry." She wiped her hands on a towel. "Have you read the letter?"

"No, because it's not my letter." He pulled an envelope out of his overall's pocket. "This one is addressed only to you."

When he slid it across the table toward her, she didn't immediately snatch it up, as much as she wanted to. If Jed was writing this close to Thanksgiving, it was unlikely to be good news. As anxious as she was to hear from him, she couldn't quite bring herself to open the letter. She used the excuse that the kettle was boiling to delay picking up the envelope.

She quickly made the tea and then set out a handful of cookies for her father to eat. It was a sign of how distracted she was that she let him find out about her favorite hiding spot, one of the few that he hadn't yet discovered. Right now she had more on her mind than whether or not her father cleaned out her supply of cookies.

They sat at the table in silence. If her father thought it strange that she wasn't reading Jed's note, he didn't say so. Finally, he finished his tea. With a sly smile, he slipped a couple of extra cookies into his pocket before reaching for his coat. "I'd better go see to the stock. It's getting dark earlier every day."

"Wear your hat, Pa." She looked up only to realize he already had put it on.

He walked out the door shaking his head. No doubt he thought she was losing her mind, and maybe she was. Nothing had felt the same to her since the night before Jed had ridden out. Still, she couldn't quite bring herself to reach for the letter; instead she clasped her hands in her lap as she tried to muster up the courage to read Jed's message.

Finally, she picked it up. Using her paring knife, she carefully slit the top open. With fingers that were none too steady, she pulled out the single sheet of paper and unfolded it. The note, written in Jed's familiar scrawl, was short and to the point. It was so typical of Jed that, if she closed her eyes, she could almost imagine him standing there talking to her.

He was coming home for Thanksgiving and bringing his friend with him. She read the letter again, sure that she'd misread it. Bart Perry was still recuperating from his recent injury, but he'd insisted on accompanying Jed to the farm. Because they were coming by wagon, it would take them longer to arrive, but they hoped to arrive the day before Thanksgiving.

Her eyes burned and her hands were even more

shaky as she tried to return the letter to the envelope. Jed was coming home. For Thanksgiving. She counted the days off on her fingers. Today, tomorrow, and the next day and Jed would be home.

With renewed energy, she began making plans for the unexpected visit. She'd recently aired out all the bedding and beaten the rugs clean. It wouldn't take much to sweep the house again and dust everything. The hard part would be making up beds for both Jed and his friend. The hayloft in the barn had been adequate while the weather was mild, but it was getting too cold now, especially for a man who was still recuperating from his wounds.

There was a small room tucked up under the eves upstairs across from her room. Only a few feet away from where she slept. Just a short distance from her bed where she slept alone. She closed here eyes and imagined Jed crossing that short distance to share the warmth of her blankets, the warmth of her bed, the warmth of her body. The idea had her squirming in her chair and aching in all those private, needy places that Jed had known how to soothe with his touch.

The direction her thoughts had taken her had her blushing. What if her father, or worse yet, Hawk were to walk in and catch her daydreaming about such things? Ruthlessly, she forced her attention back to making plans. The room upstairs would do for Jed, but his friend would likely have a difficult time with the stairs. She'd have to talk to her father about sharing his room with Hawk for a few days. It would be crowded, but she could make up a pallet for the boy at the foot of the bed.

She'd have her father explain the situation to Hawk to make sure he understood the change was only temporary and that he wasn't giving his room to Jed. Somehow, she thought he'd have a hard time letting Jed be the one to force him out of his room.

Of course, considering his previous experience with the law, he might not be any happier about letting this Bart Perry sleep in his bed. She hoped her father could find some way to make it all right with him because she had more important things to worry about than hurt feelings. Hawk needed to know that this was his home for as long as he wanted it to be, but sometimes sacrifices had to be made for company. That's what family did.

Food was the next thing on her list. She needed to at least double everything she'd planned to prepare. Her father's appetite wasn't what it used to be, so she'd intended on cutting back on the amount she normally prepared. But with two more grown men joining them, she'd need to make sure there was enough to go around. Jed always did have a good appetite, and his friend would need to eat well if he were to regain his strength.

Feeling better than she had in days, she grabbed her coat and hurried outside to share the good news with her father. Jed was coming home again.

The wagon hit a rut, jarring Bart's leg and rattling his teeth. He knew that Jed was doing the best he could to make the ride smooth. But considering the condition of the road ahead, there was only so much his friend could do. Bart braced himself as best he could and gritted his teeth. Eventually they would reach this mysterious farm, and he could stop hurting so much.

"Are you all right?" Jed's words came out in little puffs of mist, another indication that the temperature had dropped even more.

"Hell no, I'm not all right." He softened his words with a half hearted smile. "I'm tired, hungry, and hurting. Other than that, everything is just wonderful." He yanked his blankets back up around his shoulders and tried to keep his teeth from chattering.

Jed flicked the reins to speed up the horses. Bart knew he should feel bad for snarling at his friend. After all, he'd all but ordered Jed to include him on this little trip, so it was hardly his friend's fault that it was proving to be harder than Bart had anticipated. Maybe he should have listened to Miss White and the doctor when they'd tried to tell him that he was doing too much too soon. He wouldn't be caught dead admitting that to either of them, however.

Jed was probably thinking the same thing, but at least Bart could depend on him to keep his opinions to himself.

"You should have stayed in town."

Bart sighed. So he was wrong about Jed, too. His friend shot him a look, daring him to disagree with him. Even if he was right, Bart wasn't about to admit it. He knew they all meant well, but they didn't understand. He was used to being active. If he'd had to lie there in that bed for another day with nothing to do, he would have gone stark raving mad. So he would endure a little misery in order to collect a few more pieces in the puzzle that was Jed Stark.

He'd trust Jed with his life and he considered him a good friend, but getting to know the man wasn't easy. Most people didn't get past Jed's hard-edged exterior to the honorable, caring man underneath. It wasn't that Jed didn't care about what people thought. No, he cared too much and so played his cards close to his chest. As sick as Bart had been when Jed came charging into Miss Smith's boardinghouse, he hadn't missed the genuine grief and worry in Jed's eyes.

When a man made his living hunting down liars and killers and thieves, he learned to value the few good men he met along the way. Bart couldn't claim to know everything about Jed, but he knew the important things. He wanted to know more, and this trip, miserable as it was, was his chance.

In the almost six years he'd known the man, Jed had never once indicated that he had any family anywhere. The Johansons weren't blood relatives, but they were Jed's family in the real meaning of the word. And he was willing to bet that they were just as in the dark about the life Jed had lived since leaving their home.

The man sure enough knew how to keep a secret.

But he'd let one slip. Sadie Johanson had convinced Jed to go dancing. No one else who knew Jed at all would have believed that was possible. Bart couldn't wait to meet this amazing woman.

"Tell me about Sadie."

Jed flicked the reins yet again, as if hurrying the horses would keep him from having to answer the question. "Giddyup! I swear we're going to coast to a stop and freeze to death out here."

Bart laughed at his friend. "You can ignore me if you want to, but that just makes me all the more certain that I'm right."

There went the reins again. "Right about what?"

"That this Sadie Johanson has your guts so tied up in knots that you don't know what to do about it." There, he'd said it. Let Jed dispute his opinion if he wanted to. The argument would get their blood stirring and help keep them warm.

But once again Jed surprised him. "I can't stay at the farm, but I can't stay away either."

That had Bart struggling to set up taller. "Why not? Is she trying to get you to marry her?"

"Hell no. She's smarter than to tie herself to a man who doesn't even know what his real name is. No, Sadie needs a nice steady farmer to make her happy, not a man like me." He spoke the words without a hint of the powerful emotions he had to be feeling.

Bart didn't believe in letting anyone speak badly of his friends, not even when they were the ones doing the talking. "I can tell you this much, Jed. She'd be damn lucky to have you. A woman wants a man who is loyal and can keep her safe from harm. There's not a dirt farmer in this world who'd do that better than you. If she's as special as you think she is, she already knows it."

Jed gave him an odd look. Maybe he had over-reacted, but he'd come pretty damn close to dying recently. The experience had taught him that life was too fragile to waste time being noble. If Jed wanted this woman, he should go after her with everything he had. If she was the woman Jed obviously thought she was, she wouldn't hold Jed's past or his Indian blood against him.

But right now wasn't the time to press his arguments, not when they were both cold and tired. Once they reached the Johanson farm, Bart could see for himself what was going on. It shouldn't be all that hard to determine how Sadie Johanson saw Jed—as a brother, as a former employee, or as a potential lover.

Bart couldn't wait.

* * *

She was staring down the road again, but this time she had good reason. Jed and his friend should be arriving any time now. The prospect had kept all of them on pins and needles all day. Hawk was doing his best to pretend he didn't care, but she'd noticed that he'd managed to spend most of the day working where he could see the road.

Her father had made so many trips out to the bend that he'd tuckered himself out and had to take a nap. She hoped that their guests arrived soon because she wasn't sure any of them could stand the suspense much longer. She was about to turn away from the window when a movement at the end of the road caught her eye. She narrowed her eyes and stared until she was sure that it was a wagon coming into sight.

Sure enough, it was Jed and his friend. She knocked on her father's bedroom door.

"Pa, Jed's back!" She listened to make sure her father had heard her.

The bed creaked as he sat up. "I'll be right out."

She started to grab her coat, intent on meeting the wagon before it reached the house, but changed her mind. It was one thing to go running down the road if it were just Jed, but she didn't want to appear overanxious in front of his friend. After all, they'd never met the man, but he was obviously important to Jed. She didn't want to embarrass Jed unnecessarily.

So even though it was killing her, she waited inside for the wagon to pull up by the barn. By then, her father had joined her at the window. He seemed puzzled by her reluctance.

"Is there some reason why you're not going out to make Jed's friend feel welcome in our home?" He tugged her toward the door. "You've known

Jed too long to suddenly be shy. If he likes this man, then we will like this man."

She wished she had her father's confidence, but he left her no choice but to get her coat and follow along behind him. Hawk had already come out of the barn and was untying Jed's mare from the back of the wagon. Jed climbed down and walked around to the other side to help his friend down to the ground. She gasped when he almost went to his knees as his feet touched the ground. Luckily, Jed caught him and half supported him and half carried him toward the house.

She immediately turned back to open the door and pull her mother's rocker closer to the fireplace. "Bring him in and sit him down here, Jed."

Jed maneuvered his friend around to ease him down into the rocker. The man's face was ashen by the time they had him seated. He offered Sadie a pitiful excuse for a smile.

"I do apologize, Miss Johanson. I promised myself as well as Jed that I wouldn't be a bother if I came along on this trip." He eased back in the chair and let his eyes close for a few seconds. "I'm afraid it has proven to be more difficult than I anticipated."

Jed stood back and waited for his friend to open his eyes again. "I've got to see to the horses. Will you be all right while I'm gone?"

"Damn it, Jed! Quit trying to mother me!" Bart complained with no real heat. "I'll be fine, especially with Miss Johanson here to keep an eye on me."

Sadie suspected the look he gave her was supposed to be flirtatious, but he only succeeded in looking tired. "Go on, Jed. Marshal Perry and I will do just fine. I'll dish up some hot soup for the both of you as soon as you come back in."

"I'll be right back." He disappeared back out the door, allowing another blast of cold air to sweep through the kitchen.

As soon as he was gone, his friend allowed himself to slump, as if it had taken every last bit of energy he had to have made it that far.

Sadie hurried to his side. "Let's get this coat off and then I'll bring a quilt to tuck around you. We need to get you warmed up."

"Thank you, Miss Johanson. I do apologize again for being this big of a bother."

"Nonsense, Marshal. No friend of Jed's could ever be a bother." She eased one sleeve down his arm and then pulled the coat from behind him before tugging it free of his other arm. "And please call me Sadie. We don't stand much on ceremony around here."

After checking the soup, she hurried upstairs to fetch a couple of quilts. When she returned, the marshal had dozed off. Hating to disturb him when he was so obviously exhausted, she did her best to quietly drape the quilts across his lap and up over his chest. His eyes fluttered open.

"Not very good company, am I, Sadie?" His smile looked a little more convincing this time, probably the combined benefit of the warmth of the room and that he wasn't being jostled on the wagon any longer. "I've looked forward to meeting you and your father ever since I found out about you."

"And when was that?" Somehow she suspected his answer would be significant.

"I've know Jed for going on six years. He mentioned you for the first time when that business about that boy Hawk came up." He met her gaze head-on, letting her know without words that he, too, thought it odd that Jed would keep two such important parts of his life so clearly divided.

"Well, I'm glad we've finally met, Marshal. It seems like it's about time."

Rather than hover over him, she returned to the stove to dish up the soup. She set out bowls for everyone, figuring her father and Hawk would be in before long. No doubt the three of them were out in the barn settling the horses in for the night.

After the table was ready, she ladled some broth into a thick mug for the marshal. Figuring he didn't need to be moved again, she pulled a small table within reach of his chair and set the mug on it.

"You'll probably want to let it cool a bit before you sip it. Would you like some bread and butter to go with it or a cup of coffee?"

"No, this will be fine. I'm still trying to get my appetite back." He managed to pick up the mug and cradled it in both hands. "This smells really good."

"Thank you." She kept herself busy, but kept a wary eye on her guest. Unless she was mistaken, he'd be ready to turn in for the night soon. Hopefully, a good night's sleep would go a long way toward setting him to rights.

By the time she heard three pairs of boots stomping across the porch, she had set the soup kettle on the table, ready to feed the others. Hawk was the first one through. He carefully skirted the strange lawman to take his seat at the table. She wasn't sure but she thought the marshal grinned as soon as Hawk's back was turned. No doubt it wasn't the first time he'd been snubbed by someone who'd had problems with the law.

Her father, on the other hand, made straight for their guest while Jed dropped two sets of saddlebags on the floor in the corner. "Marshal Perry, it's a real pleasure to meet a friend of Jed's." He offered his hand to the seated man. "You'll be glad you came when you taste my daughter's cooking. She'll have you up and feeling fine real soon."

"If the rest of her cooking is anything like this soup, I believe it, Mr. Johanson."

"My name is Ole." Her father patted the marshal on the shoulder. "Now, you eat that soup before it gets cold."

Jed had been silent all this time. Sadie wondered if he was feeling uncomfortable with his friend here. In all the years he'd sent letters, he'd never mentioned anyone else in his life by name. Once again, she wondered what it meant that he'd chosen to bring someone home now.

Maybe later, when the two of them headed upstairs to bed, she'd ask him. Now wasn't the time to quiz him, not in front of his friend and her father. The three males at her table were tucking into the simple meal she'd prepared with gratifying enthusiasm. It would do them all some good to get a hot meal under their belts.

A few minutes later, it surprised her to have Hawk be the one to break the silence.

"Has your mare's leg been all right?" He kept his eyes firmly on the table, but it was clear that Jed's answer was important to him.

"Yeah. I haven't had her out on any rough terrain since I left, but so far she's been fine. Maybe you can give her a good workout while I'm here, so we can see how she holds up " Jed reached for another piece of bread. "How's that ugly stallion of yours?" He softened the insult with a small smile.

Hawk seemed to sense that Jed was teasing because he didn't take offense. "He's the best, as always. I've been working with him. Ole says he's about the best stallion he's seen."

The marshal joined in the conversation. "You must be Hawk. Jed tells me you have a real talent with horses."

Hawk had been about to take a bite of soup, but his hand froze halfway to his mouth, letting the rich broth drip on the table. He looked at Jed with surprise. "He did?"

"Yeah, he did. Something about you and your grandfather having a stud horse that should breed some fine horses." Bart took another long sip of his soup. "He also said that if he wasn't careful, you'd talk him into letting you use Lady as a broodmare."

Jed entered the fray. "I almost left her back in Rosser to be safe, but then I decided that if I let him borrow her, he might let me have their second foal in trade. Eventually, I'd end up with a fine-riding horse."

The two men had clearly shocked Hawk. He sat up taller, trying to seem older than he really was. "That would be a fair trade."

"It sure would." Ole reached over to clap Hawk on the shoulder. "That would be a fine start to your horse-breeding plans, Hawk. You might think about thanking Jed."

"Thank you."

Jed leaned back in his chair and stretched his long legs out in front of him. "We'll talk about it more tomorrow. I don't know about the rest of you, but I'm really tired. I plan to turn in soon."

Bart's eyes were drooping again. "Maybe you'd better give me a hand getting settled in before you do." He blinked several times before focusing on Sadie. "Where would you like me to bed down, Miss Johanson?"

"I thought you were going to call me Sadie." She softened the rebuke with a smile. "Hawk was kind enough to give up his room to you for the length of your stay. We didn't think you'd be wanting to go up and down the stairs to sleep."

"That was kind of you, Hawk. I appreciate it."

"It was nothing." In the past, Hawk had never been treated with common courtesy by anyone but his grandfather. He was still learning how to accept someone's gratitude without being embarrassed or snarling.

"Come on, Bart. We'll make a trip outside and then I'll help get you into bed."

"That sounds good to me."

He set the quilts aside, clearing the path for Jed to help him stand up. The two friends made their way slowly outside. Ole and Hawk both watched them go while Sadie started cleaning up the kitchen. She was tired enough to actually consider leaving the dishes for morning, but tomorrow was a big day. She'd need all the time she could muster to get a proper feast prepared for their Thanksgiving meal.

After she picked up the quilts, she set them on the steps to take back upstairs for Jed and her to use. Well, not together, although the possibility of cuddling up and a whole lot more with him certainly had crossed her mind more than once. She dearly hoped that none of what she was thinking right then showed on her face, but no one was paying any attention to her. Her father was bent over, adding another log to the fire to keep the kitchen warm until they were all ready for bed, while Hawk finished drying the last of the dishes.

On any other night, they would each be preparing to retire for the night themselves. Instead, it felt as if all three of them were waiting for something to happen. But what? One by one, each of them finished the chore at hand and then stopped to stare at the door as the doorknob turned.

Chapter 14

"Go on and spit it out before you choke on it."

Jed let his friend lean against a tree to catch his breath. The bastard was too stubborn to use crutches even though it had to be an agony to put any weight on his leg at all. At first, Bart didn't answer. When he spoke, his words came as no real surprise.

"With a woman like that waiting for you, why in hell are you wearing that damn badge and living on the back of your horse?" He pushed away from the tree and hobbled forward another few steps before Jed had to take charge of getting them both back to the house.

"She's not waiting for me." She couldn't be. Other than that one night by the river, he hadn't let her get close enough to even know who he was. "If she's waiting for anyone, it's some memory that she's hung on to for too damn long."

"Jed, I always figured you for a smart man, but I'm having second thoughts about that."

They were making slow but steady progress back to the house. The light from the window shone out through the darkness to lead them back into the warmth inside. Once Bart was settled into his bed, Jed would take his pack and head out to the barn. He wasn't looking forward to sleeping in the cold, but he'd spent nights in worse places over the years.

For the moment, most of Bart's energy was focused on just staying upright long enough to get inside. That didn't fool Jed into thinking that his friend was going to stop poking and prodding at him about Sadie. And it would only get worse as Bart's strength returned. Under other circumstances, he might have resented his friend's interference. But he'd come damned close to losing Bart, first to the gunshot and then to the infection that followed.

They'd reached the two steps up to the porch. Jed braced himself and all but lifted Bart up each one. It was a close race as to which one of them was breathing the hardest at the moment. Jed reached around Bart to open the door. As soon as the light spilled out on them, Sadie reached out to help them. Bart let her take his other arm, either a sign of how tired he was or because he suspected how much it would bother Jed to see Sadie touching another man.

Or maybe he was just imagining things, assuming his friend's actions were devious and underhanded when really he was simply tired. Just then, Bart looked in his direction and winked. He'd been right all along. The no-good bastard was playing with fire. He might be safe from Jed's fists right now, but he wouldn't be sickly and weak for long. Eventually, Jed would get the opportunity to teach him a hard lesson about messing with a man and his woman.

Not that Sadie was really his, except for that one night.

"Jed, watch out!"

He snapped his thoughts back to the matter at hand, barely avoiding tangling with Olga's rocker and sending all three of them tumbling to the floor. As it was, his clumsiness forced Bart to take his full weight on his bad leg.

He yelped in pain. "Son of a bitch, that hurts!" Bart immediately apologized to Sadie. "I'm sorry for talking that way in front of you."

"I've heard worse. Besides, it wasn't your fault." She helped Bart start walking toward the bedroom again.

Jed did his best to shore up his friend before he collapsed completely. "Sorry, I guess I wasn't watching too carefully."

"Well, pay attention." Sadie gave him a thoroughly disgusted look. "Let's get him to the bed, so I can check his leg."

Oh, great. The thought that Sadie would expect to change Bart's dressing for him hadn't even occurred to Jed. After all, he'd been taking care of that little chore for days now. "I'll take care of it."

"Like you took care of helping him to bed? He'll be lucky to survive the experience."

Bart didn't help matters by laughing. "He's right, Sadie. I've been enough of a bother to you. Let him check my leg for me."

She turned sideways and led the way into the small bedroom, scuttling sideways until they were all three in the room. Someone had already turned back the covers. Jed was betting it had been Sadie. It was the sort of thing she'd think of.

"Jed, give me a holler if you need anything—

bandages and the like. Otherwise, I'll see you in the morning, Marshal."

Both men watched her walk out the door, closing it behind her. Jed ignored everything Bart was thinking but not saying. He stripped off his friend's coat and shirt and helped him unfasten his pants. Once he'd peeled them down to his knees, Jed wrapped his arm around Bart's shoulder and helped him ease down on the bed.

Kneeling on the floor, he tugged off Bart's boots, going for fast rather than gentle with his injured leg. It was going to hurt no matter what, so he settled on getting it over with as quickly as possible.

"Lean back and I'll lift your leg up on the bed for you."

Sweat beaded up on Bart's face, the only sign of how miserable he really was. "I hate this."

"You'd have hated dying even worse." Jed worked the bandage loose to peek under it. "It didn't break open."

"It still hurts like hell." He laid his arm across his face. "Would you hand me that bottle of brandy out of my bag?"

Jed didn't particularly like to see anyone get in the habit of using alcohol for pain, but it had been a long, wearing day for them both. If it took the edge off the pain enough to let Bart get to sleep faster, it was worth it.

"You want a glass?"

"No need. I'll just take a couple of good swigs and then let it do its job."

Jed brought him the bottle and then lifted Bart's head high enough to let him drink. Then he pulled the covers up to his shoulders and blew out the light.

"Where does Sadie sleep?"

Why the hell did he need to know that? Was he expecting to need help during the night? If so, then Jed needed to bed down close by.

"Her room is upstairs. Do you need me to stick close by?"

Bart ignored Jed's question to ask another of his own. "And where are you sleeping tonight?"

Bart's voice was hardly more than a whisper, but whether because he was tired or because he didn't want the others to hear, Jed didn't know.

"Out in the barn where I always do."

"Then you're a damned fool. Good night." Then he turned his head to the wall, leaving Jed no choice but to leave the room.

Out in the kitchen, Sadie stood near the window, looking out into the night. There was no sign of Ole or Hawk, so they must have gone on to bed while Jed had been getting Bart settled in for the night.

"Is he all right?" Sadie didn't look in his direction, evidently finding the cold darkness outside more fascinating than he was.

"He will be. This trip took a lot out of him, but he's alive and still has both legs. That's more than they'd hoped for when they found him."

The thought of his friend bleeding out in the dust, alone and in pain, still gave him the jitters. It had certainly made him think long and hard about his own future. When he'd taken on the job of lawman, he'd done so because it was one of the few jobs he was qualified for. He'd strapped on a gun when he'd left the Johanson's farm behind and discovered that with a little work, he'd had a real talent for it.

If a man was going to make a living with a gun, he had one decision to make: which side of the law was he going to walk on? If Jed had still been the boy Ole had first brought home, he would likely have chosen differently. But Ole and his wife had taught Jed that there was good in the world. That had left him really no choice at all.

"Hawk and your father went to bed." It wasn't a question; just something to say.

"Pa said for you to sleep late in the morning. He and Hawk will see to the chores."

"That's a nice thought, but hardly practical."

She eased closer a few inches, her expression puzzled. He stood his ground, fighting the powerful need to reach out and yank her into his arms. How had he ever thought one night in her arms, in her body would ever be enough? As tired as he was, his body was still clamoring for the taste of her kiss and so much more.

"Why isn't sleeping practical?"

"Even if they try to stay quiet, it's doubtful I can sleep through them feeding the horses and milking the cow right below me." More to keep his hands off Sadie, he reached down to pick up his saddlebags. "I'd better get out to the barn before it gets any later."

Her hand lightly touched his arm, the sweet sensation enough to freeze him right where he stood. He looked down at her soft fingers before risking a quick look at her face. When she smiled, he felt it all the way to his toes.

"Pa said it was too late in the year for you to sleep outside when there's a perfectly good bed upstairs."

There was a bed upstairs—hers. He'd dreamed about it often enough. "You father wants me to sleep in your bed?"

As soon as he said it, he knew it was wrong. He'd forgotten about the other small room up under the eves. He'd never spent much time upstairs, even when he lived in the house. "Forget I said that. Put it off to me being too tired to think straight. He meant the other room."

She had the nerve to actually laugh at him. Taking his hand in hers, she tugged him toward the steep staircase. "Bring the lamp."

He grabbed it off the table on their way by. Once they reached the bottom of the stairs, she had to let go of him because the steps were too narrow for them to walk up together. Putting a small distance between them should have eased the tension building inside him. Instead, it put him in the position of watching her walk up the stairs in front of him. He almost groaned aloud at the enticing sight of her backside swaying gently from to side to side as she made her way up to her room.

The yellow glow of the lamp chased the shadows a short distance, leaving the two of them standing in the confines of its light in the narrow hallway at the top of the steps. His hands were full with the lamp in one hand and the saddlebags in the other, a fact he was grateful for. If not, he wasn't sure he would have had the strength of mind to resist doing something stupid, like hauling Sadie up against his chest and kissing her.

"Wait here while I light the lamp in my room and then you can have this one." She took the one from his hand and opened the door to her room.

He averted his eyes. It was bad enough that he lay awake nights thinking about her without finding out exactly what her bedroom looked like. Then she was back, holding the lamp out to him.

"Your room is there." She pointed across the hallway.

Considering it was the only other door in sight, he could have figured that out for himself. Still, he couldn't quite make his feet move in that direction. She slowly set the lamp down on the floor, never taking her eyes off his face. He held his breath, afraid of what might be about to happen and even more so that it wouldn't.

She whispered his name as she stepped right into his arms. He didn't remember setting down his saddlebags. All he knew was that for the first time since that damned telegram had arrived, he was right where he wanted to be. At first, the two of them simply held on to each other, absorbing comfort and warmth from the embrace.

But hugs alone would not be enough to hold him for the night. It scared him to think that it might never be enough. Her name became a prayer as he gently tilted her face up to his, the need to taste her riding him hard. The last time he'd kissed her this way, there had been innocence in her eyes that was no longer there.

No, this time she knew exactly where they were headed if they didn't slow down, didn't back away. He tried, heaven knows he tried. But she wouldn't let him, tightening her grip on his arms, not that he would let her shoulder the blame. If he'd wanted to escape, he could have. But deep down inside him, he needed this woman.

And if she wanted him, then at least for the night he was hers.

"Come into my room." She whispered the command near his ear, sending another shiver of desire coursing through his blood.

"No, come to mine." He made a step in that direction, but she resisted.

"My bed is bigger." She planted her feet and refused to budge.

"It's also right over your father's room." Maybe she had no idea how much the sound of lovemaking could carry right through the wooden floor, but he did.

"He's a sound sleeper."

"Hawk isn't."

That was enough to convince her. "Let me get settled and then come to me." He kissed her again and then lifted her hands down from where they'd wandered up around his neck.

"I'll be there." Her smile was slow and full of promise.

If she was nervous, it didn't show, but he sure as hell was. He'd come back because he'd promised he would, not so that he could again give in to the temptation of Sadie's beautiful blue eyes. He made sure to walk deliberately and a bit more heavily than was necessary in case anyone downstairs was listening to make sure that he went to his own room.

Once inside, he eyed the narrow bed, little better than a cot, that would be his for the next few days. And nights. He had no business thinking the thoughts he was thinking, but maybe Bart's brush with death had shaken Jed more than he'd realized. If Sadie wanted to offer him the comfort of her arms for the duration of his visit, he would accept it.

But he would remind her that he was here for her father's sake, and no matter how much it hurt to hear it, their time together was running out.

She quickly stripped out of her clothes and put on her best nightgown. The flannel was thick and soft with a bit of lace and ribbon at the throat. It was unlikely that she'd have it on for long, but she wasn't brazen enough to enter Jed's room wearing nothing more than a smile. Her fingers brushed across her lips as she thought about the kisses they'd shared out in the hall that had left them feeling swollen and achy. So did her breasts and other, more private parts of her body.

Had enough time passed? She hoped so because the longer she sat there, the more likely she'd turn coward and bury herself underneath the quilts on her lonely bed. Each time Jed came home, the feelings she had for him strengthened until she had little control over them.

She'd loved him from the first day he'd climbed down off her father's wagon, his silvery eyes wary and full of anger. Now she feared she was in love with him, the kind of love that would last the rest of her life, even if he didn't want it to.

The soft feel of her braided rug gave way to the cold burn of the wooden floor. She moved slowly through the darkness, trying to avoid that one board that sometimes squeaked and sometimes didn't. But even if she stepped on it, her father likely wouldn't hear it, and even if he did, he'd think it was just the usual creak and moan of the house settling.

She didn't know what Hawk would think and didn't really care. The one man who had ever looked at her with that shivery heat in his eyes was across the hall. If the boards she had to walk on squeaked loud enough to raise the dead, well, that was too bad.

Years of sleeping in the same room and rising before the sun did had taught her exactly where the door was. Her hand closed around the knob and turned it slowly. She was rather proud of herself for her slow, sure movements when what she really wanted to do was run, hop, or skip across the hall to where Jed waited for her.

The hallway was dark and silent. She ran a nervous hand through her hair, hoping that she'd guessed right about Jed liking it down around her shoulders. She stopped outside the door to his room. Should she knock or walk right in? He was expecting her, after all, so she slowly opened the door and stepped over the threshold.

He'd left his lamp burning but with the wick turned down real low, giving her just enough light to see into the room. The ceiling angled sharply down toward the other side, making it all but impossible for Jed to stand upright anywhere but just inside the door. He stood there, only a few feet away, staring at her, waiting for her and not looking particularly happy about it.

His hair was down around his shoulders, too, just the way she liked it. His shirt was unbuttoned and hanging slightly open, and he'd already removed his boots and socks. It made him look a little wild, especially with his mouth set in such a grim line. She wanted to run her tongue down that tantalizing glimpse of his chest.

When he didn't immediately speak, she cast about for something to say. "I'm sorry the room is so small."

The bed was barely big enough for a grown man to stretch out on. How would the two of them ever . . . ? Before she could complete that thought, Jed held out his hand. That simple touch drove out any second thoughts or misgivings about the bed. It would work because it was all they had.

"Sadie, are you sure about wanting this?"

Wanting him was what he really meant. She could talk until dawn trying to convince him that this was right, not just for her but for both of them. Far simpler to show him exactly what she wanted. She placed his hand over her heart and covered it with her own.

"Kiss me, Jed."

When he enfolded her in the powerful strength of his arms, she all but purred with the pleasure of rubbing her body against his. If he'd been reluctant seconds before, there was no evidence of it now. His mouth was hot and wet and so deliciously demanding. His tongue enticed hers into meeting him halfway.

The fabric of her gown was no protection against the strength of his touch as he ran his hands down her back to her bottom. He flexed his fingers, squeezing her gently, lifting her up onto her toes to center her body against the hard demands of his own.

"Sadie, so sweet, so sweet."

His voice was a rough murmur near her ear as he tugged at the ribbon at her throat. The row of buttons proved to be no barrier at all to his searching fingers. He had her gown undone and sliding off her shoulders with none of the tremors that had taken over her own hands.

The chill of the room and the heat of Jed's hands combined to have her breasts peaking quickly. She all but melted when Jed swirled his tongue around one and then the other. When he started to pull back, she boldly tugged his head right back down, telling him without words that she needed more of that right then.

He laughed softly and returned his attention to suckling her breasts, the rhythmic tugging of his mouth melting away the last of the strength in her legs. If Jed hadn't caught her with his arms, she feared she would have collapsed in a heap on the floor. He carried her across the room and laid her, oh so gently, down on the mattress. Because of the low eaves, he had to stoop the last couple of steps to keep from hitting his head.

Her gown had fallen to the floor when he'd picked her up. She wanted to be skin to skin with Jed and told him so.

"Take off your clothes." She rose up on her knees to tug at his shirt. He stepped back where he could stand upright to unbutton his trousers and pull them off.

The state of his arousal banished any last doubt she had about Jed wanting this, wanting her. She suspected she should be a bit shocked or even embarrassed about seeing Jed unclothed for the first time, but she wasn't. That night in the woods had been special and most satisfying, but she'd missed being able to really see Jed in the darkness. Tonight, even in the dim light the lamp offered, she relished being able to admire Jed's powerful body.

He let her look her fill, patiently waiting for her to signal that she was ready for him to join her on the bed. If it hadn't been so chilly, she might have made him wait a bit longer as she tried to memorize the hard planes of his muscular body.

"Come to me, Jed." She held out her hand for his. "You have such beautiful skin." When he was within easy reach, she let go to trail her fingers down his chest, pausing while she looked up into his eyes. She wanted to see the effect her hand had continuing on farther down to caress him.

He moaned and closed his eyes.

Taking that for approval, she gently closed her hand around the hard length of him and stroked up and then down. He was leaning forward, his hands braced on the rafters overhead as she continued to learn the feel of him—silk over steel.

Finally, he clamped his hand over hers, stopping her midmotion. She'd been enjoying the play of expressions on his face, but the sudden motion startled her.

"Did I hurt you?"

He drew a shuddering breath. "Honey, you're causing me anything but pain. It's just that it felt too good."

That pleased her. When he wouldn't let her hand go, she surprised them both by leaning forward to press a kiss right where her fingers had been.

Jed jumped back slightly. "You keep that up, Sadie, and this will be over before we really get started."

He knelt on the floor beside the bed. "Come sit on the edge of the bed."

She did as he asked, spreading her knees so that he could move between them. He touched her hair, letting the strands pour over his fingers, finally settling his hand on the back of her neck. With a slow smile, he adjusted the tilt of her head to the proper angle for another bone-melting kiss. Then he eased her back against the mattress and moved even closer.

Leaning forward, he shaped her breast to fit the palm of his hand while he used the fingers of his other hand to test her body's readiness for him. She moved against his hand, letting him know how his touch pleased her and how much she wanted him. His touch was relentless, driving her closer and closer to the edge. Finally, he slid his hands underneath her, tilting her hips up slightly as he paused just short of possessing her.

"Look at me, Sadie! Watch me as I take you."

She did her best to focus on his face, the strain of holding back giving him a harsh look. The power of the moment had her smiling up at him. "Then take me, Jed. Take me now."

With a single powerful thrust, he was deep inside her. His hands supported the back of her thighs as he began sliding in and out of her, slowly at first, then faster and faster. She moaned as the sensations began to overwhelm her.

"Hush, Sadie," he whispered, his voice rough with passion. "We need to keep this quiet."

She grabbed the edge of the quilt and bit down on it to muffle the noises she couldn't seem to help making. Her very skin had become sensitive to every sensation and touch—the quilt beneath her back, the chilly air in the room, the rough calluses on Jed's hands where they cradled her body, the power of his body moving in and out of hers.

"Open your eyes, Sadie!"

She did as he demanded. If she hadn't known him so well, hadn't trusted him without question, she might have been frightened. His head was thrown back, his long hair wild about his shoulders. There was nothing gentle in the expression on his face or the glittering of his eyes as they stared down into hers. Being the focus of all that intensity only served to magnify her response to the way he was pleasuring her.

Both of them were skating close to the edge, but she didn't want it to end this quickly. She held out her arms to him. "Kiss me, Jed."

He slowed his motion and used his hands to lift her up off the bed. She slid down off the edge to straddle his lap, locking their bodies even closer together. One of them moaned in pleasure or maybe both of them did. Then his mouth was on hers as he showed her how to rock against him, letting her take charge this time.

If her plan had been to slow things down, it was destined to fail. Her body and Jed's wonderful hands seemed to be determined to have their own way. The first shudders started deep inside her and then spread through her body until she wanted to scream with the wonder of it. But she hung on to her senses enough to know that would spell disaster for them both.

She buried her face against Jed's shoulder as she shattered in his arms. Just that quickly, he joined her, his arms crushing her against him as the two of them rode out the storm.

An eternity later, when her heart had slowed to a normal pace and her arms and legs felt as if they would do what she asked of them, she nuzzled Jed's face. "Do you think we can get up off this floor if we try real hard?"

A small smile tugged at the corner of his mouth. "Maybe." Then with an amazing display of strength, he managed to push himself up to his feet, while still cradling her in his arms. He sat down on the bed, his back to the low wall, and settled Sadie in his lap. She contributed to the effort by pulling the quilt up over the two of them, content to shut out the rest of the world from this warm nest they'd built for themselves.

For the longest time neither of them spoke. For her part, Sadie couldn't think of a topic of conversation that wasn't fraught with peril. Her father's health wasn't going to improve, although his condition hadn't worsened appreciably in the past few weeks. She suspected that he had somehow determined to make it through the holidays, and especially Christmas. And since Jed had promised to return as long as her father was alive, spring could well mean the loss of both of the men in her life.

Jed's profession was a matter of great concern to her. The ambush that had all but killed Marshal Perry had given her nightmares. Although Jed had his reasons for being a lawman instead of a farmer, she didn't know what was driving him to carry a gun and live such a dangerous life. It was just part of who he was. She'd give anything if he would set aside his badge and come home to stay. Her own pride wouldn't let her beg.

Jed stirred slightly, settling her more firmly against the smooth heat of his chest. She closed her eyes and took a deep breath, memorizing the moment. After a bit, she reached up to touch Jed's cheek. She liked the prickly feel of his face, so different from her own skin. He caught one of her fingers with his lips and nibbled on it, making her giggle.

"I'm glad you're back, and I like your friend." She wanted to ask why Jed had never mentioned Bart Perry in any of his letters to her parents.

"I almost lost him."

She felt him shudder. "We'll feed him up good while he's here. I bet he'll be back to his old self real soon."

"I hope so. He has a long way to go." He ran his hand up and down her arm. "I want to be the one who finds the bastard who shot him. I'll settle for seeing him hanged, but I'll shoot him myself if I have to rather than let him roam free to kill again."

She wasn't shocked by his cursing as much as the powerful hatred that dripped from each word, showing her a side of Jed she hadn't seen before. Suddenly the peaceful mood was gone. She tried to put a little space between them as she considered retreating to her own room. Jed tightened his arms around her.

"I'm sorry, Sadie. I didn't mean to upset you." He kissed the top of her head, making his hold on her feel more like a hug and less like a trap. "Sometimes it seems I've spent so much time with scum like the man who shot Bart that I've forgotten how to act around decent folks." He paused before adding, "If I ever really knew."

Her heart hurt for him. He'd never told her much about his life before he'd come to live with them, but she'd heard enough to know that it had been violent and ugly. He'd reacted to kindness with the same distrust that a mistreated dog did, growling and showing a lot of teeth. Maybe if she'd been older when they'd met, she would have known to be wary of his anger. Instead, she latched on to him and never let go.

"You did fine at the dance a few weeks ago. Several people have asked about you, in fact." She shifted so she could look at him more directly. "In fact, if Pa had been willing, Meg and her husband had invited all of us to their place for dinner tomorrow."

"That was nice of them."

His assumption that he wouldn't be welcome among their neighbors bothered her. Some folks were narrow-minded enough to hold his Indian blood against him, but that was their problem. She'd been raised to judge people by their actions, not by superficial differences. Besides, his black hair and startling gray eyes made him one of the most handsome men she'd ever met.

"Kiss me, Jed."

He dipped his head down to brush his lips across hers. "You're playing with fire again, Sadie. I was pretty rough with you before. I don't want to make you so sore that you hurt tomorrow."

"You weren't too rough with me, Jed. I'm not a fragile flower." She lifted his hand and set it right on her breast. "Touch me again, Jed, and let me touch you."

Feeling bolder for having tasted his passion, she spread her own hands on his chest, enjoying the play of his muscles under his skin. She kissed the base of his throat, touching the pulse there with the tip of her tongue. His skin tasted warm with a flavor that was all his own. Her daring led her farther down, rubbing his flat male nipples with the palm of her hands. He didn't say anything, but his breathing quickened.

He captured both of her hands with his. "It feels damn good to be here."

"This is where you belong, Jed. It always has been."

"For a time it was." He leaned his forehead against hers. "Sometimes I have no idea at all where I really belong, but right now, this feels pretty damn wonderful."

Then he kissed her again and no more words were needed at all.

Chapter 15

Hawk filled the bucket and headed for the barn. The sun was bright, the temperature fairly warm, and the last few birds of the season were singing. It was enough to make him sick.

Thanksgiving was not a holiday that his family had ever observed, but he didn't necessarily object to it. In fact any time Sadie wanted to spend all day cooking just for him and Ole was fine with him. He and his grandfather always had enough to eat, at least most of the time, but neither of them had been a good cook. Right now, the entire house smelled wonderful—spicy and full of promise.

But he wasn't sure if he could stomach sitting down and acting grateful for having not one, but two lawmen sitting right there with him. It wasn't fair, but then life wasn't often fair, not to him. Maybe he had nothing to fear from Jed and his friend, but he had a hard time convincing himself of that. His family's experience with the law in general had not been good. But for Sadie's sake, he'd do his best to get through the meal without being rude to their guests.

Inside the barn door, he set down the bucket and stared. Wind Son, his sole possession and friend in this world, had once again betrayed him by warming up to Jed Stark. He would protest and tell the man to get away from his horse, but Hawk didn't want to risk making Jed mad enough to withdraw his offer of letting Hawk breed his mare to Wind Son. Jed's interest in the stallion was understandable, but that didn't mean Hawk had to like it.

"That stallion of yours is a dandy, Hawk."

Hawk hadn't noticed that Jed's marshal friend was sitting on Ole's bench against the wall.

"He is that." That comment came from Jed as he patted Wind Son on the neck. "Wonder what kind of cross we'll get out of the pair."

Now that was a subject Hawk could show some interest in. He carried the bucket of water over closer to Wind Son's stall. "Strong and fast."

Marshal Perry pushed himself back up to his feet. Using a makeshift crutch, he hopped his way across to where Jed and Hawk stood admiring the horse. "I'd guess in the next few years, people will be lined up to buy horses from you, Hawk. Your grandfather must have had a real talent for breeding."

It had been a long time since his eyes had burned with tears over the loss of his grandfather, but he felt their sting now. He blinked several times and pretended that pouring fresh water for Wind Son took all of his concentration. Luckily, neither of his companions seemed to notice.

Honesty made him admit, "My grandfather would have admired your mare for her strong soul. She'll drop strong foals with big hearts, the kind that will risk their own well-being for the sake of their owner. A man has to be careful not to abuse that gift."

Jed jerked his hand back from Wind Son's neck

as if he'd been burned. He took a quick step back and shoved his hands into his pockets. If Hawk didn't know better, something he'd said had caused Jed pain. Even his friend was looking at Jed strangely.

"Look, Bart, will you be all right alone for a while? I promised Sadie that I'd chop wood for her." Jed was already reaching for the axe and was halfway to the door before Bart could answer.

"I'll be fine, and besides, I'm not alone. Hawk's here with me."

Hawk whipped around at that comment, ready to protest that he wasn't going to hang around in the barn just to keep a lawman company, especially one stupid enough to get himself shot up. But before he could get the words out, the man winked at him and smiled. He knew full well how Hawk felt about him and Jed; he just didn't care.

"Give a yell if you need help getting back to the house." Jed turned his icy stare on Hawk. "And don't let him do a damn thing except admire your horse. He'll try to deny it, but he's weak as a lamb right now and too stubborn to admit it."

The other lawman laughed. "Gosh, Jed, maybe you ought to trade your badge for an apron if you're going to insist on mothering me like this."

"Somebody needs to watch out for you, since you can't be trusted to take care of yourself. Damned fool!" Jed stomped out of the barn, leaving his friend staring after him, his mouth hanging open in shock.

"Well, I'll be." Marshal Perry shook his head. "I didn't know he cared so much."

Rather than involve himself in their conversation, Hawk turned his attention to grooming Wind Son. After a bit, the marshal hobbled back closer and leaned over the top of the stall to watch. Hawk figured the man had something he wanted to say; he wasn't sure he wanted to listen.

"I owe you, boy."

Now that surprised him. "Why is that?" He ran a comb through Wind Son's mane.

"Because there's something about you that caught Jed's interest."

Hawk snorted. "I was wanted for horse theft, or didn't he tell you that? All he was interested in was adding another name to his list of arrests." He started checking Wind Son's feet and the soundness of his legs.

"Oh, he told me all right. He also said he'd gone against all good sense and brought you here instead of back to stand trial. Then he risked his own life to clear your name. If that crooked rancher's men had backed his play, Jed would likely be dead right now."

Perry picked up a piece of hay and chewed on it. "In the five years or so that I've known him, I've never once known Jed to do anything but follow the letter of the law. He has a reputation throughout the territory for being absolutely ruthless in his pursuit of criminals. You're the only exception. Why is that, do you think?"

Hawk didn't want to think about it because he didn't want to feel grateful to Jed for anything. His friends, the Johansons, were a different matter. Ole and Sadie had proved themselves to be Hawk's friends, too, over and over again since he'd come to live with them. And if the doctor was right about Ole dying soon, well, Sadie was going to need him to stick around to help with the farm. But Jed's reasons for bringing him here bothered him something fierce, even if he didn't want to admit it.

Had he done it because he had Indian blood

just as Hawk did? Or because he'd been an orphan, too? Or maybe he'd used Hawk's problem as an excuse to come back to Sadie? That last one bothered him the most. When Jed was around, her eyes seemed to follow him constantly as if she couldn't get enough of him. But then Hawk had heard her crying each time Jed left.

"I don't know why that man does anything. I just wish he'd stay gone." His stallion bumped him hard with his nose, hinting he was more than ready for the treat he knew Hawk had in his pocket. Hawk pulled out the carrot and let the horse lip it up off the palm of his hand.

"Well, I'd have to agree with you that Jed is something of a puzzle. But thanks to you, I know more about him now than I did a few months ago. He and I have been friends, or at least I liked to think so. But, you know, he never brought me here to meet the Johansons until now. You might not want to hear this, but I'd have to say that he had done you a powerful favor, finding you a new home where they need you as much as you need them."

The marshal pushed away from the stall and started the long walk back to the house. When he reached the door, he paused to catch his breath. Evidently he wasn't done saying his piece. "But you know, Hawk, unlike you, I had to get myself almost killed before he introduced me to his family."

Hawk waited until the marshal was gone before stepping out of the stall. The man was right, of course. Without Jed's help, there's no telling where Hawk would have ended up, and most likely without Wind Son. He owed the man, as much as he didn't want to.

In his grandfather's memory, he would find a way to thank the lawman for all that he'd done for him. But if he made Sadie cry again, all bets were off.

Ole sat quietly, waiting for the pain to lessen. This time, the attack had come on quicker and lasted longer. At least Sadie had been too busy to notice. She would have had Jed riding for the doctor, dragging the poor man away from his own Thanksgiving dinner for no good reason. There was nothing he could do to fix the damage done by a lifetime of hard work and plain old age.

The truth was, as much as it would hurt Sadie to hear it, he was tired and ready to lie down to rest beside Olga. Sometimes he missed that woman so badly that he could hardly breathe. He loved this land, but it was time to pass its care on to the next generation. It would be in good hands.

He closed his eyes and thought past his hurting to the people who mattered so much to him. He worried about leaving Sadie alone. Hawk might be good company for her, but she needed more. And she had her heart set on Jed.

The pain had eased to the point that Ole could smile a bit. He'd heard his daughter lead Jed up those stairs last night. No doubt they'd both thought such an old man would be sound asleep and deaf to the world around him. But most nights, he spent a great deal of time lying awake, content to listen to the familiar sounds of the darkness and enjoying his memories. But if a man knew what to listen for, he might very well have heard soft footsteps overhead and the sound of a door opening and closing. After that, he'd made himself drift off to sleep because Sadie and Jed deserved a little privacy.

He supposed he should be upset if, as he strongly

suspected, Jed had taken his daughter's innocence outside of the bonds of the marriage bed. But he knew his daughter, and she definitely had a mind of her own. If Sadie had decided that she wanted Jed, no matter what the circumstances, Ole doubted the big tough lawman had stood a chance against her determination. He smiled. Sadie had a lot of her mother in her.

The bands of pressure slowly eased in his chest. He waited another minute or two to make sure the episode was over, at least for now. He needed to have a talk with Jed, one he'd been putting off for a while. Knowing his friend's pride, he wasn't going to be very happy with Ole, but that was too bad.

He pushed himself up off the bed. His legs were still a bit shaky. Surely Sadie was so wrapped up in preparing her feast that she wouldn't notice. Once he got past her, he would find Jed and hope that he was alone. If not, well, he'd just have to be rude enough to ask that other marshal to leave so they could talk. Jed's friend would understand.

"Sadie, I'm going outside."

She didn't respond. Rather than interfere with whatever she was so engrossed in, he took his jacket down off its peg and slipped out of the door. Marshal Perry had just stepped up on the porch. Ole stood back and held the door open for him.

"Thank you, Mr. Johanson. I thought I'd take a nap before dinner." He drew a deep breath. "I'll need all my strength to do justice to the dinner your daughter is preparing. My landlady is a good cook, but I suspect Sadie's efforts would put poor Miss White's to shame."

His comment pleased Ole. Sadie was putting everything she had into making this Thanksgiving unforgettable. It was nice that someone besides Ole appreciated that.

"I thought I'd check on Jed, so the house should be quiet for you."

Bart pointed toward the farside of the barn. "Jed said something about Sadie needing wood chopped."

"Thank you. That saves me having to hunt him down."

Once the marshal managed to cross the threshold with his crutches, Ole closed the door and started across the yard.

Hawk came out of the barn leading Jed's mare. "I'm going to take her out for a run." He mounted up and fought to keep the mare from taking off on him. "Tell Sadie I'll be back in time for dinner."

Then they were off and flying. As usual, Hawk looked happier whenever he was astride a horse. Having a chance to put Jed's horse through her paces was an extra-special treat for him. Ole waved him on and continued on his way to where Jed was working.

Jed had stripped off his jacket and tossed it on the ground. He'd worked up enough of a sweat to have his sleeves rolled up despite the cool temperature. He was so intent on swinging the axe he didn't notice when Ole pulled up a log and sat down to watch. Judging from the pile of freshly split logs, it appeared that there was a lot of temper in the way Jed was working.

Ole decided to let him work off some of that anger before he talked to him. Besides, it was a real pleasure to watch his friend work. Jed always did move with a grace that most folks—and especially the women—admired. As far as Ole could tell, Jed had always been unaware that he drew the eye of most of the females that saw him.

Except for Sadie. Jed had known the minute her interest in him had changed, and it had sent him into an all-out panic. That was six years ago, and Ole regretted every minute of that time. Maybe if he'd sat Jed down back then and begged him to stay, they wouldn't have lost so much time. Despite his rough upbringing, Jed had a powerfully strong streak of honor running through the heart of him. He'd felt unworthy of Sadie's interest, so he'd left.

Now Ole was going to have to find a way to bring him back for good. After a bit, Jed planted the axe in a log and left it there to begin stacking the wood he'd already split.

"Pretty impressive pile of wood there, Jed." Ole thought about offering to help but decided not to. He'd only be in Jed's way, and he didn't want to risk setting off another attack so soon.

"Sadie said she needed wood." Jed kept working. "I'll try to lay in a good supply before Bart and I have to leave."

"I'm sure she'll appreciate it." He scooted over and patted the space beside him. "Take a break and come sit down. I want to talk to you and watching you do all that work is making me feel guilty. Besides, it's Thanksgiving. We can afford to take a day off from everything but feeding the stock."

Jed gave him a considering look, not at all sure he wanted to listen to what Ole had to say. Finally, he picked up his jacket and put it back on before taking a seat.

"I've got some things to say to you, Jed. Some of them are going to be hard for me to say and harder for you to hear, but I'm running out of time and chances to talk to you."

"Ole, you've got plenty of time ahead of you." Jed's eyes gave the lie to his words.

"Don't lie to me or to yourself, Jed. I know for a fact that Sadie told you all about what that fool doctor said. Don't you think I know why you've been coming back here so regularly? I appreciate the effort, but let's not play games." He reached over and put his hand on Jed's shoulder and drew some comfort from the fact he didn't flinch.

"Now, I've lived a long life and a good one. No man gets through it without his own share of troubles, but I've done better than most. This farm has provided a good life for me and my family and will continue to do so after I'm gone." He let himself look around, taking in all the familiar sights he would miss so very much.

"Damn it, Ole, I don't like hearing you talk this way." Jed kept his eyes focused firmly on the ground at his feet. "The doctor could be wrong."

"Maybe he could. It wouldn't be the first time. But my old body is telling me he's right." Ole looked up at the sky, soaking up the bright sunshine. "Now, mind you, I'm not saying this to make you feel bad. Dying is part of life, Jed. Ain't no changing that."

"Doesn't mean I have to like it." Jed finally looked at him, pain etching heavy lines around his eyes and mouth. "I almost lost Bart to a coward's bullet. I don't want to think about losing you, too. Not now."

"I know, and that means a lot to me. You don't let many people close to you, so it hurts extra bad when you lose one." He mustered up a smile, trying to reassure his friend. "But like I said, this isn't about making you worry about me. I'm not afraid to meet my maker, and my sweet Olga will be waiting there for me. There's nothing like the love of a good woman to make a man's life worth living."

It was time to get on with the matter at hand. "Jed, Olga and I took in more than our share of needy children over the years. Each one of them was special to us, but you were different. I couldn't love you more if you'd been my own flesh and blood. You are the son we never had."

Jed squirmed in his seat. "Ole . . ."

Ole held up his hand to stop him. "Now, I plan to speak my piece. It can be now between just the two of us or at dinner tonight with everyone listening in." The threat had the desired effect of hushing him up.

"Now, don't think I'm selling my daughter short. Sadie is everything in a daughter that a man could wish for, and I'm proud of her. She's a strong woman and will make the right man a good wife. I probably won't live to see her wedding, but it's enough to hope that she'll bear someone strong sons and daughters to pass this farm on to."

He ignored the way Jed flinched when he said that. Jed might not be thinking about marriage for himself, but he obviously didn't much like the idea of another man in Sadie's life, especially one making babies with her. Good.

"I've seen a lawyer fellow and had a will drawn up. I'm leaving half the farm to you." He braced himself for the explosion he was sure to come. He didn't have to wait long.

Jed was on his feet and glaring down at Ole in a heartbeat. "Are you crazy? This farm is Sadie's home. You can't go giving it away to the likes of me! What were you thinking of?"

"This farm is almost too big for one man to work by himself, especially with that new parcel of land I bought a couple of years ago with just this in mind. Sadie will inherit this half with the house and barn. You'll have to build your own place, of course, but the land is the important part." He pointed toward a stand of trees on the far side of the field they'd harvested a few weeks ago. Your piece of land starts where those trees are. Once you get it cleared, it should provide a good living for you and your wife."

"Damn it, Ole! First you're turning me into a farmer and now you're marrying me off! What if I don't want either of those things to happen? Don't you think I should have some say in the matter?" He stomped back over to where he'd left the axe and jerked it free from the log. After shrugging off his jacket, he started splitting wood again.

Ole let him work off some more of his temper. Somehow he had to get Jed to see himself as Ole did, a strong man with a lot to offer the right woman. Did he think they should hold his mixed blood against him? Or that he'd learned to kill in the defense of the innocents of this world?

Finally, he decided enough was enough. He waited until Jed set the axe down to get more wood before approaching him. Jed had the same look about him as one of the barn cats, ready to bolt if Ole moved too fast.

"Jed, I'm not done talking to you and I think I've earned the right to have my say. Now stand there and listen to me." He risked another step closer. Jed seemed to brace himself, as if to ward off a blow. Maybe he was. Words could hurt a man as much as a fist.

"I don't know exactly what happened to you as a boy. When you came to us, for certain you'd been beaten and starved. From the way you hated being touched, I've always suspected that somewhere along the line, a man tried to use you in ways that makes me sick to think about."

Jed slowly shook his head, but it wasn't in denial. More likely he was remembering the ugliness and trying to shove it back down where he didn't have to think about it. Ole ached for the boy he'd been and the man he was.

Finally, Jed raised his eyes to meet Ole's. "It was my mother's brother. She protected me as long as she could, but he had a bad temper and big fists. I learned early not to let him catch me alone, especially when he'd been drinking. That worked as long as my mother was alive. But when she died, he tried to sell me to some men. None of them ever said what they had in mind for me in so many words, and I didn't stick around to find out."

Ole let his own tears fall because he knew Jed never would. He kept quiet, hoping that his friend would finally let it all out, lancing a wound that had festered for far too long.

Jed shuddered. "I stole, I lied, I cheated, I did everything you can imagine and some things you probably can't just to survive. Then one winter, I got sick. Someone found me in an alley, more than half dead, and took me to the local church. The pastor's wife nursed me back to health." He finally stepped closer to Ole. "That's when they sent me here. Until then, I never knew what it felt like to be clean or have enough to eat. That minister and his wife saved my life, but you and Olga saved my soul."

"It was one of God's miracles, Jed. You have to believe that. It was his plan for you to find us." Ole pulled out his handkerchief and dabbed at his eyes. "We needed you and you needed us. And Sadie is going to need you more once I'm gone."

Jed was already shaking his head. "Ole, she deserves better than me, and you know it."

"I don't know any such thing, Jed Stark! How can you say that? My Sadie wants a man to care for, one who will care for her right back. You're one of the best men I've ever had the good fortune to know. I'm so proud of what you've done with your life, and you should be, too. I know you love Sadie. It's there on your face as plain as day."

He shook a finger in Jed's face. "Don't try to tell me that you didn't give your heart to my daughter the first time you met her. I was there and I saw. That hasn't changed no matter how far you've run because you're foolish enough to think you're not good enough for her. And she loves you right back. Don't make things complicated when they aren't."

There was more he could say, but it would have to wait until Jed was ready to hear it. He could only hope that that time was soon.

"Finish what you're doing and then get cleaned up. Sadie will want us all at the table on time for this big dinner. And when it's time for someone to say grace, think long and hard about all that you have to be grateful for. You don't have to spend the rest of your life fighting the evil in this world. You've done your share. Just look at Hawk. Where would he be without you stepping in and setting things right for him? It's time you found some peace for yourself."

The sound of the axe biting deeply into wood rang out as he made his way back to the house.

Everything had turned out just perfect, and all the men arranged around her table were on their best behavior. Her father had led them in grace, and then asked each person to add something he or she was grateful for. It had come as no surprise that Hawk said Wind Son. Good friends, was Marshal Perry's offering. He'd looked Jed right in the eye and smiled, making his friend squirm a bit. Jed muttered something under his breath that no one could really hear. When Sadie's turn had come, she had smiled across the table at Jed and said, "Loved ones." Let the others make of that what they would.

Then for the first few minutes, everyone was too busy passing platters and bowls to say much of anything. They all tucked into the meal with satisfying enthusiasm. Even Sadie's father seemed to eat more than usual.

When they seemed to be slowing down to a stop, she asked, "I hope all of you saved room for dessert."

"I did," Hawk told her. "I've been waiting all day for some of your pie."

She didn't know how, considering how much he'd already eaten, but she'd take him at his word. "Anyone else?"

"I'll have some a little later. I think I'll check on the stock first." Ole pushed away from the table. "I won't be long."

"I'll give you a hand." Jed was right behind him, without saying a word to Sadie about dinner or her apple pie, which she knew was his favorite.

Marshal Perry smiled at her. "I was going to ask for a big piece, but maybe I should wait until everyone else is ready." Then he winked at her. "Or you can cut me a small piece now, and I'll have another when they come back."

"That's a deal, Marshal."

She tried not to let Jed's slight hurt her, but maybe he was worried that her father would overdo it if he wasn't there to keep an eye on him. While they were gone, she served up good-sized pieces of pie to both Hawk and Jed's friend. Then she started the long process of cleaning up the kitchen. When she had the sink full of hot water, she realized she was no longer alone. Bart had joined her, towel in hand.

"You should sit down. I can handle this."

"I know you can, but I need to do something to

earn my keep around here. Even if I could do anything to help Jed and your father, they'll be done with the chores before I even make it to the barn. Let me do this much at least."

"Thank you. I have to admit that I love cooking, but cleaning up afterward isn't nearly as much fun."

The two of them fell into an easy rhythm, making quick work of the piles of dishes. Since he didn't know where things were kept, he stacked everything back on the table. To her surprise, Hawk finished his pie and then started putting away the clean dishes. They were just finishing up when her father came back in the door.

She watched for several seconds, waiting for Jed to come back inside. When he didn't immediately appear, she asked, "Where did you leave Jed?"

Her father shrugged. "He wasn't ready to come in." He sank down in the rocker and closed his eyes, clearly not wanting to say any more.

Something was wrong. She should have guessed it from the way Jed acted at dinner. He was never very chatty, but he'd been more forthcoming with his friend there. What had happened to upset him?

"Pa, did something happen?"

Her father had been looking at the fireplace, holding out his hands to gather in the warmth. For a minute, she didn't think he'd heard her, but then he seemed to shrink in on himself. "I think I scared him off, maybe for good this time."

"What the hell—?" Bart bit off his words midsentence, as if he sensed that this problem belonged to Ole and Sadie alone.

Even Hawk looked worried, although he was always the first to be glad whenever Jed rode out. But right now Sadie didn't care what the marshal

did or didn't say or how Hawk felt. Her attention
was completely on her father. What had he done?

"Pa?"

"I'm sorry, daughter. I did my best, but he won't
listen." His voice broke as he turned toward her, a
few tears trickling down his face.

Sadie was torn between wanting to comfort her
father and running for the barn to find Jed. What
had happened to break her father's heart? Finally,
she settled for half measures. She gave her father a
quick hug and helped him to a chair at the table.

"Now, I'm sure that it's not as bad as all that. I'll
go talk to Jed." She patted him on the shoulder.
"Hawk, you stay with my father while I go find out
what's wrong."

She had started for the door when Bart called
after her. "You'll need your coat. It's getting awfully cold out there."

Even that much of a delay was almost more than
she could bear. After grabbing her coat off its peg,
she headed out into the night, pulling her coat on
as she all but ran across the yard toward the barn.
There was a narrow strip of light spilling through
the doors, lighting her way. Inside, she looked
around for Jed, but he was not in sight. Wind Son
and Hopeless stirred restlessly in their stalls, but
there was no sign of Jed. At least his horse was still
there. That calmed her. A little. For now.

"Jed?"

The silence had that heavy feel of someone listening but refusing to answer. She cocked her head
to one side, hoping to pick up some clue as to
where Jed might be. There weren't that many hiding places where he could fit. He had to be up in
the loft, probably hoping to be left alone. As upset
as her father was, Jed had to be in a similar state of

mind. It almost broke her heart to think he might be in such pain.

He wouldn't seek her out for comfort, undoubtedly thinking he was unworthy or that she'd be angry with him for upsetting her father. No matter what had happened between them, she loved Jed too much to leave him out here in the cold without trying to help.

She gathered up the front of her skirt and climbed the ladder that led to the loft overhead. It took her only a few seconds to reach the top. The light from the lantern below did little to dispel the darkness, but one of the shadows had more substance than the others. Crawling in a skirt was awkward, but she didn't hesitate.

He should have known she'd come charging out to the barn to find him. Short of saddling up and riding out, there wasn't much he could have done to avoid her. So he sat in the dark and the cold and waited. It didn't take long for her to find him. Her skirts slowed her progress down as she tried to crawl over the loose piles of hay.

"Jed."

"I'm here." As much as he didn't want to be.

She finally made it. To give her credit for good sense, she left a bit of distance between them when she sat down and stretched her legs out.

"Want to tell me what happened?" He could feel her eyes on him even though it was too dark for either of them to see much.

"No."

She played her trump card. "Pa was crying."

"Oh, hell, Sadie. I never meant for that to happen." He wished he could see her eyes. They would tell him if she believed him.

"I know that, Jed. But I need to know what you

said that upset him so much. The only time I've ever seen him cry was when my mother died."

She must have decided that he wasn't going to bite, because she inched closer to him. He could feel the warmth of her body all along the side of his. Instead of talking, he would rather kiss her, lay her down on this soft cushion of hay, and plunge his body into hers. But that wasn't likely to happen, not if they had this talk she was so intent on.

"Come on, Jed. Just tell me."

This time she fumbled in the dark to find his hand and threaded her fingers through his. The connection hurt him in ways he had no words for. How could he ride away from here, knowing he'd never know the comfort of a simple touch?

"He wants me to have half the farm."

A quick intake of breath was her only reaction for several seconds. "And that made him cry?"

"I turned him down." It hurt to feel her move away again. "I can't accept it."

"Because you're afraid it would bother me? If that's the case, you can relax. I've known for some time that he'd bought that extra parcel of land with you in mind. I'll have plenty of land for my own needs, Jed."

"That's what Ole told me earlier." He closed his eyes and tried to find words for what he was feeling. "He said I was like his son, Sadie."

"You've had to know that's how he and my mother felt. The other orphans stayed here long enough to learn a few skills before moving on to other places, other jobs. But my parents—and me, as well—felt differently about you from the very start."

"I can't stay here, Sadie. I know I promised that I would, at least until your father . . . until he . . . as long as he's . . ." The words choked him, but he made himself say them anyway. "I know I promised to come back until he dies, but I don't know if I can."

Anger tainted her words. "You mean won't, don't you, Jed?"

He could feel anger coming from her in waves.

"Listen to me, Jed Stark! If you can face down armed killers without flinching, you can handle an old man loving you enough to offer you his life's work. Once he's gone, you can sell the place and he'll never know."

"But I will, and so will you."

"What do you want, Jed? Loving someone comes with all kinds of tangles wrapped around your heart. Pa wasn't offering you the land to put you in some kind of cage. It's just like when he opened our home to you, he's trying to offer you a chance to do something different with your life."

"And if I don't want to do something different? What if I like my life?" Not that he did, but he didn't know anything else anymore.

"Then that is your choice to make." She leaned her head against his shoulder. "If you like hunting down killers and thieves better than farming, better than you like me, then that's your choice."

He was scared, but he couldn't admit to that. What if he did take the farm and couldn't raise enough food to feed himself, much less a family? He knew he could track, and he knew he could kill. How could he use those skills to plant hay and breed horses? Hell, Hawk was a mere kid, but he faced his future with more courage and hope than Jed was able to.

"Then you'd have me lie to your father, tell him I'm grateful for a piece of land so he can die easy?"

"No, I want you to tell yourself the truth, Jed. That there is so much more to you than a man who is quick with a gun. You're a son to that man in there, a friend to Bart. You're even a friend to Hawk, despite the fact he didn't want you to be."

"And what am I to you, Sadie?" Tempering his strength, he dragged her across his lap to face him. "A lover? A man you take to your lonely bed because he's handy?"

"Jed! Don't talk that way!" She struggled to break free.

"It's the truth, Sadie."

"Maybe it's your truth, Jed, but it's not mine. What we shared was beautiful. Don't try to destroy that."

"I'm not a civilized man, Sadie, no matter what you think. Not like those farmers at the dance. I've seen so much ugliness in my life that there's nothing left inside me for anything soft. I will leave when your father dies, and I won't look back."

All the fight went out of her then. It was like holding a rag doll in his arms, one that was torn and tattered and losing its stuffing.

Chapter 16

After a bit, she stirred. When Sadie pushed against his arms, he let her go, wishing things were different. Wishing he was different, but maybe it was for her own good. She thought she loved him, and maybe through some kind of miracle, she really did. But if he were to stay, gradually she'd come to hate the man he was.

"Come in the house when you're ready. Don't let my father think that he's driven you away for good. It will kill him." She crawled away, fumbling in the darkness until she reached the ladder, and then disappeared into the light below.

He closed his eyes, not wanting to see her face, not yet. He knew he'd hurt her deeply but was at a loss what to do about it. He'd planned to head back to Rosser day after tomorrow, but maybe it would be better if they left sooner.

Once he had Bart safely back to Miss White's, Jed could make his own plans. Bart was strong enough to resume some of his duties, especially the paperwork and administrative ones that Jed had been trying to do for him. Once they had that settled, he could hunt down the bastard who had shot Bart. One way or another, Jed would see that justice was done.

Then, if his quest was over, he'd come back here for Christmas. He shivered, feeling the winter's cold although it was little more than late fall. On more nights than he cared to remember, a bed in a hayloft would have been a vast improvement over his usual sleeping arrangements out on the trail. But having spent the last two nights with Sadie in his arms, he found this pile of dry grass hardly welcoming.

He stretched out and stared up at the dim outline of the rafters. This barn had been built to endure. Ole knew what he was doing when it came to creating something that would stand against the ages. He and Olga had been solid in their partnership and in their faith, so Christmas had always been special in their home, a time to celebrate a season of miracles and love.

For a few short years, Jed had been part of that celebration. The first time there had been a package under the tree for him was burned into his memory. Olga had knitted him a pair of warm socks. No gift from the fanciest store in the world could have been better than that. With his background, he hadn't even known he was supposed to give presents to the Johansons, but they hadn't felt the lack. There'd been enough love and joy to go around.

How had he forgotten that for so long?

It was time to go back to the house. Ole might go to bed before Jed came in, but he wouldn't sleep. No words would make everything all right, but he could ease the old man's mind that he wouldn't disappear again without saying good-bye.

Sadie, well, he didn't know what to do about her. His chest hurt just thinking about it.

He sat up, preparing to climb down the ladder, when he heard someone sneaking around outside. Old habits, the kind that had kept him alive all these years, had him reaching for the gun he wasn't wearing. Carelessness like that could get a man killed. Cursing under his breath, he looked around for another weapon. He spotted the axe on the far side of the barn, too far to do him any good. He jumped to the ground, flexing his knees to take the shock.

Crouched on the near side of the door, he stood ready to defend himself with his bare hands.

When Hawk stepped through the door, Jed let out a long string of cusswords. The boy looked startled, but then he grinned at Jed's colorful use of the language.

"Did I spook you, lawman?"

"Shut up, Hawk." Jed straightened up, trying to regain some of his dignity. "What are you doing out here?"

"I came to talk to you." Hawk straightened his shoulders, trying to look older than his years. "I've got something to say."

The last thing Jed wanted was another confrontation. The talk with Ole had taken a lot out of him; the one with Sadie had all but finished him off. "You've got nothing to say that I want to hear."

"Too bad, lawman." Hawk crossed his arms over his chest and planted himself in front of the door, saying without words that if Jed wanted to leave, he'd have to go through him.

Great. Resigning himself to his fate, he said, "Will this take long enough that I should sit down?"

Hawk rolled his eyes. Some of the tension

drained out of his shoulders now that he knew Jed would listen. He left his spot by the door to stand near his horse, no doubt drawing comfort and courage from the solid presence of his friend.

"You made Ole cry, and then you made Sadie cry." His mouth was a straight slash of disapproval.

"That's none of your damn business."

The anger in Hawk's eyes showed he felt differently, but he didn't pursue it. "I hear you're going to leave again. Ole's afraid you won't be back."

"Again, not your business."

"I just wanted to say thanks." He kept his eyes firmly on the ground as he dug a hole with the toe of his boot. "You know, for bringing me here."

Shock rolled through Jed, sending him staggering back a step or two. Suspicion made him ask, "Who put you up to this?"

Hawk rolled his eyes. "No one, lawman. My grandfather taught me that a man should be grateful for the gifts he is given. I had nothing but Wind Son. Now I have a family again."

"I don't need your gratitude. I was just doing my job." That was a lie. His job had been to bring the boy in to stand trial. Instead, he'd taken justice into his own hands and protected Hawk from the law until he could find out the real truth.

Hawk stood quietly, perhaps to judging Jed's reaction to his words. After a bit, he continued. "I just want you to know that I will watch over them for you while you're gone."

If the boy could say it, so could Jed. "Thank you."

Then, before the discussion could go any further, Jed stalked out of the barn. If not for Bart's presence, he might have given in to the urge to run again. But at least for this night, he would have to stay.

Bart was still up. Staring into the dying embers of the fire, he barely glanced up when Jed entered, bringing a blast of cold air with him.

Jed stopped by Bart's chair. "Do you need help getting ready for bed?"

"No, I'm fine. I'll turn in when Hawk comes back inside. You go on to bed." He waited until Jed's foot was on the first step to add, "I assume we'll be leaving tomorrow?"

"Yeah, we'll be leaving."

"Have I ever told you what a stubborn, hard-headed fool you are sometimes?"

"Bart, not now." He climbed another step and then another.

"Fine, we'll talk whenever you're ready. I just wanted to make sure you knew what I thought." His friend softened the words with a small laugh.

Slowly, Jed walked up the stairs feeling more alone than he had for a very long time.

When he reached the top, he paused outside Sadie's door, wishing he had the right to open it and walk inside. He could use the comfort he knew he could find in her arms, but he'd destroyed any chance of that out in the barn. Shuddering against the chill in the air, he walked on past to his own door. Before he could open it, he noticed a sliver of light coming from underneath it.

Had Sadie left a lamp burning for him, no matter how badly he had treated her? Another weight of guilt settled on his shoulders. He shook his head at her folly. But a bigger shock yet waited for him inside.

"Sadie?"

She was stretched out on his narrow bed, her glorious hair a halo around her face and shoulders. Her smile was a bit shaky, but the hand she held out toward him wasn't.

Neither of them spoke. Maybe that should have worried him, but so far, words had done nothing but hurt the people he cared most about. He'd made Ole cry, he'd made Sadie cry, and he'd come damn near making himself cry, something he hadn't done since he was old enough to walk.

He knelt by the bed to kiss Sadie, wanting desperately to convince her that her decision to share his bed was the right one. At the same time, he had to wonder what she was thinking. Even that little delay had her looking worried, so he immediately brushed his lips across hers. Then he wrapped her in his arms, wishing like hell that he'd never have to let her go.

Touches took the place of words, caresses hinted at emotions that were better left unnamed. Fingers fumbled with buttons and hands yanked at stubborn boots. Finally, blessedly, he was stretched out beside Sadie, skin to skin, her body cradling his. He pushed his knee between hers and ran his hand up and down her back, loving the smooth expanse of skin.

They kissed, nibbling, tasting, smiling when they accidentally knocked their teeth together as their enthusiasm got a bit out of control. When he almost fell off the edge of the bed, she managed to hold on to him long enough for him to regain his balance. Their shared laughter sent a surge of warmth through him to settle in his chest. In all his previous experiences with women, he couldn't remember ever laughing with one in bed.

Then Sadie took him in her arms and into her body. For the moment, nothing mattered beyond this time, this woman. Tomorrow and all the problems it would bring would just have to wait.

*   *   *

Sadie knew she should get up and move back to her own bed, but right now, cuddled against Jed's chest felt far too good. She kept her breathing slow and even, not wanting Jed to realize that she was awake. He shifted his legs slightly, warning her that he wasn't sleeping either.

If they were both awake, he might want to talk, and that was the last thing she wanted to do. She knew what she needed to say, for his sake, for her sake, even for her father's. Acceptance didn't mean she was in any hurry to speak her piece, not when it meant that nights like this one were likely at an end.

There were so many things they'd never spoken about. She knew she loved him and had little doubt that he was harboring some pretty strong emotions for her, even if he didn't know what to call them. They could build a good life together, but that wasn't going to happen. Not with Jed convinced that his one gift was a fast draw.

She had no doubt that he was a good lawman, one who fought long and hard for justice. But she suspected that lifestyle would slowly kill off the gentle side of Jed, the one she loved.

"No use pretending you're asleep, Sadie." Jed squeezed her shoulders.

Lifting her head, she looked up at him, frowning. "How did you know I was awake?"

The corners of his mouth tipped up in a reluctant smile. "You quit snoring."

"Jed! I do not snore." At least she hoped not. Since she'd never shared her bed with anyone else, it was hard to know for certain. Her outrage died a quick death. "Do I?"

She felt his chuckle rumble through his chest. "No, I'm sure that it was just the wind rattling the rafters."

Pretending an offense she didn't really feel, she sniffed. "I cannot believe you said that. A gentleman wouldn't say that to a lady, no matter what."

His smile dimmed a bit. "I wouldn't know the first thing about being a gentleman, Sadie."

Now that made her mad. "I was only teasing, Jed. And you're wrong, anyway. Being a gentleman is nothing more than treating a woman with respect and making her feel special. Fancy manners and fancy talk don't amount to much if there's no meaning behind them."

His ironclad hold on her eased a bit, but he didn't respond. For a short time, they lay together in silence, each lost in thoughts best not shared aloud.

Finally, she couldn't stand it anymore. "I'd better get back to my own room. It will be morning soon enough." She started to sit up, but he stopped her.

"Don't go. Not yet."

It would only hurt more the longer she stayed, the longer he let her. But despite her resolve, she was in no hurry to return to the cold loneliness of her own bed.

"All right, if you want." She settled her head back down on his shoulder.

"I want." His fingers toyed with her hair. "I'll make sure you wake up in time to get back to your bed before they stir around downstairs."

"All right." A huge yawn surprised her, making Jed laugh again.

"Go to sleep, Sadie. You've had a long day."

And the night would be too short, but she didn't say so. She dreaded morning, knowing that the hurt and tears she'd put aside to climb into Jed's bed would be back. And the hurt would likely last a long, long time.

* * *

Her eyes felt gritty and her shoulder ached from lying in one position most of the night. She kept trying to stretch the kinks out of it, but so far, nothing seemed to help. It was all she could do to lift her favorite cast-iron skillet on the stove.

She'd gotten out of the habit of cooking a big breakfast because of her father's failing appetite. But this morning, she was going to put a sizeable meal on the table. The temperature outside was definitely colder than the day before. Marshal Perry was going to need a hot meal under his belt before he and Jed had to leave.

If Jed's mood was anything like hers, he wouldn't feel like eating much. She was waiting to catch him alone, wanting to speak her piece before he rode away. Even if she had to be rude about it, she planned to tell her father, Hawk, and the marshal to give them a few minutes alone.

In fact, where was he now? She'd heard him walk down the stairs when she was getting dressed, but she hadn't seen him since. Rather than asking the others, she casually strolled over to the window to look outside. Jed was just coming out of the barn, leading his mare.

"I'll be back."

She slammed the skillet down on the stove a little harder than she'd meant to, startling Bart and Hawk. Before either of them could ask any questions, she was out the door, her coat in hand.

Jed heard her coming. He opened the gate to the corral for the mare before turning to face Sadie. He stuck his hands in his pockets and waited for her to come to him, his mouth set in a grim line. It was hard to remember that same mouth had smiled at her last night and kissed her more times than she could count.

Now it was at best a warning sign, telling her to

tread carefully. Too bad. If she didn't talk to him now, there was no telling when she'd get another chance. A glance back toward the house warned her that they had an unwanted audience. She couldn't tell if it was Hawk or the marshal watching from the kitchen window, but she didn't care.

"Jed, we need to talk."

He braced himself. "Are you pregnant?"

His question froze her in his tracks. Pregnant? How could she have not even thought about that possibility? Her hand immediately went to her stomach, as if to protect the child who might or might not be growing there under her heart.

"Well?"

"I . . . uh . . . don't know. I don't think so." It came as a shock how much she hoped she was wrong. A child born outside of marriage might horrify her friends and neighbors, but she didn't much care. Living here on the farm, she could provide a good home for the baby.

With Jed looking so impassive and stern, it was impossible how he felt about the possibility. "If that's not what you came running out here to tell me, what was it?"

He turned away from her before she could answer. Maybe he needed to say good-bye to his mare, but she wasn't going to let that horse take precedence. Not now.

She stepped between him and the corral, refusing to be ignored no matter how much he wanted to pretend she wasn't there. "Jed, I have something to say to you, and you're going to listen. Right now, we're alone. Later, we may not be."

"Maybe I don't want to hear what you have to say at all, Sadie." He sounded tired, his voice rough.

He pushed past her as if she were no more than

a pesky insect. Fine. A fair number of insects could sting if they were irritated enough. And right now, she was plenty irritated, not to mention terrified.

"It hurts when you leave." There. She'd said it. "I know I promised not to ask you for more than you could give, and I'm not. What we shared . . ." She paused to gesture back toward the house. "Upstairs last night and the night before was a gift that I'll always cherish."

She had to stop talking long enough to choke back the need to cry. "But it can't go on. Even if I'm not pregnant, I could get that way. I would love to bear your child, Jed, but that's a complication neither of us needs."

His eyes bored down into hers, silvery and cold. He laughed, but it had nothing at all to do with humor. "So that's what I am? A complication in your life?"

She fought the urge to either stomp her foot or kick his shin. "That's not what I said and you know it."

He leaned back against the fence and crossed his legs at the ankle. "Then why don't you say what you really mean, Sadie?"

She straightened, determined to finally get it all out. "Jed, I know it means a great deal to my father that you've come back. He loves you as if you're his own flesh and blood." She had to remind herself to breathe.

"But you're leaving again, this time because of what my father told you. He never meant to upset you or drive you away, Jed. You have to know that."

A curt nod was all she got. There was no sign of the man who had held her all through the night, the one whose touch had been tender and so very sweet.

"Are you coming back for Christmas?"

"I will if I can. I have to find the man who tried to kill Bart before he has a chance to try again."

"That's what I thought." His job was more important than her father was, than she was. He made her decision for her. "Your job is killing you, Jed. Every time you pull that trigger, you lose a little more of your soul."

"It's what I'm good at."

"But it's not all that you're good for." She wanted to shake some sense into him, to make him admit once and for all that he was so much more than a gun. "I love you, Jed Stark. I always have. I guess I always will."

And she hated that he flinched when she told him so.

"Sadie—"

"No, let me finish. I love you, but I can't go on hurting this way, not if I'm ever going to have any kind of life beyond waiting for you to accept the gift you've been offered." She stepped away, putting more than the distance of a couple of feet between them.

"Christmas is four weeks away. That should give you plenty of time to hunt down your man and get back here. We'll be here, ready to celebrate the season of miracles, just like we do every year. But, Jed, there's only one gift I want." Her throat closed up, making it hard to force the words out. "Either come back for Christmas prepared to stay for good or don't come back at all."

Then, coward that she was, she turned and ran for the house as if all the Furies of hell were at her heels.

He let her go because he had no choice, but he felt as if she'd gutted him and left him to bleed to death. She loved him. The words echoed in his mind, banging around with sharp points and pain. He'd always known that she had strong feelings for him, but he'd never let himself admit to knowing how strong they were.

But then a woman like Sadie would never have let him bed her if she hadn't convinced herself that she loved him. That came as no surprise. She wasn't the first woman who had claimed to love a man to justify going to bed with him, especially outside of marriage. But the queasy feeling in his stomach came from the knowledge that in Sadie's case, it was true.

Somehow, by some miracle, she'd looked at him and seen something she felt was worth the cost of her heart. He squatted down, no longer sure if his legs would support him. He wished he could go after her, but to what end? Her admission didn't change the fact that he had a job to do.

The question was what to do after that job was done. There would always be another criminal, another thief, and another and another with no end in sight. How could the world be safe for people like Sadie and Ole and Hawk if Jed didn't stand between them and the evil that walked on two legs? Why couldn't she understand that?

He heard the door open and close. His saddlebags had just been deposited on the porch. So much for saying good-bye. It was time to pack up. Sadie might not be happy with him right now, but he could trust her to see to it that Bart had a hot meal under his belt before sending him out to him.

While he waited, he could start harnessing the horses to the wagon. A movement in the corral caught his eye. The mare was trotting around in circles, her nostrils flaring to catch the wind. Damn, he'd miss that horse, but he'd promised Hawk that he'd leave her for now. In the long run, they would both profit.

Besides, looking for a replacement would give him something to occupy his time and his mind once they were back in Rosser. Once he found a suitable animal, he'd hit the trail and track down the bastard who shot Bart once and for all. Then, once that job was done, he'd figure out exactly where he'd be spending Christmas.

Alone or with Sadie.

Bart was feeling better than he had in days. If it weren't for the gloom radiating off his companion, he would have thoroughly enjoyed the trip back to town. He glanced at Jed out of the corner of his eye. His friend was never exactly talkative, but this was extreme even for him.

Considering how Sadie had been banging around in her kitchen, Bart assumed the two of them had had words. He shook his head at the stupidity of it all. Rarely had he seen two people fighting such strong feelings for each other. Personally, he thought Jed was a fool for walking away from Sadie. Hell, if it had been him she looked at that way, wild horses couldn't have dragged him away from that farm. Maybe he'd do some prodding to see if he could get Jed to talk.

"Nice day, don't you think?" He pretended an interest in the countryside he didn't particularly feel.

Jed grunted.

"We couldn't ask for nicer weather for a long drive." He stretched his arms out to the side, not quite accidentally making Jed duck to the side to keep from being hit in the face.

Jed grunted and moved farther away from Bart on the seat.

"I sure do appreciate your lady friend packing us a nice lunch to eat on the trail." He kept his eyes firmly on the road ahead. "It's a damn shame that she only has eyes for you, my friend. Otherwise, I'd be planning on doing some courting of my own. I always did like a woman with blond hair and big—"

Just that quickly, Jed had him by the front of his coat, his mouth set in a straight line of absolute fury. "Sadie is not a woman to be trifled with."

"Hey, I was talking about her eyes! I wasn't going to trifle with her." Bart held up his hands in surrender, trying not to laugh at his friend's not unexpected show of temper. "I was just testing the water, Jed. Now that I know you want her for yourself, I wouldn't dream of cutting in."

Jed immediately released him and went back to glaring at the backside of their horses. "I never said I wanted her."

"Then you're a goddamn fool, my friend." Bart sighed and stared up into the sun overhead. "I've been a lawman for a long time, mainly because no one has ever given me a good enough reason to give it up."

A glance in Jed's direction told him that he'd managed to shock him. "I can tell you this much—sleeping on rocks at night, no matter what the weather, is a pretty poor substitute for sharing a warm bed with a loving woman. I'm planning on doing some serious looking when we get back to town. I'm getting too damn old to be chasing after a bunch of lowlifes who think a gun is the answer to every question."

He slapped his leg where the bullet hole had almost cost him his life. "If he hadn't damn near killed me, I'd almost be grateful to him for making me rethink my future. If you want, I'll recommend they consider you for my replacement." Of course, he hoped like hell that Jed would come to his senses and marry Sadie.

Jed merely grunted again and flicked the reins. Maybe he thought to hurry the horses along so that he could escape Bart's company. More likely, he thought that putting more distance between himself and Sadie Johanson would weaken the hold she had on him. He should have been smart enough to know better. You can't outrun someone when you carry that person in your heart wherever you go.

But it wasn't up to Bart to tell him that. Jed was going to have to think things through for himself and make his own decision. Bart could only pray that it was the right one.

Chapter 17

Rocks and sand dug into his skin, adding to the misery of the bone-chilling cold. He'd been lying on the top of the ridge for the past two hours waiting, still and quiet, and wishing he were anywhere else. If the information he'd bought and paid for proved to be reliable, the man he'd been tracking should show up in the valley below. A ramshackle cabin sitting next to a small spring was reported to be one of Bill Thatcher's favorite hideouts.

Jed's sense of duty to Bart and the good people of Rosser insisted that he be the one to track down Thatcher and bring him back to stand trial for shooting Bart over the arrest of Thatcher's younger brother. Although Bart had argued long and hard without success to convince Jed to let someone else take over the case, it wasn't because he didn't think Jed could bring the prisoner in. No, instead, he wanted to play matchmaker. Jed tried to tell him that he was crazy, but still found himself thinking all too frequently about what Bart had been saying ever since the two of them had gotten back to town. Was Jed really a fool for not turning in his badge and heading straight back for the Johanson farm?

Maybe. Even likely.

With the wind ripping down the valley and cutting right through his coat to freeze his blood, he had to admit that Bart might have been on the right track. If Sadie was willing to overlook all of Jed's shortcomings, who was he to argue? He could build a small house on the property that Ole wanted him to have and live out his life in peace. But how could he live so close to Sadie without ever touching her again?

He kept his eyes trained on the valley below. He'd been on Thatcher's trail for two weeks now, following one step behind him through some of the roughest towns and worst terrain he'd seen. But today, he sensed a change in the outlaw's plans. Up until now, he'd been traveling steadily west, stopping only long enough to buy supplies or to bed some poor woman in a cheap saloon. A couple of them ended up sporting bruises that would take a long time to fade.

The bastard had a lot to answer for besides shooting a U.S. Marshal. Jed couldn't wait to bring him in to stand trial. He was going to give the judge a full report on Thatcher's violent habits, especially the way he treated women. Jed didn't give a damn if they were whores and earned their living selling their bodies to any man who had the money. A man who used his fists on a woman, no matter what her circumstances, deserved to spend the rest of his damn life behind bars. That is, if the judge didn't order him hanged for shooting Bart in the first place. Either way, Jed would be satisfied.

He shifted slightly, trying in vain to find a slightly more comfortable position. All he managed to do was uncover another layer of rocks to dig into his stomach. Judging by the lengthening shadows, it would be dark in another hour or so. If Thatcher hadn't shown up by then, Jed would ease back down off the slope and seek the marginal comfort of his bedroll. Then he'd try again tomorrow night and the night after that if he had to.

He hoped like hell that didn't happen. Judging by the way those clouds were rolling in, they might just be in for an early winter storm. Maybe Thatcher didn't care, but Jed did. He had decisions to make, ones he couldn't do much about until this case was closed.

And maybe he'd already made those decisions, even if he hadn't yet admitted it to himself. Sadie had made him plenty angry by issuing her ultimatum, even if he understood her need to protect herself from further hurt. It was probably best for all of them, himself included, if he quit returning to the farm unless he was going to stay.

But then why had he bought all those presents, already wrapped and waiting? It was going to be too late to have them shipped in time to get to the farm before Christmas if he didn't do something soon. Somehow, he just hadn't found the time to take care of that little chore.

He promised himself that it would be the first thing he did once he got back to town. Even if he wasn't welcome for Christmas himself, Sadie hadn't said anything about not accepting any gifts from him. Surely she'd let her father enjoy the warm shirt and coat Jed had bought for him. He knew for a fact that Hawk would like the new set of tools for caring for his beloved horses.

And for Sadie, he'd picked out some soft fabric the exact shade of blue as her eyes. The trim the storekeeper's wife had suggested was slightly darker, just the color Sadie's eyes turned when he joined his body to hers. He shifted again, this time the discomfort having nothing to do with the cold, rough ground.

Once again, he lay still, the hillside quiet except for the sound of his breathing. The temperature was dropping quickly. His breath was coming out in short puffs of white now and frost was forming on the ground. He flexed his fingers, his knuckles popping and creaking, as he tried to work out the stiffness in them. A lawman who couldn't grip his gun or pull the trigger quickly was a dead man. Shifting again, he wished he could risk walking around for a few minutes to get his blood stirring.

He could very well die out here if something didn't happen soon. Crawling forward, he raised himself up slightly, just enough to get a better look at the cabin below. Still no smoke coming from the chimney. Either Thatcher wasn't there or he liked living without the warmth of a fire.

Moving back from the edge, Jed sat up. If the outlaw hadn't shown yet, chances were that he'd found some place warmer to spend the night, which all went to prove that he was smarter than Jed had given him credit for being. It was time to do something about his own comfort. He stood up, taking several slow steps until the pins and needles in his legs quit hurting.

Taking the steep hill at an angle, he slowly made his way back down to the small grove of trees where he'd left his horse tethered. His new gelding made a decent trail horse, but nowhere near as good as his mare had been. Maybe he'd made a mistake leaving her with Hawk in order to breed her, but he couldn't find it in him to regret it. Hawk would take good care of her, and they would both profit in the long run by their partnership.

Eventually, he would have to return to the farm to pick up his mare and possibly a colt or filly.

The crack of a twig snapping from somewhere off to his left had Jed diving for the ground and rolling for cover. Silence returned, but this time it felt wrong. There was a heaviness to the air that hadn't been there before, as if time itself were waiting for all hell to break loose.

It wasn't long in coming.

Shots rained down from the slope above him, kicking up dirt and gravel on a straight path toward where he'd hunkered down behind a pile of rocks. Another round of shots rang out, this time coming from his right. Either the first shooter was moving fast or he had help. Damn, the whole time he'd been lying up on the ridge looking for Thatcher, the bastard had been circling around behind Jed. If he hadn't chosen that moment to walk down the hill, they would have had him in a cross fire.

Not that he was in a much better position right now.

He closed his eyes and listened. Sooner or later one of them would move, and he'd have a chance at picking him off. It was starting to get dark, though. It would cut down on visibility, increasing his chances of getting to his horse. But not knowing the area, he'd be risking both his mount and his own neck if they made a break for it.

No, he'd come all this way to bring Thatcher back to stand trial. He wasn't going to leave without him.

He picked up a rock and tossed it off to his right as far as he could throw it, hoping to draw their fire. A quick burst of gunfire tore into the vegetation where the rock had landed. It was dark enough now for him to catch a flash of a rifle. Taking careful aim, he returned fire. His effort was rewarded with a quick scream of pain and then a spate of cursing.

He couldn't count on the man being disabled, but he wouldn't be moving quite as fast either. That left his partner for Jed to deal with next. He doubted if the rock trick would work a second time. Instead, he started to crawl backward, keeping as low to the ground as the scant cover would allow. When he'd gone about twenty feet, he sent another round of fire back in the same direction, hoping the two men were more than casual acquaintances. If they were partners or, better yet, relatives, the injured man would be counting on the other one coming to his rescue.

Sure enough, Jed could hear someone scrambling over the loose rock farther up the hillside. Knowing this might be his only chance, he reloaded his rifle and took off running back toward the other two men. He caught a flicker of movement and adjusted his angle of approach.

He ran a crooked race, trying to avoid making an obvious target of himself. He felt as if his luck was running out, like the sand in one of those hourglasses he'd seen once. A man had only so long before trouble found him, and right now it was breathing down his neck.

Thatcher rose up out of nowhere, a look of crazed fury distorting his handsome face into something that looked less than human. His gun was spitting fire as he marched toward Jed with no concern about his own safety.

"You could have killed him, you bastard!"

"Drop your gun!" Jeb barked, hoping to end the confrontation without further bloodshed, even knowing it was unlikely. "Surrender now and we'll get your friend to a doctor."

"He's my baby brother."

"Fine, we'll get your brother to a doctor."

Thatcher shook his head. 'Why don't I kill you first and then I can get him some help?" He took aim.

Before he could pull the trigger again, Jed lunged to the side, firing as he went. Thatcher stumbled backward, circles of red blooming on his chest and thighs. Unfortunately, he managed to get off one more shot before his heart gave out. Pain burned up Jed's arm, bringing him to his knees. For several long seconds, he could do nothing more than try to breathe through the shock of being shot.

Blood ran down his arm to drip off his fingers onto the ground. Swaying, he allowed himself a minute or two to regain control of his legs before trying to stand. Finally, he managed to stay on his feet long enough to stumble to a boulder and sit down. After stripping off his coat and shirt, he realized how lucky he'd been. A deep groove cut along the outside of his arm, but the bullet missed the bone and any major blood vessels. With a little bit of care, he'd make it to the nearest town.

He worked his bandanna free from his neck and then used it as a makeshift bandage. When he was sure the bleeding was all but stopped, he put his shirt and coat back on and went in search of Thatcher's brother. He found him propped against a log, unconscious. His shoulder was a bloody mess, but he was still breathing.

Jed located the outlaws' horses and then brought his own gelding back with them to gather up his prisoner and Thatcher's body. It would be a long, painful ride back to the nearest town, but his job was done.

Maybe for good.

* * *

"Hold still, Jed, or I won't be responsible."

The fever had burned brightly, leaving him achy all over and feeling weak. He knew Bart was trying to help him, but he couldn't stand the sting of the cool cloth on his forehead another minute.

"Never knew you liked to torture people." He batted Bart's hand away from his face.

"Only those too stubborn to do what's good for them."

"Go to hell."

"Been there. Don't want to go back any time soon." Bart managed to get past his defenses to lay the wet cloth on Jed's forehead. "Doc says if your fever stays down, you'll be on the mend real soon."

"How long have I been out of it?" His throat felt like eight miles of dry dust.

"Off and on for almost a week. We still can't believe that you made it this far as sick as you were."

"If I could shoot Thatcher all over again, I would." With pleasure. The wound on his arm hadn't been all that serious to begin with, but infection had set in.

Bart laughed. "That's about the hundredth time you've told me that. Now that you're awake, I'm going to go get you a bowl of soup. Loretta left it on the stove to stay warm for you."

Jed frowned and looked around the room. "Who is Loretta?"

Bart shuffled his feet and only reluctantly met Jed's questioning gaze. "Loretta is Miss White."

"Oh, really?" Unless he was mistaken, his friend was actually blushing a bit. "Since when did Miss White become Loretta to you?"

Bart dropped back down on a handy chair. "To tell you the truth, I'm not sure. One day she was just my landlady. Then the next thing I realized what a fine-looking woman she is. We've been keeping company the past two weeks. I know it's all rather sudden, but she's agreed to become my wife."

If he hadn't already been lying down, the shock might very well have knocked Jed off his feet. He managed to muster up a smile and held a shaky hand out to his friend. "She'll make you a good wife."

Bart squeezed Jed's hand but didn't let go right away. "And I plan on being a good husband for her, one who isn't gone half the time on the trail of another killer." His smile faded a bit. "I've written my resignation as marshal. I've held off sending it in until I could ask if you want me to recommend you to take my place."

It was too much to take in all at once. "Can you give me a bit of time to think it over?"

Bart looked disappointed as he finally let go of Jed's hand. "To tell you the truth, I was hoping you would turn me down flat. But if you need time, I'll give it to you."

"Thanks." Jed let his eyes close, hoping Bart would take the hint and leave.

"I'll be back with the soup in a few minutes."

The sound of the door opening and closing told Jed he was alone again. He took a deep breath and then pushed himself up into a sitting position. For a moment, the room spun around him before settling back down. He propped his elbows on his knees and rested his face in his hands.

Things were changing too fast for comfort. Bart had been the one constant in his life for the past few years, always there, always solid. Now he was going to be a family man instead of a lawman. Jed knew he should be happy for him, but instead he was feeling betrayed. What kind of friend was he to be reacting that way?

Sure, the law always needed good, honest men to serve as marshals, but surely Bart had given enough of his life and blood to that cause. He deserved a little peace in his life. And Jed sure couldn't fault Bart's choice in wives. Miss White was a good woman. Hell, both Bart and Jed owed her more than either of them could ever repay for her gentle care when they were injured. So Jed would wish them both the best and try not to be jealous of the happiness they'd found together.

But that left him feeling more alone and dissatisfied with his own life. He looked around the small room. It was identical in most details to the one upstairs where he usually stayed; nothing about either of them marked them as home. In all of his travels there had only been one place that felt that way to him, the one place where he knew he was wanted.

The farm.

But it wasn't just the land or the barn or even the house. It was the people who lived there, and one person in particular—Sadie. Her image formed in his mind, her soft blond hair and bright blue eyes, and that woman's smile that drew him like a warm fire on a cold night.

Suddenly, nothing was more important to him than getting back to her. He lurched to his feet, grabbing on to the chair to support himself. He yelled for his friend. He hated like hell to feel this helpless, but if he was going to get all packed up and on the road toward Sadie, he was going to need Bart's help.

He yanked the bedroom door open and hollered louder this time. "Bart! Get in here!"

There was a crash followed by a string of curses that just might have Miss White having second thoughts about the gentleman she had consented to marry. Bart came into sight, soup dripping down his shirt and hands. If he hadn't looked so worried, Jed would have mustered up the energy to laugh.

"What the hell are you doing out of bed?"

"I need to leave." He bent down to pick up his saddlebags and almost fell on his face. Bart grabbed him by the arms in time to keep him from hitting the floor.

"You're not going anywhere, you idiot. You haven't eaten solid food in three days. Hell, just yesterday you were running a fever so high we could have heated the house with you." Despite his sharp words, Bart gently helped Jed back to bed, although he didn't insist that he had to lie down.

"Now, stay there. I'm going to clean up the mess your bellowing caused, and then I'll be back to see why you've suddenly lost your mind." He shot him a look over his shoulder as he went back out the door. "Again."

Maybe he had lost all good sense, but he stood to lose everything that mattered to him if he didn't make it back to the farm by Christmas. He hadn't told Bart about Sadie's ultimatum, but Jed knew she meant every word. Time was running out on him, the clock in the hall ticking away the minutes as he sat on the side of this bed.

Bart was back in a matter of minutes with a steaming mug of soup. He dragged the chair closer to the bed so that Jed could use it as a table. "Eat that and then we'll talk."

Jed wolfed the soup down, hardly taking time to chew. The thick, savory broth felt good on his throat and warmed him from the inside out. In the time it took to eat it all, he made his plans. Although he wanted more soup, he set the cup down. Right now he needed to explain the situation to Bart. Before he spoke, though, he realized he wasn't even sure what day it was.

"What's today's date?"

Bart seemed surprised by the question. "It's the twenty-second of December."

"Son of a bitch, I need to leave." Jed started to stand again, but Bart blocked his way.

"You've got time enough to tell me what's going on, Jed. One minute you're lying there weak and sickly. Now you're claiming you need to ride out. Why?"

Jed wished he could stretch out on the bed, but if he did, Bart would never let him out of his sight. "Sadie and I had words before we left on Thanksgiving."

"That was obvious. As I recall, she threw your saddlebags out on the porch rather than let you back in the house." Bart crossed his arms over his chest and leaned against the door frame. "Care to tell me what happened between the two of you?"

"Her pa wants to leave me half the farm."

"And Sadie didn't like that idea?"

"No, actually she was upset because I tried to turn it down." He kept his eyes trained on the floor. It wasn't going to be easy telling Bart the complete truth. "I don't suppose it will come as a surprise that Sadie says she has some pretty strong feelings for me."

"And you doubt that?"

Despite his earlier thinking on the matter, Jed knew Sadie loved him, just as he was, no questions asked. "No, she's not the one I doubted. It was me."

"And now?"

"I don't want to do this anymore." He held his hands out to include the bed stained with his sweat and the saddlebags that held his entire life within their narrow confines.

"Jed Stark, U.S. Marshal, wants to be a dirt farmer?" There was enough of a sneer in Bart's voice to set off Jed's temper.

"Hell yes, I want to be a farmer!" His hands clenched into fists. "It beats hunting down scum like the Thatcher brothers all to hell."

"So you're going to back to the Johansons' just so you can spend your days planting crops and watching Hawk raise horses?" Bart shook his head. "What about Sadie? You going to marry her or spend your nights sneaking into each other's beds and hoping nobody notices?"

Jed jerked his eyes up to meet Bart's all-too-knowing expression. "That's none of your business."

"Maybe not, but she deserves better, Jed. You and I both know it."

New energy fueled by anger and regret surged through him. This time when he stood, his legs held. "She might deserve better, Bart, but what she wants is me. I'm going to work damn hard to make sure she never regrets making that choice."

A slow grin spread across his friend's face. "I guess I'll be mailing your letter of resignation along with mine." Then he surprised them both by throwing his arms around Jed and giving him a back-pounding hug. When he stepped back, he said, "Now, all we have to do is get you well enough to go claim your woman."

Jed was already shaking his head. "I can't wait that long."

"Why not? You've waited this long. A few days one way or the other won't matter."

"Before we left after Thanksgiving, she told me to come back for Christmas ready to stay or not to come back at all." He hated like hell having to admit the truth. "I hurt her pretty bad."

"Not bad enough that she wasn't willing to give you a chance to come to your senses."

Jed let that idea roll around in his mind for a few seconds. Bart was right. If she really meant to end it between them, she wouldn't have allowed him one last chance to come home. "I have to get back to the farm." Even if it killed him.

Miss White stepped past Bart to enter the room. "I've never met her, but it would seem to me that Sadie would want you well more than she'd want you on time."

How much had she heard? Judging by the look on her face, too much. "But she won't know why I'm not there. She'll hurt until I get there and explain things."

"I'm guessing she's already hurting, Jed. It will be so much worse for her if you don't survive the trip."

"My fever broke. I'm a little shaky, that's all."

That's when she pointed out the window. "It's snowing. It started about half an hour ago and the ground is already covered. You could be caught out in a blizzard."

The scene outside the window only served to reinforce his resolve to leave immediately. "I've got to go." This time when he reached for his saddlebags, he managed to pick them up without too much effort.

"Look, Jed—" Bart started to protest, but Jed shook his head and repeated himself.

"I've got to go. If I leave now, maybe I can miss the worst of the storm."

His friend shook his head. "Aw, hell, then let's

get you packed up. You gather your things while I go down to the stable and get your horse saddled up. Do you need a pack animal, too?"

"Wouldn't hurt. If necessary, I can trade off riding them to keep from wearing the gelding out too soon."

His plans made, he started stuffing things in his packs as fast as he could. He barely noticed Bart and his fiancée leaving the room. All that mattered was that he was finally following the right trail, the one that would lead him right back to Sadie Johanson and home.

The cold seeped in through the walls, the floors, and the windows. Hawk had already made two trips out to the woodpile and would need to make a third before very long. The way that snow was coming down was terrible in its beauty. Unable to watch any longer, Sadie turned away.

"Hawk, we should make one more trip out to the barn soon to check on the animals. We may not be able to get there at all if we wait."

The boy looked past her at the window. "This time I'll tie a rope from the porch out to the barn. That way I can find my way back and forth if it gets really bad out there." He reached for his coat. "And maybe one to the woodpile, too. We don't want the fire to go out."

Her father stepped into the room. "I'll go with you, Hawk."

Sadie had already taken her coat off its peg. "I was going with him, Pa. You stay here and keep warm."

Ole drew himself up to his full height and glared at her. "Daughter, don't make me out to be helpless. I can walk from here to the barn."

The argument was lost before it ever really started. "Fine. On the way back, we should each carry in another load of wood."

"Fine." He shrugged on his coat. A year ago, the cloth would have stretched tightly across his shoulders. Now there was a distressing amount of room in the way it fit him. The three of them stepped out onto the porch.

"Snow for Christmas!"

Despite the cold, there was real pleasure in her father's voice. He'd always loved spending the holiday tucked up warm in the house with those he loved surrounding him. This year there was a new addition—Hawk. Two were missing—her mother and, of course, Jed. She'd so hoped that he would find it in him to come back for Christmas. For her.

She'd been so sure that she'd done the right thing in trying to force Jed to make a decision once and for all. For what seemed liked the hundredth time since the sun had risen, its light only weakly seen through the thick layer of clouds, she stared down the road and wished for a Christmas miracle.

But it was only Christmas Eve, she reminded herself. There were hours and hours left before she knew for certain that Jed had indeed chosen the outside world over her. She would not give up, not yet, maybe not ever. He was too important to her.

And with the storm building, he might just very well take shelter somewhere else or perhaps decide the trip was not worth the effort. Rather than dwell on everything that could go wrong with her plan, she shoved those thoughts aside. If Jed had left in time, he should be able to reach the farm before travel became too dangerous.

And she would rather he not come at all if it

meant risking his life just to meet the deadline she'd imposed. As she followed her father and Hawk to the barn, she held up her face to better enjoy the beauty of the swirling, dancing snow. Just as she had as a small girl, she stuck out her tongue to capture the cold, clean taste of a few flakes.

Her father was right. There was something special about a white Christmas especially sharing it with those she loved. As the three of them stepped into the relative warmth of the barn, she sent a simple prayer skyward.

"Dear Lord, wherever Jed is, keep him safe, keep him warm, and let him know that he is loved."

The chatter of his teeth was giving him a headache. Judging by the looks he was getting from his horse, Bart wasn't the only one who wondered about Jed's sanity for setting out in the first storm of the season. Jed would apologize to his gelding, but forming the words took more energy than he had. He settled for patting the poor beast on the neck.

Another gust of wind wrapped Jed in its cold embrace, setting off another bout of the shivers. It was a wonder his joints hadn't shaken apart. Hunching down to ride leaning forward helped some, but he wasn't fooling himself into thinking that he'd last much longer if the weather didn't change soon.

The clouds overhead seemed to be pressing down on him, making each step his horses took that much harder. It was starting to feel as if they were moving in fits and starts rather than making steady progress toward safety. If the weary animals finally reached the point when they could no longer go forward, the three of them would die.

Without him ever having a chance to tell Sadie that he loved her.

The wind let up a bit, allowing Jed the chance to sit up straighter and look around. With everything heaped and mounded with snow, it was all but impossible to pick out any familiar landmark. He'd lost all ability of guessing distance or time hours ago. Continuing along in the same direction was the only thing that made sense because each step took him that much closer to Sadie.

He squeezed his knees together to urge the horse onward, at the same time tugging on the lead rope to the packhorse. So far, both animals had managed to keep their feet despite having to break a new path each step of the way. If he thought it would help conserve their energy, he would have climbed down and walked for a while. But his strength was already waning. If the temperature were to drop any further or the snow to worsen again, he would need every scrap of strength he could muster.

All he could do was point the horse in the right direction and let the animal choose the best path. He looked up at the sky. The clouds were thick and gray and looked as though they were loaded with enough snow to blanket the whole world. He imagined that from inside the warmth of a cabin, it would actually look beautiful with everything outlined in frost and piled high with soft mounds of snow.

But from where he was, it looked like death.

Chapter 18

"Sadie, why do you keep staring out the window?" Her father stepped up behind her to look over her shoulder. "I've always been the one foolish enough to like snow for Christmas, not you."

She shivered and continued to watch in vain for some sign that Jed was getting close. She knew he was coming because he loved her, even if he hadn't admitted it to himself. His heart belonged here on the farm with her. It was so obvious to everyone else. Why couldn't he see it, too?

A single tear rolled down her face. Her father's health might be failing, but there was nothing wrong with his eyesight.

"You're crying. Why?" His knobby fingers rested on her shoulder, offering her what comfort he could.

She turned into the shelter of his arms. "Oh, Pa, I've done something stupid, and Jed could die because of it." All the worry and all the fear poured down her face in acid-hot streaks of tears.

Ole pushed her back from the sanctuary of his

chest. "Daughter, what have you done that makes you say such a foolish thing?"

"I told Jed to come home for Christmas."

"That is nothing to cry over, Sadie. We all wanted him here for Christmas, even Hawk. No one could have known it was going to snow like this. Jed will come when he can. You know he is not foolish enough to venture out in such weather. He is probably spending the day with his friend the marshal."

He patted her on the shoulder, trying to offer her the comfort she didn't deserve. She stepped back out of his reach. "But you don't understand, Pa. I did something terrible. I told Jed to come home for Christmas to stay or never come back again."

All the color drained out of her father's face. "Sadie, what were you thinking, to say something like that? You can't order Jed around. A man must make his own choices about his life."

Her pride stung, she lashed out. "And what about my life? Don't I have the right to make decisions about what will make me happy? Every time he leaves, he rips out a bit more of my heart until I feel like I have nothing left." The tears began in earnest again. "I love him. I always have."

"And yet this is how you treat him? Telling him that it is all or nothing? I raised you better than that. And to use the Lord's birth celebration as a tool to get what you want?"

Shame stained her cheeks. "But it was all right for you to saddle him with a farm he might not want? Weren't you doing the same thing with a piece of land?"

Her father's shoulders sank. "Yes, I regret not talking to him about it first. I knew that he has felt driven to make amends for his past, even though the only thing he was ever guilty of was trying to survive. No matter how much we showed him that we cared, he always felt unworthy. I thought maybe owning land of his own to work might finally heal him."

A sudden gust of wind rattled the windows. They both stared out into the frozen landscape. Was Jed coming? Somehow, deep inside her heart, she knew he was because the man she loved also loved her. She'd known it before he did; it was there in his touch and the way that he looked at her even when he didn't have the words to tell her.

And so she would wait, a light in the window, for her man to come home. Once he was there, safe inside the house and out of harm's way, she would beg his forgiveness for making such a dangerous demand.

The windows rattled again just as a snow-covered shape loomed up out of the night. The sudden movement startled her, but then she hurried to the door to let Hawk in. The boy had made another trip out to the barn to lay down an extra supply of feed for the animals. If the snow kept up its current pace, they might not be able to make it back out to do the morning chores.

He stomped his feet and knocked a pile of snow off his coat and scarf. Sadie slammed the door closed before all the heat from the fire and the stove could be sucked outside. While her father helped Hawk strip off his outer layers of clothing, Sadie poured a hot cup of coffee and added a dollop of the whiskey she kept around for medical reasons. She normally didn't hold with giving strong spirits to boys as young as Hawk, but he looked a bit blue around the lips. Once he was warmed by the fire, she would send him to bed with extra blankets and warm bricks for his feet.

"Do you want to open presents now, Sadie?" Ole

had pushed Hawk into the rocker by the fire and covered him up with a blanket he'd kept warm by the fire for that very purpose.

She handed Hawk his coffee. "Of course not. We'll wait for Jed. Besides, Mother always thought the proper time for opening gifts was Christmas morning."

A clump of snow chose that moment to fall down the chimney, to send up a shower of sparks, an unwanted reminder that the storm still raged outside. Anyone caught outside in its fury would be at risk. She closed her eyes and prayed over and over again that Jed had remained in Rosser for the holidays, no matter what the reason.

But knowing Jed, if he had made up his mind to come home, nothing would have stopped him, not even deadly weather. "I had better add another log to the fire and put more water on to heat. When Jed gets here, we'll need it."

"I made sure to leave feed and water in the stall for his horse. I figured to save Jed some time that way." Hawk sat huddled in his blankets, his hands wrapped around the heavy mug of coffee. When he took a sip, his eyes widened in surprise. He grinned at Sadie, nodding his thanks before taking another sip.

"Thank you for thinking of that, Hawk. I know Jed will appreciate it." She brought the coffeepot over to Hawk to top off his cup.

"I can't imagine how cold he must be by now." Hawk shivered. "And he's the kind of man who'll see to his horse's needs before his own."

That was high praise, indeed, coming from Hawk. It pleased her to know the boy had gotten past his anger to recognize the good in Jed. "Pa, why don't you go on to bed? There's no reason we all have to sit up all night."

"I'm not tired," he lied. "I'll keep you company for a while yet."

Sadie cast about for something to do as they waited to see if there would be another miracle to celebrate on this special night. Finally, she got out the checkerboard and set up a game. Her father beat her handily three times in a row before she begged Hawk to take her place. When she was satisfied that their attention was firmly on their game, she resumed her vigil at the window as she turned up the wick a bit more, hoping the light would lead Jed the last distance to her door.

He couldn't remember the last time he'd felt his feet. His hands were so numb that he had no idea if he still held the lead rope to the packhorse. None of it mattered except that he was pretty sure that he'd spotted the first of the fence posts that marked the edge of the Johanson farm. Even if he was wrong, the fence had to mean he was close to some place warm.

With a bit of luck, he'd live long enough to get the horses to a safe harbor to wait out the storm. He'd had no right to drag them out in this weather. They deserved better than to die in a misery of white and cold. He gathered up enough strength to lift his head and look around. The tree a short distance ahead on the left looked right, although it was hard to tell with the burden of snow bending its limbs down toward the ground.

His pulse sped up, sending a short-lived burst of energy through his veins. Some of his excitement communicated itself to his horse, because it raised its weary head and moved out at a faster pace.

"That's it, boy, keep moving. I know you've never been here before, but Ole Johanson's barn is one of the best in the whole region. Once you get there, you'll never want to leave. Besides, I won't be going anywhere."

He squinted his eyes and strained his head forward as if that extra inch or two would make all the difference. "Is that a light I see, boy?"

The horse didn't answer. Jed blinked several times and looked again. Sure enough, there was a small beam of light in the distance. "Boy, I think we might just make it."

The wind whistled past him and then died out completely. It had been his constant companion on the long ride, but he didn't miss it. Now that he was more alert, he realized that the snow wasn't coming down as fast. Even the clouds had broken up, revealing stretches of the night sky and a splash of stars.

That extra little bit of light revealed the truth at last. He was home, or at least only a short distance away. He urged the horse to move faster. "There's a stall filled with sweet hay and fresh water for both of you. If I know Hawk, he won't be satisfied until he checks you over from nose to tail to make sure you're all right."

The barn loomed up out of the darkness, looking solid and so damn welcoming that he could have cried. It took a couple of tries before he could swing his leg down off the saddle to dismount. Even then, he had to hold on to the saddle to keep from falling on his ass in the snow. The other horse crowded up next to him, determined to be the first one through the barn door.

Just as he expected, Hawk had a stall all ready. Luckily, it was the one really big stall so both of Jed's animals would fit in just fine. They wouldn't mind sharing. He managed to undo the cinches on the saddles and packs, letting them slide to the barn floor. The horses headed for the stall without protest, content to be in out of the wind and snow. They were both munching hay contentedly when Jed let himself back out of the door.

He almost choked himself on a rope that hadn't been there the last time he walked from the barn to the house. He ran his hand along it through the last few yards of snow, following in the footsteps left by either Hawk or Ole. He couldn't bear the thought that it might have been Sadie trudging through the icy cold to feed the animals.

It was hard to tell where the porch steps were, but he managed to get to the door without falling. It swung open before he could raise his fist to knock, and then Sadie was there, dragging him in out of the cold and into the warmth of her arms.

For the longest moment, he held on to her as if his life and soul depended on it. He could tell she was crying, although he wasn't sure why. Ole and Hawk were hovering nearby, but neither of them made a move to interfere with his need to touch Sadie.

When he trusted himself to speak, he whispered, "Sadie, why are you crying?"

She burrowed in closer and answered without looking at him. "You risked your life out in that storm because of what I said. I didn't mean what I said."

He leaned back from her and tipped her chin up with a crooked finger. "I hope like hell you did. You said you loved me."

Her beautiful blue eyes studied his face before she answered. He let her look her fill, hoping she saw something that satisfied her.

"I do, Jed. I always have." She blinked several times to clear the last of her tears as her mouth curled up in a tentative smile.

Despite their audience, he brushed his lips across hers. "I had to be here for Christmas because I wanted to give you your present on time."

"I could have waited. You know that."

"But you've already waited too long for me to see what an idiot I've been." Despite the serious nature of what he was about to say, he found himself grinning broadly, feeling lighthearted and almost merry.

"You're not an idiot, Jed, except for standing there in your icy coat and wet clothes." This from Ole, who reached up to take off Jed's hat. A small puddle of melted snow spilled onto the floor.

Sadie immediately looked distressed and began unbuttoning his coat for him. He let her fuss over him because the truth was he liked it. Ole took his coat and draped it over the back of a chair to dry.

"I'll go check on your horse." Hawk was already putting on his own coat.

"There are two of them. I needed a pack animal this trip." He pulled his eyes away from Sadie long enough to ask a favor. "I'm afraid I just dumped all my gear on the floor in the barn and left it there. When you come back in, would you bring it with you? No peeking at the packages, though. Most of them go under the tree to open in the morning."

Hawk pretended to act disappointed, but then he smiled. "As long as a few of them have my name on them."

"You'll have to wait and see."

The door opened and closed with another blast of cold air, but Jed didn't care. All the warmth he needed was right there in Sadie's sweet smile.

"Would you mind if I gave you your gift a bit early? I know your mother had rules about such things, but this time I don't think she'd care."

"I think I need to go into my room for a few

minutes," Ole announced and then made good on his promise.

Neither of them really noticed.

"Maybe he should have stayed. I meant to ask his permission before I give you the present I brought."

A muffled shout came through Ole's door. "You have my blessing, Jed. Now get on with it."

"Pa!" Sadie blushed. "Don't pay any attention to him, Jed. He doesn't know what you got me."

"Actually, I think he does." Jed managed to pull a small package out of his shirt pocket without help. He held it out to her and waited not so patiently for her to unwrap it.

She peeled back the paper to reveal a small china box. "It's lovely, Jed."

"The present is inside, Sadie, open it."

When she saw the matching gold bands nestled inside, the tears started again. "Oh, Jed."

"Sadie Johanson, will you do me the honor of becoming my wife?"

She couldn't seem to find the words to answer, so she nodded and stepped right back into his arms to let a kiss do her talking for her. As he felt truly warm for the first time in his life, he decided that as Christmas presents went, it was the best one he'd ever received.

Complete Your Collection Today
Janelle Taylor

Available Wherever Books Are Sold!

Visit our website at **www.kensingtonbooks.com.**

Put a Little Romance in Your Life With
Georgina Gentry

Cheyenne Song
0-8217-5844-6   **$5.99**US/**$7.99**CAN

Apache Tears
0-8217-6435-7   **$5.99**US/**$7.99**CAN

Warrior's Heart
0-8217-7076-4   **$5.99**US/**$7.99**CAN

To Tame a Savage
0-8217-7077-2   **$5.99**US/**$7.99**CAN

To Tame a Texan
0-8217-7402-6   **$5.99**US/**$7.99**CAN

To Tame a Rebel
0-8217-7403-4   **$5.99**US/**$7.99**CAN

To Tempt a Texan
0-8217-7705-X   **$5.99**US/**$7.99**CAN

Available Wherever Books Are Sold!

Visit our website at **www.kensingtonbooks.com**.

Discover the Romances of
Hannah Howell